BETTER ALL THE TIME

Better All the Time

a Darling Family novel

CARRE ARMSTRONG GARDNER

Tyndale House Publishers, Inc.
Carol Stream, Illinois

Visit Tyndale online at www.tyndale.com.

Visit Carre Armstrong Gardner's website at www.carregardner.com.

TYNDALE and Tyndale's quill logo are registered trademarks of Tyndale House Publishers, Inc.

Better All the Time

Designed by Jennifer Ghionzoli

Edited by Sarah Mason

Published in association with literary agent Blair Jacobson of D.C. Jacobson & Associates LLC, an Author Management Company. www.dcjacobson.com.

Better All the Time is a work of fiction. Where real people, events, establishments, organizations, or locales appear, they are used fictitiously. All other elements of the novel are drawn from the author's imagination.

Library of Congress Cataloging-in-Publication Data

Gardner, Carre Armstrong.
    Better all the time / Carre Armstrong Gardner.
      pages ; cm. — (The Darlings ; [2])
    ISBN 978-1-4143-8815-1 (sc)
I. Title.
    PS3607.A7267B48 2015
    813'.6—dc23   2014043279

Printed in the United States of America

21   20   19   18   17   16   15
7   6   5   4   3   2   1

To Noble Armstrong and Jed Armstrong:
my brothers and friends.

IN THE BACKYARD of a house in Maine, as the light was beginning to take on the peculiar slant of a late spring afternoon, the party was just getting started. The shadows had not yet begun to lengthen into evening, nor the outline of the swing set to mute and soften with twilight. That would happen later, in time for cake. For now, the air was cool and light and filled with the scent of lilacs and grilling hamburgers. This was, Ivy Darling remarked to her husband, Nick Mason, exactly one of those rare hours that people live all year for. Or at least it might have been, had not a neighboring farmer recently fertilized his fields. When the wind was wrong, a hint of rancid chicken manure tended to waft through the backyard as well and catch you the wrong way. But then again, sometimes the breeze would shift and carry in the fresh salt breath of the ocean from the cove half a mile

1

away. It was a good parable for life, Ivy thought. You took the good with the bad, and a lot of your happiness depended on just what you chose to pay attention to.

Ivy was in her kitchen, rooting around in the refrigerator for an onion, when she heard the front door open and her mother call, "Yoo-hoo! Anybody home?" Jane Darling didn't knock, but then nobody knocked at Ivy and Nick's. As a rule, people simply opened the door and called out until someone appeared from the depths and said, "Oh, *there* you are; come in!" It was a Darling maxim that you treated guests like family, and family like honored guests.

"In here!" Ivy called. She unearthed the onion and closed the refrigerator as her parents materialized in the kitchen doorway. "Hi, Mom, Dad. You all alone?"

"Sephy and Amy will be along in a few minutes. I sent them to the store first for a carton of ice cream. And David is picking up Grammie Lydia." Her mother set a plastic-wrapped salad bowl on the counter and kissed Ivy on the cheek. Ivy tipped her other cheek up for her father's kiss.

"Where are the kids?" Leander wanted to know.

"DeShaun's in the shower." Ivy frowned at the clock. "And it's time he was finished." The subject of forty-five-minute showers had become a battleground between Ivy and her new sixteen-year-old son. "Jada's setting the picnic tables in the backyard, and Hammer is . . . Oh, here's Hammer!" Her youngest, an eight-year-old who lived life in fast-forward, careened around the corner and into the kitchen.

Hammer flung himself at Leander's waist. "Grampie!"

"Hey there, buddy!" Leander rubbed the little boy's nubbly head.

Hammer looked up at both of his newly official grand-parents. "I'm adopted."

"So we heard," said Jane. "Congratulations!"

"We came because we heard there was cake," Leander told him.

"There is. It's *huge*. Ivy made it yesterday."

"Mom," said Ivy. "My name is Mom now."

"Mom made it yesterday. It's so big that Nick—*Dad*—says we'll be eating it all week."

"Lucky you," said Leander. "Wish I could eat cake all week."

"Speaking of Nick," Ivy said, "he's grilling in the back-yard. Hammer, why don't you take Grammie and Grampie out there, and while you're at it, see if Jada needs help with the tables."

She went to knock on the bathroom door and shout to DeShaun that this was not a luxury spa, and it was high time he came out and joined the party that was, after all, being thrown in his honor. She was putting drinks and glasses on trays in the kitchen when her two younger sisters arrived.

"Congratulations to you, *Mom*," said Sephy, giving her a one-armed hug as she set a plastic Hannaford bag on the counter.

"So, what's it feel like, being a mother?" Amy, the youngest in the family, came behind Sephy carrying a gallon-size glass jar.

Ivy squeezed Sephy back. "Thank you. And being a mother today feels exactly like it did yesterday, and the day before, and the twenty-two months before that, when I was one in everything but legal status. What in the name of heaven and earth is *that thing*?" She stared at Amy's jar, where a thick, pale object floated, suspended in an amber liquid. "Something you found at the beach?"

Amy set the jar on the counter, beside her mother's salad bowl. "This is kombucha."

Ivy and Sephy bent to examine the jar. Evil-looking brown tentacles trailed from the bottom of the pale thing. "I've never heard of a kombucha," said Sephy. "Is it like a jellyfish?"

"No, it is *not* like a jellyfish. Kombucha is fermented tea. Look at this." Amy unscrewed the lid. Her sisters peered in. The thing turned out to be a smooth, rubbery disc, floating on the surface of the liquid. "This is a living organism!" Amy prodded proudly at it with a forefinger. "It's a symbiotic colony of bacteria and yeast. You make sweetened tea and add this to it. The bacteria and yeast eat the sugar and turn the tea into a superfood that's packed with B-vitamins and antioxidants. It has more probiotics than yogurt!"

"That's disgusting," said Ivy.

Sephy said, "It looks like an organ that's been harvested for transplant."

Amy screwed the lid back onto the jar. "It's not disgusting, it's good for you. It's great for you, actually."

"It smells like vinegar," Sephy observed.

"What does it taste like?" asked Ivy.

"Here, try it," Amy said. "Only, I should pour it through a strainer, if you have one. Otherwise, it gets little jellyish blobs of yeast in it, and—"

"No thanks!" her sisters said, at the same time.

"It's great for arthritis."

"I don't have arthritis," Sephy said regretfully.

"Alexander Solzhenitsyn claimed it cured his stomach cancer."

"I already got over my stomach cancer," said Ivy. "Sorry."

"Fine," Amy said. "I was going to give you a starter mushroom, but forget it. I can see you don't want one."

"Well, if I ever change my mind, I know where to find you. Now, would you two mind getting out the salads while I take drinks to the others? And put that ice cream in the freezer before it melts."

When Ivy returned to the kitchen, delivered of her tray, Amy and Sephy had a small army of salads lined up on the kitchen counter and were rummaging in drawers for serving spoons. "What did I miss?" Ivy opened the refrigerator and began pulling out condiments.

"We're talking about Amy's job."

"Or lack thereof." Amy scowled.

Ivy set a watermelon on the counter and began to slice it. "What do you mean your *lack* of job? Aren't you still managing the music store?"

"Not after next week, I'm not. Elliot, my boss, met a woman online. Next thing I know, he's abandoned his lease and started selling off all the inventory in the store. He bought a one-way ticket to California, leaving me—as of next week—high and dry and unemployed."

"Just like that?"

"Just like that."

"It's a shame. That music store's been in Copper Cove all our lives."

Amy shrugged. "It hasn't made a viable profit in years. Nobody buys CDs anymore—they just download what they want from the Internet. People buy their sheet music from Amazon, and you can't keep a music store going in a town this size just by selling instruments."

"It seems so sad."

"It's the end of an era," Sephy agreed. They fell silent, recalling childhood and teenage hours spent in the metallic, oily-smelling depths of the music store. The sheet music considered and chosen, the drumsticks and violin strings bought. To a family as musical as the Darlings, the loss of the town's only music store was a palpable blow.

"Anyway," said Amy, who was less sentimental than her sisters, "I have to find a new job. I'll start sending out résumés tomorrow."

"How far away will you look?"

"Not very, if I can help it. You remember what happened last time I tried to move away." Homesickness had rendered Amy's one attempt at living on a college campus an hour away both miserable and short-lived.

"Something will turn up close to home," Ivy said, though privately she doubted it. This part of the state wasn't exactly a nerve center of enterprise. Small businesses like the music store were closing everywhere, edged out by the Internet and by big, soulless chain stores that could sell everything cheaper.

DeShaun ambled out from the direction of the bathroom then, borne on a steamy miasma of Irish Spring soap and Axe body spray. "Oh, hi," he said to the room in general.

"Hey there, DeShaun," said Amy.

"Hi, honey," said Sephy. "Happy Adoption Day."

DeShaun picked up Amy's gallon jar and peered into it. "What's this, a jellyfish?"

"It's a brain," said Sephy.

"Shut up," Amy told her.

DeShaun unscrewed the cap. "What's this thing in it?"

Amy told him.

"Cool. Can I try it?"

Amy positively glowed. "You, young man, show great promise as a human being. Ivy, I'm going to need a tall glass with ice immediately, please. And a strainer, if you have one."

"You're corrupting my son," Ivy told her, reaching for a glass.

"I know," said Amy, wiping away mock tears. "Isn't it wonderful?"

Sephy Darling, home from her third year of college, had flung wide the windows of her parents' house and was doing her best to ignore the drowsing warmth of the June day. She was studying. That is, she had been studying and would study more before the afternoon was out, but just now, she was taking a break. In the kitchen, she spread Hellmann's mayonnaise on half a kaiser roll and added a pile of shaved ham, deli Swiss cheese, jalapeño dill chips, a slice of beefsteak tomato, a lettuce leaf, rings of red onion, and a sprinkling of chopped black olives. She salted this, peppered it, covered it all with the other mayonnaised half of the roll, and secured it with a toothpick. She put it on a paper plate and picked up a bag of Doritos from the counter. Then, balancing plate, chips, and a can of Diet Coke, she took a paper napkin from the basket on the microwave and carried it all to the screened-in front porch so she could eat lunch while she tried to make her mind absorb one more chapter of *A Psychology of Nursing* by Elizabeth T. Gates, RN, MSN, PhD.

She had finished the sandwich and chips and was trying to keep her eyes open over what was surely one of the most stultifying texts to ever roll off a printing press when a knock came at the porch door. She looked up to find her neighbor and best friend, Liberty Hale, grinning at her and pressing her snub nose against the screen.

Sephy clapped her textbook shut with a snap. "You've saved me!"

Libby opened the door and came in, dropping into a chair beside her. "What did I save you from?"

"From my brain-sucking homework." Sephy held the book up for Libby to inspect.

"*A Psychology of Nursing*. I see. It sounds fascinating."

"You don't know the half of it. I no more than pick the book up and I'm asleep. Full-blown REM. I'm not kidding."

"You need an afternoon off." Libby sank back into her chair and put her bare feet on the wicker table. "What are you doing the rest of the day?"

"Spending more precious moments with Elizabeth T. Gates." Sephy shook the book at her. "I have three more chapters to read and outline. Quiz tomorrow."

Libby yawned. "I wish you didn't have to do this summer class."

"You're telling me." Still, Sephy thought, as they settled into comfortable silence, it was going to pay off in the end. Taking this class kept her busy for the summer, and it would make her workload lighter during her last year of college. With a lighter course load, she could really apply herself to her clinicals and ultimately do better on the boards next spring. She told herself this, using that loud, firm mental voice she sometimes employed when she needed to remind herself of what was really important in life.

Beside her, Libby stretched. "It's hot. Want to go to the beach?"

Sephy flicked a glance at her. "Not today. Got a date with Elizabeth T."

Libby didn't seem surprised. She was used to being refused by Sephy when it came to going to the beach. She stood up, trim and cute in her shorts and T-shirt, and smiled equably at her best friend. "I think I'll go, myself. See if I can find a volleyball game to join. Have fun with Lizzy Gates." She went to the screen door and opened it, but hesitated. "Sure you won't come with me?"

"I'd like to, but I can't. I'll call you later."

"Bye, then." Libby wiggled her fingers and let the door slip closed behind her.

Sephy shook her head and put any twinges of regret firmly away. There was no time to go to the beach. She had work to do. She looked with distaste at *A Psychology of Nursing*. Another page of it was going to plunge her into a full-blown coma. She remembered that she had seen a box of ice cream sandwiches in the freezer: instant energy. She picked up the grease-stained paper plate and the empty Diet Coke can and, struggling to her feet, went back to the kitchen in search of it.

She was washing her hands when the phone rang. It was Ivy.

"Hi, Seph. What's going on at 14 Ladyslipper Lane?"

"Not a thing. Dad's at the high school, taking inventory of the band instruments or choir music or something. Amy's babysitting, and Mom's at a meeting. I'm putting myself to sleep with a textbook."

"What meeting is Mom at?"

"Garden club, I think."

"Is Libby around?"

"She went to the beach."

"Oh. Well, I hope you're studying outside. This isn't the kind of day to be stuck indoors. Go read in the hammock or something."

Sephy was grateful that Ivy did not say, *"You should be at the beach with Libby."* Ivy understood Sephy's relationship with bathing suits.

"Want me to have Mom call you?"

"I can just leave a message."

Sephy took a jar of peanut butter from the cupboard and a spoon from the silverware drawer. "Should I be writing this down?"

"No, I just wanted to say we can't make it for family dinner on Thursday night. It's Nick's birthday, and I'm taking him out."

"Ooh, anyplace nice?"

"Some new steakhouse in Quahog. We may even get wild and crazy and go to a movie afterward."

"You're wilder and crazier than I am."

"You can't afford to be right now," Ivy assured her. "You're too busy being a nurse."

"I'm not a nurse yet," Sephy said, "and I never will be if *A Psychology of Nursing* continues to languish, unread, on the front porch while my sisters telephone me to leave messages at all hours of the day."

"I can take a hint. Tell Mom and Dad I said hello. And Amy, of course."

"I will. We'll miss you tomorrow night."

"Love you, Seph." They both made kissing noises into the phone and hung up.

Carrying the box of ice cream sandwiches and another Diet Coke, and licking the peanut butter from the spoon, Sephy went back to the porch. She picked up her book and held it between two fingers, as though it were something dead and distasteful. She could hardly bear the thought of opening it again. A breeze played through the screen windows of the porch, ruffling the pages and carrying with it the scent of some neighbor's newly mown grass. In the branches of the crab apple, a pair of birds chirped back and forth in a halfhearted way. Still, there was tomorrow's quiz, and the outlines to do, and just because it was summer didn't mean she could afford to slack off. There would be plenty of time for that after college, when her goals were met and she had made a success of herself. There would be other summers.

With a sigh, she settled herself in the wicker chair, unwrapped an ice cream sandwich, popped the top on the Diet Coke, and began to read.

Jane Darling was at the sink hulling a large flat of strawberries when Amy wandered in. Her youngest daughter hoisted herself onto the counter and sat there, swinging her legs and toying with one of her long dreadlocks.

"The economy in this country is going down the toilet," announced Amy.

Jane smiled. "Still haven't found a job?"

"I mean," Amy went on, helping herself to a strawberry, "it's not as if I'm not *looking* for work. I'm trying. I'm applying for jobs, but nobody will hire me. Do they *want* people going on unemployment? Because I'm telling you, that's what it's going to come to if I don't find something soon."

"Justin Bates's mother called this morning about drum lessons," Jane told her.

"Great, but that's one student. That will barely put gas in my car."

"Well . . . word of mouth, you know."

"I even applied at McDonald's, that's how desperate I was. Can you imagine me serving people *chicken*? And *hamburgers*?" Amy, who was a vegetarian, shuddered. "Anyway, it doesn't matter because they turned me down. What kind of loser gets rejected by McDonald's?" She took another strawberry.

"Stop eating the ones I've already hulled. If you want one, take it from there." Jane pointed her knife at the cardboard tray heaped with berries still to be cleaned. "But I did find something in the paper that you might be interested in." She wiped her hands on her apron and reached into the phone basket, riffling through directories, scrap paper, and pens before finding what she wanted. She handed Amy a newspaper page of classified ads. "I read it this morning and thought of you."

Amy read the ad circled in red ink.

WANTED: Community Arts Program Director
The Copper Cove town council is seeking an energetic, motivated person to build and direct a new community arts program. Bachelor's degree in business administration;

2 years experience preferred. Apply at www.coppercovearts

.gov or in person at the town hall. FMI: (207) 555-1478

She looked up. "I don't have a bachelor's in business administration or two years' experience."

"You never know," Jane said carefully. She had learned that it didn't do to appear too invested in Amy's decisions. "It would be interesting to at least apply for the job, see what your chances are of getting it."

Amy put down the newspaper, slid off the counter, and took a paring knife from the drawer. "Move over. I'll give you a hand."

Jane made room at the sink, and the two of them cleaned berries in silence for some minutes.

"What is it, anyway?" Amy said at last. "I didn't even know Copper Cove *had* a community arts program."

"They don't. At least not yet. The town council was awarded some kind of national grant to start one. It's quite a lot of money. They're going to use it to renovate the old Jarvis Opera House on Winter Street into a community arts center and hire someone to create an arts program."

"What, like community theater?"

"Theater, concerts, classes . . . There was a whole article about it in the paper last month. I'm sure you could still find it at the library."

"People don't find old newspaper articles at the library anymore, Mom. They find them online."

"Oh, well. Wherever."

"Anyway, I don't even fit the requirements."

"That doesn't mean you wouldn't be good at the job."

"You really think I'd be good at something like that?"

"You'd be good at anything you put your mind to. But I think this is exactly the kind of job you'd love."

Amy toyed with her paring knife. "They'd probably just reject me, like McDonald's."

"They might."

"But I suppose it wouldn't hurt to at least look at the application."

"That's true."

"Or I could call and just ask some questions."

"You could do that."

"Maybe I will." Amy put her knife down, picked up the paper, and wandered out of the kitchen.

Alone, Jane Darling allowed herself a small smile over the flat of strawberries. *You know the plan, of course,* she prayed, *but if anyone's asking, I happen to think she'd be perfect for the job.*

"ARMS UP, and deep breath *in* as you hinge *for*ward and bring your forehead to your knees. Feel the stretch up the backs of your legs. Goooood." The yoga instructor, a woman named Serenity, had a light, breathy voice and a body like Gumby's that seemed able to stretch effortlessly into the most impossible of positions.

Bent over at the waist as far as she could go, Laura Darling stretched until it hurt, but her head still hung a discouraging eighteen inches from her knees.

"Feel your aura expaaaand," crooned Serenity. "You are *calm*. You are ser*ene*. Deep breath in, now stretch even *fur*ther toward the floor as you breathe out all the tension, all the stress, all those toxic emotions poisoning your body. Let them go. They don't belong to you. Refuse to *own* them."

Laura stretched another inch and felt an alarming twang

in the back of her right knee, as though it were being plucked like the high E string on her guitar. She eased back to where she'd been.

In spite of the soothing music flowing from hidden speakers, the trickle of water in the corner fountain, and the discreet scent of sage candles in the studio, irritation stabbed through her, as fine and sharp as a needle. What did Serenity know? With her effortless vegan lifestyle, getting paid to do yoga all day, going home at night to her life partner, a gemologist named Zephyr, who sometimes picked her up from the studio and looked like something out of an Abercrombie ad. Laura had been taking the yoga class for two months, and already she knew these things about her instructor. Easy for her to talk about letting go of stress and refusing to own your toxic emotions, but what could a woman with a name like Serenity really understand about Laura and her life?

After class, she left the studio, blinking in the late-afternoon sun. The light in Phoenix was different from the light in Maine. Here there was no pine forest or ocean or swaths of green farmland to soften it, and the sun beat down from a desert's breadth of sky, as searing and bright as the bottom of a new frying pan. She drove the two blocks home. This barely gave her Saab's air-conditioning time to kick in, and she let herself into her apartment with a sigh of relief. Home. Central air.

She went to the refrigerator and poured herself a glass of white wine, which she took to the bathroom. The ice-cold wine, drunk while she took a warm shower, did more to relax her than Serenity's hour-long yoga class had. Drying her short blonde hair before the mirror afterward, she had a second glass of wine and thought about the evening ahead.

She was going out for drinks with a group of friends from the grocery store where she worked managing the office. It wasn't a great job, but it wasn't a terrible one either. She thought of it more as a stepping stone, a stopping-off place until she figured out what she really wanted to do with her life. She liked that it wasn't stressful. She could leave it behind her at the end of the day. And, of course, it was far from Copper Cove and the chaotic family that expected so much of her. But Laura had escaped all that, and she was happier for it. She was making friends and a life here, where she had the freedom to be herself at last. To do whatever she wanted.

True, it was Max who had forced her to leave Copper Cove. Afraid his wife would find out about their relationship, he had bullied Laura into moving. Had, in fact, given her ten thousand dollars to do it, which paid her moving expenses and left her some for savings. And it had turned out to be for the best. Her love for Max had been like a bad case of the flu: full of fever and aches, and all-consuming while it lasted, but short-lived and now mercifully behind her. He had shown his true colors by turning on her. She saw him now for what he was. A user. A taker. He would move on to another mistress soon. Probably already had. Laura felt not a twinge of regret over this. She was well rid of him, and she knew it.

She met the rest of the group at a downtown bar called Lustre. Kimmy and Rachel, the part-time college student cashiers, were already there with Dax, who stocked shelves on the night shift.

"Is it just us?" Laura asked, pulling out a chair and hanging her purse over the back of it.

"Jose's in the bathroom." Kimmy nodded in that direction.

A male server materialized. "Are we all set to order?" he said in a false, bright tone. Waiters who spoke in terms of what "we" were going to do were one of Laura's personal peeves.

"We thought we'd get some kale chips and nachos; is that okay with everybody?" Kimmy asked the table in general.

"I want one of those drinks they make with watermelon juice," Rachel said, bouncing up and down in her seat. "They're sooo yummy!" She sounded about thirteen years old. Laura stifled a pang of embarrassment.

The server ate it up. "One drink with watermelon juice for the beautiful brunette."

"I want the one with jasmine syrup," said Kimmy. Rachel's adolescent twin.

"Aaaand jasmine syrup for the lovely blonde." The server winked at her.

Kimmy giggled.

The server looked at Laura.

"Double vodka tonic with lemon."

"Vodka tonic with lemon for . . . You must be Mom." He wrote it down.

Laura felt her face flush. "Excuse me?"

The server looked startled, then stricken. "I'm sorry. I just meant . . . you seem a little older . . . more mature than—"

The temperature at the table might have dropped ten degrees. Kimmy and Rachel raised their eyebrows at him, all trace of giggles gone.

"Hang on, I didn't mean—" The server looked like he wanted to crawl away.

"Dude, forget about it," Dax said. "We know she's way older than us. It's not a big deal. I'll have a Coors. And wait a second, here comes Jose."

Jose, who bagged groceries full-time at the store, slid into the last empty seat at the table. "Rum and Coke," he said, sniffing. His eyes darted around the room, and he drummed his fingers on the table.

"Rum and Coke. Right." The server stuffed his pad into his pocket and hurried away.

Laura eyed Jose with interest. Two stints in rehab had taught her a thing or two.

Kimmy leaned forward. "Hey, what about that server? Totally rude, right? You're old, and we're immature? What's up with that?"

Laura didn't want to talk about it. Her thirtieth birthday was approaching, and she supposed she might be a little old to be hanging out with a bunch of college kids. Still, these were the people she knew in the city, and they had invited her along. She turned to Jose. "Feeling pretty good after your trip to the bathroom?"

He looked hard at her, then flashed a grin. "Not too bad. You wanna cut a line?"

"What?" said Rachel brightly, looking from one to the other.

"No thanks," Laura told him. "I'm not into that stuff anymore."

"What?" Rachel said again.

"You did blow?"

Laura shook her head. "Pills. Oxys and Vicodin. But I went through a couple of rehabs, and I'm clean now."

Rachel caught on. "Lau-*ra*!" she squealed. "You used to do *drugs*?"

Behind Rachel's back, Dax raised his eyes heavenward.

They were interrupted by the server, who arrived with their drinks. When he'd set them down and left, Rachel hissed, "I can't believe you were in *rehab*!"

"Well, take it from me, it's not worth it." Laura took a soothing sip of her vodka tonic. "It makes you edgy and irritable all the time. I ended up drinking just to calm myself down."

Jose smirked. "So now you're just an alcoholic?"

"I drink in moderation," Laura told him loftily.

She was glad when the rest of them finished their drinks and nachos and decided to move on to a club down the block. "Not me," she told them. "Mom's going to call it an early night." She winked as she said it and laughed along with them, but as she got in her car to go one way while the closest thing she had to friends went in the other direction, she felt small, and somehow faintly ashamed of herself.

Ivy was washing the supper dishes when the phone rang. She tucked it between her ear and shoulder, getting soap bubbles in her hair. "Hello."

"Hi, it's Amy."

"Amy! What are you up to?"

"Just finished supper. I cooked, so Mom and Sephy are cleaning up."

"Sounds like a good deal. I need to put that plan into action around here."

"Does Nick cook?"

"Well . . . no."

"Does he do dishes?"

"Okay, so it's a pipe dream. What did you make for supper?"

"A quinoa and potato casserole with curried lentils. And sprouted-wheat bread."

"Did anyone besides you eat it?"

"Ho-ho, you're hilarious. I'll have you know Sephy and Mom loved it, and even Dad ate it."

"You may convert him yet."

"I doubt it. If there'd been a New York strip on the table, my poor quinoa wouldn't have gotten a second glance. Hey, what are you doing tomorrow?"

"Working in the morning, grocery shopping in the afternoon. Want to come along?"

"Hmm . . . it's tempting," Amy said, sounding cheerfully untempted. "Actually, I have plans for tomorrow, and I wanted to know if *you* wanted to come with *me*. It's not until four o'clock."

"What is it?"

"You know the old opera house on Winter Street?"

Yes, she knew it. The moldering building had been boarded up for as long as Ivy could remember, its small front lawn racked with weeds, the walls weathered to the color of old asphalt. Over the years, different town factions had lobbied by turns to have it demolished as an eyesore or renovated as an important historical landmark. "What about it?"

"The town's just bought it. The council wants to turn it into a big center for the arts. They advertised for a full-time director, and I had an interview today."

"Amy, that's great! Sephy mentioned it, but I forgot to ask you. Why didn't you say something?"

She could hear the shrug in her sister's voice. "I thought, what are the chances they'll hire me? I don't even have a bachelor's degree. And I have practically no experience."

Ivy was indignant. "No experience? What about all those years of high school and summer theater?"

"I meant no administrative experience."

"Every member of this family can vouch for your administrative experience. You were born to organize people."

"Thank you, I think. Anyway, my lack of experience is a moot point because I got the job. They just called me five minutes ago."

Ivy let out a small scream and dropped a plate back into the soapy water. With both hands, she clutched the phone. "Congratulations! I'm so proud of you. You'll do a great job."

"I'm a tiny bit terrified," confessed her little sister. "Anyway, I'll tell you all about it tomorrow, if you can meet me at four o'clock. Part of my job includes being on the renovation committee, and the chairwoman of the town council wants to show me around the place before our first meeting.She's a dry old thing, and I could use your moral support."

Ivy did some rapid mental calculations. If she shopped fast, she could be home in time. "Four o'clock, where?"

"At the opera house. If you can make it, I'll love you forever."

"You have to love me forever anyway. I'm your sister. Okay, I can be there."

"Thanks, Ivy."

"Congratulations again, Amy. That's really, really good news. They made the right decision, hiring you."

"Wait until the end of our first season, and then tell me that," said Amy.

"Nonsense. You'll bring down the house."

Mitch Harris pulled onto Winter Street and was sizing up the place before he had his Ford F-250 in park and the ignition turned off. He let the door slam and stood at the curb, looking up at the old building. The back of his neck prickled. It was a signal he had learned to trust; it almost always meant he was in the presence of something remarkable.

Buildings had faces and stories and characters. This one had the magic too. Beneath the faded gray clapboards and the plywood nailed over the windows, he saw the bones of the structure as a sculptor sees the bones of a model. In spite of fifty years' neglect, the framework was still sturdy. In time, it would once again be beautiful.

He had arrived twenty minutes early on purpose; there were a few things he wanted a second look at. He lit a cigarette, grabbed a claw hammer from the truck, and used it to hack his way through a jungle of waist-high milkweed and timothy to the back of the building. With the hammer, he pried away a piece of clapboard and examined it. Cedar, and mostly still sound. He kicked aside the knotted and tangled grass and examined the laid-stone foundation. There were cracks in the mortar, but it was solid enough. When he'd gone through the place last spring, there had been no moisture in the basement, although the boiler was definitely going to need replacing before winter.

There was about an acre of land, he guessed, most of it in the rear. Room for either a parking lot or an addition, depending on zoning codes. Maybe for both. At the northern boundary of the property was a stream with birches growing along it, but the banks were so choked with undergrowth that it would take a bush hog to get through to the water. The right landscaper could clear that all away and do something really great with it. Mitch was happy enough to let that be someone else's headache. He'd gotten the bid for renovating the building; he would have work enough of his own.

He finished his walk around the building just as a beat-up Escort pulled to the curb behind his truck. He heard a tick in the engine as it slowed. Probably a bad lifter. He could fix that. He watched as a skinny girl in a long skirt and tank top got out. She walked toward him, shading her eyes in spite of the sunglasses she wore.

Mitch dropped his cigarette butt, grinding it out with the toe of his work boot and blowing out the last of the smoke in a long, blue stream. The girl wore her hair in dreadlocks piled on top of her head and had a canvas bag hitched over one shoulder. When she took her hand away from her face, a jolt of recognition went through him like a shot of espresso. She had to be one of the Darling girls. He did some fast mental math and took a guess. "Amy?"

"Mitch!" Her mouth fell open and she stared. He couldn't tell if she was happy to see him or not. She stepped closer and smacked him hard on the arm with the side of her fist.

"Ouch!" Mitch took a hasty step back. So . . . not happy then.

"Where have you *been* all these years?" Amy demanded. Her outraged expression might have been funny to Mitch, if his arm weren't throbbing.

He rubbed the place where she'd hit him. Little brat. He'd have a bruise for sure. "It's a long story."

She took another step toward him and pulled off her sunglasses. "Didn't it ever occur to you that the family might want to *hear* from you once in a while? That we *missed* you?"

He backed up again. "Yeah, well . . . Look at you, all grown up now."

"Oh, please. It's been fourteen years, Mitch, of course I'm grown up."

"Has it been that long?"

"None of us had any *idea* you lived around here. Why haven't you gotten in touch?"

He was saved when a white Jetta and a sleek gold Lexus pulled to the curb at the same time.

"It's Ivy," Amy said, turning to look at the cars. "I can't wait to see what *she* has to say about this." She raised her voice. "Hey, Ivy! Look what the cat dragged in!"

Ivy came, shading her eyes as Amy had done. "Mitch Harris! Oh my goodness! It's so great to see you!" She brushed past Amy and kissed him on the cheek.

It startled him, but he couldn't help grinning. It was better than a punch in the arm, anyway. "Hey, Ivy. You look great. I wouldn't have recognized you." He realized how that sounded. "I mean, you always looked great. Not that I—" On second thought, it seemed best to just shut his mouth.

"It's my hair, I think. Nobody recognizes me these days. You look great yourself—not the scrawny teenager I remember."

His neck grew warm, and he rubbed it. "Well . . . working construction'll do that for you."

The woman from the Lexus was wandering over, talking on her phone. Like the old opera house, most of her property was in the rear. She wore tight shorts that showed off the lines across her broad bottom. Mitch felt a stab of pity for her.

"Hello, everyone." She dropped her phone into her purse and surveyed them, unsmiling. "Thank you for coming. Mitch, I see you've already met our new arts director."

At first Mitch thought she meant Ivy, but then saw that she was nodding toward—

"Amy?"

The youngest Darling raised an eyebrow with a silver ring through it. "Is that a problem?"

He raised both hands. "Hey, I'm not the one with the problem."

Ivy stepped between them and held out her hand to the older woman. "I'm Amy's sister Ivy, and we've just had a great surprise. Mitch is a family friend from way back. We haven't seen each other in *years*. Wouldn't you say that's an example of how the arts bring people together?"

"Lovely." The councilwoman began to dig through her purse, either not seeing Ivy's hand or ignoring it. She pulled out a key. "Let's get started, shall we? My son has a baseball game in an hour, and I don't want to be late."

For the next forty minutes, the four of them walked through the opera house's crumbling auditorium and backstage area, while Mitch pounded walls, examined floors, and squinted up at ceilings. Ivy interrogated the council-woman with an endless list of questions, but Amy was nearly silent as she explored the rooms, scribbling pages of notes in a spiral-bound book.

Her hostility baffled Mitch. He had lived with the Darling family his last two years of high school. Amy had still been a little girl when he had left. She existed in his memory only as a vague first grader with a blurred face. He remembered long braids and a Red Sox baseball cap, but not much else. She had been a spoiled brat in those days, but he had supposed that was part of being the youngest. David had always taken Amy's side in a family argument, had let her barge in on their basketball games in the driveway, and insisted they take her with them when they drove out to Red's Clam Shack for ice cream and she begged to come along. She had shadowed them constantly back then, yet now, even as they moved through the rooms of the opera house, he could feel her animosity. It hung between them like heat waves on hot asphalt. There and not there. Invisible, but obvious all the same.

When they had finished looking the place over, the councilwoman hurried away to her son's game, leaving Mitch standing by his truck with the two sisters.

"Are you living here in town?" Ivy asked him. "Why haven't you called our parents? They would love to see you."

He blew out a breath. "It's complicated."

"I know, Mitch." Ivy's voice was kind. "Of course it's complicated. But we've missed you."

He wished she wouldn't be so nice. "I was . . . away for a while."

"We heard." She took off her sunglasses and looked at him. "But if I remember right, you were only sentenced to two years. What have you been doing for the last ten?"

He kicked at a tuft of weeds growing up through the sidewalk and wished he were doing this with a beer in his hand. "Building. I learned carpentry in prison. When I got out, the chaplain found me a job with a guy who was willing to give me a chance. I worked for him until a couple of years ago. Then he retired, and I bought the business."

"Are you living in town?"

He jerked his head north. "I got an apartment in Bucksport."

"Look," said Ivy, "we all get together at Mom and Dad's house every other Thursday night for supper. Why don't you come sometime? Everyone would love to see you."

"No, I . . . I'm probably going to be moving away after this job is finished, so—"

Ivy was already searching through her big shoulder bag, as though she didn't hear him. She pulled out a phone. "What's your number? Mom will want to call and invite you herself." She held the phone poised.

He knew when he was beaten. He told her the number and watched with a feeling of helplessness as she entered it. He could always hope she had gotten one of the numbers wrong.

"Bye, Mitch. See you Thursday night, maybe." Ivy leaned forward to kiss him on the cheek again, and this time, he was prepared. He remembered now the way the Darlings were about kissing anybody who stood still for longer than two minutes. Amy didn't say a word, just turned and followed her sister to their cars.

"Hey, Amy," Mitch called to her back. "Sounds like you got a bad lifter under your hood. Might want to get that taken care of."

She didn't acknowledge him, but Ivy turned and waved. And then they were gone, leaving him standing alone in the weed-eaten front yard of the decayed opera house. Mitch felt a fine cobweb of dread settle over him. The Darlings and their brand of big, noisy, all-encompassing love had come back into his life. He had the feeling that the world he kept wound as carefully as a reel of fishing line was about to spin out of control on him, and that when it did, there might never be any way to untangle it again.

Sephy set the last of her schoolbooks in the cardboard box by her bedroom door and consulted her list. There were only her last-minute toiletries to pack in the morning and she would be off to conquer her last year of college. Later tonight, her father would carry her boxes and bags down to the driveway and help her pack everything into the Corolla so she could get an early start in the morning.

The little Ohio town where she went to school was a good fourteen-hour drive from Copper Cove, and she always took two days to make the trip. Tomorrow she would push through to Cleveland, where she would spend the night with her mother's old college roommate Sharon DeMille, a sweet, single woman the Darling children had known all their lives. They called her Aunt Sharon, and meant it. She was family. The following day, Sephy would drive the remaining four hours, which would get her to campus while it was still morning. She would have all day to settle into her room before her RA orientation started.

She now had reason to be doubly grateful for the summer classes she had taken because last week, a letter had come informing her that she had gotten the RA job she had applied for. It would be time-consuming, and a lot of extra responsibility, and she had to be there two days early for a leadership conference, but it would pay for a good part of her room and board, and her academic scholarship would take care of half her tuition, as long as she kept her grades up, which she knew she would. She planned to find jobs babysitting and teaching piano. People in town were always looking for college kids, who would work for practically nothing, to give their children music lessons. As well, a local nursing home let her work weekends as a CNA.

Her thoughts were interrupted by a knock on the open door. "Everyone decent?"

"David!" She smiled at her big brother. "Come in, if you can get around the mess. What are you doing here? Dinner's not for a couple of hours yet."

He picked up her vanity chair and turned it around backward, straddling it, resting his arms on the back. "I left work early and drove over to see if you needed a hand packing your car."

"That would be great. It'll save Dad hauling all this stuff downstairs when he gets home."

Her brother rested his chin on his forearms and regarded her. "So, last year of college. Are you sad or glad?"

She was used to this question by now. "Am I allowed to be both?"

"Oh, that's right. I always forget you women can do that thing where you feel more than one emotion at a time."

"Well . . . you know. It comes in handy as a party trick."

"I think it just makes you needlessly complicated."

Sephy threw a pillow at him. He caught it and threw it back.

"I'm mostly glad to be graduating," she said, sitting down on the bed. "I'll miss my friends, of course, but I think I miss home when I'm at college more than I miss my friends when I'm back home. Does that make sense?"

"Perfectly. That's why I never went away to school myself. So what's after graduation?"

"I'll apply for a job at the hospital in Quahog. It's only thirty miles away, so if I get an apartment there, I can be independent and close to home at the same time."

"Like me. Living across town, but here for supper almost every night."

"Yes, David, in this as in everything, you are my inspiration. What about you? Any big plans for your life, now that summer's almost over?"

"Plans for my life? Why do you ask that?" He looked suddenly shifty.

She frowned. "Ah . . . just asking, I guess. Why?"

"No, I just wondered what you meant when you said 'big plans,' that's all. It's a strange way to put it." He examined the back of her vanity chair.

"Stop looking so guilty. What are you up to?"

"Nothing. I mean, just the usual. Working for the landscaping company. Sharing an apartment with George. Looking for the perfect girl to marry."

Sephy raised her eyebrows. "Oh-ho, finding the perfect girl is finally on the docket, is it? What are you not telling me?"

"I'm not *not telling* you anything. But now that you mention it, and since you're being such a nag, I guess I *would* appreciate your opinion on something."

"Okay, what?"

David became interested in a splinter of wood on the chair, picking at it with his thumbnail. "I was just wondering," he said in an offhand tone, "what you would think if I asked Libby out sometime. Just on a date," he hurried to add, his ears reddening. "We're not talking perfect-girl status or anything."

Sephy blinked at him, her mind wiped clean of thought. "Libby? *My* Libby? Liberty *Hale*?"

He shrugged. "Why not?"

"I just . . . No reason. None at all. Do you think she'd say yes?"

"Do you think she'll say no?"

"I don't know. I can truly say I've never thought about it. The idea never so much as crossed my mind before."

"Why? Am I that repulsive?"

"No, not that. I guess I assume she just thinks of you as . . . as a brother, but I don't *know* that. We've never talked about you that way."

"Well, it's only a simple date, maybe bowling and a walk on the pier or something. If she thinks of me as a brother after that, no harm done; it's been a fun evening between friends, right?"

Sephy squinted at him. "Do you *like* her?"

He was silent, considering this. "Let's just say that with a little encouragement, I could come to like her."

Sephy smiled. "Well, let me be the first to wish you good luck."

David looked relieved. "Thanks, Seph. But don't say anything to her about it, okay? That would be weird."

"I won't say anything."

"Or to Ivy and the rest of the pack. I'd never hear the end of it."

"My lips are sealed. But you have to promise to tell me all about it afterward."

"Won't Libby do that herself?"

She waggled her eyebrows at him. "I'll want to hear it from both sides."

He stood up. "Right. Let's schlep this stuff down to the driveway and get your car packed before supper."

David wasn't the last sibling to visit her room that night. After dinner, Sephy showered, set her alarm for 4 a.m., and had just picked up a book to read a few pages when Amy knocked and, without waiting for an invitation, came in. She sat on the end of the bed, pushing Sephy's feet out of the way. "One more year and you're done," she said, tucking her knees up under her chin.

Sephy put a bookmark in her page and laid the book on the bedside table. "One more. Probably the longest year of my life."

"I bet when you look back on it, it'll be the shortest."

Sephy smiled. "I bet you're right. That's how things usually work, isn't it? I thought my senior year of high school would never end, but once June came, it felt like I'd only been there about a week."

"I'll miss you." Amy sounded accusing.

"I'll be back in nine months."

"That's *your* story," Amy said darkly. "But you won't really be back. Even if you get a job in Quahog, you'll go off and get an apartment of your own, and we'll never see you again."

"At the very least, I'll be here every other Thursday night for supper, won't I?"

"I hope so. I hope you'll keep your head and not end up too busy for your own family. Like Laura." Amy plucked at the quilt. "Or be like Mitch and just go away and forget all about us."

"Give Mitch a break. He was probably too ashamed of himself after prison to get in touch with us again. And as for Laura, there's no law that says every Darling sibling has to be as attached to the family as you and I are. Some people just need more space to live their own lives."

"Ivy manages to strike a pretty good balance between living her own life and being loyal to her family of origin."

"Oh, Amy! If only life were so black-and-white."

"I don't see why it can't be. You have family who love you. You love them. Why can't you come for dinner one night out of fourteen? And why did Laura have to move all the way across the country anyway?"

Sephy sighed. Amy had always lacked the capacity to see a situation from anyone else's point of view. She changed the subject. "You must be excited about the new job."

"I am. I move into my office and start work on Wednesday. David and George promised to help me."

Sephy laughed. "Poor George. Is he making any progress on his Great American Novel?"

Amy shook her head. "Apparently he's nine months into a case of intractable writer's block. Meanwhile, he's working at the greenhouse out on Route 9 while his thoughts *foment*."

"*Foment?* What a great word! But nine months of writer's block . . . it sounds like he might be just about due to give birth to some staggering work of genius."

"With any luck."

"With any luck," Sephy agreed. "He's so nice. I wish him well."

They sat in comfortable silence, which Amy broke by saying, "Actually, I wanted to say something before you left for school, Seph."

"What's that?"

Amy stared at the quilt. "I don't want to offend you . . ."

Sephy felt something hard rise up in the region of her stomach. Those six words had never yet preceded something inoffensive. "Okay."

"I only . . . I want the very best for you, you know? Because I love you. You're my *sister*."

"What is it you wanted to say, Amy?"

"I was just thinking that this might be the year for you to really change your life, you know? Maybe to start eating vegetarian." Amy looked up, gaining momentum. "It makes you feel so light and clean. I mean, it's really the way we were meant to eat, isn't it? Plus, it's such an easy way to control

35

your weight." That last sentence hung lamely in the air before it fell with a heavy clang, a curious non sequitur to the rest of the conversation.

So that's what this is about. Amy, trying to be kind, was simply pointing out what Sephy was only too aware of already. She was fat.

With an effort, Sephy managed to say, "Thanks. I'll give it some thought. It might be good for me, after all." Then she yawned and added, "Well, I'd better get to sleep. I have an early start tomorrow."

Amy stood up, looking uncertain. "I'm only saying it because I love you, Seph."

"Oh no, I know that. And I really do appreciate it." Sephy gave her younger sister a bright smile. "Can you just shut the door on your way out?"

"Sure. I won't say good-bye now, because I'll be up to see you off in the morning."

"Great. Thanks."

"Love you, Seph."

"I love you too, Amy."

When her sister had gone, Sephy lay on her side for a long time, staring at the wall and hating Amy just the littlest bit. But hating herself even more. Her problem wasn't her sister's fault. Whom, after all, did Sephy have to blame but herself?

"Seraphina Darling, welcome! I've missed you so!" Sharon DeMille stepped out of her neat brick house and opened wide her arms to the daughter of her old college roommate.

"Hi, Aunt Sharon." Puffing a little, Sephy set her heavy overnight bag on the front steps and gave her honorary aunt a hug. "Thanks for putting up with me for the night."

"Put up with you, my foot! I'm delighted to have you. Come in and sit down and tell me all about your summer."

In the kitchen, Aunt Sharon opened the refrigerator and began to pull out containers. "You must be ready for a snack after your long drive."

"Sounds good."

"You could slice up some of those croissants if you wouldn't mind. I've just got to stick my finger here."

Aunt Sharon took a glucometer kit from a cupboard, and Sephy, choosing a bread knife from the block on the counter, watched her lance her finger and balance the droplet of blood on a test strip. When the machine beeped, Aunt Sharon read it. "Two thirteen," she pronounced. She tossed the test strip into the trash, dropped the lancet into a small red sharps container on the counter, and put the kit back in the cupboard, exchanging it for an insulin pen. "Aaaaand a little shot." She screwed a needle onto the end of the pen.

"I didn't know you took insulin."

"I started last winter. The oral meds weren't doing the trick anymore."

"That's too bad."

"Well, it isn't the end of the world. I suppose I've gotten used to it." She held up the pen. "I'll pop into the bathroom and give myself this while you slice those croissants, and then we'll eat, all right?"

Over chicken salad on croissants, potato salad, and root beer floats, Sephy told her about the summer classes behind her and the RA job ahead. Sharon, who normally spent a week of every summer in Copper Cove, had been laid up with varicose veins this year and had missed her trip to Maine. The year before, it was her blood pressure that had kept her home. Consequently, she was hungry for news of all of them, but particularly of David, who was her godchild.

"Why isn't that boy married yet?" she asked, half-exasperated. "He's thirty-two years old. What can the girls in Maine be thinking?"

Sephy told her about the conversation in her room the night before. "You're sworn to secrecy, though," she warned.

"If you so much as breathe a word of this to Mom or my sisters, David will never tell me anything again."

Sharon knew Libby Hale from her summers in Maine. "Does it bother you to think of your brother going out with your best friend?"

"No . . ." Even as she said it, Sephy realized this wasn't strictly true. "Actually, I'm not really sure how I feel. If it doesn't work out and one of them ends up disappointed . . ."

"But if it *were* to work out, she could end up being your sister. The question is, is she good enough for him?"

Sephy snorted. "More like is he good enough for her? Libby's the best. She's sweet, funny, loyal. No one could ask for a better friend."

"And is she kindhearted?"

"Very."

"Then I think even if things don't work out for them, David will be all right."

They finished their sandwiches in silence before Aunt Sharon asked, "What about you, Sephy? Anyone special in your life?"

"I've really been too busy with college to think about guys."

"Well, you've done well, my dear. You're always working one or two jobs, and heaven knows, nursing classes are no joke."

"How about you? How are things at the psych hospital?"

"I'm not working there anymore. In fact, I'm not working anywhere," said Sharon, pushing the potato salad bowl toward Sephy. "Have some more of that." Sephy helped herself. "I went on disability last month."

"No!" Sephy stared at her. "What's wrong?"

"It was my arthritis. I just couldn't work anymore."

"Ouch. That's too bad."

Her aunt managed a weak smile. "I'm used to it by now. The high blood pressure bothers me more. I get terrible head-aches, and . . . I worry. I think I could deal with a heart attack, if it came to that, but a stroke . . ." She shook her head. Sephy saw a flash of fear in her aunt's eyes and felt an answering fear of her own. They both knew what a stroke could do to a person, had taken care of patients whose uncontrolled blood pressure had sidelined them, leaving them forever unable to walk or talk or go to the bathroom by themselves.

"Are you taking anything for it?"

"Simvastatin. Diovan. Hydrochlorothiazide. Lopressor." Sharon ticked them off on her fingers. "Tramadol and meloxi-cam for my arthritis. Insulin. Ambien to help me sleep, and a tiny bit of Zoloft and Celexa for depression."

"How can you be taking all that? It must be wildly expensive."

"Yes, and I'll just confess right now that the doctor says I need to lose weight. I try and try, but somehow I can't seem to do it." She looked at her empty plate with an expression that said volumes. It bespoke a cesspool of emotions Sephy knew only too well: regret, helplessness, guilt. Self-loathing. Tears burned her eyes, and she reached for her aunt's hand.

"Don't give up. Keep trying." But even saying it, she felt powerless. Like she had nothing of real value to offer this woman she loved.

Later, after Sephy had a shower and a short nap, Sharon insisted on ordering Chinese food for supper. Together, they polished off a carton of hot and sour soup and one of egg drop, a pupu platter, and a large shrimp lo mein. They split an order of orange chicken and another of sweet and sour pork. Sephy could not help but feel she was aiding and abetting the murder of someone she loved. Her feeble suggestion that they order salads instead had been received in the same spirit it was offered. In the end she ate just as much as Aunt Sharon did and could not have said which was stronger: the fully sensual experience of rice, shrimp, and deep-fried pork, or the guilt of knowing they were like two drowning people clinging together, each too weak to let go and save herself, each trying to mitigate her own failure by pulling the other down with her.

Laura's birthday was the second of September. As she left the grocery store that afternoon, she checked her phone. Ivy had left a message.

"Happy thirtieth," her twin's voice chirped. "Call me when you get a chance. Love you!"

Ivy always seemed to forget that Laura worked all day and wasn't necessarily free to take phone calls whenever she felt like it, unlike *some* people she could name. Still, nobody in Arizona even knew it was her birthday. It was nice to have it acknowledged, at least.

It was a short drive to the highway. "Call Ivy," Laura told her Bluetooth system as she eased into heavy commuter traffic.

Ivy answered on the first ring. "Laura, hey! Happy birthday, twin!"

It was good to hear her sister's voice. A swell of homesickness rose up in Laura's chest, surprising and unwelcome.

"Hey, how are you doing? How are things back in Copper Cove?"

"Oh, you know. A little crazy, as ever, but it's good crazy, not bad. The kids start school tomorrow, so we're running around getting ready for that."

On the highway ahead of her, the traffic was slowing. Laura stretched to look at what was happening. All she could see was a long line of cars, disappearing into the distance. *Great.* Some idiot had caused an accident that would take hours to clean up, probably. She had been hoping to squeeze in a trip to the gym before—

"How about you?" Ivy asked. "How are you celebrating your birthday?"

"Well, it's a weeknight, so I can't go out. I have to work, actually. I picked up a second job, waitressing at a little bar in the evenings. It's just ten hours a week, but I'm scheduled tonight, so I guess that's how I'm spending my birthday." She had picked up the job because she was finding that time weighed heavier on her hands in Arizona than it had back home. Without a family to field and an affair to carry on with her boss, she was spending way too much time in her own head. She would find herself thinking at odd moments of Max and how her life might be different if they had ended up together after all. Or if she had never gotten involved with him in the first place. She would think of her parents and sisters and brother back in Maine, of all their lives going on without her, and though she was glad to be out of that particular chaos, at times she felt, perversely, like the only girl in the class who had not been invited to the party. The one sitting at home alone while all the fun went on without her. Not only did all that endless self-examination get her nowhere, it also made it easy to drink more than she should. She had put on a few pounds around the waistline recently, which she blamed on wine. Anyway, the extra money from a second job was nice.

Ivy was chattering away in her ear. "At this very minute I am, if you can believe it, having a pedicure. Nick and the kids got me a spa package for my birthday, along with a book of Patrick Kavanagh's poems. Tonight we're all going out to dinner."

Laura pulled her attention back to her sister. "Who's Patrick Kavanagh?"

"My favorite poet. You know that."

Laura supposed she had, at one time. "That's right. How are the kids, by the way? They must be getting big."

"Oh, they are. DeShaun towers over me. He's starting eleventh grade—can you believe it?"

Laura murmured something she hoped sounded disbelieving. The car ahead of her rolled forward two feet, and she followed suit.

"He's going to go mornings to the high school and afternoons to the tech school, for their culinary arts program."

"Oh, good. I remember he loves to cook."

"It's great to see him finding what he was meant to do in life, and doing it."

"If only it were that easy for all of us," Laura said. "How about Jada and Hammer? What are they up to?"

"Jada's starting sixth grade. Still taking voice and violin lessons and loving them. Hammer's in second grade. He just finished up his summer soccer season."

"Sounds like they're doing great." The traffic was barely moving. Inching ahead a foot or two at a time before stopping again.

"They are. I think having been adopted has given them a sense of stability they never had as foster children. It's the idea of permanence, I suppose."

The air-conditioning was getting cold. Laura turned the fan down. "Are you working or what?" she asked her sister.

"Just two days a week at the bookstore. The kids are involved in so much: we're heading into the busy time of year. Practices, concerts, school stuff . . . It can be pretty overwhelming. I won't have a minute to myself until maybe mid-November. Then it's the holidays, and you know what *that's* like."

Laura could take it no more. "Oh, *please*," she said, rolling her eyes at her own reflection in the rearview mirror. "I refuse to feel sorry for you, Ivy. Here I am, working fifty hours a week, while you're sitting there having a pedicure, for pete's sake. What do you have to complain about?"

Ivy was silent. Then, quietly, "I'm not complaining. I'm just . . . talking."

Great. Now her sister was offended. Laura had never met anyone as thin-skinned as Ivy. You couldn't say *any*thing to her. The line of cars in front of her began to move, the spaces opening up between them one at a time until the car ahead of her gave a hitch, rolled, and kept going. It looked like she might get home in time to hit the gym after all. "Well, I have to go," she told Ivy. "I've been stuck in traffic and it just started moving."

"Okay. Thanks for calling back, and happy birthday. I wish you good tips tonight."

Laura smiled. "Thanks. Have a good dinner out with the family." They both made kissing noises into the phone and hung up.

As the highway traffic picked up speed, Laura thought about her twin. Ivy had no idea what real life was about. What were her problems, really, except problems of excess? So she had no time to herself. She had no time because she had so many kids. Well, she had wanted kids and she had gotten them. What was she going to complain about next? Having too much money? A husband who was too good to her? Meanwhile, Laura was working two jobs at two different places, had no friends to speak of, no boyfriend, and no family around. By rights *she* should be the one complaining, but was she? No. She just sucked it up and did what she needed to do to get life done.

She was glad all over again that she lived in Arizona. Every time she talked to someone back in Maine, it was another reminder of all the reasons she had left there in the first place.

Amy sliced through the tape on the bottom of the last empty cardboard box, folded it flat, and set it atop the neat stack of other flattened boxes in the hallway, weighting it down with an iron bookend shaped like a horse's head. She had found the single bookend in the top drawer of a filing cabinet she had inherited along with her new office. The filing cabinet, two drawers high, now stood in the corner of the minuscule room. It held a collection of scripts and musical scores, alphabetized by composer, with four rows of CDs wedged in beside them. Her maple desk took up the remaining space. David and George had hauled the desk, a swivel chair, and four boxes up the three flights of stairs to her new office, and she had paid them with two loaded pizzas from Blue Yew. A city-issued computer, beige with an enormous, outdated monitor, dominated the desktop along with a phone, also beige, part of the city hall system. Her day planner lay open and ready beside a pottery mug of pens and pencils. The watercolors and sketches of a few personal friends hung on the walls. In the corner of the polished oak floor, the trash can was empty.

The job was hers; it did not seem real. Setting up her office, Amy felt like a child playing house. When her mother had handed her that newspaper clipping weeks ago, she hadn't given it any serious thought. She had applied for the job only out of curiosity, to see if she had a chance of getting it. To her surprise, they had called her for an interview, first with the chairperson of the arts committee, then with the entire town council. She still was not sure why they had hired her, unless possibly she had been the only applicant. She didn't know this to be the case, but she suspected it. Still, her age and lack of experience hadn't seemed to put them off. They told her later that the vote to hire her had been unanimous. And for her part, Amy had known as soon as they offered her the job that they might as well have created it with her in mind. The chance to combine her love of the arts with her love of being in charge, to use her creativity as well as her administrative gifts, was the very thing she was made for. And she was going to do it, as she did everything else in life, well. Really, really well.

Now, not only did she have her own office and an actual budget, but she was also expected to hire a small staff. She thought a choreographer, a combination wardrobe-and-props manager, and a music director should do it. They wanted her to plan and run a full calendar year's worth of community arts activities. As well, she was to sit on the committee that oversaw the opera house renovation. Eventually, when work on the old building was finished, she would move her office over there. For now, she had been assigned this space on the third floor of the town hall. It was a musty, hot little cupboard of a room, on a floor with one other empty office and some storage space, but there was a window down the hall, she had her desk, and it was beginning to look like *hers*.

Already, her head was reeling with ideas. Her objective for this, her first full paid day of work, was simply to brainstorm and get everything down on paper so she could begin to make concrete plans. She would draft classified ads for the staff she needed and send them to both the *Bangor Daily News* and the *Portland Press Herald*. Post them on Monster. com and Craigslist. She sat in the chair behind her desk and at once began to swelter. She turned the fan toward herself. The thin breeze it propelled around the windowless room was barely enough to make the air breathable.

With an effort, she blocked out the terrible heat and turned her mind to the job at hand. She had already decided they would put on semiannual full-scale musical theater productions using nothing but community talent: a general one in the spring and a holiday one in December. In between, they would offer weekly art classes: watercolor, pottery, and oil painting, as well as writing, cooking, yoga, and dance. Maybe foreign languages from time to time, if she could find teachers. They would invite artists from all over Maine—no, all over *New England*—to come and perform. There would be guest comedians, orchestras, dance companies, and theater troupes on every scale from high school kids to semiprofessionals. Professionals, if they could get them. She would organize an annual folk music festival, perhaps a chamber music week, outdoor art fairs in the summer, and public poetry readings on Friday nights. Every piece of artwork that hung in the opera house would be the work of a local artist.

Within minutes, she slipped into what she called her "work zone," that mental place of intense energy and creativity that some people were only able to achieve through chemicals. For her, it was an automatic response to any challenge that required the best of her. She had finished high school in three years and still graduated as valedictorian. Had earned her associate's degree in twelve months, with a solid 4.0 average, and been granted a full academic scholarship to UMO, although she could have gone to Dartmouth, or even Stanford or Yale. But she had never really wanted to pursue something as mainstream as a bachelor's degree. Stepping into this job, creating an arts program from the ground up, was exactly the right path for her. The task before her was daunting—maybe even impossible—but she would get it done if hard work, organization, and delegation had anything to do with it. *Impossible* and *daunting* were the adjectives Amy loved most.

She pulled a legal pad from the top desk drawer and took a pen from the pottery mug. The first performance, the grand kickoff to the whole thing, would be a spring production of *West Side Story*. She had always loved Leonard Bernstein's modern interpretation of *Romeo and Juliet*. So she began a new list of things that needed to be set in motion for that. May would be the right time, she decided. Before community life slowed down for the summer and people went away on vacation.

She needed to think about hiring staff first of all, then ordering scripts and holding auditions, creating a stock of costumes and props . . . Suddenly, the budget the city had allotted her, which had seemed so extravagant until now, began to look like barely enough. Amy started scribbling down numbers, even as she reached for the phone. For the rest of the afternoon, she made phone calls, sent e-mails, and did not think about the outside world again until her stomach growled. The clock on her computer screen told her it was 8:14. All at once, she felt as though she were wearing a bag of cement across her shoulders. She shut everything down, locked her office, and left the deserted building.

At home, she found a note from her parents saying they were out having dinner with friends. She was hungry, but the prospect of finding something to eat appeared an insurmountable obstacle. Even a bowl of cereal seemed too many steps to sort out and accomplish. She passed through the kitchen without turning on the lights, did not wash her face or brush her teeth, and, pausing only long enough to strip off her skirt, fell into bed in the same T-shirt she had worn all day.

The next day, and the next, and the next, Amy rose at five, ran three miles, showered, ate whatever leftovers she could scrounge from the refrigerator, then went to her tiny office and did it all over again. By the end of that first week, she had lost five pounds. She noticed this only because her mother pointed out that she was looking too thin, and she stepped onto the scale to see if it was true. Otherwise, the fact did not interest her; she thought only of her job. It was the way she did everything of importance in her life, and this was by far the most important thing that had ever happened to her. She had never felt so alive.

"Hey, Seph." Her roommate, Ann, came in from the lounge. "Leann and Shara and I are going to supper. You coming?" She picked up a brush and stood before the mirror, brushing her long black hair.

"I don't think so." Sephy kept her eyes on the textbook in front of her. "Big test in pediatrics tomorrow."

"Okay, but the caf closes in half an hour. Don't wait too long, or forget to eat or anything."

As if Sephy had ever, in her life, forgotten to eat a meal. She smiled at her roommate's face in the mirror. "I won't forget. Go ahead without me."

Ann left, and Sephy forced herself to concentrate on the page in front of her. Duchenne muscular dystrophy. *Recessive. X-linked. Eventual death . . .* The words fled her mind as soon as she read them, and she had to start all over from the beginning. She felt edgy and hollow from hunger, but she had no intention of meeting Ann and the others at the cafeteria.

Today was her second day on the 0-1-0 diet. It was something she'd found on a blog: you ate nothing for breakfast, a light lunch, and nothing for supper. The blog guaranteed you'd lose five to seven pounds a week. It had neglected to mention the part about starving to death in the process.

She hadn't been able to get Amy's little speech out of her mind. It was not what Amy had said so much as the fact that she had said it. Obesity had a way of making you feel invisible. And because she felt this way, Sephy could usually convince herself that people didn't notice her weight. But Amy had shot that illusion out of the sky. Clearly, people—even people who loved her—weren't overlooking her size. She had arrived at school determined to do something about it. Maybe her sister had a point: why shouldn't this be the year Sephy changed her life?

She was beginning to realize what being thin felt like. It felt like hungry. Grimly, she said aloud, "Get used to it, Seph." Uncapping her highlighter, she turned the page and kept reading.

Amy put the phone down without taking her eyes off the e-mail message on her computer screen. As soon as the phone touched the cradle, it rang again. She groaned and reached a hand back to massage her neck. Five days ago, she had posted ads on the Internet for a part-time wardrobe-and-props manager and a full-time choreographer, and—forced to concede that her budget wouldn't stretch far enough for an actual music director—had advertised locally for a part-time accompanist. The phone had not stopped ringing since. At first this had seemed like a good sign, but she soon learned differently. Most of the callers hung up as soon as they realized where the job was. People, it seemed, weren't all that enthusiastic about the prospect of moving to a small town in Maine, half an hour from the nearest mall and hospital, to work with community theater. Her luck with e-mail applicants had been no better. Nobody at all had asked about the accompanist job. Maybe this call would be the one, she thought.

She lifted the receiver. "Copper Cove Community Arts Center. This is Amy; how can I help you?"

"It's me," said Ivy.

"Oh, shoot. I thought you were going to turn out to be the answer to all my problems."

"Sorry, that's a service I don't provide. I'm a good listener, though. What *are* all your problems?"

"I still haven't found anyone for the wardrobe and chore-ographer positions. Nobody wants to move to Maine. And it seems that nobody in the entire community has ten hours a week to devote to being an accompanist."

"Have you asked Mom?"

"You think she'd know of someone?"

"No, I mean have you offered Mom the job?"

"Mom?"

"Why not? She's a brilliant accompanist. She'd be perfect for it."

"Mom . . ." Offering the job to her own mother hadn't even occurred to Amy. But Ivy had a point. She *would* be just right. "Do you think she'd mind having her daughter as a boss?"

"Ask her. She'll probably say that you've been the boss your whole life anyway. But seriously, she has the time and talent, and I think she'd love it."

"Ivy, you just made my day. I'll talk to her tonight."

"Glad to be of service. I'll have my assistant send you the bill."

Amy snorted. "What are you up to today?"

"I just got in from work, and I thought I'd give you a buzz in the two quiet minutes I have before the kids get home."

"How are they doing?"

"Pretty well, I think. Why don't you come over and see for yourself? We haven't seen you in a while."

Amy scrolled through her e-mail inbox, checking off messages to delete. "If you're going to be home, I'll stop by after work."

"We'll be home. Want to stay and eat with us? I'll make you something without meat."

"You know what? That sounds good. I deserve to knock off early for once."

"Oh, good! About five thirty, six o'clock then?"

"I'll be there," Amy promised. She hung up the phone and flung her arms wide. She had her first staff member! The fact that she had not yet offered her mother the job was immaterial. Jane would say yes. Amy picked a pencil out of the mug and, unearthing the legal pad with her to-do list, drew a satisfying line through *find accompanist*. She was on her way to getting this thing done.

CHAPTER

THE SIGNS HAD BEEN POSTED in the student center for a month: the Trans-Siberian Orchestra was coming to campus for a one-night-only performance on their way through from Chicago to the East Coast, where they would perform in Portland, Boston, and Hartford before winding up their tour in New York City. That the orchestra would give such a nod to a small Midwestern college was due to the fact that the group's first-chair violinist was a friend and former frat brother of the college's dean of men.

The spark of interest this news generated among the student body was fanned into a conflagration when the college administration announced that the concert was to be considered a Serious Cultural Event and instated a black-tie dress code. A formal dinner was to be served beforehand for anyone who wanted to buy tickets. Overnight, nobody could talk about anything except who was wearing what, and who was going with whom. It was bigger than homecoming. Carloads of girls made Saturday trips to Springfield, Dayton, Columbus, and even Cleveland looking for perfection on a dress hanger in every store.

Sephy had no illusions that anyone would ask her to the concert. She told this to her roommate one afternoon when Ann had returned from Columbus with a dress the color of marigolds and a new pair of strappy sandals to match.

Ann was appalled that Sephy did not plan to go. "But I wanted us to double-date!" she cried. "James has this friend Chad—"

But Sephy did not want to be set up with some man who would only be taking her as a favor to Ann. "I couldn't," she told Ann. "It would be too humiliating. It would be like my senior prom all over again."

Ann, having hung the long dress bag carefully in the closet, kicked off her sneakers and sat down on her bed. "Why? Who did you go to your prom with?"

"You've heard me talk about my best friend, Libby? Well, her brother, Justice, took me. He's six years older than me, so he was already finished with his undergrad degree by then and had no business going to a high school prom. He did it purely as a kindness. Libby and I practically grew up in each other's houses, so I was like a sister to Justice, too. He was always nice to me. Anyway, by the time I was a senior, he was in veterinary college, which impressed all the girls in my class, since the boys *they* all went to prom with still had acne and hadn't grown into their Adam's apples yet."

"So was it romantic?"

"Oh no, we were just next-door neighbors."

"Did you have fun?"

Sephy thought about this. At the time, there had been only the overwhelming feeling of gratitude for being able to go to the prom with someone at all. The relief of not being dateless, not having to buy her own corsage and be the fifth person seated at a table for four. That relief and gratitude had substituted for a lot of other things that she supposed most girls felt about their senior proms: romance, the sense of being wanted by someone. At the time, it had been enough. But now, in hindsight, she recognized the truth of it. "No," she told Ann, "it wasn't fun. I felt like second-best to every girl in the room with a date who had asked her because he wanted to go with her. And I don't want to feel like that ever again."

Ann, who was slim and exotic-looking and had already been asked to the concert by—and turned down—two men before James, had tears in her eyes. She stood up and went to Sephy, wrapping her arms around her roommate. "I think you're absolutely beautiful, Seph. Any guy would be lucky to take you to the concert."

Sephy blinked back tears of her own and tried to laugh. "Well, they're all taking their own sweet time figuring that out, aren't they?"

The next day, Sephy got an e-mail from her microbiology professor, Dr. Marstaller, asking if she would care to babysit the three little Marstallers on the night of the concert. Sephy had babysat these children before and, having enjoyed them, concluded that there were worse ways to spend an evening. One of them being sitting in her dorm room alone, while every other girl she knew waited in the coed lounge for her date to come and claim her for a night of magic, culture, and romance. She did not waste time wondering why her professor should assume she would not be going to the concert. The answer was as obvious to Sephy as it was to Dr. Marstaller, and probably to everyone else in the world. It was just as well. She had moved on to a diet where she ate only grapefruit and chicken. She was lucky to be able to avoid the pitfall that the black-tie meal before the concert was sure to be. She wrote back and said she would be glad to watch the Marstaller children.

Accordingly, on the night of the concert, she said goodbye to Ann, who was stunning in her marigold dress, and to the other girls in her suite. They were busy zipping themselves into gowns of sky blue, pink, and deep green. Borrowing each other's jewelry. Putting last touches on their nail polish. They were like a flock of bright, lovely songbirds, and Sephy slipped from the dorm with a grapefruit in her shoulder bag, feeling like an ungainly, colorless seagull among them. She drove to Dr. Marstaller's house, where her professor met her at the door dressed in a tuxedo. His wife, in a glittering scarlet sheath dress, gave Sephy a few directions about the children's routine, and they left. From the front window, she watched the professor open the car door for his wife and bend down to kiss her hand before closing it.

Turning away, she forced cheerfulness into her voice as she said, "All right, kids, how about supper? I think your mom said something about chicken nuggets and tater tots. After that, we can watch *Finding Nemo!*"

Dinner and a show. She was determined to look on the bright side of things.

She, of course, would be having grapefruit.

Sephy did not get back to her dorm until after midnight, and she was still asleep the next morning when her cell phone rang. She groped for it and answered with a groggy "Hello?"

"Sephy?" Libby's voice was breathless, as though she'd been running.

Sephy came instantly awake. "What's wrong, Lib? Why are you calling so early?" As she spoke, she pushed herself up, feeling on the floor for her slippers, casting an anxious glance at Ann who, to her relief, slept on, undisturbed. The slippers found, Sephy hurried from the room and shut herself into the empty bathroom, where her talking would not wake anyone.

"It's not early," Libby protested. "It's seven o'clock!"

"Well, there was a big concert on campus last night, and everyone came in late, so they're all still sleeping. What's wrong?"

"I'm sorry, I shouldn't have called you so early. Don't worry; nothing's wrong."

"Then . . ."

"I just . . ." Sephy heard the hesitation in her friend's voice. "I wanted your advice about something. Not your advice. Your opinion. I mean . . . your permission. I guess that's what I want—your permission."

"My *permission*? Permission for what?"

"Uh . . . It's about a guy. A man."

Sephy smiled. Libby had to be talking about David. It had certainly taken him long enough. "A man," she said.

"Yeah. Yesterday, this guy . . . this person . . . man . . . asked me out. On a date."

"Oh, good. Good for you."

On the other end of the line, Libby took a deep breath. "Would it be totally inappropriate if I went on a date with your brother?"

Sephy laughed. "You mean you would really want to go on a date with Horrible David?"

"Well, he asked me." Libby sounded defensive. "And I just wondered if you'd mind."

"Of *course* I don't mind."

"You don't?"

"No. If you want to go out with him, go ahead."

"Okay. But would it be, you know . . . weird for you?"

"What do you mean weird for *me*? You'd be the one going out with him. Are you sure it won't be weird for *you*?"

Libby's voice was reflective. "No, Seph. I don't think it'll be weird for me at all."

"All right then."

"I mean," Libby added, "it might not amount to anything. And if it doesn't, I don't want you to be hurt by it."

"Okay."

"Okay, you won't be hurt by it?"

"Shouldn't I be the one asking *you* that?"

"Maybe. I don't know. I've never dated my best friend's brother before."

"Why don't we just cross that bridge when we come to it?"

"Right. I guess I'm getting ahead of myself."

There was a little silence. Then Sephy asked, "So, where are you going on this date?"

"He asked me to a concert. The Trans-Siberian Orchestra is coming to Merrill Auditorium in Portland next week, and he got tickets."

Sephy sagged against the cold tile of the bathroom wall and didn't know whether to laugh or cry.

Jane Darling smoothed her navy-blue sweater over her hips, regarded herself in the full-length mirror on the back of her bedroom door, and frowned. Was the sweater looking a little worn under the arms? She examined it, picked off half a dozen pills, then decided to change. The sweater, originally a Christmas gift from Laura, had been a favorite of hers for nearly ten years. It had fought the good fight. Perhaps it was time now for it to take its place at the end of the closet reserved for "just around the house" things.

Leander was always after her to get herself a new outfit, but Jane hated buying new clothes. Every time she went into a clothing store, the prices on the tags nearly sent her reeling. Really, it seemed such a needless extravagance, when you could find perfectly good things at Goodwill.

She riffled through a couple of drawers and came up with a white silk shell, a long-ago hand-me-down from her pastor's wife, Constance. It looked nice under her red wool blazer, which she had found for three dollars at a yard sale in Rockport one long-ago Memorial Day weekend.

But as for the rest of the evening ahead, this was no time

to be pinching pennies. It was Leander's and her thirty-fourth wedding anniversary, and to celebrate, they were having dinner with their old friends and neighbors, Tom and Abigail Hale. They were going to her favorite restaurant, The Lobster Pot, and Jane fully intended to have mussels as an appetizer; stuffed, baked haddock for an entrée; and rum cream pie for dessert. She might even have a glass of rosé wine. None of them would order lobster. Although Jane loved lobster, she refused to order it at a restaurant. That was what tourists did. Real locals bought lobster at the fish market for a third of the price and cooked it at home. Or, if they really felt extravagant, they paid a dollar or so more per pound and bought it at the Hannaford seafood counter, where the young man with all the tattoos would steam it for free while you waited.

Opening her jewelry box, she found her gold knot earrings, a present from her mother on her sixteenth birthday. She was fastening them in her ears when Leander came out of the bathroom, a towel around his waist, fresh from the shower.

"You smell nice," she told him. "What are you going to wear?"

"I thought my blue sport coat and kha—" He gave a dry cough. "Sorry, khagh—whew! I can't get the word out." He worked his jaw from side to side and comically stuck his tongue in and out of his mouth a few times. "There. Kha. Ki. Pants. Having trouble with my *k*'s tonight. Too many in a row, I guess."

She smiled. "Try some of those vocal warm-ups that you use with the choir. Do the one that sounds like Popeye laughing. *Ga-ga-ga-ga-ga-ga-ga-ga-gaaaaaaah.*"

Leander raised his chin and looked in the mirror. "Ga-ha—" He started to cough. "Ga-ka-ha—" He stopped, swallowed, shook his head, and rubbed his throat. "Can't do it."

Jane sorted through the perfume bottles on her dresser until she found the one she wanted. White Diamonds, by Elizabeth Taylor. Leander bought her a bottle of it every Christmas. "You don't have a cold brewing?"

He frowned. "I don't think so. I feel fine. Probably a freak case of laryngitis. You know how I get them once in a while without ever feeling sick. Mark my words, I won't be able to talk at all by morning."

"Well, it's good timing at least. It's a weekend, so you don't have to teach," Jane said. "You'd better get a move on. Tom and Abigail are meeting us here in ten minutes, and you still need to put on your *Kha. Ki. Pants.*"

Mitch sorted through the pile of clean T-shirts hanging over the drying rack and found a navy-blue one that looked like it would be all right to wear to a committee meeting. All this meant was that the shirt was free of holes, paint stains, and building supply company logos. He had no wife or girlfriend, only a roommate named Pit, who was a mechanic and hardly ever home, so Mitch did all his own laundry. Although he didn't bother folding his clothes and he didn't even own a chest of drawers, he had learned that if he draped his T-shirts over the top bar of the drying rack as soon as they came out of the dryer, they would stay pretty smooth.

Mitch had few strict rules for himself, but this was one of them: hang up your shirts when they come out of the dryer.

Also, do fifty push-ups and fifty sit-ups every morning when you get up, and every night before you go to bed. Wash your dishes after you eat so you don't get bugs in the kitchen. Finish a job when you say you'll have it finished, and not a day later. No alcohol and no drugs. Those were the rules he lived by. Everything else was negotiable.

He pulled on the T-shirt and tucked it into his jeans, then shook his wet head vigorously and arranged his too-long hair with his fingers in front of the mirror. It did not occur to him to wear a tie to the meeting. He didn't own a tie in any case, or even a shirt with a collar. The battered leather bag in which he kept all the papers pertaining to his current jobs—contracts, receipts, phone numbers—was on the end of the couch, where he had thrown it an hour ago as he came in from work. He refused on principle to call this bag a briefcase, which sounded pretentious to him, but it was really just that. He grabbed it and headed for his truck.

He stopped by Irving on the way for gas and a large coffee he didn't need, then parked in the small lot of the town hall and went in, his stomach jumpy from nerves. He had no clue what was about to be asked of him. It was important that he have a say in planning the restoration of the old opera house, but he wished he could do it without sitting in a room full of arty-farty white-collar types twice a month for the next year. In the foyer, someone had written in green marker on a whiteboard:

ResToraTion CommiTTee
Room 205
2nd floor

An arrow pointed up the stairs, in case people didn't know where the second floor was.

He found the room. A long table filled the space, with an easel and a flip board of paper standing in one corner. Blue folders, yellow legal pads, and pens had been set out at every seat, along with water pitchers and glasses. Two people already sat at the table: the woman who had given them the tour of the opera house last summer, and Amy Darling. The big-bottomed woman stood when he came in and held out a hand to him over the table. He shook it.

"Hello, Mitch. So glad you could be here. I think you remember Amy Darling, the new director of the community arts program?"

Mitch nodded at Amy. "Hello."

She nodded back, unsmiling.

The older woman did not tell him her own name, probably expecting him to remember it from the day at the opera house. He didn't.

"Have a seat anywhere," she said, "and go ahead and write your name on the name tag in your folder. We'll wear these just for tonight, until we all know each other a little better. Oops! Forgot to put my own on." She let out a snorting laugh and, taking a marker from a glass in the center of the table, wrote *ELAINE* in tall capital letters. She was wearing a shiny gold blouse that looked as though it were made of rubber, and she could not get the name tag to stick to it. She clapped it to her chest, where it immediately curled up at the edges and dropped off. She tried again, holding it to the front of herself and slapping at it, making her chest bounce wildly. Mitch's neck began to burn. He looked away to write out his own name tag and stuck it to his shirt, where it stayed.

Elaine continued to assault her blouse until Amy said very nicely, "I think if you just stick the tag to your folder, we'll all be able to see it, Elaine."

Two men and another woman arrived after that, one an attorney named Steve something, one a woman Elaine introduced as "Dori, our committee-member-at-large," whatever that meant, and the town manager, Bruce Shaughnessy. Mitch had met Shaughnessy once before, when he had submitted a bid to build a sunporch on the man's house. Mitch had lost the bid, but he remembered liking the town manager, who had talked to him as one professional to another instead of as a white-collar worker talking to a blue-collar one, which was what often happened when you were in the construction business.

Elaine, minus her name tag, stood up and pounded a small gavel on the table. "The first meeting of the ad hoc Jarvis Opera House restoration committee will now come to order." She wore a long chain around her neck, from which hung a pair of thin gold reading glasses, and she put these on now, adjusting them on her nose so that she seemed to be reading over rather than through them. She announced that they would begin by electing a chairperson and a secretary for the committee, and would go on to review the budget and the architect's plans for the project. "After tonight," she said, looking at them over the rims of her glasses, "all meetings will be run on the guidelines set forth in the abridged copy of *Robert's Rules of Order* that you will find in your folders. Please take the time to review this booklet thoroughly before our next meeting so that discussion in all subsequent meetings may proceed smoothly."

Great, thought Mitch. *Homework.*

The woman was talking again. "We will now elect a chairperson, who will act as moderator of the committee, and a secretary, who will keep the minutes of each meeting. The secretary will open each biweekly meeting by reading the minutes from the last meeting. Do I have a nomination for chairperson?"

They elected Bruce Shaughnessy chairperson and Amy secretary. Mitch voted with little enthusiasm, not caring who got either job, as long as it wasn't him. Elaine seemed to be pouting as she turned the rest of the meeting over to Shaughnessy.

They discussed budget first, and Mitch began to relax. This was familiar territory. Within minutes, however, he realized that what should have been a simple, brief discussion of the printed budget in their folders was turning into a tedious blow-by-blow accounting of every dollar listed there, because Amy Darling could let no item pass without comment. She seemed to invent questions to ask, took copious notes, and had to have even the simplest terms explained to her. To Mitch's further irritation, nobody else seemed to mind this, but answered her patiently, indulgently even, taking the time to explain things that, in his opinion, should have been self-evident. They were treating her as though she were an adorable little sister instead of as a professional on equal footing with any of them. He bore it in silence until she asked what kind of flooring they had budgeted for on the stage.

"It's right there on the page in front of you," he snapped,

tapping his finger against the sheaf of papers. He was gratified when she looked startled.

"Now, Mitch, this is a learning experience for all of us,"
Shaughnessy said, and went on to answer Amy's question.
Mitch sat back and sighed aloud, his hopes for a simple half-
hour meeting long evaporated.

After an hour of this, they moved on to the projected
timeline for the renovation. Again, this was comfortable
ground for Mitch. To his relief, Amy was more subdued on
this topic. At least, she was for the first ten minutes, until
they had fixed October thirteenth as the date for beginning
construction, and someone asked when exactly they were
planning on opening the center.

"I've scheduled the grand opening for May," Amy said.

Mitch snorted. "I don't think so."

"Excuse me?"

"That's not possible."

"What do you mean it's not possible?"

"I mean there's no way a project of this size can be finished in seven months."

"Why not?"

"Because there's too much to *do*. It's too big."

"Well . . . it'll have to be finished. We're opening in May."

"Excuse me, *Miss Darling*, but when I submitted my bid
for this job, the timeline was clearly twelve months, which
means that the project will be finished next October."

Amy looked taken aback. Mitch wondered how many
people in her life had ever told her no. "Well . . . couldn't you
have part of it finished by May? Just the parts we'll need . . .
say, the auditorium and the foyer."

He couldn't believe he was hearing this. "You don't know what you're talking about. I'm not doing this project one room at a time like some kind of . . . of budget home remodeling project. The whole thing will be done in stages—"

"Just a minute, Mitch," said Steve, the attorney, holding up his hand. "There might be something in the idea of opening sooner rather than later. The moneys from the Wyler grant will cover restoration and the first two years of operation. After that, the operating expenses will come from the town budget. At some point we're going to have to make the ongoing funding of the center a tax issue. People are more likely to vote for a tax hike to fund this program if they see that they're getting something for their money. And if they're already well used to its presence in the life of Copper Cove by the time they vote, so much the better."

Mitch stared at him. "I'm telling you that's not the way to do a renovation of this size."

"What's the earliest it *could* be done?" Dori, the member-at-large, wanted to know.

"I told you: next October. And if we have another hard winter like the last one, even that's going to be pushing things."

"I'm already hiring staff with the understanding that our first show will be in May." Amy's voice was rising.

"Then you've gotten ahead of yourself." Mitch's tone matched hers. "You've done that without any kind of consensus from the committee on an opening date. And I'm telling you, we can't have the project finished by May. At least not with the budget we have. If the committee wants to let me hire twice as many men, then maybe we can start to talk about a May opening."

No one spoke for several moments as the committee members digested this. Shaughnessy broke the silence. "Fine, Mitch. I hear what you're saying. There's no way the project can be finished by May and still come in under budget. Okay. Let's start thinking about plan B, then.

"Amy, what's the minimum of space you would need for Mitch to have finished in order to welcome the public to a grand opening performance in May? I think you mentioned the auditorium and the foyer." He held his pencil poised, ready to write down her answer.

Mitch couldn't believe it. Was no one listening to him? "No," he said flatly. "No, no, no, no, no. I've already said that's not the way I do a project like this."

Shaughnessy raised a soothing hand in Mitch's direction. "All right, all right. Let's just hear what Amy has to say."

Mitch threw down his pencil, sat back, and folded his arms across his chest.

"At the very least," said Amy, "we would need the auditorium finished, and probably the foyer, if we want to give a reception after the production. And two dressing rooms. They wouldn't have to be finished, just functional. You know, have doors on them and some basic provisions for privacy."

"And bathrooms," put in Elaine. "You can't have a public gathering of that size with no bathrooms."

"And bathrooms," Amy agreed, avoiding Mitch's eyes.

He started to speak, but Shaughnessy interrupted him. "Hold on, Mitch. I understand your concerns, but for the sake of argument, just help us think this through. Is there any way—*any* way—that the renovation work can be scheduled so that these things—foyer, auditorium, dressing rooms, and bathrooms—can be finished by May? If you tackled these priority areas first, and left, say, the first-floor classrooms and the entire second floor until the auditorium and so forth were finished?"

Mitch was beginning to feel that he was stuck inside a bad dream. He picked up his pencil again, tapping it against his folder while he tried to collect himself enough to keep from biting the heads off some of Copper Cove's most prominent citizens. Finally he said, "I don't know. I'll have to do some new calculations, look at the floor plans, and budget again. That kind of thing. It'll be more expensive, I can guarantee that."

"Could you call and let me know later this week?" said Shaughnessy. "Let me know how much?"

"Yeah. Okay."

The town manager sat back and slapped his hands on the table, looking enormously pleased. "Thank you, Mitch. And thank you, Amy, for pushing ahead on this thing. Your enthusiasm is a breath of fresh air. Now, I'm sure we're all more than ready to get home. If we've no other business to attend to this evening, can I have a motion to adjourn?"

"So moved," said Elaine.

"Second," said Steve, and they all pushed back their chairs.

Mitch stuffed his folder and legal pad into his brown bag and shouldered his way through the door, hurling his empty coffee cup into the trash can on the way out.

He was in the parking lot when Amy caught up with him. "Mitch, wait!"

He stopped and scowled at her. "What was *that* in there?"

"I just . . . I thought May would be the best time to open."
She spread her hands. "It's what I've been planning on."

Mitch despised women who pretended helplessness. "And
apparently nothing is allowed to interfere with the almighty
plans of Amy Darling. Not common sense or any thought of
what might be practical or convenient for the other people
involved."

"It's not a matter of convenience. It's business."

"Maybe for you it is. I suppose it didn't occur to you that
if I can do this—and that's a very big if—*if* I'm going to fulfill Your Highness's demands by May, I'm going to be working fourteen hours a day, seven days of every week between
now and then?"

"Oh, Mitch, I can't imagine that will be necessary."

"I'm sure there's a lot about this project that you haven't
imagined. You have no idea what you're talking about."

"I wasn't trying to make things difficult for you."

"Well, you are. If I didn't need the work, I'd quit right
now." He slammed a hand down on the hood of his truck
in frustration.

She twisted her hands together. "I guess I wasn't thinking
about that."

"No, you never did think about other people, did you?
You may be fourteen years older than the last time I saw
you, but you haven't grown up at all." She looked as though
he had slapped her, and this made him feel savagely happy.
"You're still the same spoiled little girl, expecting the world to
stop and make way for your every whim." He leaned close to
her face and she drew back a little, watching him with wide,
apprehensive eyes. "Well, I've got news for you, Amy: the rest

of the world isn't like the Darling family, thinking the sun rises and sets on your cute little behind. Maybe it's time you grew up and learned that." He yanked open the door of his truck and threw in his bag. "Now get out of my way before I run you over."

Even from behind the wheel, he could see the tears in her eyes. Good. Let her cry. The restoration, which until tonight had seemed like exactly the kind of challenge he loved, now loomed before him as daunting as Everest itself. He peeled out of the parking lot and left Amy standing there, looking small and alone in the dusk. He hoped she felt as lousy about the whole project now as he did.

5

DAVID STEPPED OUT of the shower and wrapped a towel around his waist. Libby was on his mind, as she almost always was these days. Their date to see the Trans-Siberian Orchestra had been a blast. They'd been talking to each other all their lives, so conversation was no problem. And they had nearly everything in their worlds in common, so there wasn't the awkwardness of trying to get to know someone from scratch. For the first time in years, David had found someone he wanted a second date with. Three days after the concert, he'd called and asked her to walk to Red's Clam Shack for dinner. Three days after *that*, she'd invited him to go for a walk on the beach, and he'd kissed her. He'd texted her this morning to ask if she wanted to have dinner together, but she had to work a closing shift at Sears. He was thinking of heading into Quahog anyway, because there was a Burger King there. Maybe he'd stop by the mall and say hi.

The apartment buzzer startled him. Clutching the towel around his waist, he glanced at the clock, which read 6:10. He wasn't expecting anyone. He pressed the intercom button. "Yeah?"

"It's Amy."

He looked at the intercom panel in surprise. His youngest sister had never visited him at his apartment before. "Ah . . . come on up," he said and pushed the button to unlock the gate. With unprecedented speed, he leaped into the bedroom, grabbed the first clean T-shirt and pair of jeans his hands touched, and was dressed by the time he heard her knock at the door.

"Amy!" he said, throwing it open. "What are you doing here?"

She stepped inside. "I was just passing by and wondered if you'd let me buy you supper."

"That's the best offer I've had all day. Where are we going?"

"Blue Yew?"

"Sounds great. I haven't had pizza in, like . . . forty-eight hours."

"Is George here?"

"He went to a poetry slam at the college."

"Good, because I didn't want to feel like I had to invite him. I want to talk to you alone."

At the restaurant, they ordered a large meat lovers' pizza and an Allagash White for David, two slices of mushroom and spinach and a green tea for Amy.

"It's not like you to ask me out for dinner," David observed when the waitress had delivered their drinks and gone. "What's up?"

Amy leaned forward. "Mitch Harris is back in town."

"I know that. You've mentioned it about forty times since you got the new job. Not that you're bitter, of course."

"I'm not bitter. I just . . . don't trust him."

"Why in the world wouldn't you trust him?"

"He was in prison."

"Oh, get over it, Amy. Everyone knows he was in prison. He did his time, paid his debt, or whatever it is they say. Give him a break."

"If I'm going to have to work with him, I want to know his story."

"So ask him. I'm sure he'd tell you."

"I'm asking *you*."

"What is it you want to know, exactly?"

"Why did he live with us? I was so young, I don't even remember how long he was there. Why did he leave? What's he been doing in the years since he left?"

David considered her questions. "He moved in at the end of our tenth-grade year, and he lived with us until the summer after we graduated. I can't remember why he left. He was supposed to go into the Army or something and then he just . . . didn't. I was starting at the community college, and Mitch started drinking pretty heavily. First it was weekend parties; then later he was hiding bottles in his room. Dad and Mom caught him a few times and tried to help, but finally he moved out. He went to live with friends somewhere. Rhode Island or Connecticut, maybe. The next thing I remember, he'd been arrested. He did time in prison. That's all I know."

"You don't know why?"

"It was drugs, I think."

"So he's an alcoholic and a drug addict." Amy sounded satisfied.

David raised his eyebrows at her. "Are you asking me or telling me?"

Their pizza arrived. "Do you want to pray, or do I?" Amy asked him.

"I will." He reached for her hand and held it, grinning and saying aloud, "Thanks, Lord, for this food and for my crazy little sister. Thanks for the new job she has. Please make her a huge success at it. And now that we know Mitch is back, help us to know how to love him. Amen."

"Amen," said Amy. "And I'll love him if absolutely necessary, but it doesn't mean I have to like him."

Sephy dumped the pile of textbooks she was carrying onto her desk with relief. Everything was so much more exhausting when you hadn't had anything to eat all day. For ten grueling days, she had stuck to the chicken and grapefruit diet. When she weighed herself on the eleventh day and found that she had lost only five pounds, she had skipped her afternoon class and driven to McDonald's, where she ordered two Big Mac extra-value meals, super-size, and ate them straight down, right there in the parking lot. The last french fry was hardly in her mouth when she had been engulfed with shame and regret so overpowering that she had begun to weep.

For a week, she did Atkins, which had given her a cold sore and made her constipated, but had nonetheless taken off a further five pounds. The week she gave it up, she gained back seven.

Her newest hope was a protein shake program. She had one premade chocolate shake for breakfast, another for lunch, and a salad for supper. It was an improvement over the 0-1-0 diet, but not by much. After two weeks, she had lost ten pounds, but she was constantly tired. At the moment, after a full day of classes, she wanted nothing more than to crawl under her quilt and sleep for about three years. It wasn't an option, though. She had drunk the last of her protein shakes for lunch, and she needed to drive into town and pick up some more for tomorrow.

Longingly, Sephy eyed her bed. Maybe just a fifteen-minute nap first. Twenty, absolute tops.

She was drifting off when she heard a tap at the door, then, "Sephy?"

She cracked an eyelid. It was Leann from across the hall. "Mmmmm," she mumbled.

"Ooh, Sephy, I'm so sorry—I didn't know you were sleeping! You should put a sign on the door or something."

Sephy opened both eyes and yawned. "It doesn't matter. It was just a quick nap." She propped herself up on one elbow. "What's up?"

"I have a really, really big favor to ask."

"Ask away."

"Could I borrow your car to go to Dayton? I, um . . . This guy Sam asked me out for dinner. He's in my differential equations class? He thought he could borrow his roommate's car to drive us, but it turns out he can't."

"You mean tonight?"

"Right now, actually."

Sephy pushed herself into a sitting position and squinted

at the clock, trying to gather her thoughts. "What time would you be back? It's just, I have to go to the store for a few things tonight."

"Well, we thought we'd go out to a movie afterward, so it might not be until late." Leann clasped her hands in front of her heart. "Please say yes, Sephy! I really, really like this guy. I thought he would never ask me out and now that he finally has, I'd be *so* embarrassed if I had to cancel because I didn't have a car. Oh! And I would *totally* be happy to stop by the store for you and pick up whatever you need. Can I do that for you? Please?"

Sephy stared at her in dismay. She had to get to the store for those protein shakes, or that would be the end of her diet. Yet Leann was a friend. And she looked so hopeful and imploring that Sephy didn't have the heart to turn her down. She smiled when what she really wanted to do was cry. "The keys are in my top desk drawer."

"Oh, thank you, thank you, *thank* you!" Leann crowed. "I will absolutely take good care of it, and put gas in it, and oh, what is it that you need me to pick up at the store for you?"

She wasn't about to tell Leann about the diet shakes. She waved her hand. "Forget about it. Go have a good time with Sam."

When Leann had gone, closing the door behind her, Sephy lay down again. Fear snaked in tendrils around her thoughts. Her resolve, all her careful building up of her willpower, was beginning to weaken and sway like a rock wall whose mortar had crumbled. For two weeks, she had deprived herself of everything she'd wanted to eat, had worked so hard to lose the ten pounds. She couldn't bear the thought of gaining it back. Of being right back where she'd started, with only one more failure to show for it. Yet she could feel that the battle was already over. And once again, she was a casualty.

She got to her feet and reached for her hairbrush. The cafeteria would be opening soon, and she was sick and tired of eating nothing but salad. Maybe it was just as well that she couldn't continue this diet. Truth be told, sometimes the thought of facing another chocolate protein shake made her want to throw up. Tonight she would have whatever she wanted—whatever looked good. She would eat without guilt, would not despise and berate herself with every mouthful. Tomorrow was another day, a second chance. She would find a new diet, one that suited her better.

She did not meet her own eyes in the mirror as she twisted up her long red hair, then went to the closet to find a jacket for the walk to supper.

If anyone had asked Laura six months ago, she would have said that a little Presbyterian church in the country outside of Phoenix was the last place she would ever be caught dead. Nevertheless here she was putting on lipstick at eight thirty on a Sunday morning, her old Bible and a notebook waiting on the kitchen table next to her purse and a thermal cup hiding a mixture of vodka and cranberry juice. The notebook was purely for body armor. She had no intention of taking notes or of listening to the sermon. But she had found over the years that carrying a notebook to church as well as the obligatory Bible put a bigger barrier between you and any tiresome person who might decide to corner you and start asking questions about the status of your spiritual life.

Going to church had nothing to do with her spiritual life, and everything to do with the fact that she was finding it almost impossible to meet people and was nearly going out of her mind with boredom. Last night, she had sat home alone and watched a Jimmy Stewart movie marathon on AMC while she drank an entire fifth of vodka. That's how pathetic she had become. She was feeling the worse for both the vodka and the self-pity this morning, which was what had prompted her to even think about church in the first place.

She had already tried the bar scene and been seriously unimpressed. For one thing, the men in Arizona all wore cowboy boots. And she was sorry, but she just couldn't look at a man wearing boots with high heels and pointy toes without wanting to break into peals of hysterical laughter. All the men at the bars she had been to were either the hunched-over-a-beer-bottle-eyes-on-the-TV-in-the-corner type or the eyes-darting-everywhere-looking-for-the-hottest-chick-in-the-room type. When she tried to picture coming home to either one of those options every night for the rest of her life, her skin crawled. The truth was she didn't want the kind of man who went to bars to hook up with women. It just wasn't her style.

She wasn't meeting anyone at work either, where all the men were college students or married. And with Max, she had learned her lesson on *that* score. All the men she said a passing hello to at the gym were gay or full of themselves or already had girlfriends.

Church was her desperate plan D.

But it wasn't just men she wanted to meet. She had no female friends to speak of either. To be fair, Laura hadn't ever had many of those. She'd always been more the type who got along best with the opposite sex. And she'd spent her life so surrounded by sisters, girl cousins, aunts, and grandmothers that she'd never felt the lack of girlfriends.

What she was missing was a place where she belonged. A fundamental sense of roots. Maybe . . . okay, she would admit it: *family*. And with all its imperfections and potential for disappointment, church had always been a second family for her. So she was trying it. How bad could it be? Nobody was going to make her go back if she didn't like it.

She picked up her purse and books, glanced around her neat kitchen to be sure everything was turned off and in order, picked up the thermal mug of vodka and cranberry juice, and headed off to a place she hadn't been to in a long time. She hoped she hadn't forgotten how to go through the motions.

Laura had noticed the church in the spring and had settled on it because it looked so innocuous. It was a small, low building with vinyl siding and a thin, ugly steeple pointing aggressively skyward. When Laura had first seen it from the road, that steeple rising from the squat fist of the building had struck her as a rude gesture. The notion offered a complicated comfort, as though here was a place where she might walk in, pretending to be nothing more than herself, and it would be okay. It was a lot to surmise from a drive-by glance or two: probably nothing more than wishful thinking. The building was set in a dry, bare yard with patches of scrub brush in the background. What had drawn her in was a garish sign, hand-painted on a bedsheet, that stretched along the front edge of the parking lot, announcing:

Vacation Bible School!
Putting On the WHOLE Armor of God!
Ages 2–12 Welcome!
June 13–17th 10:00–11:30 a.m.!

A clunky-looking suit of armor painted in gray took up one whole end of the sheet. There had been something both pathetic and endearing about that sign. It brought back the vacation Bible schools of her youth. Water balloon games and relay races with cheap, satisfying prizes. Puppet shows and Bible memory contests where you tried to outshout the other team. Big plastic pitchers of Kool-Aid and store-bought cookies. That slightly musty, familiar smell of the church basement on the one day of the week when it inevitably rained and all the activities had to be modified and moved indoors. Fifty kids who were crazed with the energy of summer, and of being somewhere without their parents for two hours. Knowing for that window of time, you could misbehave in any way you liked and the slightly strained-looking woman in charge, with her army of teenage helpers, would never even think of reprimanding you. All because they wanted to win you for Jesus.

Strangely, the memory had made her feel homesick.

So finally she went to church, and it was more or less what she recognized. A piano played by an earnest-looking woman in her seventies. Songs sung from both a hymnal and a book of praise choruses. Kids running around everywhere before the service. Broken air-conditioning, and everyone sweltering and making their bulletins into fans. Laura positioned herself strategically in the back row, where she could observe and get away early if need be.

The pastor looked far too young. If she was any judge, he would be straight out of Bible school. Seminary, if he was lucky. It was mildly disconcerting to find herself lectured on moral issues by someone six or eight years younger than herself. Sephy's age, maybe.

He was reading from the book of 1 John, one of the books Laura had always prized for its brevity. The Darling children had never been allowed to bring any sort of outside amusement into Sunday morning church services, so left to their own devices, Laura and Ivy had resorted to spending sermon time reading through all the shortest books of the Bible. Ruth was a good one, especially during their teenage years, when they had appreciated the impoverished-younger-woman-snares-wealthy-older-man plotline. The book of Esther had been boring until Laura had somehow learned that the "beauty contest" Esther spent a year preparing for had actually been a one-night stab at seducing the king of Persia. And she had succeeded, which Laura admired her for. Other short books of the Bible—meaning they could be read with a fair degree of interest in the course of one of Pastor Ken's sermons—included Philemon, Jude, and 1, 2, and 3 John.

So Laura was familiar with the passage this pastor named Evan chose to read, from 1 John chapter 4.

> "My beloved friends, let us continue to love each
> other since love comes from God. Everyone who
> loves is born of God and experiences a relationship

with God. The person who refuses to love doesn't know the first thing about God, because God *is* love—so you can't know him if you don't love. This is how God showed his love for us: God sent his only Son into the world so we might live through him. This is the kind of love we are talking about— not that we once upon a time loved God, but that he loved us and sent his Son as a sacrifice to clear away our sins and the damage they've done to our relationship with God."

As he talked, Laura scanned the congregation in the rows before her. Lots of people in their twenties and thirties. A million kids—didn't they have junior church or something? It seemed not, because the children were all sitting with their families, coloring away at pictures from Sunday school pages or kicking their heels and poking at each other or looking plain old depressed and helpless about being there. Laura understood how they felt.

In a lapse of judgment, she stayed for the final hymn and the closing prayer, and though she tried to slip out afterward, she somehow found herself wedged into a corner behind the back pew, surrounded by an unwelcome crowd of people.

They all wanted to know her name. Where was she from? Where was she working? What had brought her clear out here to *A-ri-ZO-na*? If she answered a question once, she answered it half a dozen times, voiced from well-meaning young mothers, middle-aged women, and eventually from at least one interesting-looking person, a woman who said her name was Theo.

"Theo?" Laura couldn't help saying. "I've never heard that as a woman's name before."

"I know, right?" The woman, several years younger than Laura, rolled her eyes. "It's Theodora, actually. I had very progressive parents." She had a silver hoop in her nose, wore camouflage combat pants, and her head was shaved nearly bald. Laura felt warmer toward her than anyone she'd met thus far.

"Well . . . parents." Laura shrugged. "What do they exist for but to screw us up, right?"

Theo laughed. "Don't get me wrong. My parents are pretty awesome. They just had no clue how to name their children. All right, I'm going to confess something to you. Ready?"

"Okay."

"I have twin brothers named Stacey and Tracey."

Laura clapped a hand to her mouth. "That's terrible! What were they *thinking*?"

"According to them, they were just thinking outside the box. Apparently Theodora was a woman's name, back in the year aughty-aught, and Stacey and Tracey were boys' names long before they became girls' names."

"Really?"

"I kid you not. Look, there they are." Theo pointed her chin toward a sedate-looking middle-aged couple talking with the pastor. "Talking to Evan."

Laura looked. "Evan. Right. Good message." She didn't know if it had been a good message; she hadn't paid enough attention. But it seemed like the right thing to say.

"He's a great preacher. Great husband and father too. And pretty hot, if I do say so myself."

Laura felt the look of horror flash across her face before she could stop it.

Theo beamed. "I'm allowed to say that. I'm married to him. Anyway, let me give you my number and e-mail." She held out a little card to Laura. "Text me if you feel like it. It'd be fun to see you again. And do you mind giving me yours? I'd love to give you a call."

Numbly, Laura obeyed, wondering what kind of alternate universe she had stepped into where pastors' wives wore piercings and Army-Navy surplus clothes and referred to their husbands as "hot."

When she had made it all the way across the parking lot and had her keys in hand, she began to imagine she had escaped. She imagined foolishly, because just as she clicked the unlock button, someone stepped into her path. A man. Her own age.

"Hey," he said, holding out a hand. "I'm Rob. I didn't want to let you get away without saying hi."

Laura looked down. Cowboy boots. Pointy toes. She took a long and hearty swig from her thermal mug. "Hi, Rob." She gave his hand a brief, anemic shake. "It was a great service, but honestly, I'm just passing through on my way to, um, New Jersey. I won't be back." She sidled by him to the driver's door and with a bright smile and a cheery wave, slid inside.

It hadn't been a 100 percent lie. At the moment, she felt like New Jersey, or anywhere on the Eastern Seaboard, might be the very best hope she had. It didn't seem like a bad idea to just put the car in drive and see how far she could get before her gas tank ran dry.

Wherever she ended up, it would have to be better than this place.

Amy was still having no luck hiring someone for the job of wardrobe manager and props master.

One Friday, she interviewed a college student who ran for the door as soon as she realized the job involved working weekends. The next week, she interviewed a man in a wheelchair. He was part of a government-sponsored employment program for the handicapped, but it was clear he would be unable to do many of the things the job required. She let him down gently, then spent the rest of the day alternating between guilt and fear of a discrimination lawsuit against the town.

One woman showed up with her unemployment form in hand and simply asked Amy to sign it, saying she had been there to apply for work but had been turned down. Amy refused on principle to either sign the form or interview her for the job.

"Your problem," Ivy said, when Amy told her about it later, "is that you're trying to buy caviar on a tuna fish budget."

"You didn't see these people," Amy said. "No one could have hired them."

"You're being too picky."

Amy was sure that Ivy was wrong, but her lack of staff was beginning to be worrisome. She had begun waking up in the middle of the night, pulse pounding, certain that *West Side Story* would open in May without a single prop or costume and with no one having learned any of the dance steps because she had never managed to find a choreographer.

About a week after her conversation with Ivy, she was eating a banana at her desk and answering e-mails when the phone rang.

"Yes. Hello. My name is Karen Lutz, and I'm interested in applying for the job you advertised in the paper. The wardrobe manager and props master one. Is the job still open?"

Amy swallowed a bite of banana without chewing it. "Yes, the job is still open."

"Well, is there an application form or something? It's not very easy to find it online, if there is."

"There's no application form. Why don't we schedule an interview?" Amy pulled her planner toward herself and flipped a page. "What hours work best for you?"

"I'm a stay-at-home mom, so really any hours are fine. As long as I can bring my son with me."

"I don't think that would be a problem. How about . . . tomorrow, at ten thirty?"

"I can't do it tomorrow. Chaz has a swimming lesson in the morning and a piano lesson in the afternoon."

"How about the next day, then? I'm free in the afternoon."

"Oh no, Chaz and I have a Cub Scout meeting that day. I have to be there—I'm a den mother."

"Mmmmm . . . how about evenings? I could do tomorrow evening."

"Goodness, evenings wouldn't work. Chaz has T-ball practice every evening."

"Well, when *are* you free?" Amy asked.

"I could do Friday morning, as long as it's between eight

thirty and nine thirty. Chaz has a dentist appointment at ten thirty, and his art co-op meets here after that."

"You sound like a busy person," Amy observed. "I wonder, have you thought through the time requirements of the job? It would require a fair amount of flexibility on your part."

"The ad *said* it was part-time." Karen Lutz sounded offended.

"And it is. I just wanted to be sure you understood that there would be time requirements. And around production time, twice a year, the hours may be closer to full-time than not."

"Excuse me, I don't think I need to be lectured on time management by someone who's never even met me," said the other woman.

Amy remembered what Ivy had said about being too picky, and quickly and silently counted to ten. "Why don't you come in on Friday morning at eight thirty and we'll talk about it."

On Friday morning, Karen Lutz came, hauling six-year-old Chaz along with her. In the course of the twenty-minute interview, the boy continually climbed onto and off of his mother's lap, knocked over Amy's mug of tea, ran up and down the empty corridor, slapping the wall as he went, and demanded drawing paper and a pen, which Amy supplied in the hope that it would shut him up long enough for his mother to finish one sentence uninterrupted. She did manage to learn that her applicant had done some work with summer theater in Connecticut, in the nineties, which gave her a reason to hope. She offered Karen Lutz the job with mixed feelings. On the one hand, she had a much-needed staff member at last. But looking around her paper-strewn office, Amy realized that she was really getting two for the price of one. It seemed she had not only hired Karen Lutz for the job; she had hired the fearsome Chaz along with her. She'd better have a word with Mitch Harris and tell him to reinforce the opera house walls while he was renovating. With steel bars, if possible.

AMY WAS DRIVING HOME from work one night, through a bitter, drenching rain, when she passed the opera house and noticed a light in the window. It wasn't her usual route, but she had swung by Hannaford after work to pick up bread and eggs for her mother and had come this way instead. Through the downpour, she saw Mitch's truck parked at the curb. She was startled. What in the world was he doing, still working at this time of night? It was miserable out, and the opera house was bound to be unheated. She frowned.

At the next intersection, she made an unplanned left turn and headed back into town.

Outside the walls of the opera house, rain fell in a cold and dismal torrent. Gusting winds flung water against the broken windowpanes with a sound like pebbles rattling in a tin can. For three days, it had rained without ceasing. In one corner of the second floor, water leaked through a hole in the roof, caught by five-gallon paint buckets that had to be emptied every ten hours. The regular crew had left for home hours ago. Mitch, huddled in a flannel-lined Carhartt jacket with nothing but a lamp and a radio for company, was still working. He was hanging drywall in the auditorium, a tedious job to do alone, and in a room this size, an endless one.

Just to the corner, he told himself. *I'll quit when I get to the corner, empty the stupid buckets, and go home.* On the radio, a man was singing about beer chasin' his blues away. That sounded pretty good to Mitch. Not for the first time, he thought that as much as he liked country music, those kinds of songs sure didn't make it any easier for a man to stay sober. Sober or faithful. Not that he had anyone to stay faithful *to.* He reached over and shut off the radio. No sense courting temptation. He turned back to the sheet of drywall in front of him and held it in place with a forearm while he fumbled with the nail gun. Somewhere, the wind banged a door open and then shut again.

"Mitch? Mitch!"

He half turned, not willing to let go of the drywall. Beyond the harsh circle of light from the floor lamp, all was darkness. "Who's there?"

"It's me, Amy." She stepped into the circle of light. "It's freezing in here. How can you work when it's this cold?"

He gave up and lowered the sheet of drywall, letting it lean against the studs behind it. "The work has to get done. We have a deadline." He didn't bother trying to sound friendly.

"I drove by on the way home from work half an hour ago, and I saw your truck. Are you—have you had supper yet?"

He remembered how long ago lunch had been. "No."

"I thought you wouldn't have. I brought you some soup and a sandwich. I mean, if you want it."

She was holding up a canvas bag, and Mitch looked from the bag to the drywall, torn. He had meant to work to the corner, and if he stopped now, he was fairly sure he wouldn't finish tonight. But there were seductive smells coming from the bag, and hunger won out.

"Are you staying to eat too?"

"If it's okay with you."

The idea of company on this raw and cheerless night was appealing. "I have a couple of sawhorses. We could make a table." He found the sawhorses and a sheet of plywood, and Amy helped him drag them into the light and fashion a table. He went to the foyer for a pair of buckets to sit on, and when he got back, she had set out paper bowls and was pouring soup into them. She had brought sandwiches as well—a hot meatball sub for him and something unidentifiable for herself.

"It's all from Amato's," she said, "and the soup is vegetarian. I hope you don't mind."

Mind? It smelled better than anything he'd eaten in about a year. She had brought coffee, too, and a handful of creamers and sugar packets. He ate with enthusiasm and didn't slow down until the sub was gone and he had started on the soup. "You didn't have to do this," he said at last.

"I wanted to." She put her sandwich down and wiped her mouth with a napkin. "You said I wasn't thinking about how inconvenient it would be for you to open in May, and you were right. I mean, I still think it's the right thing to do—right for the community as a whole—but I didn't consider how complicated it's going to make your life for the next·six months."

He took the lid off his coffee cup and stirred in sugar and cream.

She went on, talking fast. "I'm really sorry that you have to be here late, alone, on such a miserable night. I thought, if there's anything I can do to help, even just bringing you food . . ." She waved her hand toward the bowls.

Mitch sipped his coffee. He was warm now, from the inside out, and comfortable within the circle of lamplight, with the wind raging outside. "Why are you working so late yourself?" he asked her.

"What do you mean?"

"You said you finished work half an hour ago." He checked his watch. "More like an hour, now. It's nearly nine o'clock."

"Oh. No, I usually work until about eight."

"Why? Do you start later in the morning?"

"Eight o'clock or so."

"So . . . you work twelve hours a day."

She shrugged. "I guess."

"What, five days a week?"

"Sometimes I come in on a Saturday morning. But I always take Sundays off."

He raised his eyebrows and whistled. "You're a workaholic."

"No, I just have a big job, and it has to get done somehow. It's no more than you're doing," she pointed out.

All at once, Mitch felt tired. The good kind of tired that came from a long day of hard physical labor. He stood up.

"Then I think we both need to go home and get some rest. Let me take care of one or two things, and I'll walk you to your car." He put away his hand tools, locked the radio in the tool chest with them, and unplugged the lamp while she cleared away the wrappers from their meal.

"I just need to empty the buckets before I go," he said.

"I'll help."

"Thanks." By the beam of a flashlight, he led the way upstairs.

"If I move this full bucket out of the way, can you stick that empty one under the leak?" he asked.

"Sure." She grabbed the empty pail, and they made the switch. "Great teamwork," she said, and he heard the smile in her voice.

Back downstairs, they pulled the collars of their coats up around their necks. "Ready to make a run for it?" he asked.

"Ready!"

He held open the door and she dashed for her car through the icy, sheeting rain. He paused just long enough to be sure the door was locked before running to his truck. "Thanks for supper!" he shouted, just before her door slammed shut.

Amy stuck a hand out and waved it to show that she'd heard, then pulled away. Mitch sat in the parking lot waiting for the windshield to defog while he reexamined his prejudices. He was surprised and impressed that Amy seemed to be working as hard as he was to get this thing done. At least she wasn't asking something of him that she was unwilling to ask of herself. And it had been nice of her to bring him something to eat. He put the truck in gear and headed for home. Maybe she wouldn't turn out to be such a bad kid after all.

"Honey, you've hardly eaten a thing," said Jane reproachfully. "There's nothing wrong with it, is there?" Haddock was $4.99 this week, so after breakfast, she had run over to The Oyster Net and picked up five pounds to make Leander's favorite fish chowder for supper.

He prodded at a cube of potato. "It's fine. I'm just having a hard time swallowing. Coming down with a cold, I expect. It's this raw weather. I don't know when we've had such a wet and miserable November."

"Too bad. I'll put it in the fridge and you can have it tomorrow night. It's better the second day anyway. I'll make you some hot tea and find you the bottle of Chloraseptic."

"That would be nice." He rubbed his throat. "I'll feel better by morning."

Sephy hitched her carry-on bag over her shoulder and looked around the terminal for the right check-in desk. She spotted it, naturally, at the end farthest from the door at which Ann had dropped her.

The space between was a teeming mass of bodies and baggage. Small children whined. Mothers shushed or snapped at them. Grim fathers hauled small mountains of suitcases along the mazelike ropes of the check-in lines, already exhausted before the real traveling had even begun. College students, flying home for the Thanksgiving weekend, made out with their boyfriends or girlfriends, with no attempt at discretion. Women wearing hijabs or saris called shrilly to their families in foreign languages. An entire college basketball team strode through the crowd, which parted like the Red Sea before them. "Mommy!" cried a little girl near the JetBlue counter. "Look at those tall men!"

Sephy smiled. She had always loved the energy and humanity of airports.

She worked her way through the crowd, which—notably— did not part for her as readily as it had for the tall men. When she reached the check-in counter, she found a kiosk and scanned her credit card. Her parents, not wanting her to waste twenty-eight hours of the holiday weekend in round-trip driving, had put the money in her account for a plane ticket. Sephy touched all the right places on the screen, and her boarding pass dropped into the tray. She had no luggage to check, only a carry-on, but as she turned in the direction of the gates, a smiling woman in an airline uniform stopped her.

"Did you get checked in all right, miss?" the woman asked.

"I'm all set, thanks." Sephy motioned to her carry-on. "I did it online last night, and I only have this, so . . . no bags to check."

She started to move away, but the woman stepped in front of her. "Mind if I just take a look at your boarding pass?" Before the question was out of her mouth, she had neatly pulled the slip of paper from Sephy's fingers and begun to examine it.

Sephy bit back her irritation. Airline employees always seemed determined to help you whether you wanted to be helped or not. Oh, well. She supposed it was a security thing.

"Hmmm . . . I was afraid of that." The woman looked

up, her smile gone. "There's a bit of a problem here, miss. If you'll just come with me."

"What's the problem?"

"Don't worry. This won't take long. You have plenty of time to make your flight." Still holding Sephy's boarding pass, the woman turned and walked toward the desk. Sephy had no choice but to follow her. To her relief, they skirted the long line of other passengers waiting to check in and went straight to the VIP counter. The woman handed Sephy's boarding pass to a man behind the counter and said something too quiet for Sephy to catch.

"Mmmmm. Hmmmm. Yes, I see," said the man. Both of them turned and squinted at her. Sephy felt a sudden kinship with the specimens of mold in petri dishes at the college microbiology lab. The woman hurried away without meeting her eyes.

"Now, Ms., ah, Darling," said the man, consulting her boarding pass. "Unfortunately, the seats in our coach class are on the narrow side, and it appears that you, ah, may exceed the size limits."

It took a moment for his meaning to penetrate, and then Sephy understood. Horror washed over her. Her face burned. The man was saying she was too fat to fit in the airplane seat. She had flown home for Thanksgiving last year, and this had not been the case. She had been uncomfortable for the entire flight, it was true, but no one had told her she could not fit in the seat. But then, that had been a different airline. Maybe their seats were wider. It had never even occurred to her that her size would be an issue, this time or ever.

A lump pressed on the back of her throat and it took every

ounce of willpower she possessed to force back tears. What did people do in situations like this? Surely she wasn't the first person this had ever happened to. When you didn't fit in the seat, didn't they make you buy a second ticket? She couldn't *afford* a second ticket. She couldn't have afforded the first one, had not her parents put the money for it into her account.

She had to get home for Thanksgiving. Two days ago, she'd gotten an emergency call from Libby, at 1 a.m.

"Sephy!" her best friend had wailed. "Please tell me you're coming home. . . ." Then, slightly hysterically she told Sephy what she had done. Libby Hale was never hysterical; it was clear she needed Sephy to be there. To not get home wasn't an option.

Oh, God . . . help somehow.

Facing the man across the counter, she forced herself to ask the question that had to be asked, and when the words came out, she sounded calm and in control. Not as though she were a woman who was about to vomit from shame. "What do you suggest?" she said.

"Wellllll . . ." The man was pecking away at his keyboard, staring at his screen. "Normally we'd ask you to purchase a second ticket, but with the holiday weekend, our coach cabin is entirely booked. Howevvvvvverrrrrr . . . Ah!" He looked up, triumphant. "We do have one seat available in first class." He leaned across the counter and whispered, "The seats are wider there."

Pure, golden relief washed over Sephy. She was not going to be kept off the plane. She was not too fat to get home for Thanksgiving. "Fine," she told the man, "I'll take it."

"All righty, then!" The man rattled away at his keyboard

with dazzling speed for a moment, then, with a flourish, pulled her new boarding pass from the printer. He looked at her, beaming. "That'll be $395."

Sephy stared at him, and whereas before, her face had flamed like a hot coal, now she had the sensation that it was a frozen, bloodless white. For a moment, she thought she might faint. Of course they didn't let you upgrade for free; how stupid was she? She fumbled her credit card and driver's license out of her wallet and slid them across the counter, feeling numb and disembodied. How she was ever going to pay the credit card bill when it came, she had no idea. One thing was certain: there was no way she was going to ask her parents for the money, or even to tell them that this terrible thing had happened.

The man returned her credit card and license and handed her the new boarding pass. "There you are, Ms. Darling. Enjoy your flight and your holiday weekend."

"Thank you," she managed and hurried away in the direction of the gates before the man could see the tears of humiliation that had begun to overflow her eyes.

Karen Lutz was turning out to be a problem. She brought the charmless Chaz to work with her every day. He was a destructive child, loud and dissatisfied unless he was being given constant attention. Amy couldn't get a thing done when he was in the building. Although Karen Lutz (Amy found it impossible to think of her as just plain Karen) had an office of her own, next door to Amy's, she gave her son free rein of the third floor while she was there.

Amy tried to ignore this, because Karen Lutz was at least good at her job. Somehow, in spite of her child, she had managed to paint two entire backdrops for *West Side Story*, and the third-floor storage room now held a small collection of the costumes and props that Amy had begun to despair of ever seeing.

Still, there was no getting around the distraction of Chaz. He spent his mother's work hours running up and down the corridor, poking his head into Amy's office and throwing things at her, or blowing raspberries at her from across the room. When she tried closing her door, he adopted the amusing game of pounding on it and then running away. At last, something had to be said. Amy thought it over and decided it would be best to do it on her own turf.

On the day before Thanksgiving, she called Karen Lutz into her office. "Have a seat," she said. Chaz went to the filing cabinet and began pulling on the drawer handles.

"It's locked," Amy told him. "Please don't pull on the handles like that. You'll tip the cabinet over."

"I want a cookie!" He knew about the box of biscotti Amy kept in the bottom drawer. Turning to his mother, Amy said, "I'm afraid I'm going to have to ask you to make other arrangements for Chaz while you're here at work."

"What do you mean other arrangements? He's not bothering anybody."

"I. Want. A. *Cookie!*" roared the little boy, yanking at the drawer handle. The cabinet rocked.

Amy put a hand out to steady it. "Please stop doing that to my filing cabinet, Chaz. Actually, Karen, I find it distracting to have him here. It's hard for me to get anything done while he's running up and down the halls and . . . playing."

Karen Lutz withered her with an oh-please look. "He's just a child, Amy. You're an adult. You should try to be a little accommodating."

Chaz, unused to being ignored, let out a piercing shriek.

"Hey!" Amy turned on him. "That's enough of that."

He looked her straight in the face and shrieked again.

"Chaz," said Karen Lutz calmly, "Amy doesn't want you to do that."

Red-faced with rage, he bellowed, *"Cookie!"*

Karen Lutz looked at Amy in exasperation. "Could he please just have a cookie? He knows they're in there."

But Amy had had enough. "No. He can't have a cookie. And no, you can't bring him to work with you anymore. If you can't make other arrangements for him, then maybe you'd be better off to find a different job."

The other woman's mouth fell open in astonishment. "I thought this was supposed to be *community* theater. A welcoming place for *everyone*. And now you're discriminating against me because I have a child. Is that even legal?"

"I assure you it's perfectly legal," said Amy, who had no idea whether it was or not. "This is a long weekend. That should give you time to make whatever arrangements you need to make. Please don't bring him in with you on Monday."

Karen Lutz stood up. "I've never heard of anyone being so unsupportive in my life. He's just a child. A *little boy*." She reached for her son's hand and pulled him to her.

Chaz kicked his mother hard in the leg. "I want a cookie!"

"Don't look for me on Monday," Karen Lutz said over her shoulder as she dragged the howling Chaz back to her office.

In spite of herself, Laura had gone back to the little Presbyterian church six times. Each time, she had relaxed a little more, until one week, without consciously thinking about it, she had poured coffee into her thermal mug instead of vodka. She was beginning to remember a few names here and there. Jenny, the young, distracted single mother whose autistic daughter had a tendency to shout out loud in the middle of the sermon. Carmen, soccer mom to five boys, endlessly enthusiastic, and always bearing a platter of brownies for the preservice coffee hour. Lance and Wendy, the middle-aged couple who arrived last and left first every week and seemed to bear a secret sadness inside themselves. Milton, the old, stooped man who smelled terrible, but smiled and bowed and handed out Werther's caramels to everyone as he leaned on his cane. And Rob, of course. Rob, of the pointy-toed cowboy boots, who always hung around Laura after the service, making small talk. Rob, who was clearly Single and Looking.

The second time she had visited, Rob had approached her at the end of the service and, smiling, said, "So . . . never made it to New Jersey, then?"

He was teasing her, and she felt mollified. "Sorry. I was having a bad day. A bad year, actually."

He waved this away. "Oh well. Anyone can have a bad year."

He was a police detective, she learned. A Navajo. He had moved to Phoenix from a small town called Greasewood. He never said as much, but she gathered it was a reservation.

Although services started at eleven, Laura had taken to

coming at ten for the coffee hour between Sunday school and church. She still skipped Sunday school, though. Sitting in a class of adults where she would be expected to contribute thoughts on a weekly Bible study that she hadn't done was more than she wanted.

One Sunday at coffee hour, Theo, the pastor's wife, had found her. "I don't know what your plans are for Thanksgiving," she'd told Laura, "but the church always sends a team to the homeless shelter to serve a meal that day. Evan and I are going, and a few others from the church. Afterward, we're all meeting at our house for Thanksgiving dinner. We'd love to have you join us."

So, with no other plans of her own, Laura had signed up.

They met on Thanksgiving Day in the church parking lot. The rest of the team was already milling around the white church van when she arrived. Theo and Evan were there, as well as the sad couple, Lance and Wendy. Laura's heart sank just a little to see that the other person in the group was Rob. Locking her car, she nailed on a cheerful smile and headed toward them. She reminded herself that she did not, after all, have a better way to spend her holiday.

The sky was low with clouds, and a chill rain had begun to clatter on the roof of the van by the time they arrived at the shelter. They entered the kitchen through a basement door. Inside, the air smelled of canned green beans and harsh dishwasher detergent, tinged with a faint underlayer of cooking grease. In the overbright fluorescent lighting, Laura found the atmosphere unexpectedly evocative. It reminded her of the old school cafeteria on winter days. A warm, safe place in the midst of a cold and threatening world. She felt the loosening of a tension somewhere inside her. This was familiar, she thought. It was going to be okay.

She was assigned the mashed potato station. As each person arrived from the turkey station on her left, she was supposed to drop an ice cream scoop's worth of potatoes onto his plate and wave him on to the gravy station on her right. It all felt so wrong to her. She came from a home where no one had been limited, on Thanksgiving or ever, to a four-ounce scoop of mashed potatoes. Two slices of turkey. A two-ounce ladleful of gravy. Meals in the Darling family were always lavish and marked by an exuberant nonchalance about the abundance set before them. And yet, although she had expected serving institutional food to homeless people on a family holiday to be depressing, she found that it was not. Instead, the humble gratitude of the ragged men, women, and children who came through the line brought tears to her eyes. Somehow, it felt like a privilege to serve them.

Afterward, as she and Theo and Wendy washed chafing dishes and serving utensils at the enormous sink in the kitchen, Theo said, "Thanks for coming and helping out."

"I'm glad I did," Laura said. "I had no idea how many hungry people there were in a city this size."

"It's pretty appalling, isn't it? Our church serves meals here once a month. We'd love to have you come with us again sometime. And if you're around at Christmas, a team of us helps out on that day too."

"I think I'd like to do that," Laura told her, and meant it.

When they finished at the shelter, Laura, Rob, Lance, and Wendy all went back to the pastor's house, where Theo's parents, along with Evan and Theo's two tiny sons, had a

Thanksgiving dinner of their own ready for them. Laura found herself seated by Rob at the table. She didn't even spare a sigh. They were, after all, the only two single adults. It was inevitable.

After dinner, when the table was cleared and the dishwasher loaded, Theo and her mother shooed them all out of the kitchen. They retired to the living room to watch football while they digested their pie.

Rob sat on a hassock beside Laura's chair. "How did you find the shelter?" he asked.

"It was more . . . hopeful than I thought it would be. Still, I don't like the idea of doling food out to people. It seems to point out their poverty all the more."

"I know what you mean."

"Really?"

"Things weren't like that when I was growing up," he said. "I have one of those huge, loud families that's always eating and kissing and talking. Thanksgiving is very different back home than at the shelter."

She laughed. "I have exactly the same kind of family."

"It's great, isn't it?"

"What? No! It's anything but great."

He looked disbelieving.

"It's true," she insisted. "A family like that always *expects* something of you. You have no secrets. Somebody's always up in your business."

"Okay," he said, "I'll give you that. There are trade-offs in every relationship, whether individual or family. I guess the question is, what are you willing to put up with in order to gain that which sustains you?"

"The question every addict throughout time has had to ask himself," she said dryly.

"Interesting that you'd jump from the subject of family to the subject of addiction."

Laura was surprised. "You're good."

"I'm a professional investigator. It's my job to spot jumps in logic."

She saw no reason to be less than honest. "The two seem very similar to me. I was—*am*, I suppose—a prescription drug addict."

"Oh? Tell me."

"My sister introduced me to Vicodin. I had a legitimate case of tendonitis, and she gave me a prescription pain pill for it. It was irresponsible of her. Once I'd started, I was hooked. I had a boyfriend, at the time, with connections to doctors who could write me prescriptions for my 'chronic pain.'" She made quote marks in the air with her fingers. "For a year or so, I had all the Vicodin and oxys I wanted. But . . ." Here she hesitated. Nothing said she had to tell him about the drinking that had gone along with the pills. "I had a car accident and ended up in rehab. I don't know, it just . . . took." Max and his supply of doctor friends had dried up by the second stint in rehab, but Laura did not feel this was pertinent to the conversation.

"So, you're clean?"

She gave a little bow. "For a year now."

He smiled. "Congratulations. That's a big deal."

She smiled back. "Thank you. It is. It *is* a big deal."

"Tell me more about this big, intrusive family of yours."

So, while the others watched the Giants slaughter the

Cowboys, she told him. Of Ivy, who played big sister to the whole world; about Sephy, who seemed to have been born without a backbone. She described David, who always did what was expected of him, and Amy, who never missed a flaw in anybody. She tried to explain her parents' unpalatable expectations. "Mom's highest aspiration for any of us is that we'll be nice and well-behaved and never make a scene," she said.

"That's tough," he agreed. "I, on the other hand, have the kind of mom who always encouraged us to be ourselves no matter what. Of course, there are nine of us kids, so maybe she just didn't have the time and energy to impose her own standards on us. We did grow up kind of wild."

"What about your father?"

"He was an alcoholic. Sometimes he was around when I was growing up, sometimes not. Mostly not. He died three years ago."

He was the fifth of nine, he told her. "A candidate for Middle Child Syndrome if there ever was one." But he did not seem to mind. On the contrary, he took out his phone and proudly showed her family photos that included a pediatrician sister, a brother with a wife and six children of his own, another brother who was now in jail, and a younger sister with Down syndrome. The rest of them, Laura soon lost track of.

When the game was over (Giants 27, Cowboys 6), he asked her, "Can I call you sometime?"

She had been afraid of this. She gave him her number only because it would have been rude not to. He was a nice guy, but there was no reason to encourage him. She tried to imagine dating someone who wore cowboy boots, being sucked into a family even bigger and more dysfunctional than her own. Both notions made her shudder.

But driving home with a container of leftovers that Theo had made her take, Laura had to admit she was happier than she'd been since . . . well, since she had moved out here. It wasn't only Rob; it was everything in this day. Doing something worthwhile in the community. New friends to celebrate with. For the first time in a long time, she was beginning to feel like she belonged somewhere.

It was Nick and Ivy's year to spend Thanksgiving Day with the Darling family. At two o'clock, Ivy put Hammer, Jada, and DeShaun in the car and meted out the food they were each to hold on the way: a chocolate cream pie for Jada, a jar of mustard pickles and another of homemade applesauce for Hammer, and on DeShaun's lap, the pumpkin cheesecake he had made by himself the night before.

She handed it in to him on its decorative plate, covered in Saran wrap. "It looks beautiful. There's many an experienced cook who still can't make a decent cheesecake. And, Hammer," she added, "stop knocking those jars together. They *will* break."

She put a green bean casserole on the floor by her own feet, along with two bottles of wine and a pound of butter in a paper bag. She looked back at the kids. "Everyone present and accounted for? Good. Jada, don't let the pie tip like that." To Nick, she said, "I think we're ready to go."

Halfway there, Nick slowed and signaled for a right turn.

"What are you doing?"

"I thought we should stop and get some shrimp to take to your parents'."

"Oh, that's a nice thought."

They bought three pounds of shrimp at a tiny fish market that was open because it was run by Heath and Tina, a middle-aged, part–Micmac Indian couple who lived in a blue bus behind the fish shack. With them lived two dogs, five cats, two guinea pigs, a rabbit, and an assortment of birds, all uncaged. Heath and Tina did not observe Thanksgiving.

"It's a bogus holiday," Heath told Nick and Ivy, weighing out the shrimp. "The English settlers exploited the native tribes for help when they needed it, then killed them all off. What's to celebrate about that?"

Tina, a tiny, knotty-looking woman with long, graying braids, was sitting cross-legged on the counter, smoking. She cocked one corner of her mouth, letting a thin stream of sweet-smelling smoke trickle up into her nostrils. "Plus, all those animals that had to be sacrificed for that first 'feast'? The very concept of Thanksgiving is a vegetarian's nightmare."

Nick eyed the bag of shrimp Heath handed to him. "But you have no problem eating fish?"

"Heath's a *pescatarian*, not a true vegetarian," Tina said with a trace of bitterness. "*He* eats fish."

Heath shrugged. "What can I say? Fish have primitive nervous systems. They don't even notice if you eat them." He handed Nick his change.

"Thanks," said Nick. He hitched the bag under one arm. "Happy Thanksgiving."

Tina put down her joint and stared. "Is that some kind of sick joke?"

Nick looked aghast. "Oh, wait—sorry. I wasn't even thinking. It just came out."

"Yeah, right. You English are all the same."

Ivy managed not to laugh until they were in the car and had pulled back onto the road.

Her mother's kitchen was too warm, and packed to bursting with Darlings. "Mom," Ivy called above the din, "I need a big bowl and some ice for these." She held aloft the bulging paper bag of shrimp.

"Oh, that was nice of you, Ivy. David and George brought some too. There's a bowl already going in the family room; you could just add yours to it."

Ivy passed the bag to Nick, who was edging out of the kitchen in search of the other men and the refuge of a television showing a football game in a quieter room. "Add those to David's shrimp, will you?" she said. Nick took the bag and made his escape, followed by DeShaun.

The doorbell rang, and Ivy, who was closest, went to answer it. Her parents' neighbors Tom and Abigail Hale stood there with Libby. "Mr. and Mrs. Hale, happy Thanksgiving! Hi, Libby. Are we all celebrating together this year?"

"Your mother invited us," said Abigail, who had never, in all the years they had been neighbors, been to Thanksgiving dinner at the Darlings'.

"What a great idea," said Ivy. "Come in. Let me take your coats."

Mr. Hale thrust a fish market bag at her. "We brought this."

"Thanks! What is it?"

"Five pounds of shrimp."

"Shrimp, great! Thanks for thinking of that." She led them into the kitchen. "Mom, look who's here."

Jane left the potatoes she was draining and came over to kiss Abigail and Libby. "I'm so glad you could come. And shrimp! What a nice surprise."

Ivy edged her way over to Amy, who was shaking up salad dressing in a mason jar. "Why are the Hales here?" she hissed.

"I don't know, because Libby and David are dating?"

"They are? I mean, is it that official?"

"I guess so. It's been six weeks. Did Mom tell you she invited Mitch?"

"No. Is he coming?"

"What do you think?"

"I think it was a nice gesture, anyway."

Amy sighed. "Poor Mitch. He'll probably work all day at the opera house, then order Chinese food and eat it in front of a football game. I hate to think of him alone on Thanksgiving."

"Maybe he'll surprise us and show up after all," said Ivy, knowing neither one of them really believed that.

Mitch did not show up, but the Hales and David's roommate, George, were crowded in with the rest of them and treated like family. The plates had been cleared, the coffeepots started, and Sephy, carrying a bowl of stuffing and one of mashed potatoes into the kitchen, announced, "That's the last of it."

"Give them here," said Amy, who, with Jada, was scraping the leftovers into plastic containers for the refrigerator.

Sephy handed over the bowls. "Should we start taking dessert orders?"

Libby turned from the dishwasher, where she was loading dirty plates and silverware. "Can I talk to you for a minute, Seph? Alone?"

"Hey, no private confabs out in the hall, while the rest of us do the dishes!" Ivy protested.

"We're just going to bring in the pies," Sephy said. She took Libby by the arm and led her through the hall and into the back entryway.

Behind her, Ivy muttered, "I've heard that one before."

The entryway was a catchall space. One wall was taken up by a row of hooks filled with John Deere caps and the kind of coats no one ever seemed to wear. A pair of red plaid Woolrich jackets had always hung there alongside an assortment of faded chamois shirts and a single blaze-orange hunting vest, although none of the Darlings were hunters. Over the years, the vest had made an occasional appearance as part of a Halloween costume or neighborhood play, but other than that, Sephy had never known it to be used for anything. An old bookcase stood against the opposite wall. Jane Darling had lugged this home from a yard sale the summer Sephy was eight. In the summer, it became a repository for flip-flops and sneakers, baseball mitts and tennis balls. In the winter, however, this was all cleared away to make space for leftover food, the unheated entryway being as good as any refrigerator. Today, the shelves were lined with pies and a roasting pan full of leftover turkey bones. The bones were cooling under plastic wrap, waiting for the next day when Jane would make soup out of them.

Sephy shut the door and turned to Libby. "What's the matter? Tell me quick, because it's freezing out here."

"I feel sick."

"You're not sick."

"I should never have done what I did."

"Are you having a change of heart?"

"No. At least I don't think so. But what if it was the wrong thing to do?"

"Do you think it was?"

"I don't know. What if it's too soon?" Libby covered her face with her hands.

"Take a deep breath," Sephy advised her. "Come on now: in through the nose, out through the mouth."

Libby closed her eyes and obeyed. "Yes," she said, after a moment. "I did the right thing. I think I did." She looked at Sephy. "I did, didn't I?"

"You did the right thing. It's going to be okay."

Libby sighed miserably. "I just wouldn't want to . . . you know, act in haste or anything."

"I don't think you did that. You and David have been going out for a month and a half, but you've known each other all your lives. That's long enough to know."

"It is: it's long enough. And I *do* know. So I made the right decision. Thank goodness I always have you to talk me off the edge, Seph."

"Oh, stop. You're never anywhere near the edge. You did

the right thing. Just keep telling yourself that, and you'll get through the rest of the day."

"But David—"

"David's going to be fine. Now enough! Stop second-guessing yourself. Let's bring in the pies, or Ivy'll be out here hunting us down." She handed Libby a blueberry pie and a mince from the shelves and opened the door for her. "I'm right behind you with the pumpkin pie and DeShaun's cheesecake."

But when Libby had left her alone, Sephy leaned against the doorjamb and gazed at the orange hunting vest. Imagine having a choice. To break up or not to break up. To stay together, to get married, or just . . . anything. Loneliness pierced her like an awl, taking her breath with its sudden sharpness. She squeezed her eyes shut against the pressure of tears. *Take your own advice, Seph. In through the nose, out through the mouth. In through the nose . . .*

From the hallway came Amy's voice. "Who left the door open out here? Were you all born in a barn?"

Sephy stood up straight. Amy, with her unerring perception, must not be allowed to find her like this. "It's just me, bringing in pies," she called back. Somehow, her voice sounded steady.

"Well, hurry up. You're letting in a draft!" Amy's footsteps receded back to the kitchen.

Sephy gave her head a shake, picked up a pie and the cheesecake, and went back in to the family.

Ten minutes' worth of cutting pies in the kitchen restored her equanimity enough to sit down at the table again with a smile on her face.

Amy, who had been on coffee-pouring detail, had just returned the pot to the kitchen and was about to sit down when David told her, "Get Mom in here."

"Go get her yourself."

"Do you have to be such a brat about everything? You're still up, and Mom should be here before we start dessert."

Amy sighed gustily, but went back to the kitchen to fetch their mother. Jane emerged, looking distinctly weepy, Sephy thought.

"She always cries on holidays," Amy said as an apology to the room at large and took her seat. "You can't stop her. We've tried all our lives."

But as the rest of them picked up their dessert forks, David stood and cleared his throat. Everyone looked at him, and Sephy felt her nose recommence the traitorous prickling that meant her composure was about to disintegrate. She twisted her napkin and blinked hard.

"When we were little," David said, "we had a tradition of going around the table at Thanksgiving and sharing the thing we were each the most thankful for. We all said things like friends, family, our house . . . Sephy was always thankful for her rabbit." The general ripple of laughter held more of politeness than of sentiment. David went on, "Somehow, as we got older, that tradition sort of disappeared. I don't remember when we stopped doing it. But today, I'd like to resurrect that old custom in a way. I'd like to share with you the thing that I'm the most thankful for this year." He turned to his right and looked down at Libby.

Sephy couldn't help it then. Her eyes filled and she

clapped a hand to her mouth, although not before a little choked sound escaped.

"This week, Libby—if you can believe it—asked me to marry her," David said, grinning. "And I said yes. We wanted you all to be the first to know."

There was a single moment of shocked silence before the room erupted in bedlam. "Libby! Go, Libby!" Amy called above the din, banging her fork against her water glass. Sephy's tears overflowed and ran down her cheeks. From Ivy's direction, a clean napkin materialized in her hand. She took it and blew her nose with gusto.

When the uproar was more or less under control, they were all made to understand that the wedding would be a year from now, at Christmas; that only Sephy and Grammie Lydia and their parents had known about the engagement beforehand, so none of them were to feel slighted because they hadn't been told. Grammie Lydia had given the couple her own engagement ring, which was sixty years old. All day, Libby had worn it on her right hand with the diamond turned into her palm, so no one would guess, but now David took it from her and slid it to the ring finger of her left hand, to the sound of whistling and pounding silverware.

"Blood diamonds," Amy muttered darkly. "How can he give her that with a clean conscience?"

"Shut your mouth," Ivy hissed, and for once, Amy listened.

Sephy stared at herself in the mirror. In the unforgiving light of her parents' bathroom, she looked pallid, bloated. Her skin dry and lifeless. *I hate Thanksgiving.* There had been a time when it had been her favorite holiday. But in her teenage years, when she had grown fatter every year, the day had become little more than a minefield of fats and carbohydrates to be navigated. Her favorite things in the world—stuffing, squash casserole, Grammie Lydia's rolls with butter, mashed potatoes with gravy, pumpkin pie, chocolate pie, pecan pie, all with billows and billows of rum-spiked whipped cream— were the very things that haunted her for days before and days after the great meal itself. How did people do it? she wondered. How did thin people eat whatever they wanted on days like today and walk away from the table not hating themselves? She stared at her reflection in despair. She both hated the girl reflected there and was at the same time overwhelmed with sorrow for having allowed her to become what she was.

And now, there was David and Libby's wedding looming in a year. Was that enough time to transform your entire life? Or would next Christmas find Sephy standing beside her best friend at the altar, broad, bulging, and as defeated as ever? The real question was, did Seraphina Darling have what it took to be anything different?

Whatever the answer was, she was afraid of it.

She turned away, determined to rid herself of the guilt of the Thanksgiving meal. As far as she could see, there was only one way out of it. She knelt by the toilet bowl and, bending over it, stuck her finger as far down her throat as it would go, and began to heave.

CHAPTER

7

ON THE FIRST DAY after the Thanksgiving weekend, Amy awoke and remembered that Karen Lutz had quit her job. She felt like Sisyphus, watching the boulder she had just pushed to the top of the hill roll all the way back to the bottom.

She told her mother this, as she bolted a slice of whole-grain toast with almond butter in the kitchen before work.

"Oh, Amy, none of us have to push the boulders in our lives uphill all alone. That's God's job."

Amy, washing the sticky mouthful down with a swallow of kale and mango smoothie, had to admit she hadn't thought of it that way.

"Well, stop pushing and start praying, then!" said her mother. "After all, God knows the plan. You might as well ask Him about it."

So Amy had prayed about it, out loud, on her way to work, her breath making little white puffs in the air as her aged Escort's heating system fought valiantly to warm the car. "God, I have these positions to fill, and no one to fill them. Could You send someone? The right people? And I'm sorry I didn't bother to pray about it sooner, but now it's starting to be a crisis. The grand opening is in May, and I need a wardrobe person, and a choreographer. And . . . I kind of need them soon, if You don't mind. Please?"

Still, when a Crystal Baker called that very morning, asking if there was a job available, Amy did not feel hopeful. Her mood did not lift when Crystal appeared, a waiflike creature a few years older than herself dressed in a tailored velvet jacket and three skirts of varying lengths over leggings. Amy accepted the résumé the girl handed her and waved her toward the other chair in the office.

"Tell me about yourself, Crystal." She glanced at the paper in her hand. Oh. A bachelor's degree in theater. Amy sat up straighter.

"Well, I grew up near Boston, and I've been working down there, as you can see." Crystal nodded at the résumé. "I used to vacation in Rockport with my family when I was younger. I love the coast of Maine, and I happened to be ready for a change right around the time my aunt, who lives in Copper Cove, went through a divorce. I moved up here to live with her."

"It says here you have some film experience."

Crystal's pale cheeks flushed. "It's not as exciting as it sounds. I got hired to do a couple of parts last year for a company that makes corporate safety videos."

"Really? What parts?"

"In one, I played a dead body. Electrocuted by a poorly

grounded wire, if you must know. In another, I was the woman who started CPR."

Amy raised her eyebrows. "Ah. So do you consider yourself an actress?"

"Well . . . I do a very good dead person. Want to see?"

Amy laughed. "Sure, go ahead."

Crystal stood up from her chair, then collapsed gracefully to the floor, sprawled on her stomach with her legs and arms splayed, her eyes closed. After several seconds, she cracked one eye. "What do you think? Were you convinced?"

"I really was. I was just about to call 911."

The other girl got to her feet and rearranged her several layers of skirts. "The trick is holding your breath. Everyone forgets to do that."

Amy regarded her with approval. "Well, it's a great talent, but unfortunately this job doesn't require you to do any acting. How's your sewing?"

"Outstanding. I made this outfit." Crystal turned on the spot.

Amy blinked. "You did?"

"Yep. I cut these two skirts down from a set of old drapes and sheers I found in my aunt's attic, and this top one was, until last night, a child's christening dress I found at the Salvation Army. The jacket was an old coat of my grandfather's. I ripped out a few seams, nipped here and tucked there, and Bob's your uncle, it's a jacket!" Crystal sat down and crossed her legs. "I did buy the leggings at Target, but I try not to talk about that."

"You're hired," Amy said in disbelief.

"Really, I am?"

"Really, you are. How soon can you start?"

"This afternoon, if you want."

Thank You, God. It seemed things might finally have taken a hopeful turn.

✦

Jane was at the piano, working through the complicated accompaniment for "Gee, Officer Krupke," when Leander wandered in. An unexpected snowstorm in the night had closed school for the day. It was nice to have him home. Not for the first time, she wished his retirement were not still so far away.

Leander sat on the couch, picked up an issue of *American Music Teacher* from the end table, and began to leaf through it. "Sounds good," he told her.

She stopped and sighed. "Lots of syncopation. And sharps. I've always had a difficult relationship with sharps."

"You can do it. Keep beavering away."

She found her place and began to play again. Within moments, she had lost herself in concentration over the tricky bars of *"And, sociologically, he's sick! I am sick! We are sick! We are sick, we are sick, sick, sick."* Over and over she played them, struggling with the accidentals and the timing.

When at last she stopped, she saw that Leander had fallen asleep on the couch. She frowned. Her husband never slept at ten o'clock on a weekday. Although lately, come to think of it, he had been napping in the afternoons, when he got home from school.

Something felt out of place. A syncopated beat in the pleasant, predictable rhythm of their lives. Jane pushed back the piano bench and went to cover him with an afghan. He did not stir. She sat back down at the piano and found her place in the music. *"We are sick,"* she played. *"We are sick, sick, sick."* Abruptly, she closed the music and pushed it aside. She took "Tonight" from the stack instead. *"Tonight, tonight, I'll see my love tonight . . ."*

It was a much better key for her.

"Do you have a minute, Seph?"

Sephy wedged the phone between her chin and shoulder and wished, not for the first time, that cell phones were a little bigger. It would make talking with your hands full so much easier. "I have just about a minute, Lib. I'm on my way to a nursing research class. Is everything okay?"

"I have a huge favor to ask you."

"How huge, and is it related to the wedding?"

"Really, really big, and yes."

"I'm already your maid of honor; how much bigger does it get?"

"Would playing the music for the reception be too much?"

"What?"

"Well, not just you, obviously. I mean you and your sisters. All four of you together. David and I want you, Ivy, Laura, and Amy to provide the music for our wedding reception."

"What, like DJs?"

"No, like a *band*. Like, singing and playing your instruments. For the entire reception."

Sephy literally felt her mouth fall open.

"Seph? Say something."

"Ah . . ."

Libby spoke very fast. "Say yes. Come on! You're all so talented. You have a beautiful blend. Between the four of you, you play enough instruments to be your own group. And the truth is, when David and I started looking at what's out there for bands, we didn't like any of them half as much as we like listening to the four of you sing and play together. Please say you'll do it, Sephy! It would mean the world to both of us."

Sephy gazed at a single spot on the wall of her room and tried to think of a way to refuse. But that was the trouble: she had never been able to say no to anyone, least of all her best friend and brother. "Um . . . ," she croaked. "I'd have to ask the others. . . ."

Libby squealed with delight. "I knew you'd do it! Oh, Sephy, you have no idea how happy this makes both of us. Thank you. *Thank* you . . ."

Sephy hung up and looked at her phone blankly, wondering how she had just agreed to do something she didn't remember saying yes to.

"Amy, do you have a second to talk?"

"David, where are you calling from? Why aren't you at work?"

"You're the one who works the crazy hours. The rest of the world clocked out half an hour ago. I'm driving home."

"David! You shouldn't be talking on the phone while you drive. It's really dangerous."

"I'll make it quick, then. I have a favor to ask you. It's about the wedding reception."

"Let me guess. You want Ivy and Laura and Sephy and me to play the music for it?"

"What—? Did Ivy already talk to you?"

"No, but I was expecting it. It just makes sense. I mean, you have this ready-made band in your own family; why would you hire strangers to do the music?"

"Oh. Then . . . you'll do it?"

"Of course I will. I mean, if the others want to."

"Okay. Well, that was easy. Thanks, Amy. Thanks a million."

"No problem. Glad to help. I even have a great idea for a name."

"Really? What?"

"The Darlings, of course. What else could it be?"

Laura had just gone to bed when her phone rang.

"Laura, guess what?"

"Ivy? I just got to sleep."

"Oops, sorry. You're in bed early."

"I had a long day." Laura sighed. "What is it?"

"I have an incredible proposition for you. A completely once-in-a-lifetime deal. You're not going to believe this."

"Just tell me."

"David and Libby want you and me and Sephy and Amy to form a band and play the music at their wedding reception."

"No way."

"'No way' as in you can't believe your good luck, or 'no way' as in you won't do it?"

"The second one. No. Way."

"Why not?" Laura heard her sister switch to a wheedling tone. "That doesn't sound like fun to you?"

"No, it sounds like *work*! And stress, and nerves, and more time than I have to devote to a project like that for the next year."

"Oh, come on, Laura! Please just say you'll think about it. This is our only brother! It's Sephy's best friend. It'll be *fun*."

"Ivy, go away."

"Just promise to think about it."

"I'm not promising anything. I'm going back to sleep. Good night." Laura hung up and stared at the ceiling above her. She would not get sucked into this. Saying yes meant committing to hours of practice on her own, and expensive, time-consuming trips across the country to rehearse with her sisters. It meant bickering, and being mercilessly bossed by Ivy and Amy. And who knew? In the end, they could end up disappointing the bride and groom anyway.

The phone rang again. She looked at the caller ID: Ivy.

Laura tapped Reject Call and turned the phone off.

No way.

"David? I talked to Laura. She's thinking about it."

"Really? That's great! I was sure she would say no."

"I'm pretty sure she's going to say yes. I'll keep working on her and get back to you."

"Wow, that's great. Thanks a lot, Ivy."

"My pleasure."

"So . . . it's a band?"

"I think it's safe to say that it's a band."

THE FIRST WEEK OF DECEMBER, Laura made up her mind: she would fly home to Copper Cove for a visit. There was something about this time of year that made her homesick for Maine. Her mother's wistful hints over the phone were one factor. Another was that she was longing for a real white Christmas.

Although she felt more at home in Phoenix now, she didn't have a lot of what might be called friendships. At a flea market, she had found a hand-painted Victorian Christmas ornament for Theo and Evan. She bought half a dozen Macanudos for Rob, who occasionally smoked them, and wrapped them in a felt Christmas stocking. Other than that, Laura had no one here to buy Christmas presents for. There was no one from whom she expected to receive a gift. She did not bother to put up a tree or decorate her apartment, since there was no one to see it.

The grocery store chain threw their employees a bleak little party with crackers and cheese and punch in the break room during one lunch hour, and that was the extent of her celebrations in Phoenix. She discovered that she felt sorry for herself, and if there was one thing Laura despised, it was feeling sorry for herself. She bought a ticket home for Christmas Eve.

It was better than she had imagined to see everyone again. Still, she had the good sense to realize, homecomings invariably seemed ideal for the first day or two. Experience had taught her that it would not be long before their quirks—her mother's solicitude, Amy's brutal honesty, Ivy's carelessness, and Sephy's unrelenting niceness—would start to get under her skin. By December 28, which was the date she had scheduled her return ticket, she would be only too glad to get back to Phoenix. Her father alone had no capacity for irritating her. No matter what issue the rest of the family was battling out, Leander sat amid the chaos, calm and supportive. On the rare occasions when he spoke up, everyone listened. None of them, no matter how badly they had behaved, ever doubted that their father loved them and thought them perfectly wonderful.

Christmas Eve was Amy's birthday, which the family always celebrated with lobster stew and Christmas carols. Amy, who did not eat fish, made a roasted red pepper soup for herself. Laura was introduced to her new friend Crystal, a dreamy, malnourished-looking girl. She already knew David's roommate, George, and Libby Hale was there, as well as Grammie Lydia Darling. Mitch Harris had been invited, their mother told them, but had not shown up.

When supper had been eaten and Amy's presents unwrapped and they were singing carols around the Steinway baby grand in their parents' living room, Sephy said, "I have an idea. Let's go to the basement and practice for the wedding. Maybe Jada can sing a number or two with us."

"Now?" said Amy. "We don't have anything to rehearse. Any songs, I mean."

"So?" Sephy said. "We'll play Christmas carols. And we know about a hundred hymns. Your drums are set up, there's a keyboard down there for me, and Laura can play David's old guitar. Ivy, is your old violin still around here somewhere?"

Ivy looked at her mother. "Mom?"

"It's in the closet downstairs, right where you left it."

"Well?" said Sephy. "Why not?"

Amy shrugged. "Sure, let's give it a try."

"I'm in," said Ivy.

Laura felt her nostrils flare. She should have seen this coming. When had anyone in this family ever listened to her? "Excuse me," she bit out. "I've already told Ivy I'm not playing in the band."

They all turned to stare at her.

"What do you mean you're not playing in the band?" said David.

"I'm not! I don't have time to practice—"

"You're not refusing to play at your own brother's wedding?" This from Amy.

Laura gasped. "Don't make me the villain here! I have a demanding job. A lot of commitments between now and next Christmas."

"So?" said Amy. "You're not the only busy person in the world. We all have a lot of commitments."

"It's *David*," Ivy said.

Crystal, George, and Libby had begun to shoot sideways glances at each other.

"You're always thinking of yourself first, aren't you, Laura?" Amy's voice was beginning to rise.

"Now, Amy. That's not a very nice—" began her mother, at the same moment that Sephy said, "Could we please not fight?" Nobody paid attention to either of them.

"That," Laura cried, "is a completely unfair statement! I do *not* always think about myself first. But I refuse to be guilt-tripped into—"

David turned to Ivy. "*You* told me she said yes!"

"I thought she would," Ivy said. "I was sure she would come around. You're going to come around, aren't you, Laura?"

Laura gaped at the circle of accusing faces around her. Unbelievable. Absolutely impossible. How had she thought she would be free to make her own decision? When had she ever been before? She held up her hands. "You know what? Fine! All right. But you realize I'm not going to be home more than once or twice between now and the wedding to rehearse."

"But you'll try," Amy filled in for her. "You'll come home when you can."

An uneasy silence fell.

"Maybe we could rehearse by FaceTime," Sephy ventured.

"You can't hold a band rehearsal by FaceTime," Laura snapped.

"It was just an idea."

"Bad idea."

"I'm sorry." Although Sephy looked away, Laura saw tears in her eyes.

She sighed. "It wasn't *that* bad an idea, Seph. We'll figure something out. We'll have to, I suppose."

In the silence that followed, David stood up. "I think that's my cue to leave. Nick, you up for a little ESPN action? DeShaun? George? Dad?"

"Me too!" Hammer cried.

"Of course you too!" David rubbed Hammer's nubbly hair. "Jump on, buddy." He crouched and Hammer took a flying leap onto his uncle's back.

"I hate to disappoint," said Leander, "but I think I'm going to call it a night."

"You're not going to bed so soon, honey?" said Jane.

"I'm just worn out. Probably fighting off a cold. An early night will do me good." He held up a hand. "Good night, everyone. Drive carefully, and merry Christmas."

Jane watched him go. "He seems to be tired all the time lately." She shook her head. "Ah, well. There isn't a one of us getting any younger."

No one answered. A residue of anger still hung in the air.

When Jane spoke again, her voice was determinedly cheerful. "Now, Crystal, Libby, Mom, it seems we're to be the groupies for the band. How about some more coffee while we watch?"

She went to the kitchen for a tray and the rest of them made their silent way downstairs to the finished basement, where Amy's drum set and Sephy's electric keyboard lived.

They found the guitar and violin, as promised, in a cupboard full of games, and tuned them. Gradually, warmed by the sharing of music, the atmosphere between the sisters began to thaw.

Jane appeared with a tray of mugs and a plate of Christmas cookies, taking a seat with Crystal and Libby and her mother-in-law on the basement sofa. Jada, torn between the equal delights of cookies and watching Ivy tune her violin, hovered somewhere between the two groups.

"Everyone ready?" called Sephy. "What should we warm up with?"

"Something slow," said Laura, at exactly the same moment that Amy said, "Something fast."

"Something slow," Amy conceded.

"'The Peace Carol,' then. Key of D," said Sephy. "Who's singing? Laura? Good. I'll sing harmony with you on 'the branch that bears the bright holly,' et cetera, and Ivy and Amy, you two give us some backup vocals."

They sang it through once, a bit roughly, and a second time, better. They moved on to hymns and a few gospel choruses they'd known forever. Laura found herself relaxing into the session. The old familiarity of playing with her sisters, of finding harmonies and communicating in the language of music, was soothing and insidious. Music made it easy to get carried away. To forget all your reasons for standing firm. By the time their mother stood up and began to clatter the coffee cups on the tray, Laura had nearly forgotten all her objections.

"Time to wrap it up, girls," called Jane. "Santa will be here soon."

"Is it that time already?" said Ivy. She checked her watch.

"Oh my goodness, what am I thinking? I need to get these kids home to bed." She looked at the others. "Well, what do you think? How did we do?"

"I hate to be the one to say it," said Sephy, "but I think we're pretty good."

"Or we will be, with a little more practice," Amy amended.

"Laura, are you going to stick with us?" Ivy asked her.

"I said I would, and I have to admit that after tonight, I'm a little more hopeful about the whole idea."

Sephy turned off the keyboard and began to arrange the cover over it. "What's your verdict, Lib? Do you still want us at your wedding?"

"I wouldn't have anyone else. You already sound incredible."

"That," said Laura, "is because you don't know anything about music. But thanks for saying so."

"So what are you calling yourselves?" Crystal wanted to know.

The four sisters looked at each other and answered together. "The Darlings!"

"All right, Darlings," their mother said drily, "mind your mother now. It's off to bed or off for home, take your pick, but this joint's closing down in ten minutes."

The Darlings, yawning and chattering, finished packing up their instruments and minded their mother.

At five o'clock on Christmas morning, Sephy's phone rang. Before she was fully awake, she knew who it would be. Disappointment and relief washed over her together. Sour and sweet. Already, she knew her answer. In the dark, she groped on the table for the phone.

"Hello?"

"Hi, is this Sephy?" The voice on the other end was apologetic.

"Yes. Hi."

"This is Gwen, the night supervisor from the hospital. I'm sorry to bother you on Christmas morning, Sephy, but we had a sick call this morning. I was wondering if, by any outside chance, you'd be interested in picking up a shift? It's time-and-a-half pay."

Sephy did not allow herself to sigh. After all, no one was forcing her to say yes. "What time?"

"Seven o'clock."

"All twelve hours?"

"If you can manage it. If not, any part of the shift you can work would help."

"Which floor?"

"Four east."

That wasn't the worst news in the world. Four east was a respiratory floor. Sephy liked the staff there. The manager was a despotic tyrant; but then, the manager wouldn't be working on Christmas Day.

"Okay, I'll be in."

"And . . . do you think you'd be interested in all twelve hours, or . . . ?"

She had to smile at the barely disguised hope in Gwen's voice. "Sure. I'll do the whole shift."

"Oh, Sephy, thank you! You can't believe how much easier this makes my life. We really appreciate it."

Sephy hung up and rolled onto her back, staring up into the darkness. She didn't *want* to work all day on Christmas—who did?—but money was money. More important, it was an escape from the temptations ahead at home today.

She reached for her nightstand and opened the top drawer. Inside, she found the little bottle of drops she had been taking for ten days now. A dropperful three times a day, before meals, and then she was only allowed a few ounces of broiled chicken breast and a small salad. . . . She was perpetually starving, but in ten days, she'd already dropped seven pounds. A record for her.

When she had forced herself to throw up on Thanksgiving, the experience had so filled her with revulsion that she could not have done it a second time, even had she wanted to. No, better to miss the Christmas meal altogether than to be faced with that alternative again. By working a twelve-hour shift, she'd be able to avoid the pitfalls of breakfast, lunch, and Christmas dinner, as well as the endless bowls of nuts and candies and the platters of cheeses and salamis and cookies her mother was sure to set out all over the house. By the time she got home, she'd have missed the enormous meal. She'd make her excuses by saying she'd eaten at the hospital, and she'd open a few gifts, maybe sing a few carols, if that was what everyone wanted to do, and escape to bed. Tomorrow would be an ordinary day, when her minuscule meals of chicken and lettuce would go unnoticed and uncommented upon by a household of concerned parents and siblings.

She sat up and squeezed a dropperful of the magic liquid under her tongue. Time to shower and put on some scrubs and find her way to her parents' bedside in the dark to whisper the news that she was going to be missing Christmas this year.

But it was a gift—the best gift she could have asked for, under the circumstances. It meant that, for today, she would not gain any weight. She swallowed the drops. "Merry Christmas to me," she whispered.

"Hey, Laura!" Rob caught up with her as she was leaving church one morning, just after the New Year. "Thanks for the Christmas cigars. Wow, great gift. I feel bad that I didn't get you anything."

She waved this away. "I'm glad you liked them. How was your Christmas?"

"Great. Busy. You know. I went home to see Mom and the kids, so it was a little chaotic. Fun, though. How was yours?"

"Not too bad. I have a brother getting married next Christmas, and while I was home, I got railroaded into playing in the family band for the wedding reception. I'm flying back for a week in April. My sister who's in college will be home then, so we'll get a chance to practice all together."

"No kidding? What do you play?"

"Guitar. Acoustic and electric. And I sing a little."

"Wow, that's unbelievable. You just might be the answer to my prayers! You wouldn't consider helping out with the youth group band, would you? They're all . . . ah . . . willing, but not necessarily able."

"Youth group band?" Too late, she remembered a motley cluster of teenagers who had stood onstage and played for the worship service once or twice. Listening to them had been a fairly painful experience. "Oh, right, the youth group band."

"The thing is, I'm the youth pastor, but I don't know a thing about music, so . . ."

"You're a youth pastor? I thought you were a cop."

"I am a cop. But I'm also what passes for the youth pastor here. It's a volunteer position."

Laura was half-ashamed at the disappointment she felt. She had thought Rob was more sophisticated than that. All the youth pastors she had ever known seemed little more than teenagers who had never really grown up. Hooting and throwing dodgeballs around the church gym. Pranking the younger youth group guys. Speaking in a slang they were a decade too old for. Even as a teen herself, she had sensed this. Not that it mattered. Why should she care how Rob volunteered in his spare time?

"Sure," she managed. "Anytime. I'd be glad to work with the kids. I mean, I'm not an expert, but I could maybe give them a little guidance with their music. Help point them in the right direction."

"Yeah?" A smile split his broad, dark face. "That's awesome, Laura, thanks! I'll give you a call about it."

"Okay," she said, trying to sound bright. She left him and stalked across the parking lot to her car, feeling far more disgruntled than she had reason to feel. So she had been conscripted to tutor the church teenagers in music. So what? Teenagers weren't the worst thing in the world. And it was a worthy cause. It would be fun.

Her tires chirped on the blacktop as she peeled onto the main road. Every head in the parking lot turned to stare at her. Laura, feeling let down and angry, could not have cared less.

A light tap on the open office door made Amy look up from her computer.

It was Crystal, with the mail. She handed Amy a stack. "Ready for a break?"

Amy rubbed her eyes and peered at the clock on her screen. "Is it that time already?"

"It's ten o'clock. You've been staring at that computer for two hours without blinking."

"It seems like I just sat down." Amy pushed her chair away from her desk and stood up, stretching. "There are never enough hours in a day to do what needs to be done around here."

Crystal shrugged. "So you do the best you can and let the rest of it sort itself out. It always does, somehow."

Easy for her to say, Amy thought with a trace of irritation. Crystal wasn't the one responsible for getting the arts program off the ground four months from now. Or hiring a choreographer. *That* search was still going nowhere. She had learned to stop mentioning it at home, where her mother was sure to counter with, "Well, are you praying about it?" And Amy, although she did not like to be nagged, *was* praying.

You couldn't grow up in Jane Darling's household and not have prayer be a reflex action to every need that presented itself. So Amy, prodded on by her mother's frequent reminders, had taken to saying, *Please, God, I have to have a choreographer soon* about twenty times a day. And, the experience with Karen Lutz still fresh in her mind, she had begun adding, *And the right one, please. It would be great if I could find the right one the first time.*

She had prayed for Crystal, and there was no denying that her props master was a godsend. Although Amy had only hired her to work part-time, she was tireless. The week she moved to Copper Cove, Crystal had found a second part-time job as a cashier at Hannaford, and in her twenty hours a week allocated for the arts program, she was already amassing an enviable wardrobe and collection of props for *West Side Story*. She hardly ever asked for help, and she ran errands, made tea, and was turning out to be a good friend, to boot.

Amy moved to the filing cabinet where the electric tea-kettle sat and switched it on.

"So, guess what?" Crystal said, folding her long legs into the tiny room's second chair. "I asked Mitch out."

"No!"

"Yes. And he turned me down."

Amy paused in the act of dropping mint tea bags into a pair of mugs and stared at her. "He did not! Why? Did he give you a reason?"

"I asked him to meet me at Shooters' Bar, and he said he doesn't go to bars. In fact, he said he doesn't even drink." Crystal accepted the box of biscotti that Amy held out to her and wrinkled her nose. "What kind of man doesn't drink?"

Amy smiled. "Lots of men don't drink." She took the kettle off its base and poured hot water into both cups. "Lots of *people* don't drink. I don't, in fact. It's terrible for your health."

"You don't count; you're a vegetarian. But . . . a construction worker? I thought they were all into the bar scene. You know, beer and wings and big-screen-TV sports."

"Guess not. Did he tell you why he doesn't drink?"

"No. Do you think it's a religious thing?"

Amy said wryly, "I'm pretty sure it's not."

"Anyway, I told him we didn't have to go to a bar. We could just go out for dinner or something. And he still turned me down." Crystal sipped at her tea. "Do you think it's my face? Maybe he thinks I'm ugly."

"Nobody could think you're ugly, Crystal. Don't take it personally. Mitch has had a hard time in the last few years. To be honest, you might be better off with someone else."

"Really? How's he had a hard time?"

But Amy found herself feeling oddly protective. It was one thing for family to discuss Mitch's mottled past, but Crystal didn't *know* him. She shrugged. "He disappeared from town for a while, and when he came back, he was different. Mom's tried to get him to come to the house for dinner and holidays and that kind of thing, but he won't. He has his own demons, I imagine."

"Does he have family?"

"We're his family. Or we used to be."

"I mean besides you Darlings."

"His father's still around somewhere, but I don't think they have much to do with each other."

"He sounds like a hero in need of rescuing," said Crystal in a satisfied voice. "I think I'll rescue him."

Amy raised her eyebrows. "I don't think Mitch exactly wants to be rescued."

"Well, obviously I'm not going to *advertise* it to him. But you've made up my mind for me: I'm going to ask him out again, and this time I'm not taking no for an answer. Do you think he'd go to a hockey game with me?"

"Ah . . . I guess you'll have to try and see."

"Okay, I will. On my lunch break, I'll run over to the opera house and ask him. Will you come with me?"

Amy tried to suppress a smile. "What if he turns you down again?"

"He's not going to say no. The first time was just because I didn't know about the bar thing."

"The possibility of rejection doesn't bother you at all?"

Crystal made a noise of derision. "What is this rejection you speak of? Mitch Harris wants to go out with me; he just doesn't know it yet."

Amy had to laugh. "Are you always this confident?"

"Confidence," said Crystal, "is my middle name." She stood up and stretched like a cat. "Lunchtime, you and me at the opera house, then?"

"It's a date."

"That's one down, one to go," said Crystal.

Mitch sensed rather than heard the front doors close as Amy and her friend left the opera house. He pulled the safety goggles from his forehead, where he had pushed them while he had talked with . . . what was her name? Christy? Carla, maybe. He polished a fine layer of sawdust from the goggles with his sleeve, trying to put the last uncomfortable ten minutes out of his mind.

"So, are you going out with the tall one?" It was Brian, one of the carpenters, who had watched his interaction with Christy-Carla from the other end of the room, where he was supposed to be installing insulation.

"No," said Mitch shortly. "I'm not going out with her."

"Was she your girlfriend before?"

"I don't even know her." Mitch leaned over a two-by-four and made an elaborate show of measuring it.

"So what'd she want?"

Mitch shrugged, but Brian was not to be put off.

"Come on! A hot girl shows up to talk to you, and you have no idea what she wants? She ask you out?"

He shrugged again, but after a minute was forced to admit, "Yeah. She asked me to go to a hockey game."

Brian whooped. "Nice work! So . . . ? When are you going?"

"I'm not. I said thanks but no thanks."

"What?" Brian swore colorfully. "Are you crazy or just stupid? She's hot!"

Mitch looked at the door through which the girls had disappeared. "*Her?* No, she's not."

"Stupid and blind," was Brian's pronouncement. "Well, she obviously thinks *you're* hot. Isn't this the second time she's asked you out?"

Mitch shrugged, wishing Brian would shut up and disappear.

"I don't suppose she'd look twice at me, if it's you she's really after," Brian mused. "What about her friend? She was cute. She seeing anybody?"

"Amy? Ah . . . I don't think so."

"Maybe I'll ask her out. Hey, I got it!" Brian snapped his fingers. "You and the tall one, me and Amy—double date. Huh? Huh? Come on, we'll go to that hockey game together."

"Listen, I really don't want to go out with her."

"You won't be going out with her; you'll be going out with *us*."

"I don't think so."

"I'll just ask Amy out myself then."

Mitch had heard enough of Brian's stories to understand what he expected from a date with any woman. A small wave of panic washed over him. "Look . . . all right. We could do a double date, I guess."

"Good. It'll be fun. You have Amy's number?"

Mitch did, but he wasn't about to give it to Brian. "No."

Brian cursed. "Well, can you get it for me?"

"I don't think so."

"How am I supposed to ask her out then?"

Mitch hesitated. Then, "She works at the town hall. You can probably find her there."

He turned away from Brian's salacious leer and muttered, "That insulation needs to be finished."

❧

The ladies' room of a sports arena during a hockey game is a revolting place, Amy thought. In the small space that was overwarm with the body heat of hundreds of women, all odors were magnified. Amy and Crystal could hardly hear each other over the chatter and the sounds of running water and electric hand dryers. By the time they made it to the head of the line, the cloying potpourri of perfume and cigarette smoke, urine and hand soap, had begun to stir a faint nausea in Amy. They left with relief and elbowed their way back to their seats, where Brian and Mitch waited for them.

"Thanks for doing this!" Crystal shouted above the roar of five thousand Black Bears fans. "I think Mitch only agreed to come because you and Brian would be here. He seems shy."

"No problem." Amy, who hadn't been to a hockey game in years, had been surprised when Mitch's good-looking coworker had turned up at her office the week before and asked her to the game.

"It's for Mitch's sake," Brian had said, looking very humble and clean-cut. "He really wants to go out with your friend, but he's too . . . well, you know Mitch. So I thought, I'm his friend and you're *her* friend, and maybe we could help them get together."

So for Mitch's and Crystal's sakes, she had agreed.

On Friday night, the four of them had piled into Brian's extended-cab pickup and driven an hour to the University of Maine's Orono campus to watch the Black Bears take on the Terriers of Boston University. On the trip down, Amy, Crystal, and Brian talked animatedly about hockey and the future of the arts center. Mitch was mostly silent, adding to the conversation only when Crystal asked him a direct question. Amy was annoyed. For a man who had been so eager to go out with her friend, he didn't seem to be trying very hard.

Back at their seats, Amy bought Brian a program. He bought a Pepsi for himself, a spring water for her, and nachos for them to share, which Amy did not touch. They spent the pregame minutes poring over the player bios and watching the team mascot do cartwheels on the ice. From the corner of her eye, Amy noticed that Crystal was trying to make conversation with Mitch but having little luck.

Her friend cast her an agonized look that clearly said, *What's* wrong *with him?*

Over the noise of the crowd, Amy shouted, "Be patient. He doesn't get out much." As a great roar signaled the entrance of the Black Bears, she leaned behind Crystal and pulled on Mitch's sleeve.

He looked around. "What?"

She cupped her hand and spoke into his ear. "You need to pay attention to your *date*."

Mitch looked at Crystal, clapping and cheering as the players were announced, as though he had never seen her before. "What? I *am*."

"No, buy her a Pepsi or something. Talk to her."

"I am talking to her!"

"No, you're not. And unless you start, she's going to think you're a real jerk."

Mitch looked uncertain.

"Ask her if she wants a hot dog. Then go get her one."

She did not miss Mitch's small sigh, but was relieved, a moment later, to see him bend and speak into Crystal's ear. He left his seat then, edging his way along the row of knees between him and the aisle. Ten minutes later, he returned with a cardboard box of hot dogs and sodas that he offered to his date before helping himself. Amy, satisfied, turned her attention back to the game. She kept her eye on them throughout the first period and into the second and saw that Mitch was making an effort. Still, she felt sorry for Crystal. Even a seat removed from Mitch, Amy could tell he wasn't exactly scintillating company.

But halfway through the second period, something happened that blew thoughts of Mitch and Crystal from her mind. She was squinting at the program, trying to find the name of number 29, when Brian slipped his arm around her shoulders. She shot him a startled glance. He grinned at her and gave her shoulder a little squeeze. She forced herself not to flinch. He kept his arm there, heavy across her shoulders, making it hard for her to sit up straight. When the Bears scored a goal, she seized the chance to jump up and throw off the arm.

She had been too optimistic. As soon as she stopped clapping, Brian reached for her hand and caught it in his. Trying not to cringe outright, Amy looked to Crystal for help, but her friend flashed her a triumphant smile, as though they both understood that something wonderful had just happened. Crystal, getting into the spirit of things, snuggled into Mitch's side and slipped a hand through the crook of his arm.

The rest of the period seemed endless, and Amy, her captive hand sweating inside Brian's, spent the time contriving plans to get away from him as soon as possible. She got her chance as the second period ended. Jumping up the moment the buzzer sounded, she yanked her hand back. "I need to use the bathroom," she gasped, and fled.

She did not go to the restroom but leaned against a wall

by the soft pretzel stand, where she could keep an eye out in case Brian should come looking for her.

A soft touch on her arm made her jump.

"Excuse me, miss. You're right in front of my basket." A custodian stood there, gesturing at the overflowing trash bin beside her.

"Oh, sorry." Amy moved to one side.

The custodian began picking up the empty cups and paper trays scattered around the trash can and stuffing them in with blue-gloved hands. "You waiting for someone?" he asked. In spite of the noise in the arena, Amy had no trouble hearing him.

"Hiding from my date," she confessed. "He seems to have more hands than an octopus."

"*Arms*, you mean. An octopus don't have hands." The man spoke in a strong New York accent. For some reason, his comment struck Amy as funny.

She smiled. "You're right. I never thought of that." She watched him tie up the top of the full trash bag and pull it out of the bin. "You're not from Maine," she said.

"Nah, Brooklyn."

"I don't think I've ever met anyone from Brooklyn. What brought you all the way up here?"

The man, who was probably nearer forty than thirty, took a spray bottle from his caddy and began to squirt cleaner on the side of the trash can, where something red had run down and congealed. "Wors' reason onna planet: love." He said it like *luff*. "I met someone in New York, fell in luff, followed 'im up here. Gave up a good career to work for 'is old man inna furniture store. By the time he dumped me, I was too old to get back inna my own business. I'll probably be doin' this for the resta my life." He nodded at the trash can and snapped open a clean plastic liner. "So, ah . . . you in luff with this . . . Octopus Arms?"

"No. In fact, I don't even like him very much."

"You a student here?"

"No, a group of us just drove down for the game."

"You got a good career?"

"Yes. At least, I've just started one."

"That's good. Hey, let me give you some advice. Don't get all tangled up wit' some man who's gonna mess that up for you. Do your thinking here—" he tapped the side of his head—"and not here." He tapped his chest. "You're young. You got pleny'a time to fall in luff later on."

Amy glanced at the electronic clock that hung above the center of the rink. There were still two minutes until the game recommenced. She had no desire to go back to Brian earlier than she had to. "What was your other job?" she asked the custodian. "The one you gave up to come to Maine?"

"I was a dancer," he said, now flicking a cloth along the edge of the pretzel counter. "Well, a choreographer really. Worked fifteen years off Broadway. Not much in that line a work up here, though, and like I said, I'm too old to get back inna the business in the big city."

Amy stared at him. "You—you're a choreographer?"

"Nah. I *was* a choreographer. Now I'm a janitor."

The warning buzzer sounded. The man stuffed his rag back into his caddy and raised a hand to her. "Well, good luck. And remember what I tol' you." He tapped his head again.

"Wait!" Amy dug in her purse for a business card. "I'm the

director of an arts center in a little town about an hour from here. I'm looking for a choreographer. And a dance instructor. Can you teach dance?"

Now he was staring at her.

"Anyway, if . . . if you're interested, give me a call and we can talk about it."

He took the card she held out to him and looked at it. "Amy Darling. Sounds like a stage name."

She grinned. "It's not."

He held out his hand to her. "Nice to meet you, Amy. I'm Paul." He pronounced it *Pawl*. "Pawl Zamboni."

She raised her eyebrows. "A Zamboni, working at a hockey game? Now *that* sounds like a stage name."

He grinned back at her. "Yeah, I get that a lot. I'll maybe give you a cawl."

"No, wait—can I get your number too?" She dug out another business card and a pen and handed them to him.

He scribbled down a number and gave them back, then saluted her with the business card she had given him to keep. "Thanks."

Amy went back to her seat, hardly daring to believe her luck. When the final period started, she kept her hand carefully out of reach, under the program cover. She hadn't reckoned on Brian's determination, however. Half a minute into the game, he put his hand on her knee and squeezed, then moved it higher. Amy all but yelped aloud and clapped her hand over his. Suddenly holding hands didn't seem like such a bad idea; at least that way, she got to control where all the limbs went. To her great relief, he seemed satisfied with this.

The game ended late, and since they had a long drive ahead of them and all had to work in the morning, they agreed to go straight home. They dropped Amy off first. Brian walked her to the door while Mitch and Crystal stayed in the truck with the engine running.

Under the porch light, Amy turned to face him. "Thanks. It was really fun," she lied, shivering in the frigid air.

"Yeah, me too." She could see his intent on his face. He was going to kiss her.

"Well, g'night!" she squeaked and tried to duck out of the way. He was too fast. Blocking her with one arm, he pinned her against the porch door with his body and kissed her. Amy tried to turn her head, but he was surprisingly strong. His lips were wet and cold, and she shuddered.

The truck's horn sounded and they both jumped. Brian pulled away. "We should continue this later." His voice was husky.

The horn sounded again, startling and abrasive in the stillness of the night. Amy groped for the door handle behind her, pushed it open, and ducked under Brian's arm, silently blessing Crystal for saving her.

Her mother had left the stove light on, and a single mug sat on the counter beside the box of tea bags. The sight lifted Amy's spirits. She was home; she never had to see Brian again if she didn't want to—and she *didn't* want to. And best of all, she just might have found herself a choreographer tonight. She would call him first thing in the morning. Butternut the cat wandered into the kitchen and rubbed against her ankles, as if in approval. *Cawl Pawl,* Amy thought, as she turned on the gas beneath the kettle.

She hummed a few bars of the UMaine college fight song and did a little twirl, sidestepping the cat. *Thank You, God, for sending me a choreographer.* In spite of Brian, all seemed right with the world.

CHAPTER

10

Rob was as good as his threat. The very week he asked Laura to help with the youth group band, he texted to pin her down to a date and time.

Laura was half pleased, half exasperated. She had always hated to have her time encroached upon by someone with an agenda. On the other hand, she did know music. And the church was the only thing she had that passed for a social life out here. It was gratifying to be needed. And wanted. She texted him back and agreed to a Sunday night.

The band, it turned out, had some good raw material to work with. There was a thirteen-year-old girl named Cassie on keyboard, who could read music but had no real grasp of theory and therefore lacked the confidence to improvise. There were two Trevors: one on bass and one on drums. Both seemed to know their parts but had no notion of following together as a group. The same was true of the guitarist, Adam, a skinny, bewildered-looking fourteen-year-old in glasses, who blinked around at everyone while playing with the artistry of a future Bob Dylan. The real weakness was the trio of girls who led the singing. Their voices were thin and breathy, and they possessed an irritating tendency to dissolve into giggles at any given moment.

Halfway through the rehearsal, Laura took them in hand. "Girls!" she said sharply. "What are you giggling for?"

They quieted at once and stared at her, shooting each other apprehensive sideways glances.

Laura sighed and approached the stage, where the three vocalists were huddled around the microphone like a clutch of fledgling chicks around a feed pan. "Look," she said, "this is no good. When you start giggling like that, you just look dumb."

The girls' appalled faces were a mosaic of pinks.

"I mean," Laura went on reasonably, "you're not dumb, right? You're smart. I'm assuming you're bright. Don't sell yourselves short. There are enough weak, brainless women in the world. You be *strong*. Find your voices and let them be heard!" She raised a fist in the air. Getting no response from the girls, she retired to her seat. "Now, let's try that from the top." She pointed at Drum Set Trevor. "And three and four and—"

The tremulous music wavered forth again. The three terrified vocalists came in on their cue.

"Amazing grace! how sweet the sound—
    That saved a wretch like me!"

Not wonderful, but stronger this time. "Good!" Laura called. "But *louder!*"

From the seat beside her, Rob leaned over. "Don't hold back, Laura. Tell us how you feel."

"I see no reason to mince words. What I said was true. Girls who act helpless and stupid will be treated by the world as if they're helpless and stupid. I'm doing them a favor by teaching them that."

"Is it possible there may be kinder, gentler ways to speak the truth? You know, without crushing the human spirit in the process?" He was smiling, which took the sting out of his words.

She smiled back. "Well, my way seems to be working." She was right. Already the vocal trio sounded stronger. They had made it all the way to the end without collapsing into hysterics, a first in the evening's rehearsal.

She broke for a few minutes to show Cassie some chord patterns. She bullied Adam and the Trevors into watching her for cues. And somehow, although the kids looked stupefied, and she was pretty sure they all hated her by the end, they left that night sounding better than when they had started. Rob sat in the front row and watched, shaking his head all the while. But he didn't stop smiling.

Sephy was leaving Dayton Children's Hospital after a day of pediatric clinicals when Libby called. "You'll never guess who David asked to be his best man."

She smiled at the smugness in her best friend's voice. "You'd better tell me, then."

"Okay. Ready? Gorgeous Gabe Michaud."

"Gabe *Michaud*?" Sephy stopped right there, in the middle of the parking garage. Gabe had been in David's class. Far older. Practically an adult by the time Sephy became besotted with him. Soccer captain, prom king, student body president, Gabe had been Copper Cove's golden child. After high school he, like David, started community college in Quahog, and many weekends and evenings found him in the Darling home. It was during those years that Sephy's wide-eyed admiration of him had turned into a serious schoolgirl crush. "*The* Gabe Michaud?"

"The very one. You were in love with him from the time we were in third grade."

"Who wasn't?"

"Me, for one," said Libby. "But the salient point here is that *he* is going to be David's best man and *you* are going to be my maid of honor, which means at the wedding, you'll be thrown together all the time. You'll be expected to walk up the aisle, and dance together, and all kinds of things like that. Who knows what might happen?"

I do, Sephy thought. *The same thing that always happens with me and men: nothing.* She could dance all night in Gabe Michaud's arms, and she would still be as invisible to him at the end as she had always been. But Libby obviously thought this was great news, and Sephy couldn't bring herself to ruin her best friend's moment of triumph.

"That's amazing." She managed to inject some enthusiasm into her voice. "I can't wait."

They said good-bye, and Sephy put the phone back in her coat pocket. The parking garage was damp and cold and smelled like an unpleasant combination of engine oil and old banana peels. It didn't help her feel better.

She had nearly reached her parking space when, ahead of her, a red Kia took a corner too fast and came straight at her. Sephy knew a moment of throat-stopping panic before she jumped to one side. The Kia veered back on course, so close she felt the heat from it as it passed. The driver didn't even sound his horn. Heart juddering like a jackhammer in her chest, Sephy stared after the car's taillights as they receded down the ramp. Was it possible, she wondered, that she really *was* invisible?

Since work at the opera house was well in hand, the renovation committee had voted to scale their meetings back to once a month. Amy pulled her battered Escort into a parking space at the town hall, locked the doors, and, thermal cup of chai in hand, headed for the second floor. Mitch's truck was in the parking lot. She glanced at her watch, wondering if there was time to catch him alone. She wanted to find out how he had liked Friday night's date and to ask if he planned to see Crystal again. She hadn't been able to ask Crystal about it, since her wardrobe manager had left early Saturday morning to spend a long weekend with her parents in Boston.

Amy had telephoned Paul the choreographer-janitor on the Saturday morning after the hockey game, interviewed him by video call on Monday morning, checked his references Monday afternoon, and offered him the job half an hour ago. He had accepted and was to start the following week. Meanwhile, Amy had promised to do some apartment hunting for him since he would need a place to live in a very short space of time. Shunning the elevator to the second floor, she ran up the stairs with a lightness she had not felt in months. She had her wardrobe and props master. She had a part-time accompanist. And at last she had a choreographer. Now they could really get the show on the road.

At the top of the stairs, she all but collided with Mitch, who had just stepped out of the conference room. She stopped herself in time, but some of her chai slopped out of the cup and onto his shirt.

"Hey, watch it!" He pulled his sleeve over his fist and began to scrub at the spots.

"I'm so sorry!" She dug in her shoulder bag and came up with a paper napkin. "Here, let me; you're only smearing it."

He pulled away. "I can do it myself."

She watched as the spot on his shirt grew worse. "Bad day?"

"You could say that, yeah."

"Any particular reason?"

"No." He sounded peevish. "Yes. It's this stupid deadline. If I'm going to finish on time, every hour counts. Today the flooring for the stage was delivered, and it was the wrong kind." He gave up scrubbing at his shirtfront and wiped his sleeve on his jeans, scowling at her as though she, personally, had delivered the wrong flooring. "We got nothing accomplished today. *Nothing.* I'm telling you, Amy, I'm only human. Many more days like this and you can kiss your grand opening in May good-bye."

"Sisyphus," she said.

"What?"

"He was a Greek king who was condemned to spend eternity pushing a boulder uphill."

He stared at her.

"My point is, you're not Sisyphus. You don't have to push this boulder uphill all by yourself, Mitch. Are you praying about it?"

"Give me a break." He shouldered past her and stalked toward the restroom.

Amy glared at his retreating back. Why was he being so miserable? She dismissed the idea that his bad mood was about lost time at work. It had to be Crystal. Things could not have turned out well for them on Friday. After the meeting, she would talk to him. Help him figure it out.

But after the meeting, Mitch slipped out the door and was gone before she could reach him. She tried calling him on the way home, but he wasn't answering his phone. She would text Crystal, then, and ask how Friday night had gone. Something must have happened that she didn't know about.

Sephy couldn't sleep. Since Libby's phone call that afternoon, her thoughts had been like a hamster on a wheel, running faster and faster but never making any progress forward. *Gabe Michaud.* She was going to have to walk up the aisle at the end of Libby's wedding with Gorgeous Gabe Michaud. And dance with him at the reception. And talk to him. And on the off chance that he happened to notice Sephy at all, what was he going to see? But that was a moot question, because how could he see someone who was invisible?

Her self-pity disgusted her. It was time to switch gears. She sat up and found her slippers, then made her way through the dark room, past Ann, whose heavy, rippling breaths could almost—but not quite—be called snoring, and into the bathroom. At the sink, Sephy turned the water on and examined her face in the mirror. For almost twenty-three years, this skin had been her home. Sometimes her reflection was the most familiar thing in the world to her and at other times, like now, she might have been examining the green eyes and freckles of a stranger. She stepped back and frowned at the girl she hardly recognized.

From a dispenser on the wall, she took a paper cup and filled it. Beside the dispenser was a green card she herself had taped up at the beginning of the school year. It was part of a packet the RAs had been given during a training session about campus resources. Back in August, Sephy had presented the information to the girls in her dorm, as she was supposed to, then forgotten all about it. Now, she drank her water and read it with new eyes.

Feeling overwhelmed? Does it seem like no one understands what you're up against? Don't go it alone! Visit the campus counseling office in Gleckler Hall today for free and confidential help. Or call ext. 2307 to make an appointment with a professional counselor.

Counseling. She had always thought of it as the kind of thing other students did, people who had come to a point of desperation and despair.

But then, didn't that describe her exactly?

She tossed her cup into the trash and went back to her room. Could this be the answer? She kicked off her slippers and climbed under her quilt, then turned over, trying to find a comfortable spot. It couldn't hurt, and it might do some good. *May as well make an appointment.*

If she remembered, she'd call in the morning, as soon as the campus offices opened.

Sephy sat rigid in the reception area of the counseling office and willed herself to blend in with the furniture. She recognized the student receptionist from the Psych 101 class she had taken freshman year, a pale young man whose sculpted blond hair blended into his waxen skin. His lips were an unsettling, vivid red. He wore a headset for answering phones and a name tag that announced him as Ian. When Sephy told him she had a two o'clock appointment with Dr. Fielding, Ian showed neither interest nor recognition. Well, it had been a big class.

The office was busier than Sephy had expected. Students came in, made appointments, and left again. Faculty members strode through, swinging briefcases, harried and important. A counselor appeared from a back office and handed Ian a file. She muttered a few words in his ear and disappeared again. Meanwhile, another student, presumably just through with her session, stood shuffling in front of the desk, looking drained and bemused while she waited to make her next appointment. Sephy recognized this girl from around campus. Her head was shaved bald, and on the back of it, a tattooed eagle perched atop a skull with a rose in its beak. Sephy studied the tattoo as, behind the desk, Ian assaulted his keyboard in short, staccato bursts. He exchanged a few sentences with the shaved-head girl, wrote something on a card, and handed it to her. As she left, the girl glanced at Sephy, and her knowing look seemed to say, *You and I are not so different. Wait and see.*

Sephy was clammy with anxiety. *Please, God, don't let me run into anyone who knows me.* From the expressions of the students emerging from the offices, something was going on in there. Maybe something helpful. Possibly something life-changing. *I'm ready for my life to change. I'll do whatever it takes if this could just be the thing that finally works.*

The counselor's name was Carl. Or, "Dr. Carl Fielding, but just call me Carl," as he introduced himself. He was a small, middle-aged man with a high forehead and wild curls that stood straight up and out on all sides of his serene face. *It must be impossible to comb,* Sephy thought. On the beige filing cabinets along one wall, plastic dinosaurs fought a mock prehistoric battle. Sephy, taking a seat across from Carl, did not feel hopeful.

She told him it was her first time ever seeing a counselor.

His first question was easy. "Why are you here?"

"Because I want to lose weight."

"Tell me more about that," Carl said. "Why do you want to lose weight?"

The question threw her. "Why wouldn't I want to lose weight?" she asked him. "Nobody wants to be fat."

"I would have to disagree with that, actually," said Carl. "There are plenty of overweight and even obese people in this world who make peace with their bodies, love themselves the way they are, and live perfectly happy lives."

Are there?

"But you are not choosing that path, or at least you don't want to," Carl went on. "Tell me why. Why do you want to lose weight?"

She told him about the Trans-Siberian Orchestra concert, then went further back and told him about her prom.

He interrupted her. "But why are you assuming that your weight was the reason you didn't have dates for those events?"

"I . . . because . . . Isn't that why?"

He smiled—a gentle, beatific smile. "Plenty of overweight people have normal, satisfying love lives, Sephy."

They do?

"So let's go back to my question: Why do you want to lose weight?"

She thought she had known the reasons, but maybe she didn't. All right, why then? Certainly good health was a reason. She didn't want to end up fifty years old and a physical train wreck like poor Aunt Sharon. But that was more of an academic worry, a vague idea of what might or might not happen sometime in the future. Concern for her health was not the thing that drove her every minute to unzip this fat suit of a body, climb out of it, and leave it as far behind her as she could. She told Carl this.

"Hmmm. Interesting analogy," he said, writing something down on his notepad. "So if you could unzip your body and step out of it and walk away right now, what would you be like? Who would that girl inside the fat suit be?"

"You mean, what would she look like?"

"Sure. Look like, feel like . . . What kinds of things would be possible for her?"

"She would be free." Sephy hadn't even known the words were there, yet the suddenness with which they came out made her wonder how close to the surface they had always been.

"Free of what?"

"Free of fat."

Carl shook his head. "That's the easy, obvious answer, but not the real one. As we move ahead, I want you to try to be aware of the times you use the word or idea of *fat* as a smokescreen for other, deeper issues."

"What do you mean?"

"I mean it's easy to say, 'I'm fat,' when what you might really mean is 'I'm inadequate' or 'I'm embarrassed because I failed at something.' Your weight is just the symptom. We want to get to the root of the problem."

It had never occurred to Sephy that her weight itself was not the root of the problem.

Carl went on. "Let's explore this idea of unzipping a fat suit and stepping out of it. What else, besides fat, would the girl inside the suit be free of?"

She thought about it. Somewhere, a phone rang. In the corridors, she heard the faint buzz of voices as people passed by.

"Just say whatever comes to your mind," Carl prompted her.

"I'm not good at saying whatever comes to my mind."

"Why not?"

She shook her head. "I don't want to offend anyone."

"I see." Carl made another note. "That can be a form of false humility: an excuse to avoid conflict. I'd like to come back to that later. But for now, tell me: Would the girl who unzipped the fat suit and stepped out of it feel free to speak her mind, regardless of what people thought of her?"

Why not? They were, after all, still talking about the realm of impossibility here. "Yes. Yes, she would."

"What else?"

"She would be brave."

"Brave enough to do what?"

Sephy turned her attention to Carl's bookcase. Three odd, brown pieces of pottery stood on the top of it. She wondered if they were historic. Valuable. *Brave enough to do what?* She ventured an answer. "Maybe . . . brave enough to say no?"

"Are you asking me or telling me?"

"Telling you."

"Then tell me."

Looking at the pottery, Sephy lifted her chin. "The girl inside the fat suit would be brave enough to say no to people when she felt like it."

"Good for her!" Carl sounded happy about this. "What else?"

She thought. "Mmm . . . She would have the courage not to care what people thought of her."

"And . . . ?"

"I think she would be athletic."

"Really? What kind of athletic things would she do?"

Sephy shifted her gaze to the frosted windowpanes. She couldn't see outside, but she could hear the laughter of students walking by on their way to classes. Nobody out there could hear a single thing she was saying in here. "Oh, everything. Hike, swim, play beach volleyball . . ."

"You're smiling."

"It sounds like fun."

"Has your weight held you back from doing those things?"

"Yes. At least from doing them the way I'd like to."

"And how would you like to do those things: hiking, swimming, volleyball, and so on?"

She sat up straighter, aware of her anonymity. "I'd like to have the stamina to go on long, rugged hikes. Climb Mount Katahdin someday. Maybe do part of the Appalachian Trail. And if I played beach volleyball, you know—just at home with friends, I mean—I'd like to be . . . fast. Agile."

They sat in silence, and Sephy felt a stirring somewhere inside her. It was as faint and fragile as the beating of a butterfly's wings, but it was there all the same. It felt like hope.

"I notice," Carl said at last, "that you haven't talked about the way you would *look* if you lost weight."

I haven't? "Well, obviously, that would improve too."

"But it's not the first thing, or even among the first several things you talked about. I think that's significant."

"Why?"

He smiled at her. "Good question. Why don't you think about that this week and come up with an answer for me for next time? That will be part of your homework."

"Okay."

"Now tell me this: What's holding you back from losing enough weight to live the kind of life you envision?"

"I have no willpower. I can't say no to food."

"Okay. Certainly there are physical reasons why people overeat, or feel unable to say no to food. Carbohydrate addiction, insulin resistance, and so forth. I'm going to send you to the health clinic here on campus for a workup just to rule out physical problems. Meanwhile, tell me, in what other areas of your life do you lack willpower? How do you do in school, for instance?"

"I have a 3.7 GPA."

"Impressive. So you don't lack willpower in getting your schoolwork done."

"No."

"Do you have a job?"

"I work weekends as a CNA at a nursing home. And I give piano lessons to a few kids in town. Oh, and I babysit for some of the professors once in a while."

"How's your social life? Are you satisfied with it?"

"I am. I have plenty of friends."

"Boyfriend? Or . . . girlfriend?"

"Boyfriend. And no."

"Do you date much?"

"Not lately." That was the understatement of the year, she thought.

"It must take a fair bit of time management and hard work, juggling all those jobs and an active social life *and* maintaining a GPA of 3.7."

"It does."

"You don't sound like somebody who lacks willpower. In fact, you sound like a pretty self-disciplined person."

Do I?

"I'm wondering," Carl continued, "why you choose to define yourself by an area in which you're *not* succeeding—your lack of willpower over food and exercise—instead of by all those other areas where you're, in fact, succeeding very, very well."

She stared at him.

"Earlier, you told me that you're afraid to speak your mind because of what people might think of you. Why is that?"

"I guess I'm afraid people won't like me if I disagree with them."

"Why would people dislike you for disagreeing with them?"

She didn't know.

"Do *you* dislike people who disagree with you?"

She smiled. "No. If I did, I wouldn't be on speaking terms with any of my siblings."

"Is there a lot of conflict in your family?"

"No. I only meant my siblings never hesitate to speak their minds on any given subject."

"But you do."

"I'm different, I guess."

"When your siblings are speaking their minds, does it ever get heated?"

"Sometimes."

"And what do you do then? What's your role?"

"I smooth things over and pat down the ruffled feathers. My mom always says I'm the peacemaker of the family."

"Ah. So you're a peacemaker. How do you feel when these arguments at home get heated?"

"I don't like it."

"Meaning . . . ?"

"It makes me uncomfortable."

"Why?"

She thought about this. "I guess I don't like conflict."

Carl said, "That's worth looking into, but let's leave it there for this week. I have a few more questions I want to ask you about your history of dieting and exercise and other things you've tried in order to lose weight. Then I'd like to schedule you for a few tests to screen you for anxiety and depression before next week."

They talked for a few more minutes before Carl said good-bye and sent her back out to Ian.

Sephy stood in front of the reception desk feeling as though she'd just awakened from a dream. An hour ago, she had sat in this lobby and watched people like herself emerge from their sessions looking pensive. Now she knew how they felt. Her thoughts surged and churned with the things she had said in there—things she hadn't even known she felt until now. Mechanically, she answered Ian's bland questions about dates and times when she could take the screening tests and have her physical workup and make her next appointment with Carl. She scheduled it all, took her appointment cards, and left.

As she crossed the campus to her dorm room, she felt the flutter of hope again, stronger this time.

The butterfly effect. The thought came out of nowhere. The idea that a butterfly beating its wings in one hemisphere could eventually cause a hurricane on the other side of the world.

There were things about herself that she had never known before. Parts that were as unfamiliar as if they belonged to a stranger. In the weeks to come, she was going to get acquainted with a whole new side of Sephy.

The butterfly wings beat faster. She wondered: Was it possible that she might even turn out to be wonderful?

CHAPTER

11

Sephy sat in the circle with her arms and ankles crossed
and listened to the man next to her talk about all the things
he had and hadn't eaten in the past week. It was her third
meeting, and already she hated it.

Until mid-January, she had continued taking the magic
drops and eating chicken and salad three times a day, until
one day the chicken had literally gagged her, and she'd realized she could no longer stomach one more meal of it. Sephy
counted it among her life's great achievements that she had
not, at that point, simply gone on a fast-food-and-ice-cream
binge and gained every one of the pounds back. That, after
all, had been her pattern in this war she had been fighting since childhood. Instead, she had forced herself to eat
sensibly, and she had somehow managed not only to keep
off the pounds she had lost, but to add to them, so that her
grand total of weight loss—between near starvation, protein

shakes, grapefruit, salad, magic drops, and what seemed an entire poultry farm's worth of chicken—was now twenty-three pounds. It had been exhausting. She couldn't bear the thought of living much longer on the dieting Tilt-A-Whirl her life had become.

"Your weight is just a symptom that something is out of balance in your life," Carl told her. "Let's try to figure out what that could be." Meanwhile, he had pointed her here, to this dim church basement, where a schedule on the wall informed her that the weight-loss program held its meetings on Mondays, Al-Anon was on Tuesdays, and youth group on Wednesdays. It would help her begin to learn what balance looked like, he promised.

The problem was, Sephy found it discouraging to listen to other people discuss how they had tricked the system in order to eat large amounts of food with relatively few calories. Substituting applesauce for oil; baking with artificial sweeteners instead of sugar; buying the program's special snacks and premade meals that were simply unaffordable to a college student like her. Through all of it, Sephy could not shake the idea that these things were just another form of Band-Aid on a problem that was really, in the end, going to require some major lifestyle surgery. She loved food. She didn't want to spend her life eating brownies made with Splenda and applesauce and chewing gum that was flavored like apple pie and sipping constantly on diet soda like the other people in the program. She didn't want to write down every bite she ever put in her mouth.

If there was one thing the program did for her, though, it was to get her over her fear of the number on the scale.

At her very first session, someone had directed her to a folding table set up in one corner of the basement. She went over to it, filled out a few papers, paid her fee, and took the plastic bag of literature someone handed her.

Then the slim, curly-haired woman behind the table said, "Step onto the scale, please."

Sephy stared at her. There was no way she was weighing herself in front of another person. A thin person, no less.

"Come on, step up," said the woman.

"I can't," she said. "I already ate breakfast. I'm wearing a sweater. And boots."

"Slip the boots off, if you want, but let's go. There are other people waiting."

Sephy glanced behind her. It was true. So, feeling as though she had been asked to strip naked and walk down the main street of her hometown, she pulled off her leather boots and set them to one side. She stepped onto the small digital scale and, with a sense of dread, watched the black numbers until they stopped changing.

"Okay," the woman murmured, writing the number down in a little book and handing it to Sephy.

"I ate a big breakfast," Sephy explained.

But the woman wasn't listening. "Next?"

"If I'd known I was going to have to weigh in, I wouldn't have worn this heavy sweater. It's wool."

"Step to the side, honey. There's a line."

Sephy obeyed, feeling dazed. To her, the number on the scale was the very representation of failure. The other woman, however, didn't seem to care about it in the least.

And as she moved on to the circle of folding chairs at the

other end of the room, it occurred to Sephy for the first time that the number might be just . . . a number. It did not seem to be, in this other person's mind, a gauge of Sephy's success or failure as a human being. It signified nothing to this neutral third party about Sephy's moral character or work ethic or potential or intelligence or anything, beyond the simple evidence that here was a person who ate more than she should and didn't exercise enough.

And maybe, even if it meant coming back week after week to these meetings she didn't want to sit through, those were things she could learn to change.

The day she turned her calendar to February, Laura experienced a twinge of apprehension. Valentine's Day was looming. Already, the drugstore on her block had stocked its windows with stuffed bears, Russell Stover marshmallow hearts, and Whitman's Sampler boxes in every size and color of heart imaginable. The hosts of her favorite morning radio show joked over love-themed trivia and announced contests and special playlists for the big day. Laura had done her best not to give Rob any hints that would lead him to think she was interested. To encourage a camaraderie devoid of any romantic undertones. While he seemed to respect the line she had drawn, she sensed that he would not be opposed to something more. She dreaded the thought that he might make some embarrassing gesture, come the fourteenth.

With this in mind, she began to avoid him. She circled the church basement during the Sunday morning coffee hour, always keeping a crowd between Rob and herself. She spent the final minutes before the service in the ladies' room and slipped out during the last hymn so he wouldn't have a chance to talk to her. She cried off two youth group band practices in a row—once by claiming she had a headache, and the second time by texting him with the shameless lie that she had to work late that night.

Valentine's Day fell on a Saturday. She worked a busy shift at the bar, came home, and went straight to bed. On Sunday, she got dressed for church with the grateful sense that she had dodged a bullet. It was February 15, and the world's expectations of romance were on hold, at least for another year.

At church, Rob was sitting with a woman she didn't recognize. Not a *woman* after all, she decided, scrutinizing them narrowly throughout the opening hymns, but a *girl*. A college-age girl, at best. Short. Warm-skinned and curvaceous. When the service was over, Laura watched them walk out of the sanctuary together, talking and smiling. Rob did not even look her way.

She stood by her seat with an odd sense of betrayal until the sanctuary was empty and it was only her and nodding, smiling old Milton left. He tottered over to her, holding out a Werther's caramel, wrapped in its gold foil, as though it were some rare and precious jewel.

She took the candy. His gesture, no different from what he did every week, today brought tears to her eyes. On impulse, she bent over and put her arms around his stiff, thin body. "You're so kind, Milton. Thank you." She held him for a moment, and when she stood back, she saw that his eyes had grown red and rheumy, and his small frame was racked with silent sobs.

"Oh, Milton, I'm sorry. I didn't mean—"

But he held up a hand. "It's all right. You're such a nice girl, Laura. Always such a nice girl." His voice cracked and, leaning on his cane, he made his way past her out the door. Crying because she had hugged him.

Laura wanted to weep herself. Had there ever been a person as doggedly self-absorbed as she was? Someone so certain that the world revolved around her? Rob had not been pining away, waiting for a chance to pounce and railroad her into romance. He wasn't even interested in her that way. Meanwhile, had it ever occurred to her to look around and notice that there were lonely people in the world, and to think of making Valentine's Day about one of *them*? Laura had never felt so small, and at the same time so ashamed of her smallness, in her entire life.

"So much for my visions of a romantic Valentine's Day." Crystal settled into the extra chair in Amy's office and hugged her arms around her knees. "I haven't heard one word from Mitch since the hockey game last month."

Amy, busy comparing five different caterers' menus on the desk in front of her, was only half listening. "Mmm," she murmured. "Why don't you ask him out again?"

"I do have some pride, you know. I mean, it's one thing to ask a guy out. It's another thing entirely to chase him down when he so clearly doesn't want to be caught."

"Mmm . . . What's your opinion about phyllo dough? Too messy?"

"What are you talking about?"

"The reception after the grand opening. Are hors d'oeuvres wrapped in phyllo dough too hard to eat in a crowd?"

Crystal considered this. "The pastry does kind of blow around as soon as you bite into it. Whenever I eat it, I end up covered in crumbs."

"That's what I thought. No phyllo dough, then." Amy drew a line through something on one of the flyers.

"Why are you thinking about the reception already? That's not for ages yet."

"It'll be here before we know it. Besides, I want to book the caterer early so I get exactly what I'm looking for. If I put it off, I'm liable to end up with someone who only knows how to make carrot sticks and French onion dip."

"Take a break from that and tell me what to do about Mitch," said Crystal.

Amy sighed but sat back in her chair and gave Crystal her full attention. She had tried talking to Mitch after the hockey game, but getting him to discuss his feelings was like trying to mine for gold with a teaspoon. She had been just as happy to let the subject drop. Busy with work, it had been easy enough to dismiss Crystal's perplexity as well. Now, against every shred of better judgment she possessed, Amy succumbed to a guilty conscience. "Look, do you want me to talk to him for you?"

"Would you? Really? Just find out if he's at all interested in me. Hint that I'd be more than willing to go out again if he asked me."

"All right, all right."

"Will you do it today? Like . . . maybe run over to the opera house on your lunch break and talk to him then?"

"What is this? Are we all in fourth grade again?" But she couldn't help smiling at Crystal's enthusiasm. She would be good for Mitch, Amy thought, if he ever gave her half a chance.

But Mitch's response, after the promised talk, was less than heartening. "Leave me alone, Amy," he told her, loading a lethal-looking strip of nails into a nail gun. "I need a girlfriend now like I need a hole in the head."

"She's a wonderful person, Mitch."

"I'm sure she is. But when, exactly, am I supposed to find the time to date anyone, even assuming I'm interested, which I'm not? I'm married to this opera house project for the next three months." He brandished the loaded nail gun at her. "Now, unless you're prepared to hold drywall for me, I suggest you get out of my way and let me get back to work."

She turned to go.

"What is this anyway?" he called after her. "Fourth grade?"

"Sort of," she muttered. But he was too intent on his task to hear her.

"It was a wonderful meal, my dear, as always." Leander draped the damp dish towel over the handle of the oven door and untied the half apron he had been wearing to wash the dishes. He passed it to his wife, who hung it up on its hook in the pantry, along with her own.

"Thank you, but I can't take credit for this one. Ivy brought the chicken parmigiana and Amy made the eggplant. Libby baked the cake and David picked up the bread on his way from work. The only thing I did was put together the salad, and if Sephy had been home, I wouldn't have even had to do that."

Jane was following her husband into the living room when Leander caught his foot on the edge of the braided rug and stumbled. Reflexively, she grabbed for the back of his flannel shirt and kept him from falling.

"That darn rug. Can't we fix it? Seems like I'm always catching my foot on it."

"I'll find some double-sided tape," Jane said. They settled themselves, with the ease of old habit, on either end of the sofa. Obliquely, she watched Leander. Maybe the edge of the rug did need to be taped down, but surely that was not the problem with the hardwood stairs? Or the walkway from the driveway to the house, or the half-inch threshold from the front steps into the entryway? It was not like him to trip everywhere he walked. Yet he did. Well, she supposed it was one of the unpleasantries of middle age. You weren't as coordinated as you used to be. She herself found it increasingly difficult to concentrate on more than one task at a time. Where once she had been able to write out a grocery list even as she chatted on the phone with a friend, she now found that either task required her full attention in order to be done well.

Jane kicked off the wool clogs she always wore around the house and propped her feet in Leander's lap. Butternut jumped heavily onto her legs and began to knead at one of her knees, preparing to nap. She picked up the thread of their conversation. "I find it very convenient to have adult children who can cook."

Leander began to rub her feet. "You found it convenient to have small children who couldn't do anything but cry and wet their diapers, Jane."

"I don't know that *convenient* is the right word, but I certainly did love those years when they were young." She sighed. "That time went by so fast." After a moment, she corrected herself. "No . . . the days themselves went slowly; it was the years that somehow flew."

"And now that they're grown up, we get to enjoy them in a whole different way." Leander cocked an ear toward the floor. Faintly, they heard the sounds of music going on below. Ivy, declaring that—their absent sisters notwithstanding—they had to start practicing for the wedding *sometime*, had brought her violin to supper. Amy was playing her drum set, and David was standing in for Laura on his old acoustic guitar. "They don't sound half-bad, do they?"

"They sound pretty darn good," said Jane. She got up and opened the basement door so they could hear better, then went back to her seat and the footrest of her husband's legs. "Any idea where the younger kids are?"

He resumed massaging one of her feet. "I think the boys are upstairs, watching a basketball game on the big TV. Jada's downstairs watching the band, and Libby's with her, watching David."

"She's such a nice girl."

"Good enough for your only son to marry?"

"You can't ask better than for your son to marry the girl next door. It makes you feel kind of safe, somehow."

"Is that all she has to recommend her: being the girl next door?" He was teasing her.

"Of course not. You won't meet a nicer family than the Hales. Libby's a Christian girl, and she's been a stalwart friend to Seraphina all these years. Not because she's kind, but because she really likes Sephy for who she is."

"Who wouldn't like Sephy?"

It was a rhetorical question, but Jane answered it anyway. "Plenty of people who never bothered to look past her weight, that's who. All those years of middle school, then high school, when people were so cruel. I somehow felt she could bear it all because Libby was such a friend to her. She made the other girls be nice to Sephy, include her. And they *did* like Sephy for herself, once they gave her a chance."

"More than one boy found himself taken to task by Libby Hale, and rued the day he ever picked on Sephy."

They smiled, although there was little humor in the memories. Much hurt, some gratitude, and a guilty sense of vindication, but not much that was funny, even after all this time.

"Well, Libby's been so much like family all these years, I'm glad she found a way to make it official," Leander went on.

"And will she make David happy?" Jane was the slightest bit anxious on this score.

"Of course she will. She's sweet, endearing, and on top of being wildly in love, they're really good *friends*, which, as you know, is the key to a happy marriage." He leaned over to kiss the tip of her nose.

"I'm glad I married you, Leander Darling."

"I wouldn't go through this life with anyone else," he said, massaging her other foot.

Sephy set her alarm for four in the morning. When it went off, she sat up at once, leaving herself no time to reconsider the momentous step she was about to take. Careful not to wake Ann, she groped under her bed in the darkness for the bag she had packed the night before, containing her swimsuit, towel, and a pair of goggles.

The dormitory corridor was silent and dim, lit only by the night sconces. There was a certain gravity to the hours just before dawn. An isolation. A person awake and purposeful in them was all alone. Yet there was a solidarity, too, with the other keepers, few and faceless, of this secret part of the day. Newspaper carriers, night shift workers. And herself, Sephy Darling, on her way to the first day of the rest of her life. She let herself out into the bitter cold of the night's end and headed toward the athletic center.

CHAPTER

12

At the end of February, FedEx delivered the rented scripts for *West Side Story*. Amy, Crystal, and Paul looked them over with delight.

"I always love getting packages," Crystal sighed. "No matter what they are, they're so much better than the utility bills and credit card offers you get the rest of the time."

"This," Amy pronounced, "is like Christmas and my birthday all rolled into one."

"Your birthday is on Christmas Eve, so that's not really saying much," Crystal pointed out.

"Don't confuse me with the details," said Amy. "My point is that now we can really get started."

Amy had found Paul a one-bedroom apartment in a block of four overlooking the river, and Paul had bargained, over the phone, for a lower rent by agreeing to give the landlord's

daughter a free Irish dance lesson every week. He moved
to Copper Cove the week after Amy hired him, with three
cardboard boxes, a futon frame and mattress, an espresso
maker, and a cat carrier. Amy and Crystal had been on hand
to help him.

"Are you allowed to have a cat?" Amy had asked as they
passed on the stairs, she empty-handed, he with the carrier,
which, even from a distance, smelled strongly of animal.

"No, they said absolutely no cats or dawg," he told her
with a wink. "Good thing this ain't a cat or a dawg."

Amy and Crystal had brought him a philodendron in a
brass pot and a pan of vegetarian lasagna, which he invited
them to stay and share with him when the transfer of his
possessions from U-Haul trailer to apartment was complete.

Crystal confessed this was just what they had been hoping for, and while the lasagna was heating in the oven, Paul
opened the cat carrier and introduced them to a pair of
ferrets.

"Fred and Ginger," he told them, stroking his hand along
the back of one of them as the other snaked its way up his
arm and settled itself like a fur collar around his neck.

Amy was delighted. "I vote we make them the official
mascots of the arts program," she said, scratching one of the
ferrets between its silky ears. Crystal, who was not a fan even
of less-aromatic animals, stayed clear. One of Paul's three
boxes contained the pieces to an elaborate cage and tunnel
system, which he assembled as they waited for their meal to
be ready.

Over dinner, eaten from paper plates while sitting on the
floor, they acquainted Paul with the fledgling arts program

and their great plans for its future. They talked of *West Side Story*; of great and not-so-great productions they had seen and what, in their opinion, had made each one so; of Paul's ideas for the choreography; of a timetable for auditions, callbacks, and rehearsals. On this matter, they'd been unanimous: they should begin as soon as possible.

Accordingly, the day after the scripts arrived, Amy posted notices all over town. She also took out a half-page ad in the weekly edition of the *Copper Cove Courier*, gulping a little at the price of it, to announce that auditions for *West Side Story* would begin on Monday and that all questions should be directed to the number listed below.

She continued the same routine she had followed since Christmas: up at five to spend an hour at the gym, at the office by seven, and home by eight at night, unless she had a meeting. Nothing had changed in that respect, but she felt that something had finally, subtly shifted. Where before, it had been like spinning her wheels, laying groundwork, getting through the countless necessary and unrewarding details of launching the program, now it suddenly felt as if it were all beginning. They had lifted the wheels. They were nearly flying.

She always sent Paul and Crystal home at five. Unlike her, they were paid by the hour and the budget would not stretch to paying them overtime. Amy was firm about this. One night, she left the office with them. She had a renovation committee meeting at six thirty, and she thought she'd stop by and see if Mitch was still at the opera house. If he was, she'd offer to take him somewhere for dinner.

He was there, wearing a hard hat and safety goggles and

using some loud power tool. He did not hear her come in, so Amy approached him at a wide angle. She startled him anyway, but at least he did not cut his hand off when he jumped.

He switched off the tool and spoke over the powering-down whine of it. "What are you doing here?"

"Hello, yourself. Nice to see you too. I came to see if you want to go get dinner somewhere before the meeting."

He swore colorfully. "I forgot about the meeting."

"Oops."

He pushed the safety goggles up onto his forehead and swiped at his face with a sawdusty hand. She saw that he had dark smudges under his eyes. "I can't go."

"To dinner, or to the meeting?"

"Both. Neither. Look at this place." He gave a general sweep of his hand, indicating the whole auditorium, and cursed again.

It was true that equipment was strewn everywhere, and a thick layer of sawdust coated every surface, but to her eyes, it looked like he was making enormous headway. The stage had been completely rebuilt, all the drywall was up, the floor replaced. "I can see how much you've done already, Mitch. It's looking really great."

"You have no idea what you're talking about."

"Okay, no; no, I don't. But it looks like you've made a lot of progress—"

"Does it? *Does* it?"

And heeeere we go again, Amy thought, bracing herself.

Mitch's face was a flushed, mottled red. "Let me tell you about progress. One of my guys quit yesterday. Just quit! And Brian is taking the week off to have—of all things—his tonsils out. His *tonsils* out, for pete's sake. What is he, six years old?"

"Are you praying about it?"

"Don't preach to me, Amy."

She frowned. "Maybe you'll feel better with some food in your stomach."

He glared at her. "Oh, you're a fine one to talk to me about food in my stomach. When's the last time you ate anything yourself?"

"At one o'clock, thank you," she said.

"Anything besides an energy bar."

She cleared her throat.

"You go eat something. I don't have the time right now."

"Can I at least bring you a sandwich?"

"No." His hand strayed toward the safety goggles. "Thanks, though."

"Look, Mitch, it doesn't have to be perfect," she said. "The auditorium . . . the lobby . . . definitely not the dressing rooms. They just have to be functional for the opening week. Please don't kill yourself over this."

"Easy for you to say," he grunted. "It's not your name all over the construction. Can I get back to work now, please?"

"Should I tell them you won't be there, at the meeting? They won't be very happy."

He told her in no uncertain terms what the committee could do with its unhappiness.

"Fine. You don't have to be rude."

He pulled the goggles down over his eyes, picked up the saw, and switched it on.

"Good-bye to you too," she said, her mouth moving

futilely against the roar of the machine. He didn't look at her as she backed up to the auditorium door and left.

Amy drove to Amato's, where she bought him a meatball sub, a liter bottle of water, and a large coffee. She remembered that he liked his coffee loaded, so she added to the bag a handful of sugar packets and several little tubs of the vile chemicals that passed for cream in the coffee-drinking world. She returned to the opera house and walked through the auditorium, moving ostentatiously through his field of vision. He gave no sign that he was aware of her, so she left the food and the coffee balanced on a sawhorse where he would find it. She knew he saw her, but he didn't so much as glance up from the screaming saw as she came and went.

Sephy kept going to the meetings in the dank church basement. They were predictable. They felt like a class. But Carl reminded her, "People need people, Sephy. There's great power in going through this journey with others." And he was right. In spite of her resistance to sitting around in a circle comparing points and recipes, the weekly meetings did give her a sense of hope. There were others out there fighting the same fight. Some of them were winning.

Balance was another thing Carl kept insisting on. Part of balance was doing the things you didn't want to do now, for the sake of the payoff later. Going to meetings. Eating salad and skipping dessert. Swimming laps alone at four thirty in the morning. In her purse, she kept the little book wherein was recorded the evidence that she had lost a further ten pounds. She carried that number around with her like a talisman, holding on to it in her mind when she got hungry. And every time she successfully navigated the cafeteria, each night that she made it to the finish line of bed without sabotaging herself, she allowed herself to imagine that maybe, just maybe, her life was going to change this time.

She had begun having dreams that she was standing at the edge of a black and yawning abyss. On the other side stood a small child in some kind of nameless danger. The child was frightened and weeping, and it was up to Sephy to save him. In order to get to him, she had to cross the chasm on the slenderest of wires. She could not do it. Each time, she fell, jerking awake, chilled and sweating, pulse hammering in her neck. She didn't need a Jungian textbook to interpret the dream for her. She was desperate not to fall. And although she didn't understand it, somehow she felt that staying away from home was one of the things she needed to do to keep herself balanced.

The phone rang. Jane, who was dusting the living room, dropped her damp rag back into the bucket of hot water and Murphy Oil Soap to answer it. "Sephy! How are you, sweetheart?" Oh, it was good to hear her girl's voice. They spent a few minutes catching up on family news before Sephy dropped the bomb.

"Not coming home for spring break!" Jane schooled the dismay from her voice. She prided herself on being a mother who never employed guilt or shame tactics with her children, but oh, she was tempted sometimes. "If you need money for the ticket, we can send you that."

But according to Sephy, money wasn't the issue. "Surely you don't have to work the whole week, then?"

It seemed she did have to work at least the first half of her break. Sephy was right, of course, when she pointed out that it would hardly be worth the cost of a plane ticket to fly home for three or four days. And she did promise to spend her free days at Sharon DeMille's house, which made Jane feel a little better. At least her daughter wouldn't be alone in the dormitory for a week. She would be fed and taken care of, and be with someone who was as good as family.

Jane hung up from her conversation with Sephy with the dull weight of disappointment in her heart and dialed the number of her old college roommate.

March, as expected, came in like a lamb. Temperatures soared to the high thirties, and a softness in the air hinted of June days just around the corner. Two days later, the weather repented of its promises and assaulted the down east coast of Maine with a vicious onslaught of sleet and freezing rain. At midnight, the front shifted. The lashing rain changed to a wet and heavy snow that fell like flour from a sifter, with the single-minded determination of covering everything and halting all progress in its tracks. By morning the second day, the snow had stopped, although most of the roads remained impassable. Amy, having seen the forecast, had transferred enough files to her laptop to keep her busy for two days. She worked in her bedroom all morning, sitting cross-legged on her bed with her back against the wall until her mother called up the stairs to her.

"Amy, can you find time to walk to Price Mart for a gallon of milk?"

She surfaced from the copy of the script she had been making notes on and looked around, bemused. It surely wasn't eleven o'clock already? It had been an unsatisfactory morning's work. Her mind felt foggy, slower to see ideas or to seize on solutions to problems she would normally have considered simple. She knew this was because she was working outside of her regular environment, and she chafed at the storm that had closed down the town offices. She would have loved a chance to talk to Crystal and Paul about some of her ideas, but it didn't seem fair, somehow, to intrude on their unexpected day off by calling.

She put the script aside and stood up, stretching. One leg cramped, suggesting that a good, brisk walk was just what she needed. "Coming," she called back, rubbing out the knot before skipping down the stairs for her mother's grocery list, which was bound to be considerably longer than just a gallon of milk.

In the end, she wore a backpack to the store, because her mother wanted not only a gallon of milk, but a pound of butter, a dozen eggs, and a bunch of cilantro. Amy, opening the fridge herself to take quick stock of the situation, saw that they were low on soy milk as well, which was the kind of thing her mother never kept track of.

The day had turned crisp and sunny, the blue of the sky as sharp on the retina as the blade of a knife. The white landscape glittered with blinding brightness even as a certain warmth to the sun promised that winter could not last much longer. Already, the eaves were dripping. The wet, heavy snow was perfect for making a snowman, and the two boys across the street were doing just that. They had rolled a ball nearly as high as the younger one's head, although to call it a ball was generous, Amy thought, shading her eyes and squinting at them. It looked more like the rolls of insulation that Mitch's crew had stacked in the corners of the opera house.

Amy had babysat for these boys many times over the years, and now she picked up a handful of snow, shaped it into a quick ball, and lobbed it across the street at them. It missed, but it caught their attention. They waved frenetically at her and threw a snowball back. They were too far away to do any damage, but as she laughed and walked on, they shadowed her, keeping even with her on the other side of the street, throwing snowballs at her until they got to the end of the block, which seemed to be as far as they were allowed to go. Amy waved again and yelled, "You throw like girls!"

"*You* throw like a girl!" they called back, laughing.

Price Mart was the small neighborhood grocery store. Amy hadn't been inside for nearly three years. Still, when the automatic door swung open to let her in, she saw at once that almost nothing had changed. There were the same dusty shelves full of overpriced off-brands, the narrow aisles and yellow hand-lettered sale signs. The same two cash registers in front, manned by middle-aged clerks in red polyester smocks.

Kids in town called it "Nice Fart," each generation thinking themselves clever for inventing something everyone had already been saying for years. In spite of the bleakness, there was something nostalgic about the place. Being nearer the high school than the Hannaford supermarket, it had been the popular place to stop by on the way home, or between classes and basketball practice, for a Dr Pepper and Hot Fries or a pack of AirHeads. When Amy was in third grade, Price Mart had hosted an elementary school Halloween art contest. She had drawn a green witch flying on a broom and had won first prize in her class. The picture had been displayed on the big plate-glass store windows with the winners from all the other classes, and she had been allowed to pick an item from the toy aisle as a prize. She had chosen a pack of modeling clay in four colors and had later ruined the carpet in her bedroom by pressing the green clay into the nap, to see if she could make a mold of it.

She was thinking about these things when she rounded the end of an aisle and quite literally ran into someone.

"Oh, I'm so sorry—" she began.

"Oh, excuse—" he said.

She laughed. "Mitch! We have to stop running into each other like this. What are you doing here?"

"Picking up a few groceries on my lunch break." He nodded toward his cart. A discreet glance showed it to be full of frozen dinners and packages of meat. He made a motion as if to move on past her, but she put a hand on his arm.

"Wait, don't run away."

He stayed, but there was tension in him, like a coiled spring. She sensed his desire to bolt.

"What's the matter, Mitch? Have I done something to upset you?"

He looked through her. "No. I'm just busy, same as you. Thanks, by the way, for leaving me the sandwich and coffee the other week."

"I'm afraid you're working so hard you're not eating right."

"Pot, meet kettle."

Inspiration struck her. "Why don't you come home with me right now, and we can have lunch at my mom's? We can be kind of a . . . a mutual help society, make sure each other eats and all that. Come on, Mitch, *please*. Mom and Dad would love to see you again."

"Yeah, thanks, but I have to get back to work. I can't really spare the time."

"Oh."

He cleared his throat. "I, ah, have some good news. I'm moving to Florida."

"Florida? When?"

"As soon as the job's done."

Amy felt a strange, small panic. "But it won't be. Not in May. There's still so much to do."

"I'll stay until it's all finished. My original bid was for doing the job in twelve months. I can have it done by then."

"So . . . is that October, then?"

"Yep. September, if I'm lucky."

"Oh." She tried not to scowl. This was good news. She must be happy for him. "We'll miss you. Do you have family down there? Friends?"

He shrugged. "Not really. About like here. But I know a guy who has work for me in Trenton, and that's the important thing. It's a good job. Pays more than up here."

She felt as though he had slapped her. "You *do* have family here. Why do you insist on pushing us away when we want you to be a part of us?"

He rubbed the back of his neck. "Look, I have to go. Give my regards to your parents, okay?"

"Give them yourself. We still have dinner on Thursday nights. Why don't you come? They'd all love to see you again."

"I'll think about that." And then he was gone, and she was sure he had no intention of thinking about it.

Amy shopped slowly, giving him time to get through the checkout and leave. She didn't know what she had done to offend him. She shifted the heavy basket on her arm. Exhaustion soaked through her like water through a dry sponge. The walk home, and the rest of the day spent in work, seemed all at once more than she could bear to contemplate.

After exams on Friday, Sephy waved her friends off to their own homes and families. She felt light and effervescent, buoyed up with excitement about the days ahead. She was most successful with eating well when she was busiest, in a routine that did not leave long stretches of time to reconsider and negotiate her fledgling self-discipline. For the next three days, she went to her job as a nurse's aide at the nursing home, working double shifts on two of the days. She swam at the college pool in the mornings, attended her meeting in the church basement, and at her weekly weigh-in, was down another two pounds. On Tuesday morning, she packed a suitcase, locked her textbooks in the dorm room, and drove the four hours to Sharon DeMille's house in Cleveland, ready to rest.

Aunt Sharon, as always, was down the steps and on the sidewalk with her arms outstretched before Sephy was out of the car. "Seraphina!" her surrogate aunt cried, pulling her into a bosomy hug. "It's about time you got here. Your mother's been on the phone every half hour since dawn, asking about you. Go right in now and give her a call before you do anything else. No, leave your bag in the kitchen, I'll take it to your room while you're on the phone."

Sephy leaned against the kitchen counter and dialed her parents, glancing idly around as she waited for someone to answer. A chocolate layer cake stood under a cover on a glass stand, its glossy top encrusted with nuts. Candy dishes on every surface were heaped high with M&Ms, nuts, and mints. A box bearing the name of her favorite local bakery sat atop the refrigerator. Her heart did a slow spiral of dread. How could she have forgotten about the caloric pitfalls of a stay at Aunt Sharon's? She searched for any signs of fruit or whole grain bread. A bowl of red apples in the middle of the table was the only thing she saw.

Nobody answered at 14 Ladyslipper Lane, and after leaving a message that she had arrived safely, Sephy hung up. *Safely*, she thought, had very little to do with it. The next four days loomed before her like a veritable minefield of nutritional disaster.

To Sephy's relief, she had arrived just after lunchtime, and she shamelessly invented a story of having eaten something along the road. There was no getting around suppertime, though, when Sharon ordered two large pizzas from the mom-and-pop place down the street.

"Could one of them be just veggie?" Sephy ventured.

"Of course!" Aunt Sharon said, but when she was phoning in the order, Sephy overheard her say, "One large with everything and one large with veggies and extra cheese."

While they waited for the pizza, Sephy decided it was time to broach the subject. They might as well get it out in the open, she thought. There was no sense in trying to be evasive all week, refusing the junk food she was sure to be offered, opting out of the food orgies that were the usual MO for her weekends with Aunt Sharon. She would only wind up hurting her friend's feelings that way.

"Aunt Sharon," she ventured, tearing up lettuce for a salad, "did you notice I've lost weight?"

"Well, yes," said the older woman, with her head in the refrigerator. "I did, now that you mention it. Have you been feeling all right?"

"I feel fine. I'm losing weight on purpose, actually. I'm really *trying*." She did not go into details, because she did not want Sharon telling Jane just yet.

Sharon emerged from the refrigerator with a jar of mayonnaise and a plastic container of bleu cheese. "That's wonderful, Sephy. I'm very proud of you." But she did not sound as if she thought it was wonderful. "I thought I'd mix up a little of my famous bleu cheese dressing for the salad. You always like that."

"That's nice of you, but I'll probably just have my salad without dressing tonight."

"Oh." Sharon looked at the mayonnaise and the cheese she was holding. "I guess I'll . . . put these back, then."

"It's just that I'm trying to eat better these days."

"Of course you are. I wasn't thinking." But her friend's voice, coming from the refrigerator again, was stiff. Later, as Sephy refused a second slice of pizza, Sharon said, "If I'd known you weren't going to eat, I'd have only ordered the one." And as they watched a movie on television together, she said, with a trace of acid, "I probably shouldn't even offer you a bowl of ice cream."

"No thank you." Sephy felt like the worst kind of heel.

"Well, there's no law that says I can't have one." Sharon heaved herself out of her chair and headed for the kitchen.

God, help me get through this week; don't let me fail, Sephy prayed silently. *And if I could do it without hurting Aunt Sharon, that would be great. Help her to understand.*

But Sharon didn't understand, and by the next evening, Sephy was worn out with repeatedly refusing cake and doughnuts, bacon and eggs, and offers of Chinese takeout. Sharon's attitude was increasingly frosty; she seemed to be trying to sabotage Sephy. And Sephy wanted those things. She didn't love eating carrots and cottage cheese every day. Waking up in the morning and knowing she was miles from the nearest swimming pool was a luxurious relief. The old ways had a familiarity to them, a comfort that was absent in this long and grinding battle toward a place where she felt comfortable in her own skin.

By the time she and Sharon had settled into seats at the movie theater the second evening, Sephy had given in and let her friend buy her a gallon-sized tub of buttered popcorn. She ate the whole thing. The next morning, they went out to breakfast, where she ordered a three-egg omelet with corned beef hash. It was easier. Sharon was warmer. Sephy felt comforted. The simple truth was that she had always been far better at saying yes than saying no.

On Monday morning, back in her dorm room, she weighed herself and was unsurprised to find that she had gained six pounds. She went back to bed and crawled under the covers, unable to summon the ambition to find her bathing suit and go to the pool. She had fallen off the wire, and fallen hard. She did not deserve to like herself; she had been foolish to even hope she could change after all these years. She covered her head with the quilt and let herself dissolve again into the absolution of sleep.

CHAPTER

13

SEPHY'S BIRTHDAY was on the twelfth of March. Her suite-mates made her a box-mix cake in the microwave, which they topped with twenty-three candles. Once lit, the candles melted at once into the canned chocolate frosting, coating it with a cloudy film of wax. They ate it anyway.

"It was my French Canadian grandmother's fault," Sephy told them. "I was a C-section, and the story goes that my mother was all drugged up from the surgery, and she agreed to let her mother name me. My grandmother—Memere, we called her—was dying at that time, I think. Or pretending to be dying, anyway. She pretended to die for years. Nobody ever knew when to believe her. So Mom let her name me. Memere was Catholic, and March 12 is Saint Seraphina's feast day, according to the Catholic Church calendar, so that's what she named me. My mom didn't really wake up enough to realize what she'd done until the birth certificate had been signed. Luckily, one of the nurses suggested Sephy as a nickname." She poked with her fork at the piece of cake she was only pretending to eat. "Nobody ever spells it right on the first try. And when I was little, we could never find those cute barrettes with my name on them."

Her friends protested the unfairness of this and helped themselves to more cake.

"So what's this year going to bring for you, Seph?" said Ann, with her mouth full. "Any birthday resolutions?"

"I hope," Sephy said, "that by this time next year, I'll be a different person."

"Well, don't change too much. We love you the way you are, you know."

"We do! We love you!" cried the rest of them.

Birthdays, Sephy thought, were a time for new beginnings. Like new years, they were a time of resolution. Of resolve to bury the past and give birth to the future. "I won't change too much. Just one or two small adjustments." Sephy smiled—a brief, private smile that the others, vying with their forks in the cake pan for the last crumbs, did not notice.

Auditions were over, and Amy, who for the time being was not only director of the arts program but also director of all performances, was more than satisfied with the cast and crew she had lined up for *West Side Story*. For the role of Maria, she and Paul and Crystal had been unanimous in their choice of Connie, a student at the junior college in Quahog. She was a fine arts major and had a little dance experience, which Paul said was a relief, since it meant she had a sense of rhythm and an idea of what an eight-count was. For Tony, they had chosen Def, an artsy, home-schooled high school senior who both sang and danced and was so obviously the right choice for the lead role that there had not even been any discussion on the matter. Amy, Crystal, and Paul were already plotting how they might keep this treasure involved with the arts program for as long as possible. The rest of the cast and crew were energetic and willing workers; the thrice-weekly rehearsals were proceeding as expected, the props and wardrobe departments overflowing with the abundance of Crystal's treasure-hunting forays at flea markets, and the renovations on the opera house running apace.

Mitch and his crew had finished two bathrooms and one large room behind the auditorium, which would eventually be used as a dance studio. It was here they held their rehearsals. He promised them that the auditorium would be ready by mid-April, when he would turn his attention to the foyer and dressing rooms and let them get on with using the real stage. All was going as planned.

Amy, however, was not getting enough rest. Increasingly, she had trouble falling asleep, for all she collapsed into bed exhausted at night. When she did sleep, it was patchy: an hour here, a few more there. Nearly every night she awoke at two or three o'clock, her head reeling. With every decision that had to be made, her mind was like a slot machine, whirling through a wheel of options, touching briefly on a possible winner, only to discover it wasn't what she was looking for at all, before it recommenced its revolutions. Spinning and spinning, in search of each right answer.

Two nights out of every three, she lay awake so long that she gave up trying to fall asleep again and, carrying her laptop down to the living room couch, made herself a cup of tea and worked until dawn.

The opening of the musical also meant the opening of the entire community arts program, and there were teachers still to find, a class schedule to organize, concerts to book. Rarely did Amy even take time for lunch these days, sending Crystal away without her and murmuring, "Pick me up something on the way back." More often than not, the vegetable wraps, soups, or salads Crystal brought back sat forgotten and untouched in the refrigerator until someone discovered them three days later and threw them out. Amy was not complaining. She never felt as alive as when she was working at maximum capacity, and that was exactly what she was doing now. The arts program was like an enormous plow pulled by dozens of horses at once, and Amy felt herself holding the reins of every one of those horses, steering in the right direction, creating a program that would be a hallmark of the entire community. It was going to be a huge success. She knew this already.

Still, it bothered her that she was too busy to get to the gym as often as she would have liked. When she wasn't too busy, she was too tired. Once, she had forced herself to go when she left the office at ten o'clock at night, but no sooner had she started running on the treadmill than her head began to spin and black spots to swim before her eyes. She remembered then that she had eaten neither lunch nor supper that day and, resigned, stepped off the treadmill. She drove home, determined to eat something before bed, but by the time she pulled into the driveway at number 14, she had forgotten all about it.

It was always after five, when Crystal and Paul had gone home for the day and she was alone in her little third-floor office, uninterrupted by phone calls, that Amy got the most work done. She was sitting at her desk during one of these after-hours marathons, absorbed in an e-mail from a music teacher in Boston who was interested in giving string lessons in the summers, when a tap came at her open office door. She looked up to see Mitch.

"What are you doing here?" she said, glancing at her watch. "It's late."

"I was on my way home and thought I just might find you here. Wanna hear the latest?"

"Am I going to hate it?"

"Nah. You're going to love it."

She leaned back in her chair and smiled. "By all means, make my day."

"The auditorium should be finished tomorrow. They laid the carpet today, they're coming to install the seats in the morning, and after that, it's all yours."

She tried to speak and was surprised to find she couldn't say a thing. Worse, there were tears in her eyes. She felt all at once unraveled and knew that she must not let herself begin to cry or she would crumble completely. She hid her face in her hands and took several deep breaths.

"Are you okay?"

It took so much effort to make everything look effortless. But she was the leader, and that was what she had to do. She looked up and managed a smile. "Thank you."

He frowned. "You look terrible."

"Thank you," she said again, her voice prim.

"When's the last time you ate something?"

"I'm fine. Just a little busy, which I'm sure you can understand."

"When's the last time you slept?"

"I'm *okay*. I really am."

"Let's go get something to eat. You can leave whatever you're working on until morning."

"I can't. I'd like to, but I really can't. I just have too much to do."

"Then they're asking too much of you. If you can't do this job in forty hours a week, they need to hire a second person."

"I have Crystal and Paul."

"And you're still working too hard. You're going to make yourself sick."

"No, I'm not," said Amy, who had been nursing a headache and a sore throat since just after breakfast.

"Come on, put that away and let me buy you something made of tofu for supper. We'll celebrate the auditorium being finished."

"It won't be finished until tomorrow."

"And tomorrow if I come back, you'll still be too busy to celebrate."

"I'm sorry, Mitch, I *can't*. We open in just over a month."

"And we will open. But not everything has to be perfect when we do. Give yourself a break."

"*Give yourself a break* is not part of my vocabulary."

"You say it like it's something admirable, but it's not. You know what's admirable? Balance. *That's* what's not in your vocabulary."

She tried to make him understand. "You, of all people,

know what it's like to be at the top, in charge. To have it all depend on you."

He shook his head. "It does not all depend on you. You're expendable. Everyone is. If you couldn't finish this job, someone else would step in and do it."

She was stung. "What a *mean* thing to say."

His voice softened. "I'm not trying to be mean. But you should get over the sense of your own importance to this project. Get some help. Let somebody else share the load."

She stared at her computer screen, her lips tight. "I have all the help I need."

"Amy." He waited, but she refused to look at him. "Whatever. If you want to kill yourself with work, I can't stop you. Good night." He pushed himself away from the doorway. She heard his footsteps retreating down the hall.

Remorse flooded her. Jumping up from her chair, she went to the door and called after him. "Thank you for finishing the auditorium, Mitch. I can't wait to see it." She wanted to tell him that she knew the hard work and long hours he had put in to finish on time, indeed a week and a half early. She wanted to say that she appreciated it. But Mitch did not look back at her, merely raised his hand in acknowledgment and kept walking away.

Jane's voice came through the phone. "You're not coming home for Easter break either? Oh, honey . . . I don't want to nag you, but we miss you so much, and your sisters are counting on you to practice with the band at *some* point."

Sephy, who was more susceptible to guilt than any of the

other Darling girls, cringed at her mother's words. "I'm sorry, Mom, but Ivy sent me the music, and believe me, I've been practicing my part. It'll be no problem for us to get it all together when I'm home this summer. And I really do need to work at the nursing home here while I have the chance."

"I'm glad you're willing to work, Sephy, but you don't have to overdo it. We'd really like to see you."

"I want to see all of you, and I *will* see you, next month at graduation."

"Are you sure there's nothing wrong?"

"Not a thing. I'm doing great. In fact, in a way, I'm better than ever."

"Is it . . . it's not a boy, is it?"

Sephy hated the note of doubt in her mother's voice. As if, with Sephy, no one would believe it could be a boy. "No. No boys. Guys, men, whatever. None of that."

"You just want to work extra hours."

"That's all."

"Everyone will be so disappointed. Laura's not coming home either."

"I'm sorry, Mom. But everyone will just have to get over it. I'll see them next month, and then I'll be home for good, right?"

She heard her mother sigh. "All right, then. Do you think you'll get to Cleveland to see Sharon at all?"

"I have a couple of days off from work, so I'll drive out and spend Easter with her."

"That's sweet of you, Sephy."

"Not at all. Aunt Sharon's family. Why isn't Laura coming home?"

Jane hesitated. "She says she has to work."

"It'll all turn out just fine, Mom. Try not to worry."

"You're right, of course. We miss you; that's all. Oops—Ivy and Nick and the kids just showed up for supper, so I'll let you go."

"Oh, that's right; it's Thursday. I wish I were there."

"We wish you were too, sweetheart."

"I will be soon."

They made kissing noises into the phone and hung up.

Sephy planned to work a night shift on Friday, then sleep a few hours on Saturday before driving to Aunt Sharon's, where she would spend two nights with her old friend. On Monday afternoon, she would drive back to campus and be ready for classes on Tuesday. She was glad to have the shift at the nursing home, but that was not the main reason she had stayed in Ohio. If she worked hard, and was careful, she figured she could lose another ten pounds before her family arrived for graduation in May. She had taken a chance and ordered her graduation gown in a size sixteen. It wasn't yet where she wanted to be, but it was a long way from where she had been.

On Saturday afternoon, Sephy made the four-hour drive to Cleveland. She remembered her last visit and took the precaution of packing a soft-sided cooler with low-fat yogurt, fruit, and vegetable sticks. This she had hidden inside a suitcase so as not to offend Aunt Sharon. It was too big a bag to bring for such a short stay, but as she lugged it down the hall to the guest bedroom, she waved it away by saying, "I never know whether to pack for warm weather or cold this time of year, so I packed for both." When Aunt Sharon, coming behind her, looked unconvinced, Sephy added, "Plus, I brought my review books, in case I have a chance to study for the boards while I'm here."

That night, Aunt Sharon was peevish and out of sorts. She served a lasagna dripping with sausage and cheese for dinner and eyed Sephy critically as she ate. "Well," she said, when Sephy had finished one endless square, "I wasn't sure you'd like my lasagna anymore. I thought all you ate was rabbit food now."

Sephy, stricken, shook her head at the offer of another plateful. Aunt Sharon helped herself, saying, "Well, I hope you won't think less of people who take seconds," and Sephy felt about two inches tall. She was gratified later to see that low-fat ice cream had been added to the freezer, but when they were scooping it into bowls, in preparation for an evening spent on the couch, in front of the TV, Aunt Sharon had much to say. Every comment, of course, was spoken jovially, in a no-offense-meant sort of tone.

Adding chocolate syrup and whipped cream to her bowl: "I like a little something on my ice cream so I can *taste* it."

Going back to the freezer: "Hope I don't offend you, but I believe I'll have a little more."

Opening a package of cookies to go with her ice cream: "We big-framed people have to keep our strength up. Of course, a skinny little thing like you only has to worry about how you're going to look in your bathing suit this summer. . . ."

At this, Sephy finally put her spoon down. "Aunt Sharon," she said, with her heart hammering a drumroll in her ears, "does it bother you that I'm trying to eat healthier and that I've lost weight?"

"I don't know what you mean," said Sharon, scraping the bottom of her ice cream dish with great concentration.

"It just . . . Sometimes it sounds like you're a little offended because I'm not eating as much as I used to eat."

"You're imagining things, sweetheart." Sharon's eyes stayed fixed on the television, where eight contestants of a reality TV show took turns standing on livestock scales to broadcast the particulars of their gross obesity to the entire world. But Sephy was sure there was nothing imagined about her friend's aloofness.

On Sunday morning, she navigated breakfast at a pancake house before Easter Sunday service at Aunt Sharon's church. Afterward, they went to the mall for an all-you-can-eat buffet. Sephy visited the salad bar first, but it was uphill work, eating lettuce and bell peppers with vinaigrette for Easter dinner, when across from her, Aunt Sharon was putting away roast beef, gravy, mashed potatoes, creamed spinach, and pie with such obvious enjoyment.

"Don't be shy, honey," said Sharon more than once, gesturing with her fork. "Have whatever you want."

There was what she wanted *now* versus what she wanted in the long run, Sephy kept reminding herself. So, regardless of what she wanted now, she went back to the salad bar for a second plate of vegetables.

She was better at knowing her own limits this time, and with the memory of her last visit to Aunt Sharon's, which had ended in disaster, Sephy made the decision to leave on Sunday afternoon.

"But I thought you were staying until tomorrow!" Aunt Sharon was dismayed.

"Oh, I just . . . There was a book I didn't bring with me that I really should look at before tomorrow. It's for a test on Tuesday." They both pretended not to recognize the thinness of the excuse.

"All right. Just be sure you call and let me know you got back safely. And take a lunch along with you. I'll make you one while you put your things in the car." So Sephy packed her suitcase for the drive back to college, a day earlier than planned, relieved beyond words that she was returning to a place where she would not be punished for aspiring to something better for herself.

Mitch parked his truck on the street outside 14 Ladyslipper Lane but did not get out at once. He felt jittery, as though he had drunk too much coffee, which, come to think of it, he probably had. That was the trouble when you didn't drink alcohol: you tended to compensate with caffeine and nicotine, which were just as bad for your nerves. Worse, probably. A large coffee urn was a fixture of every AA meeting he'd ever gone to—and he'd gone to plenty. Still did. Alcoholics were the worst people in the world for drinking coffee and smoking cigarettes. Somehow you never lost that instinct for calming yourself by putting something in your mouth. The trouble was, it tended to backfire on you at times like this, leaving your heart pounding and your hands sweaty.

The cigarette he had smoked at home helped a little, but not much. He considered having another one now, before he got out and knocked on the door. But someone was bound to look out the living room window. They would see his truck and maybe see him smoking. With his luck, it would be Amy, who thought all chemicals would kill you instantly. Besides, he didn't want to go in smelling like an ashtray. No cigarette, then. He would have to do this on sheer nerve.

It was strange to be so worked up about seeing a family he had once lived with for better than two years. Of course, that was before he'd sat right here in a truck one night and watched Amy kiss that jerk Brian under the porch light. He hadn't been able to stop himself from leaning forward and laying on the horn. That had made them jump apart in a hurry.

Since that night, his disgust for both of them had been so great that he'd almost made up a reason to fire Brian three or four times. It was only the looming deadline that stopped him. He couldn't afford to lose a worker right now, and if Brian knew nothing else in life, he at least knew the job. Mitch had taken it out on Amy instead, which was easier. Whenever he thought of her kissing Brian, each time the disgust rose up, he used it to fuel his anger against her. Every time he snapped at her or gave her the cold shoulder, a little curl of shame would begin to smolder in his stomach. At the same time, there was something satisfying about seeing the hurt and bewilderment flash across her face. It felt like justice. A sharp pain shot up the side of Mitch's face and reminded him that he was clenching his jaw again. He opened his mouth and worked it side to side, loosening it. He didn't need a tension headache on top of everything else.

He was not sure why he had come tonight. Maybe because the way she had asked him, when they had run into each other at the grocery store, made him think she really meant that she would like it if he came. He guessed that what he really wanted was to see if that was true, if Amy would be happy to see him outside of work.

"Just do it, Mitch," he muttered to himself. "It's only Amy." It took all his will to peel his fingers away from the steering wheel, jump out of the truck, and make his legs carry him up the front walk. He was saved the torment of knocking because the door flew open before he got to it, and there she was.

"Mitch, you came!" She was tickled, he could tell.

"I came."

She was dressed in a long, green, soft-looking skirt and a drapey sort of sweater, and with her elf-like face and huge brown eyes, she looked like the kind of thing that would come floating out of a dream. He stuffed his hands into his coat pockets and looked at the doorstep.

"Well, come in. Don't stand out there in the cold. Supper's almost ready."

He followed her inside and was at once enveloped in a sense of home. This house was the one place in his life where he'd ever felt he belonged. There was the big mirror on the wall, with the table standing under it, holding a dish full of keys and library cards and other assorted junk. There was the dark-blue rug lying over a polished wood floor, and the orange-striped tail of Butternut the cat just disappearing around the corner. The same cat, after all this time. Jane Darling had gotten it as a kitten when Mitch had lived here. For an instant, he felt confused, unable to remember why he had ever walked away from this the way he had. Or maybe he hadn't. Maybe he had been here all along and it was the years in between that had been the dream.

"Give me your coat."

He obeyed, and Amy hung it on a wooden hanger in the front closet.

She reached for his hand, and his heart lurched. He felt a hot flush spreading upward from his neck and hoped she didn't notice.

Of course she noticed, but she misunderstood. "Don't be nervous; it's just family." She gave his hand a little squeeze and tugged him after her, laughing at him. "Look what the cat dragged in," she crowed when they reached the kitchen.

"Mitch!" The cry was instant and gratifying, and he couldn't hold back the grin that took over his face. Ivy was there, and Jane, and Libby from next door, and Ivy's little black daughter that Amy had told him about. He nodded at all of them and answered the questions they fired at him as best he could. When you got the Darling women together all in one room, it was a little like being in a henhouse, everyone clucking and talking at you at once.

Amy, still clutching his hand, spoke up. "I'm taking him away to watch the game with Dad and the others, where it's quieter, and people won't be talking him to death."

Still smiling, she pulled him through the kitchen to the living room, with its glossy black baby grand piano and white built-in bookshelves lining two walls, and beyond that, to the family room. Leander was there, and David, and Nick, and Ivy and Nick's adopted sons. They were watching a basketball game. Celtics and Lakers, he saw with a quick glance at the screen.

"Mitch!" Leander cried, standing and coming toward him, arms outstretched. "If this isn't a surprise!" He embraced him in a hearty, back-thumping hug that made Mitch's throat tighten up. "Come on and sit down and watch the game with us, and tell me how you've been. I was beginning to be afraid we'd seen the last of you."

Mitch looked toward the door, but Amy had already disappeared. "Move over there, DeShaun," said the man who was the most father Mitch had ever known. "Make room for our boy here. We have a lot of catching up to do."

One Friday morning in mid-April, Laura awoke with a scratchy throat and stuffy nose. She pulled herself out of bed, forced herself to stand in a hot shower, and dressed for work. But by the time she got home that evening, she was well and truly sick. She put on her pajamas, made herself a cup of tea with whiskey and honey, and crawled into bed. She spent Saturday alternately napping and reading on the couch.

On Sunday morning, she was running a fever, and her whole body ached, right to the bones. Won't be @ band practice tonight, she texted Rob. I think I have the flu. The real one.

He texted back, Bummer! Want me to stop by afterward?

She smiled at the phone and typed in, I don't want you to catch it, but if you feel brave enough, it would be nice to see you.

I got my flu shot this year. Can I bring you anything?

No thx. I have everything I need. Door unlocked, in case I fall asleep. Just come in.

She was lying on the couch, the coffee table littered with tissue boxes, a Tylenol bottle, a mug of tea that had gone cold, an empty water glass, and several novels, when he arrived. He held up a paper bag. "I brought soup."

Laura was touched. She propped herself up on her elbows, aware that her face was bare of makeup and her hair was most likely sticking out everywhere. "That's really nice of you."

He pulled a takeout container from the bag, along with a plastic spoon and a handful of napkins. "Luckily, the salad bar at the grocery store has chicken noodle on Sundays."

More to please him than because she was hungry, Laura sat up and opened the container. However, a few spoonfuls and she had to confess herself defeated. "I just don't have any appetite," she told him.

"I'll put it in the refrigerator for you. You can eat it later." He picked up her empty water glass. "How about I refill this while I'm at it? You need to push fluids."

She heard him in the little kitchenette, opening the refrigerator door and rattling around in the freezer for ice cubes.

When he returned, he handed her a glass of water. "I see you're a vodka girl."

Oops. Laura had forgotten the bottle she kept in her freezer. "From time to time," she said. She supposed he had seen the three-liter box of wine in the refrigerator, too, although he didn't comment on it. "Thanks for the water." She sipped at it. "Hey, I never got the chance to ask you: Who was the cute girl with you at church the day after Valentine's Day?"

"That was my sister Naomi. She's a teacher on the reservation. She came down for the weekend to hang out with me and do some shopping. Sorry I didn't get a chance to introduce you, but you . . . ah . . . seemed pretty busy." His smile was enigmatic; he knew perfectly well that she'd been avoiding him, and why.

Laura could do nothing about the heat that suffused her face. "Oh, nice," she forced herself to say. "I hope I'll get to meet her next time."

He stayed only long enough to give her a report on the youth group band's progress, then said, "I can see you're tired, so I'll let you rest. Are you sure there's nothing else I can get you?"

She was sure.

"Well . . . don't hesitate to ask if you think of something. You have my number."

When he had gone, Laura marveled that the simple offerings of soup, a glass of water, and tacit forgiveness could make her feel so cared for. She fell asleep then, and really rested for the first time in a long time.

CHAPTER

14

AMY RESTED HER ELBOWS on the desk and pinched the bridge of her nose. She'd been fighting a headache all afternoon, and she had never really kicked her sore throat of a few weeks ago. Concentrating on the e-mail in front of her seemed a Herculean task. It was an application letter from someone who did something or other with children's puppet theater. Amy tried to remember if she had advertised for such a person but could not seem to think straight. She squinted at the e-mail once more and could make no sense of the words. She pushed herself away from her desk. Maybe eating some lunch would help.

"Crystal!" she called. There was no answer.

"Paul!" No answer.

She was exasperated. It would be really nice if someone were around who could go out and pick her up some soup or something. Soup would feel good on her scratchy throat. She tried once more. "Crystal!"

She squinted at the clock on the wall. The hands pointed to 9:25. Or was it 5:45? She frowned, trying to puzzle it out. One hand on the 9. One hand on the 5. If it was 9:25 in the morning, shouldn't Crystal and Paul be here? But then— here, she groped for the desk calendar, as if that would help her decipher the clock—it would be far too early for her to be wanting lunch. But surely it couldn't be 9:25 at night? She got up from her chair and began walking down the deserted hallway toward the third floor's only window. Moving her legs was like moving two cinder blocks. Pick up, heave forward, set down. Pick up, heave forward, set down. When she gained the window, she peered owlishly out. All dark.

But then, maybe it was really 5:45. Except that this was April, and it should be light at that time of evening. Or morning, for that matter. Could it be 5:45 in the morning? Amy leaned against the wall and considered the problem. At last she came to the weighty conclusion that such darkness outside the window, coupled with the ambiguous arrangement of the clock's hands in her office, could only mean that it was 9:25 at night. Which meant that it was much too late for lunch, and in fact, probably time to think about heading home. Only then did it occur to her that a glance at her computer or phone's clock would have solved the mystery in the first place.

Amy groped her way back to her office, put on her coat, and found her purse and car keys. Her head was pounding, and she thought she might be sick. Around her, the walls began to tilt strangely, as though the roof were about to collapse. A cold chill of fear broke over her, and she bolted for the stairs. She misjudged the first step and felt her foot hit only air. As though she were standing to one side watching a play, she saw herself sliding in slow motion down the length of the staircase.

At the bottom, she crumpled to a stop, only vaguely sore. "Ouch," she said aloud in surprise, and began to cough. Her overwhelming feeling was one of gratitude that no one else had been around to witness her gracelessness. She giggled and, still clutching her shoulder bag, picked herself up and made her way through the darkened foyer to the parking lot, humming a song from *Show Boat* under her breath.

Her car . . . her car . . . Her eyes focused on the only car in the lot, a small, beat-up-looking thing sitting under a lamp-post. It did not look at all familiar, but she felt sorry for it, and went over and tried her key in the lock. It fit, and the door clicked open. She felt giddy with happiness that her key—the only key she possessed—had worked to open the only car in the whole parking lot. She laughed aloud, feeling as though she had won some prize, and flung her arms to the sky. The keys slipped from her fingers and soared into the air. She watched them make a slow arc up, then down again and land a few feet away, still within the pool of light from the streetlamp.

Admiring her own patience, she started over to retrieve them, but noticed that the pavement under her feet was behaving oddly. As she walked, the parking lot began to heave and pitch like a storm-tossed ocean, and when she bent to pick up her keys, a wave of blacktop rose up and hit her on the forehead. She collapsed, exhausted, to the ground. Her last thought was that the pavement was blessedly cool against her face, and the drops of rain that were beginning to fall sounded like a lullaby as they struck the ground around her. She closed her eyes and rested.

❧

She smelled the antiseptic before she even opened her eyes. The odor made her stomach turn.

"Look!" someone said. "I think she just blinked."

"Amy? Amy, honey, can you hear me?" It was her mother's voice.

"*Unnnh,*" she managed. She tried to open her eyes, but someone had taped them shut.

"She's waking up. Leander, look!"

"Hi, sweetheart." It was her father this time. "Can you hear me? Blink if you can hear me."

Couldn't he see that her eyes had been taped shut? Amy tried again to open them and realized with horror that they had not been taped at all; they had been *sewn* shut. "Dad," she croaked. "Dad, help." Then she drifted away again into darkness.

Later, she did open her eyes, but it was dark in the room. She raised heavy hands and rubbed at her eyes, clearing the blur from them. She was lucid enough this time to realize she was in the hospital. That one of her arms was rigged to an IV, and that she had oxygen tubing in her nose. Also, there was the shadowy form of a man slumped, asleep, in the chair beside her. *Dad.* She felt a rush of love and, on the heels of this, wondered what had happened to land her here. She probed her mind tentatively and came up with some vague recollections of being at the office. That was all.

"Dad," she whispered. He didn't move, so she tried louder. "Dad!"

He came awake with a start and rubbed his eyes, then sat forward, squinting at her in the semidarkness.

"Mitch!" she said in surprise.

"Hey there, kiddo." His voice was sleepy and pleased. "We were beginning to think you wouldn't wake up 'til morning. I sent your parents home a few hours ago."

"How long have I been here?"

He looked at his watch. "They found you unconscious in the parking lot about six hours ago. Do you remember what happened?"

"Not really. Who found me?"

"Some lady on her way to work the night shift at the Super 8 saw you and called the police. It was pouring rain, and you were out cold."

"I don't remember."

"They checked your blood for alcohol and drugs, and you came up clean."

"Of course I did." She was trying for indignation but sensed she sounded only tired.

"Turns out you have pneumonia. Plus, you're dehydrated and malnourished and just plain exhausted."

Amy *felt* exhausted. She let herself slump back against the pillows. "Are Mom and Dad okay?"

"Out of their minds with worry, but otherwise fine. I convinced your father that you wouldn't wake up until morning, so they should go home. Plus, the nurses told them you weren't in any immediate danger."

"You have to work in the morning."

He shrugged. "So I'll work in the morning."

She held out a hand to him, and as he took it, her eyes swam with tears and spilled over. "I'm sorry, Mitch."

"Sorry for what?"

"For being such a bother to everyone. For making you stay here all night when you have to work tomorrow."

"Don't be stupid; you're not a bother. And nobody's making me stay. I'm here because I want to be."

"I *am* stupid. I'm so embarrassed that this happened."

"The only thing you should be embarrassed about is not knowing when it's time to stop working. You're going to kill yourself at this rate."

"I'm almost done. Opening night's just a couple of weeks away."

He was shaking his head. "But once opening night's over, you'll be running yourself ragged over the next show. And then the next one, and the one after that. You don't know how to slow down, Amy. How to . . . I don't know . . . how to delegate and relax and let go of things."

She stiffened. "Don't lecture me. You don't understand all the things I have on my plate."

"Actually, I kind of do. You dumped some of them onto my plate, remember? Remember that impossible deadline I'm working night and day to meet?"

She felt tearful again. She was a rotten friend to him. A terrible sister. "I'm sorry," she whispered. "You're so good. You work so hard. I *do* remember. I'll never forget."

"Ohhhhh no. No way. Now you're going to say things you'll wish you hadn't. Time to go back to sleep. I'm calling the nurse, and then I'm calling your parents." He reached over and pushed the call button fastened to her bed rail.

She felt beleaguered by a sense of urgency, and she tugged on his hand. "Don't go, Mitch. You're the best friend I have. You're the only person who will tell me the truth about myself."

"Oh brother, Amy. I hope you don't remember any of this when you're finally better. Trust me, you'll be embarrassed."

"I love you, Mitch."

The nurse bustled into the room, switching on the small light over the sink as she came. Amy felt the warm pressure of Mitch's lips on her forehead and heard him whisper, "Me too." After that, she slept again for a long, long time.

They kept her until the next afternoon, then let her go home with strict instructions that she was not to go to the office for a full week. She was allowed to work from home for three hours every day. Her mother annoyed her by hanging around Amy's bedroom, making pointed comments about the clock and taking her laptop away when the allotted work hours were up. Jane herself called Crystal and Paul to explain Amy's need for rest and ask that if they needed their boss for anything, would they please contact her only during her three work hours. In truth, Amy was a bit hurt that neither Crystal nor Paul called more than once a day, and in fact seemed to be getting along very well without her. And to her intense disappointment, Mitch didn't call or text at all, although he did send a large arrangement of wildflowers, which she set on her dresser and admired from different angles several times a day. She sent him a proper thank-you note for being a good friend to her in the hospital, then tried to settle down, with the cat on her lap, to devote the rest of her endless free hours to rereading *Gone with the Wind*. It was uphill work.

Seeing Rob with another woman on Valentine's Day weekend had been a wake-up call for Laura. She knew now that it was only his sister, but for the first time, she realized there might be other women interested in him. The fact that he had brought her soup during her bout with the flu made up her mind for her. She wanted him. But it had been weeks, and Rob did not seem to be any closer to asking her out. He was always friendly, sought her out at church on Sundays, and texted her with little amusing observations about his life and job throughout the week. It was clear enough to Laura that he liked her, so what was taking him so long? She was not used to waiting around for a man, once she had set her sights on him. Maybe he was afraid she would say no if he asked her out. Well then, Laura would leave him in no doubt of her interest. *She* would ask *him* out. She had not the slightest doubt that he would say yes.

She waited for a Sunday night, when the youth group band, which had vastly improved under her supervision, had packed up their instruments and were shooting hoops in the church parking lot while they waited for their rides. She and Rob were supposed to wait until everyone had been picked up before they left.

"Listen," she said to him as they watched one Trevor shoot a basket over the other Trevor's head, "I was wondering if you'd be interested in going out to dinner with me some night."

He was silent for so long that her face began to burn. She realized, too late, that she had misinterpreted his friendliness.

"Hey, you know what? Never mind," she said. "It was just a thought. Dinner between friends, that's all."

"No," he said, looking down at his Sauconys. "I like you, Laura. It's just—can I ask you a question?"

"Okay."

He looked into her eyes. "What part does God play in your life? Any at all?"

She could not have been more startled if he'd slapped her. She should have known, though; this was exactly the kind of question she'd heard all her life from Christians. She sighed. "It's complicated, Rob."

"Is it? Why don't you try telling me?"

Laura watched as two cars pulled into the parking lot. Cassie, Adam, and one of the vocalists peeled off from the group around the basketball hoop and headed for the cars, yelling good-byes to the others as they went. Rob and Laura both waved.

"I grew up in a church kind of like this," Laura said. "But I don't know, it just never really . . . took with me. I can give intellectual assent to the existence of God, but the truth is I don't really care." And because she felt that she could trust him not to think less of her for it, she said, "I'll be perfectly honest, Rob. I know that if I were to have a relationship with God, I would have to let Him be in charge of my life. And right now, I'm not interested in that. I like things the way they are."

He nodded, looking at his sneakers again. "Well, that's honest, all right. Thank you for telling me. But, Laura . . ."

He hesitated. "Don't overplay your hand. If God wants your attention, He's going to get it, one way or another. I wouldn't want it to be harder for you than it has to be."

"Thanks for the warning." There was no one else she could think of who could say those words to her without raising her ire. But from Rob, somehow, she felt a concern behind them that was entirely without judgment. "Believe it or not," she added, "I understand why you can't go out with me."

He smiled. "I pray for you, you know."

Again, because it was Rob, she said, "Thank you. I appreciate that." And she was surprised to find that she actually meant it.

"So, everything's ready for opening night, then." Amy held a binder stuffed with schedules, lists, program templates, ticket sales reports, and caterers' menus for the opening-night party. "Crystal, I am officially passing the baton. I won't be back until four days before we open, so it's up to you to iron out the last of the details."

"Everything's ironed out," said Crystal with a trace of exasperation.

"Amy, go away," said Paul. "The arts program will still be standing when you get back."

"I'll be here for the dress rehearsal."

"We know you will."

"Don't forget to call the florist and confirm the flowers for the party."

"It's on my calendar for tomorrow."

"Did you get hold of the paper in Bangor to see if they'd do a story on opening night?"

"Yes, and Portland, too. They're both sending reporters."

"I don't suppose this is big enough for Boston?"

"Not yet, Amy."

"I feel like I'm forgetting something."

"You are," said Paul. "You're forgetting to let go and have fun."

"Has anyone seen Mitch today?"

"No, but I talked to him last night," said Crystal, "and he told me the spindles and banisters will be installed on the staircase on Thursday, so we can open the second-floor bathrooms to the public for both the play and the party. The rest of the upper level won't be finished, but he'll rope it off. It shouldn't be a safety issue."

Amy frowned. "Why did he call you last night about the staircases, instead of just e-mailing me about them this morning?"

"He didn't call me; I called him. I thought it might give him a little nudge to ask me out."

"And did he?"

Crystal sighed. "No, and I can't figure out why. It's been four months since we went to that hockey game, and he hasn't made a single move. I *thought* he had a good time, but I guess not."

"You could always ask him out again."

"It's his turn," Crystal said irritably. "Anyway, never mind that. You go off and have a good time at your sister's graduation."

Amy looked around, trying to find something that had

been left undone. "Well, if there's nothing else, I guess I have no excuse for hanging around, do I?"

"Nope," said Paul. "Get out of here."

She obeyed and went home to pack, feeling oddly disappointed, as though she were about to miss out on a party she had spent a very long time planning.

Sephy got Ivy's call just after two in the afternoon. She shrieked with joy when she heard her sister's voice. "I'll be down at the front door in a second," she told Ivy. When she hung up, she took a minute to stand in front of the mirror that hung on the back of her door.

What would her family think when they saw her? Sometimes—most of the time, in fact—she had a hard time remembering what she had looked like fifty pounds ago. The change was so gradual when you looked at yourself every day, it was easy to forget how far you had come. However, reason— and the numbers on the scale and on the tags of her clothes— told her that her family was going to notice right away.

For some reason, this felt terrifying.

But she couldn't think about it any longer; they were here. She turned from the mirror and headed for the door.

The car was not fully in park when Ivy and Amy scrambled out.

"Girls! You'll kill your—!" Sephy heard her mother cry from the passenger seat. Then Ivy and Amy were smothering her, wrapping her in their arms and squeezing as though breath and oxygen were optional things for the well-being of a long-unseen sister.

"Se-phy!" Ivy cried. "*Look* at you!"

"You've lost weight!" Amy said at the same time.

Sephy managed to free her arms and worked one around each of them. "A little, yes."

"How much?" Amy demanded.

"Amy!" said Ivy.

Sephy rolled her eyes. "About fifty pounds, if you must know."

Her parents had found a space and parked the car, and they came toward them now with Aunt Sharon.

"Oh, my heavens, Sephy!" Jane, exclaiming with tears in her eyes, flung her arms out to enfold Sephy in an embrace as familiar as Sephy's earliest memory. "You look—what have you done?—just *wonderful*!"

The only one, it seemed, who had nothing to say was Aunt Sharon. She stayed in the background, fussing with the straps of her purse and the hem of her blouse, and beyond a stiff, "Congratulations, my dear," had nothing else to say.

Sephy was nearly finished packing, so she was free until graduation the next day. They asked if she wanted to spend one last night in the dorm with her friends. She did not. There had been a big party the night before, she told them, and they had all said their good-byes then. She wanted to stay with her family, whom she had not seen in nearly five months.

David had not been able to come because of work, and no one had heard from Laura at all. But the rest of them spent the night at a hotel, playing canasta until after midnight. In the morning, they ran Sephy back to campus for graduation lineup.

The ceremony itself was long and faceless. Except for the moment when she, Seraphina Louise Darling, stepped across the platform to graduate magna cum laude with her bachelor of science in nursing degree, it did not interest Sephy in the slightest. Afterward, they went back to the dorm and, maneuvering around hundreds of other students and parents, began to truck her boxes down to the little U-Haul trailer their father had rented that morning. The afternoon was hot, and Sephy went to a vending machine and brought back a spring water for Amy and Diet Cokes for the rest of them. She and Amy sat on the lid of a plastic bin in the parking lot to drink theirs.

Amy swept an arm at the boxes around them. "Where'd you get all this stuff, Seph?"

"I honestly don't know. My few possessions have multiplied over the school year, that's for sure."

"I have this recurring dream," Amy told her, "where I'm packing up to leave college. I'm supposed to be out of the dorms by a certain time, maybe five o'clock on graduation night, and I'm packing and packing, but I can't get it done. Everyone else finishes and leaves, but I'm still working all alone. It's a terrible dream."

"That's an easy one," said Sephy. "It means you're afraid you won't be able to fulfill all your responsibilities."

"Oh, so you're an interpreter of dreams?"

"Yep." Sephy put her fingertips to her temples and closed her eyes. "Your dream says that although you see other people doing the things they have to do and succeeding, you're afraid you don't have what it takes to do it right."

"Huh. I have a sister who's a mystic. Who knew? Do you read palms and tarot cards too?"

"It's not mysticism; it's pure psychology. Dreams reveal our innermost fears, and sometimes our hopes. The emotions we can't access have to surface sometime, and it's usually at night, when our psychological defenses are at their lowest."

Amy pointed her water bottle at Sephy. "Someone's been seeing a counselor."

Sephy didn't mind admitting it. "That I have."

"And what do *you* dream about when your defenses are at their lowest?"

Sephy glanced around the parking lot. "I dream about Aunt Sharon. That I have to go live with her so I can take care of her. And she's really happy about it, but I'm not. I try to escape, but all the doors are locked." She could not bring herself to smile.

Amy put an arm around Sephy and squeezed. "We're not going to let that happen. You're going to come home to Copper Cove and get a job, and finish losing the weight you want to lose, and have a successful, *healthy* life."

"Do you think so?"

"I know so."

"Amy, thank you for not saying that I don't need to lose any more weight."

"I do think you're beautiful the way you are. If you didn't lose any more, you'd still look great."

"I'd look okay, but I'm not where I want to be. I need to keep going. Mom's already trying to persuade me that I've lost enough."

"Don't listen to Mom or Sharon or anyone else. Not even me. You're the one who has to live with yourself. Do what you need to do to be healthy."

"Thank you."

"Let's go back up for another load before Ivy catches us shirking. We'll really be in trouble then."

Sephy gave a mock shudder and stood up. "Too late. Here she is now." She nodded at the front doors of the dorm, which were propped open.

Ivy lugged a suitcase over and dropped it, panting, near the pile of baggage. "Hey, you two, get in there and give the rest of us a hand. We're not your pack mules."

"Yes, ma'am," said Sephy.

Amy smirked. "Told you so."

Amy, Ivy, and Sephy made the drive home from Ohio in Sephy's car, followed by their parents, who were pulling the U-Haul trailer. Between Buffalo and Rochester, Amy made an executive decision that they must have more landscaping done around the opera house before the grand opening. Technically speaking, it was too early, in a zone where the mantra was *never plant before May 31.* Amy wasn't bothered by this detail. They could cover the plants every night until the danger of frost was past. So far it had been warm, though, and she didn't think anything would freeze. Having decided this, Amy spent a happy couple of hours in the car drawing plans for flower beds, helped by Ivy and her mother—consulted from the other car by Bluetooth—who knew more about gardening than she did. Sephy, who did not, but who was a voice of common sense nonetheless, contributed from the backseat.

"You can't put everything in at once," Sephy pointed out,

squinting at the scribbles in Amy's notebook. "For one thing, there won't be time. For another, what if they really do freeze? Think of the waste."

"Sephy's right," said Ivy. "There's no sense wasting time and money hurrying to put in plants that won't mature by the end of the week anyhow. I think you should just do azalea bushes, maybe some hostas, and a lot of mulch."

"Mom?" said Amy, who felt that her sisters were purposely trying to rain on her parade. "We should have more plants for the opening, shouldn't we?"

"I have to agree with your sisters on this one," came their mother's voice through the speaker. "Although I might add some pansies. They're bright and colorful, and hardy too. Bleeding heart is a good early plant. Creeping phlox . . . And nothing says you can't have the rest of the flower beds ready. If they're dug and nicely edged, people will see that there's more to come as the weather gets warmer."

"You could have pots of bulb flowers set out in the gardens," Sephy suggested. "Tulips, daffodils, that kind of thing."

Amy was aghast. "That's a horrible, tacky idea! I suppose I should have them all leaning around in green plastic pots with the price stickers from the local grocery store still on them?"

Sephy did not sound offended. "It doesn't have to be tacky. It could be very nice. If anyone can figure out how to do it the right way, it's you."

"Why don't we just plant them in the ground?"

"You plant bulbs in the fall, not the spring," Ivy reminded her.

Amy knew when she was outnumbered. "Oh. Well . . . I'll think about it."

On Monday morning, Amy was back in the office at seven. She spent the morning making phone calls and placing orders, and on Tuesday, four men from the parks department showed up at the opera house armed with shovels, edgers, and a truckload of bark mulch. Amy hung around giving advice and instructions and being generally helpful until she overheard one of the men mutter to another, "Miniature Genghis Khan." And though she was not sure, she thought the second man replied, "Makes my mother-in-law look like a canonized saint." She went back to her office and left the men to their work.

Thursday's dress rehearsal was a disaster. Def, who was playing Tony, misjudged one of his jumps in a dance sequence and strained an ankle. Riff, Chino, and Anita all forgot lines. Maria, who had a sore throat, kept cracking on the high notes of "I Feel Pretty," and a backdrop fell over, punching a gaping hole in the skyline of New York City. By the time it was over, Amy was fighting back tears, in spite of assurances from Paul and Crystal that everyone knew a bad dress rehearsal portended a good opening night.

She left the opera house, planning to go back to the office at the town hall and pick up her laptop. When she stepped out into the spring dusk, she found Mitch leaning against his truck, waiting for her.

"How did it go?"

"Don't ask. Terrible."

"Isn't that supposed to be a good sign?"

She could only shake her head.

"Come on, get in the truck. Your father sent me to pick you up and bring you home."

"I have to go back to the office first and get my laptop."

He shook his head. "Sorry. Not allowed. Your father said not to let you go to the office, or you'd get sidetracked and be there all night."

"I won't!"

"Liar. Of course you will." He opened the passenger door. "Come on."

Amy was outraged. "I have my own car, thank you very much. I can drive myself home."

"You can pick up your car tomorrow. For now, you're going home and getting some rest. You have a big weekend ahead, and nobody wants you to end up in the hospital again."

She crossed her arms with a mutinous glare.

"Don't make me pick you up and *put* you in the truck." He looked at the cast and crew still milling around the parking lot, chatting with each other or waiting for rides. "You don't want me to do that in front of everyone."

"Why didn't my father come get me himself?" she hedged.

Mitch rolled his eyes, and before Amy knew what had happened, her feet had left the ground. She shrieked with rage and surprise, and suddenly everyone in the parking lot was looking their way.

Someone whooped. A few others applauded.

"Put me *down*!" She hammered on Mitch's shoulder with her fist.

In a single, easy motion, Mitch deposited her on the seat of the truck and pinned her there with one arm. "Don't make a scene," he advised. "I already have a criminal record. If they arrest me for kidnapping, I'll really be in trouble." He slammed the door shut, went around to the driver's side, and got in.

Amy considered jumping out and running for it, but there was no point. Her father was only trying to take care of her. And Mitch was right: she did not want to make a scene in front of the very interested crowd of actors in the parking lot. She glared at him. "That was not necessary."

"Put your seat belt on."

Fuming, she obeyed. "You're a bully."

He started the truck. "Just following orders." He pulled into traffic, and as they left the opera house and her car behind them, Amy felt a kind of knot begin to loosen somewhere deep inside. It seemed it was always her job to tell everyone else what to do, to carry the weight of the world. It felt rather nice to be given orders for a change. She would not like it all the time, of course, but at the moment it was . . . restful. She felt a great wave of affection for her father. He knew her well.

She let herself lean back against the seat and sighed. "I'll be glad when this is all over," she confessed.

"I don't believe that for one minute."

She considered her own words. Would she really be glad when opening weekend was over? It was true that she was in every way exhausted. It would be a relief to settle into the slower, more normal schedule of classes and concerts that she had planned for the summer. But she did love the excitement of working to deadlines, of pulling so many impossible details together into a successful, seamless whole. She was discovering that there was no high like the high of being proud of yourself for a difficult job well done.

"I think I *will* be glad when it's over," she said, "but only because I know I get to do it all again for the December show. Once the grand opening is behind me, the hardest part will be finished, and I think the rest of it will be more fun."

"Are you sure you'd recognize fun if you saw it?"

She was stung. "I know how to have fun!"

"Sure you do."

"I do! I have fun all the time."

"Okay, how about having some fun right now, over at The Lucky Panda?"

"I thought you had orders to take me home."

He shot her a sideways glance. "I'm allowed to feed you along the way."

"Oh."

"So . . . something with bean sprouts for you, spare ribs for me?"

"That . . . that would be very nice. Thank you."

Friday night's production of *West Side Story* was to be by invitation only, with a reception afterward in the opera house foyer. Mitch, who would have given anything to skip this, was expected to be there, and in a coat and tie no less. He put off actually shopping for these foreign items until Friday morning when, determined to face it like a man, he drove to the mall in Quahog. Every particle of his being rebelled at the idea of spending several hundred dollars on an ensemble he would likely never wear again until his own funeral.

He shopped haphazardly, his method being to pull a few sport coats off one rack, shove them back, and move on to the next. Early on, he discovered that anything with an acceptable price tag was either shapeless or shiny or too tight across the shoulders. In Sears, he got sidetracked buying himself a new pair of Carhartt pants and examining an air compressor he had been wanting. After that, he spent an increasingly desperate half hour searching Macy's and JCPenney for a sport coat he did not hate before he gave up and headed for the food court. He would reassess his options over lunch.

He was standing in line at Taco Bell when he heard his name.

"Mitch! Mitch Harris! Over here!" It was Crystal, waving at him from a table. He left the line and went to her, relieved to see a friendly face in the bewildering crowd of shoppers.

"What are you doing here?" she asked him.

"Buying a sport coat and tie for the party. What are *you* doing?"

"Getting my hair and nails done. Isn't it exciting? It's like prom night all over again!"

"I wouldn't know. I didn't go to my prom."

"Oh." She looked at the bag in his hands. "So what did you find?"

"Nothing yet—not for tonight." On impulse, he said, "I could use some advice."

"Ooh, I love to give advice."

"I haven't worn a sport coat since . . . Actually, I've never worn one. I don't even own a tie. Any ideas where to start?"

"Macy's," she said at once. "They do custom tailoring."

"I already looked in Macy's. There was nothing."

"You just didn't look in the right place," Crystal said, sounding a bit like his third-grade teacher. "Come on. I have an hour before my hair appointment. I'll go with you and tell you what looks good on you."

He forgot about lunch and let her sweep him like a current down the mall to Macy's. There, Crystal summoned, as if by magic, a man wearing a diamond pinkie ring, who brandished a measuring tape along Mitch's shoulders, armpits, and waist, turning him this way and that as easily as if he were a floor mannequin. Like an obedient puppet, Mitch tried on one coat after another, with Crystal pursing her lips and shaking her head while she and the salesman talked to each other in a language of fashion that was foreign to him. On the sixth or seventh coat, Crystal suddenly smiled and Mitch had his first inkling that the ordeal would, in fact, end. The salesman began to pinch and tuck and pin and measure some more. The coat came off, and the man announced, "You may come back for it in an hour, sir."

"What?" He looked at Crystal in alarm. "I can't just buy it now?"

"No, silly, they need to make the alterations first."

"But . . . it fits, doesn't it?"

Crystal and the man exchanged knowing glances, and Crystal said, "It doesn't fit *right*. But an hour from now, it will. Now, how are you set for the rest of the outfit?"

"The rest?"

"Shirt, tie, pants, socks, shoes."

"Uh . . . I hadn't thought that far ahead."

"Well, it's a good thing you have an hour to kill," she said cheerfully. Mitch followed her to the other side of the store, feeling as though he were walking to the guillotine.

Afterward, Amy couldn't remember breathing once through the entire show. It was, as Crystal and Paul had predicted, a stunning success. When the final curtain fell, the crowd—two hundred of the political, financial, and artistic elite of the entire state, including four mayors, a senator, and the governor, all specially invited by engraved invitation—rose to their feet as one person for a thunderous standing ovation that went on and on. It rose to a crescendo when Jane, Crystal, and Paul took the stage, and when Amy joined them, the noise nearly took the newly replaced roof off the opera house. They bowed and bowed, and people came and put flowers in their arms, and then it was over.

Amy floated through the champagne reception afterward in a happy daze. She made a little speech, in which she introduced Mitch and the rest of the renovation committee, then gave a brief rundown of the events lined up for the summer. No fewer than six people approached her to offer their services to the program, including a violinist, an art professor from the community college in Quahog, a voice teacher, a dance instructor, a graphic artist, and a landscaper. The governor and the senator shook her hand and congratulated her; three reporters interviewed her, and about a dozen people asked when auditions would be held for the next production.

Ivy, Nick, and the kids, full of shrimp and quiche and

cheesecake, came to congratulate her and say good night. "We'll be here tomorrow morning for the family day," Ivy promised.

"And the face painting and karaoke," said Jada.

"And the hot dogs," Hammer put in.

Amy looked at DeShaun. "What about you?"

He shrugged. "I guess I'll be here too."

"There'll be break-dancing demonstrations and a hip-hop workshop."

"A'ight, that's cool," he said, one corner of his mouth tugging upward.

David and Libby said good-bye, and then her parents and Sephy and Grammie Lydia left. After that, things wound down quickly. At last, there were only her and Crystal and Paul and Mitch left, with the team of caterers doing their lightning-fast cleanup in the background.

Amy sat down on the second step of the sweeping staircase beside Crystal and slipped her shoes off. "My poor feet will never forgive me for this night," she groaned, flexing her cramped toes.

"It was great, wasn't it?" sighed her prop master/wardrobe manager/Girl Friday, swirling the remains of her champagne around in the bottom of a plastic flute. "The cast did a fantastic job. I was so proud of them."

"It was better'n I hoped," agreed Paul. "If they do half as well tomorra an' Sunday, I'll be the proudest choreographer inna the state a Maine."

Amy looked at Mitch. "What's your expert opinion, Mitch?"

"Perfect." He smiled into her eyes. "Perfect in every way."

Crystal stood up and took his arm. "Come on, Mitch. I'll let you take me home."

They said good night and left together, and Paul said, "I guess I'd better call it a night too." He bent to kiss her on the cheek. "Congratulations, Amy. Really, really great job. Broadway couldn't have topped it."

She fluttered her fingers at him, too tired to form an answer, and when he had gone, she sat on the steps, dreamily replaying scenes from the evening in her head. It *had* been perfect in every way.

The caterer stuck her head around the door and said, "We're finished here, Miss Darling."

"Oh, wait," Amy said and, pulling herself off the stairs, retrieved the envelope of cash she had put aside for the caterers' tip. "The committee wanted me to thank you on their behalf for such a lovely party. It was really great."

"Thank you, ma'am," said the woman, slipping the envelope into a large shoulder bag. "We'd be glad to work for you anytime."

"We'll be sure to call you the next time we have something like this."

"I'd appreciate that. We just started this company fourteen months ago, and we're still trying to build up the business."

"Keep doing great work like this, and you'll have a name for yourselves before you know it," Amy said. "I'll be glad to spread the word when I can."

"That's really nice of you. Here, let me give you a couple of cards." The caterer dug in her bag and pulled out half a dozen business cards. *Butter Side Up*, they read.

Amy smiled. "That's such a nice, optimistic name for a catering company."

"That's what we thought, but I'm glad to hear someone else say it. I never know if people will get it or not. 'Night now."

"Good night."

Amy closed the door behind the woman and stood alone in the foyer. The walls, with their lovingly restored mahogany paneling, rose around her, enveloping her in the nearly tangible personality of this place. Mitch had done a beautiful job, had given life and presence to what should have been only plaster and wood. It was her privilege to fill it with music and art and a chance for people to gain a better appreciation for the lovely things in life. She put out a hand and touched the chair rail. The wood was warm under her fingers. She was a lucky, lucky girl.

CHAPTER

16

With the warmer weather, Thursday night Darling family suppers once again moved outside. The grill was pulled out of the garage, the plastic tablecloths unearthed from Jane's tote labeled *Picnic Tables*, and new citronella candles purchased. On the night of their first cookout of the summer, Jane looked out the kitchen window to see Ivy and her family arriving. Last, as usual. *Ah, well.* Jane remembered the ordeal it could be to corral a family of children into the car with the hope of arriving anywhere on time.

She picked up the old green Tupperware container of picnic flatware from the counter. It had been a wedding gift from her sister, Ellen, thirty-four years ago. A celery keeper, she thought the thing was called. Jane had only ever kept knives, forks, and spoons in it. She carried it outside.

"Hi, Mom!" Ivy called. She came over and set a bowl

of pasta salad on the picnic table. "Want me to count out silverware?"

Amy came out of the house with Mitch at that moment, letting the screen door slam behind her. "Hi, Ivy!" she called. "Hi, Nick. Hi, kids!"

"You!" Ivy cried, pointing a finger at her.

"What about me?"

"What did you *say* to our sister?"

"Which one?" Amy's eyes were wide and innocent.

"You know perfectly well which one. I talked to Laura today. She told me you called and read her the riot act because she forgot about Sephy's graduation. Said you ripped up one side of her and down the other for a good ten minutes."

"Amy!" Jane protested. "You didn't!"

Amy tossed her dreadlocks. "Of course I did. It was rotten of her to forget such a big occasion. She never acknowledged my opening night either. Never called, never sent a gift or even a card. I didn't mind so much for myself, but I couldn't stand to see Sephy overlooked. She never stands up for herself, so I stood up for her."

"Oh, *Amy*," said her mother. "You can't talk to Laura that way. We'll be lucky if she comes home in July now, like she was planning to."

"You know it's two steps forward, one step back with her," Ivy added.

"Well, somebody had to hold her accountable."

"Don't worry, Mom. I patted down her feathers," Ivy said. "I assured her that Amy will be calling to apologize in a day or two, once she thinks better of her rash words."

"I'll be doing no such thing!" Amy cried.

"I wish you would," said Jane.

"And *I* wish Laura would think of somebody besides herself for a change, but that's probably not going to happen either. Come on, Mitch. Let's see if Nick and the kids want to shoot some baskets."

Mitch flashed an apologetic look at Ivy and Jane as he followed Amy to the basketball hoop at the end of the driveway.

Jane sighed. "I hope she hasn't done too much damage."

"Laura's still planning to come home in July, as far as I know," Ivy told her. "No thanks to Amy. When it comes to putting people's backs up, she takes the cake."

"She certainly believes in speaking her mind. I suppose we should have curbed her more when she was a child. We probably spoiled her because she was the youngest."

"Don't beat yourself up over it, Mom. We all spoiled her."

"I suppose so," Jane said. "But I do hate a rift in the family."

"Let it go. It'll blow over soon enough."

"I certainly pray it will," replied Jane, who had her doubts.

Jane watched from the front porch as her son and husband heaved the last of Sephy's cardboard boxes into the bed of David's truck, pulled a tarp over everything, and began to fasten it down. She did not even try to keep the tears from running down her face. *One more flying the nest,* she thought. *Next it will be Amy, and then the child years will be all over.*

There was still the prospect of grandchildren to fill the rooms, of course. Hammer, Jada, and DeShaun were already there nearly every week, and as dear to Leander and herself as if they'd been theirs from the day they were born. She hoped David and Libby would decide not to wait too long to start a family. Jane and Abigail Hale had agreed over shared cups of coffee that if they promised not to nag their children— indeed, they decided, it might be best to pretend profound disinterest in the subject—then maybe, just *maybe*, they would find themselves sharing a grandchild a year or two after the wedding. For now, Sephy had a job on a respiratory floor at the hospital in Quahog and was at this very moment moving to her first apartment. She would take a few days to get her things arranged, and at the end of the week the girls, spearheaded by Libby, would throw her a housewarming party. Jane and Leander's gift was an apartment-size washer and dryer. Ivy was giving her pots and pans; Amy had chosen two oil paintings. Laura, harangued by Amy, had ordered sheets and towels and had them shipped from L.L. Bean. Libby and David's gift was six months of cable and Internet service. Other friends and extended family would bring smaller items to the party: cutlery, dishes—

Her thoughts were interrupted by Sephy herself, who came through the kitchen door clutching a floor lamp. Jane hastily wiped her eyes. It wouldn't do to be caught crying.

"You've been crying," Sephy said at once. "You don't have to, you know. I'm practically next door."

"I'm just being silly," Jane said with a shaky laugh. "I know we'll see you all the time."

Sephy leaned over the lamp and dropped a kiss on her mother's cheek. "I love you, Mom. I'm glad the thought of my leaving makes you cry. It would be worse if it made you sigh with relief."

"You've always been one to find the silver lining, Seraphina."

Sephy smiled. "Can I have this lamp? I found it in the attic."

Jane squinted at it, trying to think where it had come from. "Oh, that was your Grammie Thibodeau's. It used to stand in the porch of her summer cottage. Make sure your father checks the cord; it might need to be replaced after all these years."

"Thanks. And you're coming for the party on Saturday, and lunch on Sunday afternoon, right?"

"We wouldn't miss it."

The truck's horn sounded. "Gotta go," Sephy said. "See you Saturday, Mom." And then she was gone, running down the three front steps, carrying her floor lamp. Jane's heart swelled with gratitude at the simple fact that her daughter had the freedom to run like that. It had not always been so. Sephy had so many tools to give her freedom: a good education and job, a wise and steady character, a loving heart, a supportive family. And now, the confidence that came from having conquered a once-insuperable part of her life.

Help her to make the most of her freedom, Jane prayed. *To use it wisely and not to squander it.* She said the words for two of her girls at once, and although she did not think Laura's name, even in this prayer, she did not have to. At every moment, God knew both the lightness and the heaviness of her heart.

Sephy stood at the nurses' station and examined the assignment board with dismay. Jennifer, her preceptor, stood with her, shaking her head. "That's not fair. Everyone else has five patients; you have seven."

"It must be a mistake. Char just didn't notice it when she made out the assignments."

Char, the day-shift charge nurse, joined them at the board. "It's not a mistake. I'm really sorry, Sephy, but Jan made me give you a heavier assignment than everyone else. She was specific that you were to have seven patients."

"Why?" Jennifer said. "There's no reason for that."

"She said Sephy has to learn to cope with heavy assignments before she finishes orientation."

"But I already know how to cope with heavy assignments!"

"That's true," Jennifer put in. "She's right on track. She takes a full assignment every night and does a great job. She's ready to be done with orientation."

Char held up her hands. "I know that. But Jan's the manager, not me. She said give you seven patients; I gave you seven. If it helps, I at least gave the heavier patients to other people."

When she had left them, Sephy turned to her preceptor. "What's Jan doing interfering with patient assignments anyway? That's Char's job."

"Who knows? But if there was ever a person who was mean just for the fun of meanness, it's Jan Winston-Jacobson."

"But why me? What did I ever do to her?"

By now, everyone at the nurses' station was listening. Bree, an older, brassy CNA who had worked the night shift for over twenty years, spoke up. "You're an easy mark. New grad, not a lot of experience . . ." She looked at Sephy over the rims of her half glasses. "And you don't stand up for yourself. Jan knows she can push you around and you won't complain."

It's not my fault. Sephy didn't say it aloud. She felt the dangerous weakness that meant she was about to dissolve into tears. She would not cry in front of everyone. "I'm going to run to the bathroom. Be right back," she squeaked and hurried to the locker room.

In the bathroom, she leaned against the sink and studied herself in the mirror. Reflexively, she thought, *She picks on me because I'm fat.* But another voice, one she was just beginning to know how to listen to, spoke up too. *Fat is a convenient excuse.* Carl had worked with her on this. All her life, she had blamed any difficulties that came along on her weight. But there was less and less weight to blame. She couldn't even honestly use the word *fat* anymore. She thought of the word Ivy always used to describe herself: *zaftig.* That's what Sephy had become. No longer a fat girl. A zaftig one. The thought that the problem lay elsewhere was oddly frightening. Being fat was familiar. She had the tools now to deal with that. She wasn't equipped for other issues.

Bree had put her finger on it, of course: the real problem was that Sephy had never known how to stand up for herself. But surely now was not the time to start. She couldn't get on anyone's wrong side this early in her career. It paid to get along with the people you worked with, even when it took an effort. For the most part, if you were nice to people, they were nice back to you, and everything went along smoothly. Jan just needed a little more kindness than most. And if there was one thing Sephy was good at, it was being kind.

She straightened her back. She would positively kill Jan

with kindness, if that's what it took. Sephy knew she was already a good nurse: smart, compassionate, highly regarded by her coworkers and patients. At some point, Jan would have no choice but to acknowledge that. If human effort could achieve it, Sephy would win her manager over yet.

With the community's unanimous praise of May's grand opening still ringing in her ears, Amy plunged into the summer with more energy than ever. December's production was only six short months away. Hardly enough time, really, to get a wardrobe and cast together for the blowout holiday musical production she had in mind.

This show would be different from the first in many ways. For one, it was to consist almost entirely of music and dancing, and although Amy had grown up with music, was musical by nature, it was a weak point of her education. She would have to rely much more on the expertise of others this time around. She was not comfortable with that idea; she didn't mind admitting it. At least in her mother and Paul, she felt sure she had the best accompanist and choreographer in the state.

She met with the whole team in her office one morning and laid out her plans for the program.

"This is huge!" Paul protested. "You already drive us like rented mules."

"Mom?" Amy said. "What do you think? Is it too much to pull off by December?"

"It does seem . . . ambitious," said Jane.

Amy ignored this. "We can do it," she declared. "I have faith in all of us."

"I can't believe I gave up a perfectly good job cleaning toilets for this," muttered her choreographer as he left the office.

Crystal stayed behind after the meeting. She shook a list at Amy. "There's no way I can get these costumes made and find all these props by December."

"Oh, come on, Crystal! If anyone can do it, you can."

"That's what I'm saying to you. No one *can* do it. Not in twenty hours a week, at least, which is all I get paid for."

Amy quelled the reflex to sigh out loud. Honestly, you had to wonder where peoples' work ethic was sometimes. "Remember that Mitch said the same thing about getting the opera house ready in time for the grand opening," she reminded Crystal bracingly. "He was positive he couldn't do it, but look: he did! All it took was a little confidence and some hard work. And that's what I prescribe for you. You'll get it done, just like Mitch did."

"Let me point out that—one—Mitch did *not* finish the renovations by the grand opening. He only finished the parts you insisted on, which added considerable stress to him, and expense to the project as a whole. And—two—he worked his tail end off seven days a week in order to get it done. I'll be honest with you, Amy; I'm not willing to work like that for the sake of this arts program."

Amy felt as though she'd been slapped. "I never thought of you as a selfish person, Crystal."

"*Selfish?* You want to know what's selfish? Paying me for twenty hours a week and expecting me to accomplish forty hours' worth of work."

"You know I can't pay you for any more than half time. It's not in the budget."

"That's fine. But I will put in twenty hours a week and no more. And I'm giving you fair warning." She waved her list. "I will not be able to get all this done by December."

"Well, what do you expect me to do?" Amy said, exasperated. "The show must go on. Everybody knows that."

"How about lowering your expectations? Scale back. Give us all a break. Let us *enjoy* putting on this production!"

Amy did not answer right away. She was steeling herself not to let loose a flood of tears over this unexpected betrayal. At last, she managed, "Well. I'm sorry you're not enjoying yourself. I warned you at the beginning that this job would be hard work."

"Yes, and I'm not opposed to working hard. But we're not all like you, Amy!"

"Like *me*? What's that supposed to mean?"

Crystal sighed. "Driven. Perfectionists. Workaholics."

Amy gasped. "I cannot believe you just said that. I'm not all those things!"

"You are."

"How mean! How absolutely unkind and unfair and . . . and . . ." The injustice of it choked her, and she found herself gasping for words like a landed fish for air.

Crystal's mouth was a small, hard line, but she looked steadily at Amy. Of the two, it was Amy who looked away first.

"Fine." Amy's voice was like cardboard. "You'll just have to do the best you can do. We can't ask any more than that."

"No, you can't. And I will gladly and cheerfully and willingly do the best I can do in the work hours allotted me." Crystal's tone became kinder. "It's going to be fine, Amy. If I only accomplish half this list, it'll still be the best Christmas extravaganza anyone's ever seen in these parts."

But Amy could not agree with this. The thought of doing half a job was as anathema to her as the idea of not doing the job at all. "It's your conscience, Crystal. I guess we'll all just have to live with whatever you decide to bring to the table."

Crystal stiffened visibly, and her nostrils flared. "I'm leaving now. Clocking out for the day. I have an afternoon shift at Hannaford."

Amy watched her stalk from the auditorium. She had thought Crystal was dependable, a friend, but apparently she had been wrong. Alone, she went back to her office, her heart like a stone in her chest.

In the middle of June, Amy moved her office across town to the second floor of the opera house. Unlike her stuffy third-floor closet at the town hall, this room was wide and high-ceilinged. When she opened the north and east windows, a soft breeze blew through, carrying summer with it. Robins in the oak tree. Traffic on the street below. The distant, low growl of someone's lawn mower. The scents of cut grass and of sunshine. Sitting behind her maple desk in an antique oak office chair that Mitch had found in the basement and treated with a coat of tung oil, Amy was queen of the world.

On her second morning, she was simultaneously booting up her computer and skimming through the contacts list on her phone when she heard a tap at her open door. She looked up. The sight of Mitch leaning against the doorframe made her smile.

"Mitch! Come in. I have to tell you again what people are saying about your work. They can't get enough of this place. Our summer schedule is already packed full, and we have waiting lists for every class."

He came and sat in the chair across from her. "Thanks. That's good to hear." He scrutinized her face as if looking for something that should have been written there but wasn't.

"What's up?" she asked.

"I worry that you're already working too hard again."

She rolled her eyes. "I know you do. You nag me about it enough. But I'm *okay*, really. That thing in the hospital was just a fluke. I'm all better now." She gestured toward her desktop, at the neat rows of samples, copies, and notes filed in their metal racks. "See? I'm working on December's show, and doing just fine."

He did not smile back. Instead, he leaned forward, elbows on his knees, his fingers steepled under his chin. "Are you sure you're feeling all right?"

"Never better."

"Because you still look like you could stand to gain a few pounds. And a week of vacation wouldn't hurt you either."

"But it would very much hurt progress on the new show. I'm fine, Mitch. Really. Quit worrying."

"You'll never slow down enough to have a normal life, will you?"

"Who wants a normal life?"

"I do, actually."

"I was just kidding."

He picked up a letter opener from her desk and began

turning it in his hands. "I . . . ah . . . I wanted to tell you that I finally got around to asking Crystal to go out with me."

"That's great," Amy said. It didn't feel great. It felt strange. "And did she say yes?"

"Yeah. We're going to a baseball game on Friday, then out for a late dinner."

"Oh. Well . . . it's about time. I've always thought you two were perfect for each other."

"Have you? I guess other people are always quicker to see what's best for you than you are yourself."

"I know what you mean."

"So . . . no objections, then?"

"No objections to what?"

"To my going out with Crystal."

"Are you asking my permission?"

"No. I just wanted to know what you thought about it."

All at once, Amy was exhausted. Mitch was right: she was working too hard. She had to be careful. But her e-mail was open on the monitor, and she saw there was a message from Steve Ayers (*cello,* she thought automatically; *Portland Symphony Orchestra; available seasonally*). Her eyes strayed to this, and with an effort she shook off the threatening lassitude. She had work to do. "I think it's just great, Mitch. You and Crystal have a lot in common. I really hope things work out for the two of you. Let me know how it goes." And as he stood and left her office, she called after him, "Keep me posted, okay?" He did not answer.

She reached for the phone.

CHAPTER

17

THE FORECAST FOR INDEPENDENCE DAY was perfect, as it
was almost every summer in Copper Cove. A week beforehand, the airwaves were thick with phone calls between
the various Darling women. They would celebrate at Piper
Point Beach. Jane and Leander would provide the hot dogs
and hamburgers, condiments and buns. Amy was making
hummus and tabbouleh. Ivy and Nick volunteered a potato
salad, chips, and a cooler full of sodas. Libby and David
were contributing paper napkins, plates and cups, and plastic
utensils. Sephy would bring a whole-wheat pasta salad and
watermelon, and Laura, who was home for a whole week to
see the family and practice with the band, had promised five
pounds of shrimp and sparklers for the kids to light after
dark. Jane had invited Mitch, but he hadn't committed one
way or the other.

The Fourth of July was not only the birthday of the nation; it was Libby Hale's as well. Coincidentally, Libby's older brother, Justice, had the same birthday. "It's uncanny," Libby had been known to wail to Sephy, or more recently to David. "To think that two fanatical patriots like Tom and Abigail Hale—direct descendants of *the* Nathan Hale, no less—should have only *two* children, and that *both* of those children should be born on the Fourth of July, six years apart, and that they should name one of them Justice and the other one Liberty . . . It's freakish! Nobody else has a family as weird as mine."

She never found a sympathetic audience among the Darlings. They merely thought it was funny. Besides, having grown up next door to the Hales, it was old news to them.

The Hales were invited to the cookout, whither they came, bearing a Jell-O salad and a bushel of clams. Libby's father had dug them himself and soaked them in several changes of cornmeal and water to clean the grit from their bellies. At the beach, he planted himself in a folding camp chair with the cooler full of clams on one side and an empty bucket on the other. There, amid clouds of charcoal smoke from the nearby grill, he taught DeShaun the finer points of shucking clams and eating them raw. He found the boy to be an apt pupil, and Ivy spent a good part of the afternoon casting a worried eye on the progress the two of them were making through the bushel. "I hope DeShaun won't make himself sick," she said to her mother.

"If he does, it'll be the last time he overeats on raw seafood," was Jane's pragmatic but unhelpful reply.

Justice Hale had not been home in nearly three years. This, he knew, had disappointed his parents, but he made a point of calling every Sunday afternoon, and he e-mailed them often. It wasn't that he'd stayed away on purpose; it was just that his small-animal practice kept him busy, and Seattle was a long way from Copper Cove in more than just mileage.

But this year was different. His sister was engaged to David Darling, and although Justice had known the Darling family all his life, he felt the need to set eyes on Libby for himself and make sure she was really as happy as her texts and e-mails assured him she was. Accordingly, he had arranged to attend a veterinary conference at Dartmouth and to come north for a few days afterward to spend the holiday in Copper Cove.

While the charcoal grills were heating, he joined Sephy, who was setting the picnic tables. Sephy had practically grown up at his house, was as much a sister to him as Libby was. He hadn't seen her in a few years, and he had the vague idea that she had lost quite a bit of weight, although he wasn't sure. He knew she had been considered a chubby kid, and had been teased for it, just as he had been teased for being too skinny. He was pleased to see her looking so well and happy now. It was nice when the inequities of the early years balanced out in adulthood.

"So you think they're doing the right thing?" he asked her.

"I know they are. I've never seen either of them happier." Sephy handed him a box of plastic cutlery. "Here, want to count these out? There should be eighteen of us."

He began counting forks. "I hear congratulations are in order for you. On your graduation."

"Thank you. It's nice to be done with school." She told him about her job, and he told her about the conference he'd been at, on metabolic disorders of small animals.

They finished setting the tables, and Justice said, "It's good to know Libby has you to look out for her, Sephy. Thanks for being such a good friend to her."

"The pleasure is all mine," she said. "And I'm glad you found time to come home for a few days. I know it means the world to her."

"I'll be back at Christmas for the wedding."

"Then we'll get to see you twice in one year? We should have weddings more often around here."

David's roommate, George the Frustrated Writer, joined the gathering, but Jane noticed that Crystal did not come. She was supposedly in Boston, visiting family, although Jane was not entirely sure she believed this story. Crystal's name had not been mentioned around the house for weeks, and whenever anyone asked after her, Amy changed the subject. Paul was there, however, with a pair of ferrets on leashes, which he handed over to Jada and Hammer as soon as he arrived. Once, Jane had asked Ivy if she thought Paul might be interested in Amy. Ivy had raised an eyebrow and said, "Paul doesn't swing that way." At first, Jane hadn't known what she meant. Her daughter had clarified, "He doesn't like women, Mom."

"He—? Oh!" Jane had caught on then. And ever since, it

had been easier for her to think of Paul as part of the family—just another of her children, albeit older than the rest of them. Not someone who was going to eventually break Amy's heart or have his own broken by her.

Mitch was a different story. He showed up at the picnic just as they were sitting down to eat. Afterward, he spent hours bodysurfing on the incoming tide with Ivy and Amy and the kids. He helped Nick, Justice, David, and DeShaun dig a pair of holes in the sand deep enough to bury Hammer and Jada up to their necks. He threw the Frisbee with Sephy and Laura.

Jane was surprised and pleased at his apparent eagerness to once again be part of the family. Night fell, and still he stayed. When the insect repellent had been brought out and liberally sprayed on everyone except for Amy, who had her own ineffective herbal remedy, they arranged their camp chairs and blankets facing the water and prepared for the show. The tide had turned when the first of the fireworks burst from the Quahog peninsula and exploded over the ocean. A collective "Oh!" went up from the group. Ivy and Jada broke into applause. For twenty minutes, the display went on, giving Jane plenty of leisure to observe the people around her.

David and Libby lay on their backs on a blanket, her head resting on his stomach. Tom Hale sat in a chair, Abigail on the sand, leaning against his knees. Nick had his arms around Ivy. And under the lingering streaks of color in the sky, Jane Darling did not miss the expression on Mitch's face whenever he looked at Amy. Jane closed her eyes against a pang for the man who had once been like a son to her. It was clear that

Amy was oblivious to him. But at some point, she was going to figure out how Mitch felt. And Jane knew her daughter well. Amy had tunnel vision. There was no room in her life right now for anything but her work. Before it was all over, Jane was afraid Mitch was going to be hurt, and badly.

The breeze off the ocean was cool. Laura sat on a blanket with another blanket over her lap and made a show of watching the fireworks. In actuality, her mind was back in Arizona. What was Rob doing right now? He'd texted her that morning to say he'd decided to run over to Greasewood to spend the holiday with his family. What were they like? she wondered. Did his mother spend her life feeding everyone? Were his siblings as noisy as hers? As intrusive? Probably worse, she decided, since there were more of them.

Her thoughts were interrupted by someone nudging her in the back. It was Amy, who had crawled around the back of the group to wedge her way onto Laura's blanket.

"Budge over!" her little sister hissed.

"What now?" said Laura snidely. "Come to nag me about something else?"

"Oh, stop. I just reminded you to buy Sephy a house-warming gift; that's all."

"And lectured me to within an inch of my life about missing her graduation. You're rude and presumptuous, and you don't know how to mind your own business." Laura pulled the blanket around her throat. "Go away."

"Come on, Laura!" Amy whispered. "What was I supposed to say?"

"How about nothing? How about minding your own business for once?"

"I was just standing up for Sephy."

"Sephy's a big girl. She can stand up for herself."

"Right! When has she ever?" Amy was quiet, watching the explosions of crimson and white in the sky over the water. Then, "You forgot about my grand opening too."

Laura sighed. She knew she had dropped the ball on both occasions. And as irritating as Amy might be, as obnoxious and obtrusive, as sophomoric in her black-and-white view of the world . . . it just so happened that this time, she was right. Laura had let down both of her sisters. "It's not your job to be everybody's conscience," she hissed anyway.

"You think I don't know that? I know that!"

"I'm thirty years old; I can manage my own relationships."

Amy's whisper was impassioned. "Well, what do you expect me to do? If I see that something's wrong, I can't just stay quiet."

Laura swept her a freezing look, which was useless in the dark. "You do not have to take up every single wrong that comes across your path and make it a personal cause!"

Amy did not answer until several more bursts of light had cleared from the sky. Then, "I'm cold."

Laura sighed and, rearranging her blanket, threw an edge of it over Amy's bare legs. "Here."

"Thanks." Amy nestled into her sister's arm, shoving her sideways, and pulled the blanket up around her shoulders, robbing Laura of several inches on her own legs.

After a bit, Laura said, "Congratulations on your grand opening. I heard it was really, really good."

"It was," Amy whispered. "Dad recorded it. You should watch it tomorrow."

"I will."

"And maybe you could get Sephy a pair of earrings or something."

"Mind your own business."

"It was just a suggestion."

In the darkness, Laura smiled.

In July, Aunt Sharon flew out from Cleveland for her summer visit. Sephy, who had scheduled five days off to help entertain her, drove her mother to the airport to pick her up.

At baggage claim, they searched the crowd of hot and tired travelers for a sign of her. Aunt Sharon saw them at the same moment they saw her.

"Jane!" she crowed, hurrying over and enveloping her friend in a sonsy embrace. "I know I just saw you in May, but it seems like it's been a year already." She stood back to assess her best friend. "You never change, Jane. You always look like a girl."

Jane laughed. "I don't *feel* like a girl. I feel like a very middle-aged wife and mother. But as far as compliments go, I'll take it."

Sharon turned to Sephy, and a shadow of concern flitted over her face. "Oh, Sephy, you look so thin! You're not still starving yourself?"

Sephy stiffened. "Well, I'm still losing weight, if that's what you mean."

Sharon frowned. "You don't look well, honey. Are you

getting the vitamins you need? Jane, is she getting the right *kinds* of food? I'm concerned about her."

Sephy fought back a surge of irritation. She had lost nearly seventy pounds, it was true, but at a robust size fourteen, it was ridiculous to suggest that she was anywhere near starving herself. *Boundaries,* Carl would remind her, if he were here. *You have the right to set boundaries and ask others to respect them.* Anxiety began to scratch at the inside of her skin, like a trapped creature fighting to get out. She hated these situations, where she was supposed to draw a line in the sand. It was inevitable that someone would be made unhappy. Yet it was clear that something had to be said now, before Aunt Sharon's week of vacation got any further under way. So Sephy flashed her a bright smile and said, "I'm eating well and exercising, and I feel just great. Please don't waste time worrying about me." She said this last with all the firmness she could muster, her mouth dry and her palms damp.

"Are these your bags?" she went on. "Good. No, let me take them—they're both small—and you and Mom just follow." She led them to the car, her pulse in her ears pounding a mixed message of guilt and indignation. The changes she had embraced were no reflection on anyone else. She was not pronouncing judgment on Sharon's life; she was simply choosing something different. Why couldn't her friend see that?

Early the next morning, Sephy drove her mother and Aunt Sharon south to Freeport, where the three of them put in a full day of shopping. They spent the night with Aunt Ellen, Jane's strange, formal older sister, who never called or came to visit them or invited them to come and visit her. Ellen lived alone in Durham, near Freeport, in a spotlessly clean house with a stiff couch and stiffer beds. For supper, she served them dry chicken with rice: four pieces for the four of them, and four precise salads that looked as though they had been weighed out before being arranged on her Royal Doulton plates. Dessert was cookies from a bakery box. Sephy had been to Aunt Ellen's house only once before, when she was ten. She remembered thinking then, as now, that it was so different from the way things were at home, where the furniture was soft and worn and inviting, and there was always too much food on the table, and everyone talked over each other in order to be heard. Here, they labored through the dinner conversation and went to bed early.

The next day, after breakfast (a box of granola cereal, four bananas, and four cartons of yogurt), they said good-bye to Aunt Ellen and drove the fifteen minutes to Portland for more shopping in the old port and dinner and a show.

Even the visit to Aunt Ellen aside, Sephy had never known two more stressful days. Every hour, it seemed, Sharon was pressuring her to eat something. She offered to buy ice cream from the Ben & Jerry's vendor in Freeport, and from Beals in Portland. She paid for dinner and insisted Sephy have both an appetizer and dessert. Sephy avoided the worst by ordering a small salad and a light sorbet, but it seemed to her that Sharon watched her closely to be sure she was eating every bite on her plate.

"Mom, can't you say something to her?" Sephy whispered when Sharon had stepped into the bathroom for her insulin shot. "She's going to feed me to death!"

"Oh, Sephy, don't make a fuss," Jane implored her. "She's just trying to be nice. You know how generous she is."

"I can't keep eating everything she sends my way. I'll explode."

"Couldn't you try, for her sake? She's only here for a week. Let's not spoil her visit with a confrontation. It's not going to kill you to eat a few extra snacks for a day or two."

But it was more than just "a few extra snacks." Every two hours, Aunt Sharon was ready to interrupt their shopping for a coffee break, supplemented by cinnamon buns or cheesecake. Lunch in Freeport was fried clams and french fries with mayonnaise-saturated coleslaw. Sephy began to feel a distinct commiseration with the kind of geese who were said to be raised for foie gras. These birds supposedly had grain forced down their gullets in such quantities that their livers morphed into overdeveloped, inadequate organs, until the geese were carried off to slaughter, sacrificed on the altar of someone else's greed. Never before had Sephy known such sympathy for PETA and its causes.

At first, she felt inept and apologetic for saying no thank you so often. But gradually, a new feeling began to filter to the surface. It started in the fitting room at L.L.Bean, where she was trying on a pair of shorts. They had just come from the heavy lunch of fried clams, and none of the shorts were fitting to Sephy's satisfaction. The pair she was trying on now buttoned easily around her waist, but pulled and stretched across her thighs. Feeling bulky and bloated and generally miserable about herself, she peeled them off and glared at her reflection in the mirror.

Outside the door, the discreet, polite voice of a Bean's employee called, "How are you doing in there? Can I get anything for you?"

You can go away and leave me alone, Sephy wanted to snap. Why couldn't she shop in peace? What had happened to that wonderful, old-fashioned notion? Why couldn't she *eat* in peace, or not eat if she wanted, or choose to stay fat, or work to lose weight without commentary and criticism from the people around her?

"I'm fine, thanks," she said instead to the voice outside the door.

It was then that she remembered her very first session with Dr. Fielding. There were some things she had said in that first session that they had never gotten back around to discussing. And one of them, she remembered, was that she was not a person who ever felt she had the right to say just what she wanted to say.

She began the meticulous folding of the shorts and the re-clipping onto the hanger, and all at once, she knew something that she had not known before: when you never said what you wanted to say—never expressed what you really meant—that was a problem. The thought was so startling, and held so much promise, she had to sit down on the fitting room bench, in her underwear, and catch her breath.

All her life, Sephy had listened to her sisters speak their minds, and she had cringed. But maybe speaking your mind didn't have to look the way Amy did it, plowing over everyone with her opinions. What if Sephy could learn to stand her ground without—as Laura did—hurting and alienating her family in the process? She was always going to be a person who valued tact and kindness. But didn't she have a right, maybe even a responsibility, to say what she wanted to say? Surely both were possible.

It was as though a door in a dark room had been opened just a crack, letting in a beam of light. Behind that door, there might be anything. Everything.

The day Libby's bridesmaids went for their first dress fittings, the whole of New England lay broiling under a record-breaking heat wave. The sun did not so much rise that morning as it simply appeared, burning resentfully through a thick, evil haze of sky. By nine o'clock, when Libby rang the bell of her apartment, Sephy already felt as though she were swimming through the air. The weather report on the Internet said it was eighty-two degrees.

"Eighty-two degrees at nine in the morning!" Sephy exclaimed, flinging open the front door.

Libby's face glowed damp and shiny from the heat. "I hate people who greet you by talking about the temperature," she said cheerfully. "No one ever changed the weather by complaining about it, so let's not. Think of it this way: we're going to climb into my air-conditioned car to drive to the nice, air-conditioned mall, where we'll spend the morning basking in the coolness before we have lunch in a lovely, refrigerated restaurant. The rest of Maine may swelter, but I guarantee we won't even notice."

"I hate people who always think the glass is half-full." Sephy moved aside to let Libby in.

"I learned it from you." Two strangers followed Libby into the apartment. "Seph," said Libby, "these are my other bridesmaids. Sarah, my cousin from Michigan, and Marina, my other cousin from Michigan."

"Hi," said Sephy. "Any cousin of Libby's is a friend of mine. Are you sisters?"

"Not even close," the blonde Sarah said. "Libby's mom and mine are sisters, and Marina comes from the other side."

"My father is Libby's father's brother," put in the dark-haired Marina. "Sarah and I just met for the first time yesterday. We were on the same flight."

"So we're all equally strangers. I'm Sephy, Libby's lifelong neighbor and stalwart friend."

"The best friend a girl could have," Libby added. "Plus, she's our token red-haired bridesmaid. I had to have one of each color."

"I'm so flattered," Sephy said. "I was going to offer you something to drink, but you've hurt my feelings, and now I don't think I will."

"Marina and I didn't hurt your feelings, did we?" spoke up Sarah. "Because we would *love* something to drink before we go back out into that heat. I thought Maine was supposed to be cool?"

They sat at the table drinking cold Diet Cokes and leafing through a stack of bridal magazines Libby had brought along in her shoulder bag. "Here," Libby said, finding the page she wanted and turning it so the other girls could see. "This is the bridesmaids' dress. I was going to surprise you with it, but I can't wait. Isn't it gorgeous?"

It was indeed. Sephy bent closer to examine the photograph. The dress had long, filmy sleeves and a tight bodice that laced up the back. The smooth fabric hugged the flat plane of the model's belly, the curve of her waist. Sephy tried to quell a spurt of terror. She had never worn anything that form-fitting in her life, if you didn't count a bathing suit, which she never wore except to swim laps. For a moment she saw herself standing half-naked in front of everyone at Libby's wedding, looming hugely, rolls of fat bursting from the seams of sea-green organdy while the bride stood, diminished, in the wide shadow cast by her maid of honor. Sephy recognized this as a reflex of old habit and tried to shake herself out of it. She was not fat anymore. No one was going to be looking at her. They were going to be focused on Libby, who would rightly be the center of attention the whole day. Still, Sephy thought that if she could put on a tight dress that would expose every bulge and curve and walk down the aisle and stand there for half an hour in front of two hundred guests, it might be the bravest thing she had ever done.

"We won't be able to try on the exact dresses today," Libby explained along the way to David's Bridal, "because they have to be ordered. But we'll try on some others, and they can get your measurements and find out what sizes you'll need. When the real dresses come in, they can be altered if they have to be."

At the store, Sephy slipped into the dress the salesgirl handed her. It was a stiff, shiny, royal-blue affair, nothing like the soft, clinging green dresses Libby had chosen. But it was of a similar cut, which was the point, and when she had zipped it up the back, she stood in her changing cubicle, gazing at herself in the mirror. She stood there so long that Libby knocked on the door.

"Are you alive in there?"

Sephy opened the door a crack and motioned her in.

"What's wrong?" Libby asked, squeezing into the small space. Her eyes widened. "You look great, Seph!"

Sephy looked at herself in the mirror again. "Do I? All I can think is that I'm wearing my prom dress again."

"Why? That was ages ago."

"Do you remember that day, Lib? You wore lilac chiffon and looked perfectly gorgeous."

"You wore black," Libby said, "and you looked beautiful too. We double-dated."

"Your brother was the only person kind enough to go with me. He danced with me during every slow dance so I wouldn't have to stand on the sidelines alone." Remembering it, Sephy felt her heart twist in pain for the girl she had been that night—awkward and uncomfortable in her unflattering dress, invisible to all the beautiful people in the room. "He's been my hero ever since."

Libby was silent, and Sephy felt her sympathy. One thing she had always appreciated about her best friend was that Libby did not try to pretend away her fatness, but had suffered through it with her over the years.

"Did you know I wore black that night because it's supposed to be slimming?"

"No."

"It's true. As if you could slim someone as big as I was just by changing the color of her clothes."

"Come on, Seph. Don't be mean. That's my best friend you're talking about."

"The night of the prom, I put on the dress, and I bulged out everywhere. Just fat roll upon fat roll, with my bare arms all jiggly and covered with cellulite. I looked at myself in the mirror, and I started to cry. I knew I looked like a circus sideshow."

Tears stood out in Libby's eyes. "Don't say those things about yourself."

"It wasn't just prom night. I went through that every time I got dressed in the morning, every single day of my life. It was just worse the night of the prom because it was a night when everyone was so focused on beauty."

They looked at their reflections side by side in the mirror. "You've never told me what changed last year, why you started going to those meetings, and swimming, and . . . all of this." Libby's voice was tentative. "I mean, if you don't mind my asking."

"No, you can ask. It wasn't one big thing. Maybe it was a perfect storm of a lot of little things. Like, there was a big concert at school. Everyone had a date except me. I ended up babysitting for one of my prof's kids. I suddenly saw that unless I made some changes, every special occasion in my life was going to be like that: everyone else able to enjoy it to the fullest, and me held back, holding down the fort, maintaining things so all the beautiful people could have a good time. I couldn't stand the thought of that. I wanted to have a life I could love. It was that, and . . . other things." Even now, Sephy could not bring herself to tell her best friend about not fitting in the airplane seat.

"How much have you lost?"

"Eighty-seven pounds this morning." She gestured to the dress. "This is a size twelve, but you know what?"

"What?"

"When I look in the mirror, I see myself squeezed into my

black satin prom gown, spilling over the sides of it, holding my breath so I don't split a seam somewhere."

"Oh, Sephy—"

"I'm still fat inside."

Libby bit her lip.

Sephy shook her head, and her voice became brisk. "Here, unzip me, will you? I'm going to order my dress in a size eight."

"*Eight?* Sephy, how much more weight are you going to lose?"

"I'll know when I lose it."

"Don't go overboard. Don't get . . . you know, crazy about this. You look fine the way you are. You look great."

"I'm not going to go crazy. I just know I'm on a journey that I haven't finished yet."

"Well . . . okay," said Libby, unzipping the dress. "But keep this in mind, Seph: you're never going to lose enough weight to shed the fat girl inside. You're going to have to figure out a different way to do that."

The second week in August, Laura faced a decision that had to be made. She dreaded the phone call to Ivy, who was in no way going to understand, but on a Saturday morning, she gritted her teeth and dialed the number anyway. "I'm calling to say I won't be able to come home for David and Libby's wedding after all," she told her twin.

"But David will be so disappointed. And what about the *band*!"

"I have a perfectly valid reason."

The silence on the other end was a beat too long. Then, "I'm sure you do."

Laura had expected this. "Forget it. I can tell you're not prepared to listen, or to give me the benefit of the doubt."

Ivy sounded very patient. "Tell me, then. Why can't you come?"

It was a matter of conflicting work schedules, Laura explained. And her church was serving a meal at the homeless shelter that day. Also, the plane ticket back home had turned out to be much more expensive than she'd counted on.

Ivy murmured appropriate responses, but Laura could not help feeling patronized.

"Now, don't you all be mad at me. It's not my fault," she said.

"Of course it's not." But Laura knew her sister didn't really feel that way.

She hung up and poured herself a glass of wine. Ten o'clock in Arizona was surely five o'clock somewhere in the world, she thought peevishly. It really *wasn't* her fault. She had been very clear from the start that she did not plan to play in David's wedding band. But had her family listened to her? Could they take no for an answer? Of course not. Laura had been coerced into it, and she reserved the right to change her mind if she wanted to. That David and her sisters and her parents would be disappointed was beside the point.

She sipped at her wine and fought down a rising sense of something like queasiness. Emotional nausea, she thought. What was the word for that? *Repugnance.* Self-repugnance? That was ridiculous. She was not going to castigate herself just because everyone thought she should have made different choices. It was her life to live, and no one else's.

She picked up her phone and pulled up Rob's number. When he answered, she said, "I can't go back to Maine for my brother's wedding."

He was silent, as Ivy had been. Laura had never felt so judged in her life. "Why not?" he said at last.

She gave him her reasons. "And it turns out they didn't need me in the band after all. They had another guitarist waiting in the wings all the time. Someone who's been practicing with them, standing in for me."

"Really? Who?"

"Someone from the church, I think. So . . . no harm, no foul."

"Still, your family must be disappointed."

"Not too badly. I told them a while ago that I might not be able to make it. They understand."

"*You* must be disappointed, to be missing such a once-in-a-lifetime event."

She sighed. "I am. You have no idea how disappointed. But my boss just won't cooperate. I have to work the day before and the day after Christmas."

"That's too bad."

She knew he didn't believe her.

"Oops!" she said brightly. "I have another call coming in. I'll talk to you later, Rob!" She punched End and threw her phone across the room, where the rubber case bounced off the TV. The phone skidded under the couch. She drained her glass of wine in one swallow, and poured herself another.

Ivy hung up from her conversation with Laura and dialed the direct number she had learned by heart.

It rang three times. "Bailey Darling." Her social worker cousin's voice sounded distracted, and in the background, Ivy heard the rapid-fire clicking of a keyboard.

"Bailey, it's Ivy."

The clicking stopped. "Ivy. Hey, how are the kids?" It was Bailey who had arranged for Ivy and Nick to have custody of Hammer, Jada, and DeShaun when the children had been abandoned by their mother.

"Fine. That's not why I'm calling."

"Oh. Okay, why *are* you calling?"

"Do you still play the electric guitar?"

Her cousin laughed. "Not in years. Why?"

Ivy told her what she wanted.

At her office in Augusta, Bailey hung up the phone and stared at it. She could hardly believe what she had just agreed to.

A knock on her open door brought her back to the present.

"Got plans for lunch?" It was Kevin, who worked in adult protective services down the hall. He frowned at her. "You look kind of pale. Everything all right?" Kevin was one of her best friends. He knew her well.

"Guess what I just agreed to do?"

"Umm . . . run for Congress?"

"Ha, right! No, I'm playing guitar for my cousin's wedding reception on Christmas Day."

"Sweet! I didn't know you played."

"I really don't. I haven't played in years. That's why I'm pale."

"Christmas is a long time away. You've got a few months to dust off, get back in practice. It'll be fun."

"I'm not so sure." She leaned forward and rested her forehead on a stack of file folders on the desk. "I shouldn't have said yes."

"What *can't* you do, Bailey? You're the smartest person I've ever met."

She sat up. "What are you doing on Christmas Day?"

He grinned. "Going to a wedding with you?"

"Darn right you are."

"Good. Let's get some lunch."

"Hi, Jan." Sephy stood in the doorway of her manager's office and tried not to cough. Although signs posted everywhere around the hospital announced that this was a fragrance-free facility, this rule did not seem to apply to Jan Winston-Jacobson. She moved around in a nearly palpable cloud of rank scent that had, more than once, been the subject of complaint from patients.

"One moment, Sephy," said Jan, without looking away from her computer screen. She typed a few more lines and, still without looking at Sephy, picked up the phone and punched in a number. Sephy wondered whether she was supposed to go in and sit down or just stand there in the doorway until she was invited. She stayed where she was.

"Ah, yes, Simone!" Jan exclaimed, still not looking at Sephy. "I'm glad I caught you." Everyone knew that Simone was Jan's au pair. "Listen, I want to be sure you have Apple wear her pink skirt with the striped leggings today and the rose suede shoes. It's her dance camp's end-of-summer field trip to the ballet. Yes, the pink suede Mary Janes, that's right. Mmmm-hmmmm . . . ." Pause.

"Yes, she can wear her pink leotard under the skirt if she wants, but be sure to pack a sweater in her backpack, in case the theater's cold. Pack the white one with the faux-fur collar. And if you would, put her hair up in two pigtails. Not down, in low pigtails, but *up*, on top of her head." Pause.

"Fine, fine. There are some free-range eggs in the fridge for breakfast, and some Brie, flaxseed flatbread, and apples and carrot sticks for her lunch. Oh, and I bought some organic almonds, if you could pack those separately as a snack for her."

Sephy shifted from foot to foot in the doorway. Jan finished the conversation with her daughter's au pair and hung up the phone. She closed her eyes, rolled her neck and took a couple of deep, slow breaths, blowing each one out through pursed lips. At last, she turned.

"Now, Sephy. Come in, come in. Have a seat."

Sephy sat low in a webbed chair across the desk from her boss.

"Let's see, now . . . where did I put your file?" Jan shuffled a few things around on her desk and came up with a manila folder. "Here it is. All right. Yes . . . Yes. Let me see . . ."

Jan found the reading glasses on a chain around her neck, adjusted them on the end of her nose, and opening the folder, read silently from the top page. "Hmmm . . . oh yes . . . mmmm . . ." The expression on her face did not imbue Sephy with hope.

At last, she looked up. "I'm afraid, Sephy, that we are going to have to ask you to complete another month of orientation before we can let you work independently."

If Jan had slapped her, Sephy could not have been more shocked. "*What?* Why? I'm signed off on all my skills. I've been satisfactory in everything. I take a full patient assignment every night—"

Jan interrupted her. "I can't pinpoint this need to any specific deficit in your practice, Sephy. But it's my considered, professional belief that you lack confidence as a nurse, and that your confidence, and therefore your patients' well-being, would be better served by giving you a further month of orientation. After that, we'll re-evaluate where you stand and go from there."

Sephy stared at her. She felt disoriented, unsure of her footing.

"Was there anything you wanted to add?" Jan asked.

Sephy blinked. "I'm not . . . I don't lack confidence. My preceptor says I'm doing great. I've been checked off—"

"Well, *Sephy*, unfortunately, although Jennifer is your preceptor, she does not have the last word on when your orientation is complete. Three months is standard, but I've been doing this job a long time, and it is my belief— a belief grounded in considerable professional experience, I might add—that you would benefit from one more month of orientation." Jan sat back, clasping her hands behind her head.

Sephy could think of nothing to say except, at last, a muttered, "Okay." With nerveless fingers, she signed the form Jan slid across the desk to her. She hated feeling that her boss was displeased with her. In an effort to smooth things over, she asked, "So how is Apple doing these days, Jan? She must be about six or seven now?"

"She's eight. And she's doing just fine. She's a lovely, talented, *confident* girl. In fact, I would say that's the characteristic that defines her most: her confidence." Jan looked meaningfully at Sephy, over the tops of her glasses. Sephy wanted to crawl away. Somehow, she managed to stand and find the doorway. The cloying scent of Jan's perfume followed her all the way to the elevator.

CHAPTER

18

"So, I was thinking of adding a number to the show," Amy said at her weekly staff meeting. "Just a small one," she was quick to add. Paul and Crystal protested loudly, and she held up a hand. "Wait! Hear me out. You're going to *love* it. It's a short, jazzy rendition of 'All I Want for Christmas Is You.' Not the whole song, just maybe the chorus, with a little tap number—"

"Come *awn*, Amy," said Paul. "I can't take on one more thing for this show. I mean it."

"But, Paul, I saw the cutest version of it on YouTube. We could totally do it here! It doesn't have to be complicated—"

He was shaking his head. "No way. I ain't got a single spare minute to choreograph another dance, no matta how simple, let alone teach it to the cast and rehearse it. I gotta put my foot down this time."

Amy looked at Crystal for a sign of support, but her

wardrobe girl was absorbed in studying her own shoes and would not look Amy's way.

"Crystal?"

She shook her head.

"Well," Amy said tightly. "All right, then. I guess we'll cross that idea off the list." She made a show of putting a line through the page of her notepad.

"Have mercy, Amy. We're only human," said Paul.

"Nobody said you weren't."

By the time the meeting was over, both Crystal and Paul had become noticeably cooler toward her. In fact, despite the August heat wave going on outside, Amy had to say the atmosphere in her office had turned downright frosty.

"I have a plan," Libby announced, sailing through the front door of Sephy's apartment. "It is *so* hot out there."

"I thought you never complained about the weather." Sephy took a couple of Diet Cokes from the refrigerator. "Is this plan of yours for you or for me?"

"For you. Listen to this: I think you should ask Gorgeous Gabe Michaud out while he's here for the wedding."

Sephy recoiled. "I couldn't do that!"

"Why not? I asked David to marry me, for pete's sake. Surely you can ask a man out on one simple date."

"No way. I just . . . couldn't."

"Why not? Guys are always giving you a second look these days. Gabe's bound to as well."

Libby was right. Men did look at her differently. Strangers—men and women both—smiled when they made eye contact. Just the day before, when she had gone through the line at Hannaford, the bagger had asked if she wanted help taking her groceries to the car. No one had ever offered such a thing before. With the latest five pounds behind her, it was as though Sephy had turned some kind of magic corner and become suddenly not invisible.

"Look what I brought." Libby held it up. "David's high school yearbook."

"You think of everything!" Sephy pounced on it and flipped through the pages to Gabe Michaud's senior picture. "*Look* at him!" she sighed.

"Pretty hot, all right, even with last decade's haircut. I'm sure he's only improved with age."

Sephy skimmed the list of accomplishments under Gabe's name. "Valedictorian. Prom king. I forgot he and David played football together. He used to come over once in a while on a Sunday afternoon to watch a game. Remember spying on them from the hallway?"

"And inventing excuses to go in and out of the family room while they were in there? 'Oh, excuse us. Sephy left her math book in here.' Or, 'We made brownies. Would you guys like some?' We were pathetic."

"Neither one of them so much as looked at us as long as the game was on."

Libby popped the top on her Diet Coke. "David said he has a son now."

Sephy felt deflated. "He's married? I thought you were trying to get us together."

"He's not married; he just has a son. And he works for some kind of electronics dealer in Virginia."

Sephy brightened. "I love electronics."

"Yeah, right."

"Well, I could *learn* to love electronics."

"Someone still has a cru-ush," Libby singsonged.

"Not really, but I might have one before it's all over. Anyway, it won't matter. He's bound to have a girlfriend. I'm sure he's completely unavailable."

"But if he were available, it would be a temptation."

"Libby, it's Gabe *Michaud*."

"I see what you mean."

"It would be a definite temptation."

All summer, Amy's work had been carried out in a milieu of pounding hammers and the shrill whine of electric saws as Mitch and his crew worked on the opera house's second floor. In spite of the cleaning woman's best efforts, Amy's office was perpetually covered in a layer of plaster dust. At first, she had been irritated by the mess and the noise and had threatened to go to Mitch and complain. But Crystal had pointed out that the work had to get done, and it was unrealistic to suggest that the crew only use their power tools after office hours. If they were too bothered by it, Crystal reasoned shrewdly, they could always move their offices back to the third floor of the town hall until the renovations were finished. Amy, appreciating this logic, learned to tune out the sounds of construction. For weeks, they formed a sort of white noise to her day, a sensory backdrop that, together with the scents of fresh sawdust, plaster, and paint, came to personify for her the birth of the arts program.

On the last day of August, Amy became aware that something seemed out of kilter. She looked up from a script she was reading, cocked her head to one side, and frowned. Silence. That was the problem. Or near silence, anyway. No shrieking saw, no hammers banging on two-by-fours or tip-tipping against crown molding and beadboard. No men calling to each other over the powering-down whine of machinery. Only the sound of some distant, murmured conversation. She waited. The silence seemed to ring with a high pitch in her ears. She shrugged and went back to the script.

Half an hour later, Mitch knocked at her door. His brown Carhartt jeans were coated in a film of sawdust, and he smelled faintly of gasoline. "Well, that's it," he said. "We're done."

"What?"

"We're done. Finished."

"Finished with what?"

"All of it."

"*All* of it?"

He gave a mock bow, and she could tell he was pleased with himself. "Yes, ma'am. There's just the painting of the interior walls, and the floors to be sanded and sealed, but I've subcontracted those things out to local guys. My crew will clean up our stuff here today, and the painter can start tomorrow."

"You mean you won't be working here anymore?"

"Nope."

Something had shifted from the way it was supposed to be, leaving Amy off balance. "You weren't supposed to be done for another month or six weeks at least."

"True. But I was pushed at the beginning, remember, and I finished early."

"Oh. Well . . . that's great." She wished she could sound as pleased for him as she knew she should be. "What will you do next?"

Mitch scuffed the toe of one work boot against the threshold of her office and stared at it. "There's still that job offer in Florida."

"That's a long way away."

"It's a job."

It was the same bereft sadness she had always felt when one of her older sisters went away to college at the beginning of a term. These days, Crystal spoke to her only when necessary to conduct business, and Paul was hardly friendlier. If Mitch left, she would be alone. All the fun would be gone from work. "Why does everyone have to go away?" Amy said. She had the sense that she sounded about seven years old, but she didn't care.

"Is there . . . I can't really think of any reason I should stay. Can you?"

Amy could. She could think of a lot of reasons. "How about us—your family?"

Mitch kicked at the floor. "Well . . . that's complicated."

"How about Crystal, then? You two have just started going out. Have you thought about what your leaving will do to her? Isn't *she* reason enough for you to stay?"

He raised his eyes to hers. "You think I should stay for Crystal."

"Yes! I think it's . . . it's cold and *mean* for you to go away and leave her at a time like this." Amy's voice was rising. She couldn't help it. She felt foolishly close to tears.

"Crystal and I have only been out three or four times. I'm not going to stay for her."

She couldn't believe how unfeeling he was. "You don't deserve her."

"No, you're right. Crystal deserves far better than me. I think she understands that."

Amy stared at the script on her desk. She heard the voices of the construction workers down the hall, the clunking sounds of tools and equipment being moved, and her own breathing. After a moment, she asked, "When do you leave?"

"Day after tomorrow. I'll drive down. The job starts Monday."

"Oh."

More silence. Then, "Well . . . it's been a pleasure, Amy."

Tears pricked her eyes, and through them, she smiled. "Not always."

"No, not always. But . . . eventually."

"That's right."

"I'll probably just say good-bye now, then."

"Oh." She got up and came around the desk. He held open his arms and she went into them. "Believe it or not, I will miss you, Mitch."

"I'll miss you too, little brat."

His arms were tight around her for a moment; then he gave her a rough kiss on her forehead and pushed her away.

"Text me," she said.

"Yeah, okay."

She knew he wouldn't. Mitch had never texted her when they'd worked in the same town. She tried again. "You should stop by and say good-bye to Mom and Dad. They'll be so sorry to see you go."

He cleared his throat. "I will."

"Don't just say it. Really *do* it."

"I will."

She wasn't saying any of the things she really meant. "Thank you for all your hard work, Mitch. I'm so proud of what you've done here, I can't even tell you."

He turned to go, holding up one hand in a farewell. "Thanks."

"I'll miss you," she called.

He dropped his hand and looked back. "Will you?"

"Yes." She really would. His leaving would rend a hole in the fabric of her days that she would hardly know how to fill.

"Good," he said. "I'll miss you too." And he was gone.

Sephy was finishing her documenting and looking forward to getting home to bed. It had been a busy night, her fourth twelve-hour shift in a row, and she was left with all the energy of a wrung-out dishrag. Six hours of sleep and three days off was just what the doctor ordered. She and Libby were going to the mall tonight. Sephy had finally conceded that her clothes had, once again, become too big for her. It was time to go down another size. That thought alone would buoy her through the final hour and ten minutes of her shift. Then she was out of here.

"Oh, Sephy," someone said behind her.

Sephy swiveled around in her chair. She smiled and tried to infuse her voice with warmth. "Good morning, Jan."

"I'm going to need you to stay over this morning until eleven, Sephy." Jan's voice was brisk, and she fixed her eyes somewhere over Sephy's head. "One of the day shift nurses called out with a sick child. We can't get a replacement until eleven. You can take her patients until then."

"Wha—no! Jan, this is my fourth night in a *row!*" Sephy heard the whine in her voice, and hated it. She had no patience for nurses who complained about their schedules, who went on and on about how tired they were, how busy. Weren't they all exhausted and understaffed and overwhelmed? Sephy had vowed that she would distinguish herself at work by being that person who never complained. She would do what was asked of her and do it cheerfully. Yet this protest had slipped out before she could stop it, and when it did, Jan seized on it like a cat pouncing on a mouse.

"Well, *Sephy* . . . maybe you should plan your schedule a little more thoughtfully next time. Nobody made you work four twelve-hour shifts in a row. That was your own choice." Jan went on in her patient, patronizing tone. "And now, I need someone to fill in in an emergency, and you are the nurse with the least seniority, so I will expect you to stay over until eleven and take a full patient assignment until your replacement gets here."

There was no time to protest, or to think of an answer before Jan had turned and swept from the nurses' station, perfume trailing her like a poisonous cloud.

"Janey, can you give me a hand here?" Leander went to the living room piano, where his wife was practicing that morning's prelude for the church service. He waited until she stopped. "I can't seem to get my shirt buttoned," he said, sounding helpless. "I'm just all thumbs."

Jane tutted and stood up, straightening the sides of his dress shirt. "Darned arthritis," she said, slipping the buttons through their buttonholes. "I'm telling you, Leander, this getting older isn't for the faint of heart."

"No, it's not. But I suppose it's better than the alternative."

She laughed as she finished the final button. "Here, I'll do your sleeves too."

He submitted to having his shirt cuffs buttoned. "Thank you. I feel silly, having to be dressed like this."

"Well, we're both a little stiffer than we used to be," Jane said. "Go take a few Advil. It'll help. Then we'd better head out, or we'll be late for church."

Leander went off to the bathroom to find the Advil, and Jane watched him go with concern. Other than a little stiffness in his knees, her husband had never suffered from arthritis a day in his life.

In the small town of Trenton, Florida, Mitch pulled his pickup into a parking space and punched a number into his phone. Lenny, who had set up the job for him, answered.

"Hey, buddy, I'm here," Mitch said.

"All right! You're, like, at the apartment already? Hold on. I'll be there in ten minutes with the key."

"I'll be sitting right here."

"Hey, you want me to bring over a six-pack to celebrate? Or we could go out somewhere. There's a place around the corner from you that's not too bad. Got a couple of cute college girls who tend bar. Well . . . kinda cute, anyway."

Mitch felt his stomach plummet to the floorboards. Already it was starting, and he hadn't even gotten out of the truck. If Amy were here, she would tell him to pray. He gave it a try. *What do I say, God?*

He didn't get an answer, so he ad-libbed it. "Ah . . . look, man, I've been driving twenty-five hours straight and I'm really beat. If I'm going to be up for work tomorrow, I have to get some sleep. If you can just get over here and let me into the apartment, that would be great."

"All right, dude, we'll do it another night. See you in ten."

Mitch closed the phone and let out a breath. He knew Lenny from the old days, but he'd forgotten the man's enthusiasm and stamina for a good time. For tonight anyway, he had dodged a bullet. But it was going to come at him again and again. For the first time in years, Mitch felt afraid of something.

"Oh, Sephy."

The cool, unguent voice of her nurse manager, accompanied by an offensive waft of scent, froze Sephy in place. She had just swiped her badge to enter the med room, but now she stood where she was, inert with dread.

"Please look at me when I'm speaking to you," Jan said. "It's a matter of professionalism."

Sephy turned, her face a rictus mask, and for this she was grateful. It wouldn't do, for example, to turn and face Jan snarling and spitting and lunging for her throat. Much better to look calm and neutral, which was how Sephy was certain she looked, in spite of herself. "Yes, Jan." She could not will a smile any higher than the corners of her mouth.

It was immaterial: Jan was not concerned with Sephy's reaction. At any given moment, Jan was only concerned with what Jan needed, wanted, and felt. Her voice was brisk. "I'm going to need you to work Labor Day."

"I'm not scheduled, though," Sephy said. "I worked Memorial Day." The holiday schedules were made up years in advance. There was never any question about who was supposed to work which of them.

Even as she said it, she knew that she might as well direct her words to the dispenser of hand sanitizer on the wall, for all Jan was listening. She made one more feeble stab. "It's not my turn."

"Well, Sephy, as you know, one of our day shift nurses has left, and I need someone to fill in until I hire someone new. We all have to be willing to sacrifice from time to time for the sake of the team. So I'll tell Char to write you into the schedule for Labor Day, all right?"

Jan did not wait for an answer before she turned and headed for her office. Sephy, watching her go, was suffused with a helpless outrage. Not for the first time, she wondered, *Why is she out to get me?*

Before, it had always been a rhetorical question, the kind that flashed through her mind with the simultaneous understanding that there was no real answer. It was just the way of things. Jan was unfair; Sephy was a pushover. Jan was thoughtless and rude; Sephy responded with kindness and got trampled.

She had thought, had pinned her hopes on the belief that kindness was the only weapon she needed in this fight. Wasn't there a saying about killing people with kindness? Didn't the Bible say, "Through patience a ruler can be persuaded, and a gentle tongue can break a bone"?

But it didn't seem to be working with Jan. And why *was* her manager out to get her, anyway?

This time, on the heels of the rhetorical question came the remembered words of Bree. *"You don't stand up for yourself. Jan knows she can push you around and you won't complain."*

For four years, Sephy had worked as a CNA at the hospital. Plenty of those shifts had been worked on this floor, with Jan as her boss. For years, she had known her manager as a tyrant both by reputation and by experience. Jan was probably (and at this thought, Sephy was unable to suppress just a twinge of joy) the most universally disliked person on the hospital staff. In spite of that, Sephy had always chosen to think the best of her. She had interpreted Jan's abrasive manner and coercive form of leadership as professionalism.

But now she wondered: Was it possible that Jan was just a bully?

As Sephy signed out the narcotics she needed from the Pyxis and brought them to her patient, an idea, or the seed of an idea, began to take root. At seven thirty, when the sun was fully up outside the windows and the day shift nurse had taken over her patients, Sephy went to the charge nurse.

"I wanted to check the schedule for Labor Day," she said easily. "Just want to be sure I'm not scheduled to work that day."

Char flipped the schedule open to the holiday Monday and scanned down through it. "No, looks like we're all covered. Anyway, you worked Memorial Day, didn't you? So you wouldn't be scheduled for Labor Day."

"That's what I thought," Sephy said, "but with Allison leaving, I wondered if that would affect things."

Char frowned down at the schedule again. "No, Allison wasn't scheduled to work Labor Day in any case, so her leaving doesn't change anything. You have the day off. Go and enjoy your holiday."

It was just as she had suspected: Jan had been bluffing in order to bully her.

"Thanks," said Sephy. "I fully intend to."

Jane was reading the paper at the breakfast bar one morning when Leander choked on a mouthful of his raisin bran.

"Heavens!" she said, pounding him between the shoulder blades while he sputtered and coughed.

"Went down the wrong pipe," he gasped at last, his eyes streaming.

"Leander," she said. "I think it's time to see the doctor."

He looked at his sodden cereal and nodded.

"I'll call as soon as they open," Jane said.

"Paul, what's on the agenda this afternoon?" Amy asked.

Her choreographer's answer was terse. "I'll finish teachin' the sugarplum fairies their dance in classroom 2, and we'll practice it. Your mom's got the choir in the auditorium, and other people will be comin' in and out for fittings with Crystal in wardrobe."

"What about the orchestra?"

"Dean's got his own schedule. You'll hafta ask him."

Amy had offered her father the job of conducting the twelve-piece string ensemble for the Holiday Extravaganza, as it was now being called, but Leander had regretfully declined. He just didn't have the energy for it these days, he'd told her. However, Dean Street, the local middle school music teacher, had jumped at the chance.

"I'd love to work with adults who are really *motivated*," he'd told her. They had agreed easily on the music, and he'd proven himself more than capable, even pulling in a few of the more advanced high school musicians to play with the adult orchestra. Amy liked having people of all ages involved in the programs. It was a *community* arts center, after all. At the moment, her youngest participant was five-year-old Sophie Barnes, who was one of the sugarplum fairies. The oldest was eighty-five-year-old Jessie LaRoche, who sang in the choir. Jane, as accompanist, had confided to Amy, "Her voice is a little wobbly, but after all these years she can still carry a tune like nobody's business."

Since Paul, Crystal, Dean, and her mother seemed to have things well in hand, Amy headed back to her office. She needed to call Linda from Butter Side Up Catering to finalize the menu for the cast party on closing night. As she pulled out her phone to find the number, it rang in her hand.

For a second, she was confused. Had Linda read her mind and called *her*? Then Mitch's face appeared on the screen. She answered before the second ring. "Mitch!"

"Hey, you."

"Hey, yourself. How are things going down there?" She realized she was smiling hugely at nothing but the empty stairway and sank down to sit on a step.

"Hot. Iss *hot* down here."

She laughed. "Did you think it was going to be anything else?"

"I din' think it was gonna be so *hot*."

She leaned against the wall and frowned. "You sound weird. Are you okay?"

"No. I'm *not* okay." He was forceful and petulant. "Iss *hot*. An' I miss you."

Oh. Oh no . . . "Have you been drinking?" Amy asked.

Silence. Then, "Maybe. Maybe a lil'."

Oh, Mitch . . . Despair hit her in the stomach and settled to the bottom. What did you say to one of the strongest people you knew when his strength was not enough to keep him from sliding into the pit again? Should she have been there with him? Could she have prevented this from happening? What she said, feebly, was, "You shouldn't be drinking."

"Oh, tha's right. I should listen to *you*." Mitch's voice was querulous. "You, who's . . . who've never had a good time in your narrow little virgin life. *You* wouldn't know a good time if it stood up and bit you in the—"

"Shut up!" Amy cried. Her voice echoed in the beautiful, empty stairwell that Mitch had so patiently rebuilt. "Just . . . *stop* it. You're not yourself."

"Yeah, I am," came his slurred voice across the miles. "I'm more myself than you've ever seen me. You have no idea who I am."

"I'm hanging up now. I'd love to talk to you when you're sober, but not now."

"Don't you hang up on me!" he roared.

She hung up on him.

"Sephy, what's this about?" Char stopped her on her way to the locker room as she was leaving at the end of her shift. The charge nurse read from a yellow Post-it note stuck to her finger. "'Need extra RN to work Columbus Day. Sephy Darling is up: please schedule her 7A-7P.' It's from Jan."

Sephy felt a surge of rage that was in no way moderated by her lack of sleep. She had directly defied Jan's command to work on Labor Day. Would the woman never leave her alone? She flashed a humorless smile at Char. "I'm sure it's a misunderstanding. I'll clear it up with her."

"Well . . . okay. Just let me know."

Sephy took a few minutes in the locker room to brush her hair and touch up her makeup. Might as well go into the lion's den with her best foot forward. When she felt reasonably well collected, she made her way to Jan's office.

Her manager was squinting at a computer screen.

Sephy knocked perfunctorily on the doorjamb and walked in. "Jan," she said.

Jan glanced up and said, "Oh, Sephy. Give me a moment here. I'm almost finished."

"Actually, I don't have a moment. My shift ended ten minutes ago." In the small office, Sephy's voice rang back to her own ears with a bravado that was wholly unconvincing.

Jan looked up and eyed her, with a touch of astonishment, over the tops of her reading glasses. "*Well.* You sound distressed, Sephy. Please, by all means, come in and have a seat and tell me what's on your mind." With a gracious sweep of her arm, she indicated the low chairs in front of her desk.

"No, I'll stand, thanks. This won't take a minute."

Jan's eyebrows went up.

Sephy forged ahead. "Char is under the impression that you want me to work Columbus Day."

Jan opened her mouth, but Sephy spoke over her. "I told her it's a mistake, of course, since that's not my holiday to work."

Jan said nothing.

"According to HR, I have to work one minor holiday a year, and I've worked it. On Memorial Day."

Her manager's eyes narrowed. Her nostrils flared.

Sephy took a step closer to the desk. "So . . . it seems like we're on the same page then. I shouldn't be working Columbus Day, and *you* shouldn't be asking me to work any more holidays or weekends or overtime shifts that I'm not already scheduled for. Is that right?"

Jan's face was an unattractive, mottled pink. The scent of her perfume hung in the air like a tired sachet from the drawer of someone's old grandmother. "If your shift is over, Sephy, I hope you're not still on the time clock."

"I *am* still on the clock. My work schedule is hospital business. I think it's reasonable that I conduct that business on hospital time."

"You," Jan whispered, her nostrils flared and white, "may punch out and go home."

"Sure. I just wanted to be sure we understand each other about Columbus Day."

Jan glared at her in silence. Sephy turned and left the office. By the time she had punched out and her heart had stopped hammering, she was in possession of a new piece of wisdom that she had never considered before. When you pushed back at a bully, the bully would back down. She left the hospital with a free Columbus Day weekend ahead and a sensation she had never experienced before. She felt powerful. Immensely powerful.

Bailey Darling plugged her guitar into the amplifier in her aunt Jane's basement and tried to calm nerves that were fluttering like a luffing jib. She hadn't played in front of other people in years. What if she messed everyone up?

The week of their phone call, Ivy had mailed her a thick packet of music and Bailey had been practicing every night. Still, she had always been one to have terrible stage fright. She was fine, as long as she was playing by herself in her bedroom. But the minute she had ever tried to perform for anyone at recitals or school concerts, it was as though her mind was shot through with Novocain and she couldn't remember any of the chords or notes she had learned.

To her left, Sephy said, "Okay, Bailey? Ready to start?"

Bailey gave a tense nod.

"Ivy? Amy?"

"Let's do it!" said Ivy.

"Okay . . . and three and four and—"

Bailey missed the cue. "Sorry!" she called. "Sorry, I—"

"Just keep going!" Sephy shouted. "Jump in anywhere. You're doing fine."

Bailey concentrated hard, and at the next phrase, she joined them. It felt a little like leaping onto a speeding train and trying to hold on. Ooh, this had been a bad idea. She,

Bailey Darling, was the least spontaneous person she knew. She was going to be the ruin of The Darlings.

After work on Wednesday, Mitch stopped by his mailbox in the lobby and found an envelope there. The first real mail he'd gotten since moving in, not counting Walmart flyers and a credit card offer or two. He shifted the twelve-pack he was carrying to his left arm and opened the envelope as he took the stairs, two at a time. It was the invitation to David Darling's wedding on Christmas Day.

He unlocked his apartment door and set the twelve-pack on the couch. The idea of heading north again made something in him feel whole—something he hadn't realized was broken. Part of him dreaded facing Amy after that last, drunken phone call. Still . . . at the thought of Amy in any mood, he couldn't help but smile. He would find a way to make her forgive him.

He kicked his boots off, popped the top on a can of beer, and headed for the shower, trying to decide what would be the right kind of present to buy David for his wedding. Maybe he would give Amy a call and ask her.

Bailey's second rehearsal with the band went more smoothly. Ivy, Sephy, and Amy were her cousins, after all, she told Kevin the next morning. It wasn't like playing in front of strangers. Around them, she almost found herself relaxing and having fun with it.

The real test would come a month from now at the wedding. And there was no way she felt hopeful about it. She knew herself too well.

Sephy closed her eyes and stepped onto the scale. She listened for clues from the staff member who was weighing her. What was she expecting? Thunderous applause? A cheerful, impersonal, "Good progress, Sephy. See you next week"? There was nothing but silence.

Carefully, she opened her eyes and looked down at the digital readout. Her goal weight.

She clapped a hand over her mouth and did not even try to stem the tears that brimmed up and overflowed. The woman on the other side of the desk was smiling at her. "Congratulations. You did it."

Later, after the meeting, where she had been applauded and asked to say a few words to the group about how it felt to lose a hundred sixteen pounds, she went for a walk by herself in the park. It was a golden, sunny morning, one of the last they would have this fall. Though the trees were mostly bare, on the south side of the park, near the pond, she came upon a young maple, its branches still carrying a handful of red leaves, incandescent with light. Nearby, an old man was selling bags of stale bread crusts. She bought one for two dollars and sat on a bench.

A hundred sixteen pounds. She had lost the equivalent of an entire human being. It had taken her more than a year of self-denial, false starts, mistakes, and steps backward. Month after month of swimming or walking five days a week; of deprivation; of discipline gained and ingrained inch by painful inch. It *was* painful, becoming another person. And no one, looking at her, would argue that she was a different person than she had been a year ago.

But of course, she was really the same person she had always been.

She tossed bread to the ducks as she attempted an inventory of herself. Who was she, Seraphina Darling? She was . . . She tried to think of what other people said about her. *Kind.* That was what they always said, and it was true. Kindness was important to her. Probably because she had been the recipient of so little of it in her fat years. People had overlooked and ignored her, felt free to disrespect her. Even now, when she knew it was not possible that she remembered every unkindness, she felt sure that each one had left its mark. Meanness did not create physical damage, but it chipped away at the soul as surely as knives and bullets scarred a body.

But there had been grace along the path as well. Maybe it was all grace. Because even the hardest things had shaped her for the good. Had she grown up admired and popular, she might be a less compassionate person. *"You're never going to lose enough weight to shed the fat girl inside,"* Libby had told her. And now, having reached her goal at last, Sephy knew that this was true. Perhaps it was time for her, who always had compassion to spare for others, to extend some of it to the girl she had been. To stop defining herself, as Carl had taught her, by her failures. To see both her abilities and her shortcomings for what they were and make peace with them. In the end, grace—if you accepted it—was the only thing that could heal your soul. And a hundred sixteen pounds or not, your soul was the real shape of you.

A breeze rustled the branches of the maple, and the last of the scarlet leaves rained over her like a benediction.

Jane sat down in the hard, pink-upholstered waiting-room chair and looked over the selection of magazines on the end table beside her. *Neurology. Journal of Neurology, Neurosurgery & Psychiatry. People.* She picked up *People* and opened it at random.

"Heavens!" She leaned over and showed it to Leander, who was sitting beside her. "Look at *this!*" A blonde woman in a bikini and a muscular, brown-haired man were lying together, their limbs entangled, on a deck chair near a swimming pool. Five inset shots showed them in varying stages of ardor.

"Who's that?" Leander whispered, pulling half the magazine closer to scrutinize it.

"I have no idea. She looks like a child."

Leander held his half of the magazine away, squinting at it. "She's no child."

"I *know* that," hissed Jane. "I'm just saying she doesn't have any, you know . . ." She gestured toward her own ample bosom. "Curves."

"That's Hollywood for you," said Leander sagely.

She shook her head in resigned agreement.

They had read through nearly the whole article together when a medical assistant of about Amy's age came out and called, "Leander Darling?"

They followed her, not into an exam room but into a paneled office furnished with a vast cherry desk at one end and an entire living room furniture suite at the other. They stood awkwardly, not sure what to do.

"Why don't you have a seat right here, in front of the fire-place?" the assistant suggested. "Dr. Gutierrez will be along shortly."

"Thank you," they murmured. She left, closing the door behind her, and they sat on the couch, pressed close together in the middle. A gas flame burned in the little fireplace. They held hands.

Dr. Gutierrez was immensely kind. He was a bit older than David—closer to Paul's age, really—and he sat across from them in a red leather wing chair with a manila file folder on his lap.

It was the sight of the folder that undid Jane Darling's world once and forever. It did not belong in this office. And with that incongruity she understood, before he said a word, that people did not get invited to sit in the doctor's wood-paneled office, in front of the fire, just to hear that everything was going to be all right. She watched the doctor, a man who had pictures of his wife and children sitting in lovely leather frames all around the room, open that file folder, and her heart groped for the hand of God. *Help us. We cannot do this without You.*

It was, at first, unpronounceable. Dr. Gutierrez helped them through it. "ALS. Amyotrophic lateral sclerosis," he said. "*A* means *non*. *Myo* means *muscle*. *Trophic* refers to growth and development. It's more commonly known as Lou Gehrig's disease."

He explained more in his gentle, unhurried voice, but all Jane really heard was that Leander was going to die. It was going to be slow, and it was going to be awful, and in the end, there would be no way to defeat it. It was not even worth trying to fight.

They went home in a numb kind of stupor. Jane drove, her instinct to protect him already kicking in. Somehow they reached Copper Cove. At the Tim Hortons intersection, the light was red, and she stopped. "Do you want to go in for a sandwich?" she asked. Leander always liked the Tim Hortons turkey bacon panini.

He looked at her as though he were in a dream, and she realized that, in this moment, he did not even register what a sandwich was. He did not know what anything was.

She cupped her hand to his cheek. "We'll just go home," she whispered.

The light turned green.

AMY WAS COMPOSING an e-mail to the French teacher from the Copper Cove high school to ask if the woman would be interested in teaching adult classes, when a knock on the office door interrupted her. "Come in," she called absently.

It was Paul and Crystal. "We needa talk," Paul said.

"Yes, of course. Shut the door and have a seat." Amy indicated the office's two other chairs. They sat.

Crystal was looking at her hands. It was Paul who spoke. "We cameta ask you to reconsider 'The Twelve Days of Christmas' number."

"What does *reconsider* mean?"

"Consider takin' it out of the Holiday Extravaganza altogether."

"What? No way!" The number was Amy's own brainchild. It was to be the culmination of the program. If it went as planned, the evening would end with the stage and aisles filled with lords a-leaping, ladies dancing, drummers drumming, and possibly live geese and turtledoves, if Crystal could scrape some up anywhere. It was going to be spectacular.

"Why in the world would we cancel it?" she asked.

"It's too big, too hard. People are havin' trouble learnin' the dance parts."

"How hard can the parts be?"

Paul shrugged. "These are schoolkids, Amy. Or people with full-time jobs, or retirees. They're not the Rockettes."

"Also, I don't know if I'm going to have time to finish the costumes for it," Crystal spoke up. "That one number has more props and costumes than the rest of the program put together. I still have three drummers to do, and all eleven of the pipers piping."

Amy was appalled. "How is it that you're only telling me this now, so close to the performance?"

"We thought we could do it," Paul said. "But it turns out we can't."

"Oh, please. I'm sure we can pull this off! We'll all have to work a little harder, that's all. One last push! Come on, another week and it'll be over with."

Paul and Crystal exchanged a look. Crystal said, "We can't work any harder than we already are, and it's not fair of you to ask us, Amy. Just . . . no."

She couldn't believe she was hearing this. "I don't know what to say. I really don't. I need some time to process this and come up with a solution. Why don't we meet again and discuss it at, say, one o'clock. Will that work for both of you?"

"One works for me," said Paul.

"I have to be at Hannaford at two," Crystal said.

"Let's make it twelve thirty then."

"Twelve thirty," they muttered. Paul and Crystal exchanged another wordless glance, and Paul left the office, closing the door behind him.

Amy felt all at once buoyed up with relief. Crystal had stayed behind to apologize. The coldness between them was about to be over. Her friend would say she was sorry for her defeatist attitude. Amy would say, *"I know you have a hard job. But I only ask a lot of you because I know you can do it."* And everything would be right again.

"I've missed you," she said to Crystal.

"I've been offered a full-time manager's position at Hannaford."

What?

"I love working with community theater, but . . ." Crystal began to cry. "I just want a job where I can do my best, then leave it behind me at night with a good conscience. I want a normal life."

"You're . . . *quitting?*"

"I start my new job after the first of the year, Amy. Consider this my two weeks' notice." She helped herself to a tissue from the box on Amy's desk. "I'm sorry it didn't work out," her wardrobe girl said, wiping her eyes. "I guess I just wasn't the right person for you." She forced a watery smile. "I did love it, though. Thanks for giving me the opportunity." She reached for the door handle.

Amy watched her go, speechless.

Alone again, Amy put her head down on the desk. Her mind felt on overload, refusing to compute what had just happened. She knew what Crystal had said, but she couldn't make it seem real.

Now what, God?

The phone on her desk rang. She answered dully. "Amy Darling."

"Yes, hello, Ms. Darling," said an unfamiliar voice. "My name is Cheryl McTeague. I work in human resources for the Maine adult education program statewide. I'm calling to check the references of someone who says he's employed by you?"

"I'm sorry. I think you must have the wrong person."

"You don't have a Paul Zamboni in your employ?"

Her stomach had become a hollow drum. "Yes, Paul works here."

"He lists his date of employment from January of this year; is that correct?"

"Yes."

"And is he employed by you in the capacity of choreographer and dance instructor?"

"He is."

"Very good. That's all I needed, Ms. Darling. Thanks for the help, and enjoy your holidays."

Amy hung up without bothering to return the sentiment.

So Paul was leaving her too. Her arts program was less than a year old, and already it was finished. She stared, unfocused, at the phone.

It's not your arts program. The impression came out of nowhere.

That's not what I meant, she thought irritably.

It belongs to everyone. Let go of it.

No. There was no way. She was the one with the job

of holding this arts program together. It was up to her to keep the boulder rolling uphill. If she let go, the whole thing would come crashing down. It would fail massively.

She waited for more inspiration, but none came. Numbly, she saved the draft of the e-mail she had been working on and closed out of all her screens. Taking her purse from the bottom drawer of her desk and locking the office door behind her, she left the building and drove home.

Her mother was vacuuming the stairs when she arrived. She switched off the vacuum cleaner when Amy came through the door. "Well, this is a surprise! Did you forget something?"

Amy felt her face begin to crumple, and two enormous tears leaked from her eyes.

"Oh, my dear," said her mother, opening her arms.

Amy went into them and wept until she felt wrung dry.

When the storm had passed, her mother said, "Come into the kitchen and have a cup of tea and tell me all about it."

Amy told her. "The thing is," she finished, "I know I should let go, but I can't. I don't know how."

"What are you afraid of, exactly?"

She thought about this. "That if I don't do everything myself, nothing will be done right. And my name is all over it."

"So . . . ?"

"I don't want people to think I don't know what I'm doing."

"So this has become about you and your reputation more than about the community and what it needs?"

"No! That's not . . ." Amy sighed. "Maybe a little. But I'm young, and I didn't have any experience when I started, and I just wanted to prove that I *could*."

"There's not a person in the world who doubts you can do it."

She was silent, thinking.

"You don't have to be perfect," Jane told her gently. "It should be enough to know that you're doing your best and getting better all the time."

Amy stared miserably into her teacup. "I guess we could leave out 'The Twelve Days of Christmas.'"

"Would it make that big a difference?"

"It would shorten the program by about fifteen minutes. And it would make Paul and Crystal's lives easier. And the lives of everyone who's having a hard time with the dance steps. So yes, I guess cutting it out altogether would make a big difference."

"Look at that! You've just let go of something."

"I don't like it."

"It takes practice. You'll get used to it."

Amy wiped her eyes with a paper napkin. "I have a meeting with Paul and Crystal in twenty minutes. I'll tell them we'll cut out the number. They're still going to leave me, though."

"Well . . . God sent them to you in the first place. Why don't you let Him take care of the details of how long they stay?"

When Crystal and Paul were once more seated in her office, Amy came straight to the point. "We'll leave 'The Twelve Days of Christmas' out of the program."

That both of them let out great, gusting sighs made her

ashamed of herself. Why had she not seen how overwhelmed they both were?

Because you didn't want to see it; that's why.

"I'm sorry," she told them. "I know I've asked far too much of both of you this year." Amy caught the narrow look Crystal gave her and could only hope her sincerity was apparent. "I'm going to do better," she went on. "Lower my expectations for the program, and try to enjoy it more, like you said.

"And, Crystal, you were right when you said we should all be able to leave our jobs behind us at the end of the day. I don't blame you for wanting that. And even though you won't be here after the first of the year, I want you to know I've heard you, and I'll be making some changes."

Neither Paul nor Crystal said anything.

"So . . . I hope you can forgive me," Amy prompted. "I know I can be a bit driven."

"Kind of a tyrant," Paul said.

"A slave driver," added Crystal.

She managed half a smile. "Yes. All of that. I know. And I'm sorry."

"It's okay."

"You're forgiven."

Amy gave a great, wet sniffle. "Can't I have a hug or something?"

Both of them came around the desk and hugged her.

"And . . . and if either of you did decide to stay on after Christmas—" Amy could not go on.

"We'll see," said Paul.

"I'll think about it," said Crystal.

It was the best she could hope for, under the circumstances.

For Sephy and Libby, December meant crunch time for planning the wedding. "Twenty-one more days," Libby informed her one evening when they met at Sephy's apartment, which was now a permanent repository for Libby's enormous collection of bridal magazines. "Do you realize that's only three *weeks?*"

"I do realize that." Sephy put a hand on her friend's arm. "You're being so brave."

"Oh, shut up," Libby said. "Shut up and go over this list with me one last time, so I know everything's all set."

Sephy slung her legs over the side of her favorite easy chair. "Okay, hit me."

"Let's start with the day before the wedding. Tuxes and bridesmaids' dresses?"

"Check," said Sephy, well-versed in her role. "We girls have ours already. David will pick up the tuxes Friday morning. Groomsmen and ushers, including *Gorgeous Gabe*—" they giggled on cue— "will stop by my parents' house throughout the day to get them. My mom will supervise that."

Libby prompted her. "Meanwhile, we ladies—"

"Will be at the spa, having facials and getting our nails done. Seriously, what a nice bridesmaids' gift, Lib."

Libby waved her away. "It's nothing. Purely selfish. I just don't want to get a manicure all by myself. So while we're doing that, *my* mom will be picking up the bouquets at the florist. We have to get them by ten in the morning because they close early for Christmas Eve. At the same time, David will be heading to the airport to pick up—"

"Gorgeous Gabe," they chorused again. Again, they giggled.

"Also," Libby went on, "my brother flies in later that day. My father will pick him up just before—" she consulted her list—"the rehearsal."

"Right." Sephy picked up the thread. "Everybody meets at the church at six o'clock. We don't have to decorate, because all the poinsettias and things will already be there for Christmas."

"That saved us a fortune in flowers, right there. Rehearsal dinner?"

"A buffet at the Darling home, provided by Butter Side Up Caterers. Christmas carols or not, as the spirit moves."

"Great. On to Saturday morning."

"That's when I spirit the bride off bright and early for an eight o'clock hair appointment at the salon."

"And then?"

Sephy sang a few bars of "Get Me to the Church on Time."

"Look." Libby pushed up her sleeve and held out her bare arm for Sephy's inspection. "Goose bumps!"

"So then—" Sephy changed to humming "Here Comes the Bride"— "'I now pronounce you husband and wife.'" She burst into Mendelssohn's recessional, conducting an imaginary orchestra with her finger. "And voilà! You're married!"

"But the day's not over yet."

"Oh no, it's *far* from over." Sephy waggled her eyebrows meaningfully.

Libby leaned forward and hit her on the arm with a rolled-up magazine. "Yes, but first the reception, you idiot."

"Oh, well then. The reception will be at the Jewish Heritage Center in Quahog, which was the only thing we could find that would agree to open on Christmas Day."

"It was that or a Chinese restaurant," Libby said dolefully.

"So, an entirely kosher meal—"

"They swore we wouldn't even notice. No shellfish, though; I'm still sad about that."

"And music provided by—drumroll please . . ."

Libby obliged by drumming her hands on the coffee table.

"The one and only . . . Darlings!"

Libby gave a cheer. "But only for two hours," she added. "After that, we'll use an iPod and the Jewish Heritage Center's sound system."

"We could only come up with two hours' worth of music." Sephy still felt bad about it.

"And we're grateful to have it. Besides, we want you to enjoy yourselves too. You have to be guests as well as workers."

"And the honeymoon?"

"Cocoa Beach. But the wedding night is still a secret. David won't tell me where we're going."

Sephy shuddered. "Enough. I can't think about my brother in the same sentence as the words *wedding night*."

"Please don't tax yourself on my account," Libby said loftily.

Jane was sitting up in bed, reading her Bible.

Leander shuffled out of the bathroom in his robe. "I've been thinking," he said. Already he looked older. Diminished. *"Pick up your feet when you walk!"* she wanted to snap.

"Don't just give up yet!" Instead, she closed the Bible, keeping one finger in the Psalms, where she had been reading. "What have you been thinking?"

He sat down on the edge of the bed and stared at his hands. "I'd like to put off telling the children until after David and Libby's wedding."

Jane seized on this at once. "I agree. We shouldn't do or say anything that would tarnish their big day."

"We'll tell them after Christmas, then."

"After Christmas," she agreed. He reached for her hand and gripped it. And Jane, gripping back, felt like the worst kind of coward because her motives were not for David's happiness at all. Really, what she wanted—what she longed for—was to never have to speak the terrible truth aloud to anyone at all. If they didn't think of it, or talk about it, that might keep it from happening. Maybe silence would stop it from coming true.

The Holiday Extravaganza went off beautifully. Amy privately mourned the loss of "The Twelve Days of Christmas," but she had vowed to herself that she would not say a word about it to anyone. *Next year,* she thought. *We can always do it next year.* Afterward, when she was called to the stage to take a bow, Paul came forward and presented her with a bouquet of two dozen red roses. The card said simply, *An admirer.* She was baffled, but when she showed the flowers to Ivy, her sister laughed.

"Bet you anything they're from Mitch."

"Mitch? He's in Florida."

Ivy raked her with an appraising look. "Amy, you're kind of an idiot, you know?" She walked away.

Amy knew Mitch was coming back to Copper Cove at some point for David's wedding, but she didn't know when he would get into town or where he would be staying. She'd hoped to see him at one of the productions, but if he had come, he'd slipped out before she caught a glimpse of him. She was too embarrassed to call and ask if he'd sent the flowers. What if Ivy was wrong? So she remained in the dark, but whenever she thought of those flowers in the days to come, the idea that Mitch might have sent them made her cheeks flush and her mouth go dry.

On the last night of the Extravaganza, Crystal found her at the cast party.

"I was thinking," her wardrobe manager said, "if you haven't found someone yet to fill my position, I wouldn't really mind staying."

"I haven't found anyone yet."

"So . . . I can keep my job?"

"I can't imagine running this show without you."

Crystal's smile was like a burst of sunlight on clear water.

"Do you happen to know . . . ," Amy whispered, glancing across the room to where Paul was talking with an orchestra member. "I mean . . . has Paul said anything about leaving?"

Paul seemed to sense he was being talked about. He looked up at them just then and gave a wave and a smile.

"I'm pretty sure Paul's not going anywhere either," Crystal told her.

"Good. We need him, too."

Mitch still had his old apartment key. Pit was expecting him, so he didn't bother knocking, but let himself in, trying to be quiet about it. It was after midnight. Pit had left the stove light on. Mitch could hear his old roommate's snores from the second bedroom. He smiled. It was as though he had never left. He had come for only a few days, so he hadn't packed much. He tossed a sports bag of clothes onto the floor of his old room, dug around in it until he found his toiletry bag, and headed for the bathroom. Already, in just a few weeks of Florida living, he had forgotten how cold Maine could be. He took a quick, intensely hot shower and hit the sack, his eyes half-closed by the time his head hit the pillow. His last thought was to wonder if Amy had liked the flowers.

CHAPTER

21

ON THE MORNING before the wedding, Sephy was awakened by her phone ringing at five o'clock. "Lib-by," she groaned as she answered. But it was not Libby. Instead, it was a very distraught Mrs. Hale.

"Sephy, we have such a mess on our hands! Libby has a stomach bug. She was up half the night with it. I called over to your mother's house, and she says David has the *same thing*. Can you believe it! *What* are we going to do?"

Sephy sat up in bed, her head reeling. The nurse in her kicked into gear. "Do you mean she's vomiting? Diarrhea?"

"Just throwing up. From about one o'clock in the morning on."

"And you don't think it's just nerves?"

"For both of them? Besides, you know Liberty. She doesn't really *have* nerves."

Sephy felt beleaguered. "Let me think. Ummm . . . I'll come over and we'll work out contingency plans for everything that has to get done today."

"I think you should stay away, Sephy. We don't want you catching it too. With any luck, this is only a twelve-hour thing, and she'll be better in time for tonight's rehearsal."

"Okay. Give me half an hour to figure out what needs to be done, and I'll call you back."

"All right." Libby's mother sounded close to tears.

"Mrs. Hale?"

"What, honey?"

"Everything's going to be all right."

"I certainly hope so."

Sephy made a cup of coffee and pulled out her lists. Her father would surely be able to pick up the tuxedos from the rental place in David's stead. The bridesmaids could all go to the spa without Libby. Later on, one of them could do the bride's nails for her. On second thought, who cared what the bride's nails looked like, as long as she was able to stand upright at the altar long enough to say her vows and get herself married?

Mr. Hale could probably pick up Gorgeous Gabe from the airport. Of course, he would have to go back soon after to pick up his own son, but this was an emergency, after all. They needed all hands on deck. The rest should be able to happen as planned. Everyone would just have to pray that the bride and groom were recovered by rehearsal time.

Only it wasn't that simple. It turned out that Libby's brother, Justice, was flying into Boston and taking the bus up to Bangor, where his father would pick him up. Mr. Hale would be en route to Bangor at the same time Gabe's flight would get in at the tiny Quahog airport.

"Couldn't *you* go pick Gabe up?" Libby's mother begged Sephy. "There's really no one else. And we can't let him be met by a stranger or take a taxi all the way here. It wouldn't be hospitable."

Sephy did some rapid mental arithmetic. She would have to miss the spa trip, which didn't bother her all that much. Truth be told, she wasn't really a spa kind of girl. Although she had to admit, examining one hand, her nails were a mess. It was one of the occupational hazards of being a nurse. She would think about that later. Ahead was the prospect of forty minutes alone in the car with Gabe. If she drove slowly, maybe she could stretch it to an hour. "I think I can manage it, Mrs. Hale," she said, trying not to sound too thrilled. "You just concentrate on getting Libby better."

She made a quick call to her mother to give and get updates, then headed for the shower.

She dressed carefully for the trip to the airport, in a moss-green sweater that set off her coppery hair and a pair of dark-brown, wide-wale corduroys. Then she worried that she looked too L.L.Bean, so she changed into jeans, which she decided were too casual. She put the corduroys back on and resolved not to look in the mirror again. There was nothing wrong with the L.L.Bean look. This was Maine, after all.

She was conscious of a certain breathlessness on the drive to the airport, as though she had to inhale twice as often to get enough air. The mindless DJ patter on the radio irritated her, but when she turned it off, the silence irritated her more. *Gabe,* she thought. High school football star. Soccer star. Everything star. Gabe, whom she had secretly loved since he had moved to town and begun riding her bus when she was in third grade. He had never given her a second look in his life, but she knew that this time he would, like everyone else, *see* her at last. For half a moment, she wished again for invisibility. It was easier in so many ways.

Jane Darling had called Gabe that morning and brought him up to speed on the situation. She had told him that Sephy would meet him at baggage claim and reminded him that this was David's sister with the red hair. But when Sephy got to baggage claim, she was not prepared for the crush of the crowd. She felt a moment of panic. Why were all these people traveling on Christmas Eve? She would never find him.

As it turned out, he found her first. A light touch on her shoulder startled her, and a voice said, "Stephanie?"

Sephy turned and looked into those liquid brown eyes that had bewitched every girl in school, and she felt her heart turn over. "Gabe."

"In the flesh." He made a self-deprecating little bow. He was as gorgeous as ever.

"I see you already found your bag."

"I got lucky. It was first off the belt. Hey . . ." He was scrutinizing her. "Are you sure you're David's sister? I don't seem to remember a Stephanie."

"It's Sephy."

"I'm sorry. I guess I don't remember you, Steffy."

"*Seh*-phy. I was younger than you. And I've changed a bit since school." She smiled at him. "Are you ready to go?"

"Yes, ma'am."

"Then follow me."

"To the ends of the earth," he said.

She did not miss the admiration in his eyes.

Gabe was easy to talk to, and Sephy was beginning to fear the ride home was passing too quickly when he suggested they stop for lunch. "I haven't eaten yet, and the last thing your family needs is for a hungry guest to show up on their doorstep asking about food."

They ate at a truck stop. Gabe had a fried haddock sandwich and two beers; she ordered a Caesar salad and a Diet Coke. While they ate, she brought him up to speed on what her family had been doing in the years since he and David had graduated. He told her about his son, who was four years old and also named Gabe. "His mom and I split up right after he was born. We were never married, actually. He lives with her."

"But do you get to see him?"

"Oh yeah. Me and him, we're real tight. He's my little buddy." He pulled out his wallet and flipped open to a photo of a little boy who looked to be about two years old. He was a beautiful child who had inherited his father's olive skin and dark, curling hair.

"He must be bigger than this by now," Sephy said, examining it.

Gabe frowned. "Yeah, I don't know why I don't have a newer picture. I'll have to get on his mom about that."

"So you still have a good relationship with her."

"The best. We just weren't right for each other. There were no hard feelings when we split up."

She told him about her job at the hospital and he seemed impressed. He told her that he sold wholesale electronics to retailers.

"Hey, I can hook you up with a new iPod if you want," he offered. "Latest and greatest at the factory price."

"Well, thanks," she laughed. "That's the best offer I've had all day." Reluctantly, she looked at the clock on the wall. "We should get back if we're going to get you settled in and make it to the rehearsal on time. If David's still sick, you'll be staying with Nick and Ivy for the night."

"Hey, I'm not picky. I always got along with Ivy just great."

He insisted on paying for their lunch, and as he was taking care of the bill, Sephy called her mother for an update. David, it transpired, was on the mend, having not thrown up since seven o'clock that morning. He had even eaten some toast and a bowl of soup. Gabe was given the go-ahead to come and spend the night in the house. Quickly, Sephy called Libby's mother and heard the same news there. Libby was weak and tired, but the stomach bug seemed to have run its course.

She delivered Gabe to her parents' house, where she made sympathetic noises at her pale brother before running next door to check on Libby. Her best friend was lying on the couch with a towel under her head and a large bowl on the coffee table beside her. She waved a tired hand. "What's going on, Seph?"

Sephy sat down in a chair. "I just got back from picking up Gabe at the airport. How are you doing?"

"Better. I'm drinking ginger ale." She gestured to a half-filled glass beside the bowl. "I'm so sorry about all of this."

Sephy waved her away. "Don't even think about it. Just concentrate on getting better. Listen—" Her phone rang. She glanced at it; it was Ivy. "Just a sec," she told Libby.

"What's up?" she asked her sister.

Ivy said, "I just thought: Amy and I were going to take the instruments and sound equipment over to the Jewish Heritage Center and set up this afternoon. David was supposed to help with the heavy things, but obviously . . . ?"

The answer came to her at once. "Ask Mitch. He was supposed to get in last night."

"Sephy, you're a marvel. You're like a machine. I'll get Amy to call him. What time are Bailey and her date getting here?" Their cousin had driven up from Augusta for a third rehearsal just the week before. She wasn't entirely comfortable playing in the band yet, but they were all hoping for the best.

"No idea. They'll get here when they get here."

"I was just thinking maybe the friend had some muscle and could heave a few amplifiers around for us."

"Call Bailey and ask."

"All right. Hang in there, Seph."

She related the call to Libby.

"You have to be the greatest maid of honor ever invented." Libby smiled wanly. "We couldn't do this without you."

Her phone rang again. It was her mother.

"Sweetheart, I called the girl who does Ivy's hair. She

doesn't have any openings, but she said her sister can fit you in for a manicure if you can be there by three thirty."

"Perfect."

"Then I'll call her back and confirm the appointment. You know where it is?"

"Out near the highway, isn't it?"

"That's the one. How's Libby?"

"Much better. Everything's going to be fine." She hung up, praying she was right.

Mrs. Hale popped her head around the corner. "Do you feel up to trying some chicken broth, Liberty? Or toast?"

Libby considered this. "Both, I think."

"Thank goodness," said Sephy, who was beginning to feel very worn out.

The clock seemed to leap right past two, three, and four o'clock, and the next time Sephy looked, it was time to leave for the rehearsal.

She called Libby from her parents' house, where she had stopped after the manicure to change her clothes and repair her makeup on the way to the church. "How are you feeling?"

"Much better. Not a hundred percent yet, but I'll get there. What's the report?"

"Tuxes have all been picked up; bouquets are in my mother's second refrigerator; instruments and sound equipment are set up at the Jewish Heritage Center—"

"Did Mitch come through?"

"Of course. One distress signal from Amy did the trick."

"Innnnteresting. What's going on there?"

"Oh, nothing, nothing. According to Amy."

"Ah, but what does Amy know," said Libby wisely.

"Exactly. So, I called the photographer to confirm the time. Your cousins had a ball at the spa without you and me, and my mother called to say the caterer just pulled in to start setting up for tonight's party."

"Sephy, you really are the very best of friends."

"No, you are."

"No, *you* are."

"You are."

"*You* are."

"You."

"*You.*"

"Youyouyouyouyouyouyou." They were both talking over each other. It was an old game.

"All *right*," Libby broke in. "This time there is *no* argument. I can't tell you how much I appreciate all you've done. I'll return the favor one day, when you get married."

"As if." Sephy made a kissing noise. "See you at rehearsal, you clown."

It went as badly as wedding rehearsals usually go, but everyone assured everyone else that this was definitely a sign of good luck. The main thing was that the bride and groom were both walking upright, even if they did look a little peaked.

Libby's brother, Justice, had arrived, been briefed on his usher duties, and was sitting in the back row with his parents, watching. Bailey and her friend Kevin were back at the Darling home, supervising the caterers. So everything was in place, Sephy thought with satisfaction. A near disaster had been averted because the stomach bug hadn't been serious. It had been a close call, though.

When the rehearsal was over and Gabe offered his arm to walk her up the aisle, she held on tight, lest her feet come off the ground and she float right up to the ceiling with relief and, yes, with joy.

At 14 Ladyslipper Lane, the rehearsal dinner, catered by Butter Side Up, was in full swing, but Amy was not enjoying it. She was watching the door for Mitch. He was an usher and had been at the rehearsal, but he had not come back to the house with everyone else. She was half-irritated, half-concerned. It would be just like Mitch to feel too self-conscious to show up at all. She considered texting him, but he probably wouldn't text her back. He never had before.

Justice Hale stood in the doorway of the familiar Darling living room and surveyed the scene before him. His sister and David were sitting close together on the sofa, eating from plates balanced on their knees. They both seemed to be recovered. He was happy for Libby. David had always been a good guy, though he and Justice had belonged to different circles back then. David had been a jock: a handsome, popular kid. Justice had acne and was a member of the chess club. It had probably taken some courage for David to be nice to him on the school bus and around the neighborhood, but he had done it all the same.

David's best man, Gabe, was a different story. What a jerk he'd been, always picking on someone younger or weaker or poorer than him. Justice, who was not insensible of the fact that his teenage acne had become a distant memory and that he'd filled out his height well since high school, was happy to see that Gabe's hair was beginning to recede at the temples. The difference in their heights was enough to let Justice observe that it was also thinning at the top. And Gabe had the start of a satisfying paunch above his belt. This did not stop him from looking very full of himself as he stood with a beer in his hand, chatting up Sephy Darling.

Sephy. Now there was a change for the record books. She was a different person than she'd been when he'd seen her in July. At the rehearsal, he'd nearly had to ask his mother who she was. Even knowing it now, it was hard to reconcile the sight of this slender young woman with the overweight girl who had spent half her life at his house. Sephy had always been such a nice girl. Not just nice to him, but to everyone. Even to the mean kids. Justice remembered taking her to her senior prom so that she and Libby could double-date. Sephy didn't even look like the same person now. He was nearly overcome with an urge to stride across the room and step in between her and that jerk she was talking to. The rapt expression on her face, though, warned him that she might not appreciate that.

He turned his head and concentrated on the piano instead, where a lively old woman was playing Christmas carols. At one end of the room, the caterers were keeping a long table stocked with salads, cold cuts, and finger foods.

More for something to concentrate on than because he was hungry, Justice headed in that direction.

Halfway there, Ivy intercepted him. She held a plate of salads in one hand.

"Justice! It's good to see you. I'm so glad you could come home for the wedding."

"It's nice to be back. I guess you and I will be family by tomorrow." He nodded at Libby and David, who had put their plates down and were holding hands on the couch.

"Yes," Ivy said, "but then Libby's always been part of the family, so what could be more natural?" She shifted the plate to her other hand and looked around for an empty seat. "Your mother tells me you're on your way to Africa."

"That's right."

"I'd love to hear about it. If you're not busy, why don't you get some food and come sit down and tell me."

"All right."

"I mean, if you're not sick of talking about it."

Justice couldn't help smiling. "I never get sick of talking about it."

Amy was on the verge of calling Mitch when he appeared in the doorway of the living room. He looked as uncomfortable as she had expected. She made her way over to his side. "Hi, Mitch."

The relief that broke over his face transformed him. No one would ever call him classically handsome, but when he looked like that, with his guard down for just one second, she thought he was beautiful.

"Get lost along the way?"

He shook his head. "I had to talk myself into coming. This isn't really my scene."

"I'm glad you came."

The nervous look was back, as though he might bolt at any moment.

"Come on and get something to eat. It'll give you something to do with your hands." She took his arm and steered him toward the buffet.

They filled plates and looked around the room.

"It's too loud in here," Amy called over the noise. "Let's find someplace else."

They rounded the corner and discovered that the stairs to the second floor were quieter. Halfway up, they sat side by side.

"Thanks for helping us get all the equipment over to Quahog today," Amy told him, swiping a bread stick through a pile of artichoke dip.

"Anytime."

"You saved our lives. Ivy and I could never have lifted all those heavy amps by ourselves. Not to mention wrestling with the keyboard and the drum set."

"Well, I don't mind saving a few lives for this family. You all saved mine once."

She looked sideways at him. "You know, I was only five years old when you moved in with us. Seven or eight when you moved out. I never understood all that happened."

He shrugged, toying with a shrimp puff. "It was complicated."

"Give me a little credit, Mitch. I might be intelligent enough to figure it out. That is . . . if you felt like telling me."

He ate the shrimp puff.

She let him.

At last he said, "It's not a very nice story."

"I would love to hear it anyway."

He swallowed some smoked salmon on pumpernickel, then blew out a breath. "Well, my mother left when I was young, and my dad raised me. He wasn't exactly your fairy-tale father. Smoked a lot of weed, shot up with his friends on the weekends. He gave me my first joint when I was eight years old. I had my first beer the same year."

Amy's hand went to her mouth.

"Yeah, so, not a great father, right?" said Mitch. "He had kind of a rough life before he met my mom. I think he had a lot of, whaddya call it—"

"Post-traumatic stress?"

"Something like that. He rode with a biker gang, worked at the copper mine before it closed down. When I was sixteen, he got arrested for assaulting a man in a bar. It wasn't his first arrest, but it was his longest sentence. I was left on my own. The state was going to put me in foster care, but your dad stepped in and said I could come live with your family."

"My dad was one of your teachers? I didn't know you took music classes."

"That year it was either music appreciation or family consumer science. I didn't want to spend the semester baking cookies and learning about budgeting, so I sat in your father's class instead."

"Did you learn anything?"

"I learned that I have no appreciation for music." He

grinned. "Anyway, your family was really nice. They acted like I'd always been here. David had to share his room with me, but he didn't even seem to mind. At least I never heard him complain."

"That would be like David."

"I remember your mom made me wash my own clothes. She said all the teenagers in the house were responsible for their own laundry, and she took me downstairs and taught me how to do it. I was so embarrassed to have her sorting through my dirty underwear and stained-up shirts. I wanted to die."

Amy laughed. "I can picture her doing it. But with seven people in the family, I'm sure she'd already seen it all when it came to dirty clothes."

"Not like mine, she hadn't. I'd never used a clothes washer before. My father used to take our clothes to the Laundromat every couple of months. You know, the kind where you drop them off, then come back later and they're all washed and folded for you. We'd live out of the laundry basket, wearing everything seven or eight times until he got around to going again. I learned early on how not to spill things on my clothes. I didn't want to be one of those kids at school who smelled bad, but I'm sure I did anyway. And I didn't get new clothes very often. Usually, they were things the school nurse passed on to me. I was always scared someone would see me wearing his old shirt at school and tell everyone I'd gotten it from the lost and found."

Amy said, "I was just a little kid, and you seemed so tough to me. You never smiled. But I did think you smelled good. I remember that."

He snorted. "That's because once I moved in here, I took a shower twice a day. I never wore anything more than once without washing it. I was obsessed with being clean."

"I had kind of a crush on you back then," she confessed.

"Really?" He looked thoughtful. "I don't remember you all that much."

"Thanks a lot. Anyway, what happened?"

"I stayed with your family for about two and a half years, then my old man got out of prison. He never sent for me, and I never mentioned him because I wanted to stay on here. I think your parents knew he was out, but they never said I had to go back."

"You liked it here?"

"Are you kidding? I gained twenty-five pounds just from eating regular meals. I didn't like the going-to-church part, and I couldn't figure out why everyone laughed so much. And when you all started singing, I never knew what to do. But all in all? Yeah, it was a great place to live."

Mitch ate three miniature quiches. Amy toyed with her diminished puddle of artichoke dip.

"Why did you leave?" she asked.

"I finished high school, and it didn't seem like there was any excuse to stay. David was about to start college, and your dad offered to help me fill out applications and financial aid forms and all that, but I was just never cut out for it. I thought about the Army, but . . . well, by then I was drinking a lot. The discipline of the military didn't really appeal to me. So I left."

"Where did you go?"

"Providence. I had a cousin there who got me a job in a bar."

"Weren't you too young for that?"

"Nah, I was eighteen." He nudged her in the ribs. "Are you sure you want to hear all this?"

"Don't even think of stopping now. So then what?"

"About what you'd expect when a rootless eighteen-year-old kid starts working in an inner-city bar. I got in with the wrong crowd, started drinking more and more, doing more drugs. Heroin, coke, ketamine, benzos, Suboxone . . . whatever I could buy, barter, or steal on the streets. By the time I was twenty-one, I'd turned yellow from hepatitis and had infected track marks on my arms. Twice, I ended up on life support in the hospital for OD'ing. I was on the fast track to an early grave."

Amy was holding her breath. "Our family never heard anything about that. So what happened?"

"I got arrested on a felony drug charge and wound up in prison. I was sentenced to two years; ended up doing sixteen months. It was the best thing that ever happened to me. There can't be any hell worse than detoxing in prison. For three days, I didn't sleep; I sweated and shook and puked up my guts. I saw things crawling on the walls and felt them on my skin. I heard voices that weren't there. But on the fourth day, I woke up and it was all over. For the next sixteen months, I didn't put a single pill into my body. Not even a Tylenol. I worked out and went to AA at the prison every day, sometimes twice a day. After I got out, I went back to the prison every month to speak at their meetings. Still do it."

She smiled at him. "I didn't know that."

He smiled back. "I'll bet there's a lot you don't know about me." He started to say something else but was interrupted by the crashing of fortissimo chords on the piano. The hubbub in the room below subsided.

"What's going on?" Amy asked.

Mitch shrugged. "Let's go see."

Together they crept down the stairs and looked around the corner.

Jane Darling stood in the middle of the floor banging on a cooking pot with a ladle. "Attention!" she called. "Can I have your attention, everyone?" When the room was quiet at last, she put the pot down and went on, her mother's voice carrying easily through the crowded room. "Tonight, we have a double reason to celebrate."

"Oh no." Amy drew back and leaned against the wall. "I should have known."

"What?" said Mitch.

She didn't have to answer, because Jane was calling out, "I don't want to steal any thunder from the bride and groom, but I think it's only right that we recognize someone else here tonight."

"Mo-o-o-om," Amy whimpered. "Don't."

Beside her, Mitch said, "What? What is it?"

Jane's voice continued to ring out. "David and Libby both agree with me that this is too important an occasion to overlook, so would you all take a moment and join me in singing 'Happy Birthday' to David's youngest sister, Amy, *who is twenty-two today!*" With a flourish, Jane gestured to the very corner where Amy was cringing. From the piano, Grammie Lydia struck the opening chords. As the room erupted into song, Amy felt a tug on her arm.

Ivy was standing in front of her. "Get out here! They're singing for you."

She could not be ungracious. With flaming cheeks, she joined her mother in the center of the room. As the song died away, Amy nailed a smile to her face and curtsied to the applause. "Thank you. Thank you, everyone."

"Birthday cake on the buffet table!" her mother crowed, amid the renewed wave of talking. "Help yourselves!" To Amy, she said in a low voice, "I hope you don't mind not blowing out the birthday candles. I thought it might embarrass you if I made a big deal over it."

"Gee, thanks, Mom." With only the smallest roll of her eyes, Amy kissed her mother on the cheek and returned to where Mitch was standing.

"I didn't know it was your birthday."

"Well," she said pertly, "I'll bet there's a lot you don't know about me."

"Listen, Amy . . . ," he said. It was no use. The noise from the living room had grown too loud again for them to hear each other. "Come on," he called. Taking her arm, he led her back up the stairs. They sat at the top, side by side again, he with his elbows on his knees, she with her arms clasped about hers.

"Listen," he said. "I just—the last time I talked to you. On the phone."

She looked sideways at him. His face was red. "Were you drunk?" she asked.

"Yeah. I, ah . . . fell off the wagon there for a little while." She said nothing.

"I'm sorry I called you and dragged you into my mess. You didn't deserve that."

Amy felt an unaccustomed rush of compassion. "It's okay. Nobody's perfect."

"Except you."

"No. Not at all. I've learned that being perfect and just doing your best are two very different things."

"Well . . ." He was picking at the head of a nail in the stair tread. "I, ah, went back to AA, in Florida, and I'm doing okay again. I'm not drinking. I've been sober for about three weeks."

"That's great," she said.

"Yeah, thanks. It's, ah . . . I'm glad, anyway. But listen, what I wanted to say is that with AA, they have this thing they tell you."

"Okay. What thing?"

"Like, after you get sober, then for an entire year at least, you're supposed to concentrate just on your sobriety. No, ah, other relationships or things like that."

She wasn't sure if what she thought she was hearing was what he was actually trying to say. "What does that mean: 'no other relationships or things like that'?"

He looked anguished. "I mean, if things hadn't happened the way they did—like, if I hadn't fallen off the wagon in Florida and started drinking again, I guess I would have liked to come back here for the wedding and, I don't know, ask you out or something."

She knew her own face had to be scarlet, but she didn't care. A smile broke across it from side to side. "You would have asked me out?"

He cleared his throat. "Yeah. I mean, if . . . you know . . . *if.*"

With an effort, she contained her smile to less-foolish

proportions and tried to speak rationally. "So . . . when *can* you ask me out?"

He looked helpless. "In a year?"

"Well. In a year. Okay then." She knocked him lightly on the arm. "You'd better stay sober."

"I will. I'll stay sober."

They grinned at one another like a pair of idiots.

"Sephy." Ivy was standing over her.

Sephy looked up from the couch, where she was listening to Gabe talk about the new quarterback the Patriots had just signed. He was supposed to lead them on to a great season, she gathered, although the details of it were fuzzy to her. "What?" she asked, blinking at her sister.

"Sorry to butt in, but I think Grammie Lydia's ready to go home. Nick and I can drive her, but could you take over at the piano?"

Sephy shot her sister a meaningful look in the direction of Gabe. "Can't Mom do it?"

"*Sephy*. She has her hands full enough."

Sephy looked over to where her mother was helping the caterers pass around plates of birthday cake. She sighed. "All right." She smiled at Gabe. "I want to hear more about this later."

"Absolutely." He raised his beer bottle in a toast to her and took a long swallow.

Sephy went to the piano and touched her grandmother on the shoulder. "Want me to take over here? Nick and Ivy can drive you home if you're tired."

Her grandmother was playing "O Come, O Come, Emmanuel" and, ever the artist, tapered into an arpeggio so graceful that no one would suspect it happened midstanza. "Thank you, dear. Just swap over quick here, and no one will hear the interruption."

Sephy slid smoothly onto the bench and started "Silent Night," the easiest of the carols and one she knew automatically enough to give her time to adjust to what she was doing. "'Night, Grammie," she said, raising her cheek for the older woman's kiss. "I love you."

"I'll see you tomorrow, sweet girl." Briefly, her grandmother laid her hand on Sephy's head, like a blessing, and then she was gone.

From the corner of her eye, Sephy watched Ivy come toward them with the old lady's coat and purse over her arm, and a wave of love washed over her. She had the best family in the world.

As she drew near the end of "Silent Night," her mind shifted into gear. She loved best to play when people were singing, so with great energy, she struck out the opening chords of "Deck the Halls." Loudly, she began,

"Deck the halls with boughs of holly,
　Fa-la-la-la-la la la la la.
　'Tis the season to be jolly,
　Fa-la-la-la-la la la la la."

By the time she got to "Don we now our gay apparel," half the room was singing with her, and by the start of the second verse, nearly everyone was.

Justice had been thinking that if he had to sit and watch Sephy talk to that jerk for five more minutes, he would have to find something—or someone—to hit really hard. He knew for a fact that the man was on at least his fifth beer, although Sephy appeared to be clueless about this. Justice had been on the verge of leaving the party when Sephy sat down at the piano. As soon as she started to play, he changed his mind. He now had the perfect excuse for sitting right where he was and watching her for as long as he liked. He leaned back, rested an ankle on his knee, and prepared to enjoy the show.

They had been singing for about half an hour when Sephy glanced up and caught her mother's eye. Jane tapped her watch and raised an eyebrow. The signal was clear: *Time to close this party down.* Sephy gave her mother a nod and seamlessly changed key.

"Have yourself a merry little Christmas,
Let your heart be light."

Experience had taught her it was one of those songs that people recognized but didn't really know all the words to. Sure enough, the singing dwindled after the first few lines, and Sephy was left singing alone.

"Here we are as in olden days,
Happy golden days of yore.

Faithful friends who are dear to us
Gather near to us once more.

Through the years we all will be together
If the Fates allow;
Hang a shining star upon the highest bough.
And have yourself a merry little Christmas now."

She held the final chord; then, amid a smattering of
applause, stood and said, "And with that, the Darling family
says good night. Drive safely, and we'll see you all at David
and Libby's wedding tomorrow."

Their guests took the broad hint and, getting to their feet,
began to track down their coats and purses. Sephy searched
the room for Gabe and saw him, leaning in a doorway,
watching her. Smiling, she threaded her way through the
crowd to where he stood.

"You," he said, holding her eyes with his, "have a beautiful voice."

All her life, Sephy had been told she had a beautiful voice,
and it had never meant anything like this. "Thank you," she
said, her heart giving a little hitch.

"Oh, look." Gabe raised his eyes to the doorframe.
"Mistletoe."

It was true. He had stood there on purpose and waited
for her. Sephy's pulse was beating like hummingbird wings.
"Mistletoe," she whispered.

Gabe pulled her close and kissed her.

Her first, shocked thought was that it wasn't anything
like she had expected kissing Gabe Michaud to be. It was . . .

wetter. It tasted like beer. Surprised, she pulled back and looked at him.

He smiled and brushed a strand of hair away from her cheek. "Merry Christmas, Sephy. Darling."

From across the room, Justice watched that idiot kiss Sephy under the mistletoe. A bitter taste filled his mouth, and rage flashed through him like sheet lightning. The force of it shocked him. Made him distrust himself. He should have stayed in Seattle, he realized. He had no business caring this much about what Sephy did, or with whom. The timing for it was all wrong. He watched her reach up to touch Michaud on the face, then disappear into the crowd.

Not bothering to stop and find his coat, Justice shouldered his way through the French doors of the living room and onto the snow-covered deck beyond. Sliding a little, he maneuvered down the steps, then stalked across the lawn to his parents' house next door.

WEDDING DAY DAWNED, and one of the most hectic mornings of Sephy's life ensued. She swallowed something appalling and completely destructive for breakfast in order to get Libby to the Vietnamese hair salon in Quahog by eight o'clock. It was Christmas morning, and they were the only customers in the place. Three young Asian women lay draped around the front desk, sighing with boredom. Not only did they agree to give Libby a manicure, but one of them seized Sephy and insisted on styling her hair "no chahge." Sephy was too stupefied to refuse. She cast an apprehensive glance at the girl's own high, lacquered pompadour and tried to telegraph a mute appeal for help across the room. Libby, who was sitting under a drape the size of a circus tent, shrugged and pointed helplessly to her own towel-wrapped head.

For an hour and a half, Sephy endured an agony of pinching, pulling, fine-combing, and spraying. She consoled herself with the thought that she might still have time to rush home, wash out whatever damage they were doing now, and get her hair blown out before the wedding.

But to her amazement, she loved the result. A mass of tiny, loose twists with white flowers woven into them culminated in a spill of curls around her shoulders. "Ooh," she gasped when she saw it. "How do I make it stay like this forever?" When they left the salon half an hour later, she tipped the "no chahge" stylist thirty dollars and was glad to do it.

Back at the Hales' house, they found that Jane Darling had brought the flowers over from next door as planned. Together with the other two bridesmaids, they commandeered the second floor for the important task of dressing. It was all accomplished with enough giggling and minor crises and clouds of hairspray to leave Sephy with the beginnings of a headache. When she could stand it no longer, she escaped downstairs on the pretext of looking for the bridal bouquet. In the kitchen, she ran into Libby's brother.

"Oh, Justice," she said, distracted. "I didn't get a chance to say more than hi last night. I wanted to tell you welcome home."

"Thanks," he said. "Are you—is everything okay?"

"Fine." She rubbed at her temples. "Hairspray headache."

He looked puzzled. "Is there such a thing?"

"Not really. I'm just ready to get this show on the road, that's all. I'd love a glass of water, though, and some ibuprofen, if there's any around."

"Here, let me." He got a glass, filled it with ice water from the refrigerator, and handed it to her. In the cupboard over the stove, he found a bottle of pills. "How many?" he asked.

"Three, please."

He shook them out and handed them to her.

"Thanks," she said. "Hey, are you taller than you used to be?"

"No, why?"

"I don't remember you being able to take glasses down from the top shelf without reaching."

"Well, maybe I did grow an inch or two after high school." She swallowed the pills and drank her water.

He cleared his throat. "Um. You look great."

"Really? Thanks."

"I mean—in general, you look great. But today especially." His ears were crimson, which Sephy found endearing.

"Oh, that's sweet. Thank you." She patted him on the arm and, having spotted the box with Libby's bouquet on the table, reached past him and snatched it. "I'd better take this to the bride." She set her empty glass beside the sink. "Thanks for the water. I'm starting to feel better already."

"You're welcome."

She was halfway up the stairs when he said, "Sephy?"

She turned. "Hmm?"

"Will you save me a dance? You know, for old times' sake."

She smiled. How like Justice to remember taking her to the prom. He had always been thoughtful like that. "Of course," she said, and ran up the stairs.

They were married before she knew it. Although the practical Liberty Darling, née Hale, did not shed a single tear, Sephy herself was a mess. She had more than one occasion to be glad she had worn waterproof eye makeup. In the congregation, she saw every single Darling she knew wiping his or her eyes at some point and even suspected David of tearing up once or twice. Then it was over. The bride had been kissed, and Sephy was hanging on to Gabe's arm for dear life as she followed her best friend and new sister up the aisle on the way out of the church.

Libby had made the photographer promise, on pain of nonpayment, that the photo shoot would not be a lengthy affair. The long-suffering woman shuffled the band members through the photos with gratifying speed. Then Nick hustled Sephy, Ivy, Amy, and Bailey into the car, where they cackled with high-strung laughter as they sped their way through the empty Christmas Day streets toward Quahog and the Jewish Heritage Center.

The guests started to arrive, and The Darlings played light classics. DeShaun, who had been appointed lookout, waited at the door to give them the signal when the bride and groom arrived. Amy, who was searching the crowd as she played the drums with her mind only half on what she was doing, couldn't see Mitch anywhere. Disappointed, she pulled her attention back to DeShaun and waited for his cue. When he gave it at last, she nodded to Ivy, Sephy, and Bailey, gave an extravagant drumroll, and they were off, playing a rock version of "Here Comes the Bride" that their father had arranged. The throng parted to let David and Libby into the hall. The crowd was wild, yelling and clapping and stamping their feet, and behind the drum set, Amy grinned, knowing it wasn't just the bride and groom they were cheering for. The Darlings were darn *good*.

Dinner was over. The bride and groom had danced, the bride and her father had danced, the groom and his mother had danced, the bride's parents had danced, the groom's parents had joined them, and finally the floor was opened to everyone.

At the family table, Mitch sipped ginger ale and looked around the room. Gabe Michaud, who had been an imbecile back in high school and, as far as Mitch could tell, hadn't improved much since then, was bending over a table of giggling college-aged girls.

"Hello," someone said.

Mitch pulled his attention back to the only other person at the table: a red-haired man a few years younger than himself. "Kevin O'Brien," the man said, holding out a hand to Mitch across the white tablecloth. "How are you related?"

"Sort of like a brother," said Mitch. "A foster brother, I guess you could say. You?"

"I'm not related at all. I'm with David's cousin Bailey." Kevin nodded toward the stage. "The beautiful one on the electric guitar."

"Your girlfriend?"

"I wish," said Kevin. "She'd never think of me like that in a million years."

"Why not?"

"You haven't seen us side by side. I'm two inches shorter, even when she's not wearing heels."

"So? What difference does that make?"

"All the difference in the world to her. She says she could never date anyone shorter than she is."

"That seems like a waste."

"Tell me about it."

Mitch looked at the stage, where a tall, plain young woman with mouse-colored hair and wire-rimmed glasses was playing the electric guitar with all the concentration of a brain surgeon operating inside somebody's skull. She sounded good enough, but she was different from Ivy and Amy and Sephy. She didn't have their playfulness. Or their good looks. He darted a look back at Kevin.

"The beautiful one on the electric guitar."

Huh. There was no accounting for taste.

"Women," said Mitch in disgust.

"Yeah," Kevin agreed.

Sephy was surprised when they reached the end of their sheet music and Ivy said, "Last number." Two hours had flown by. The dance floor had been packed the whole time, and the party was still in full swing. Their last number was "Evergreen," and as she reached for the high notes, which were a stretch for her contralto voice, Sephy realized she was exhausted. Without Laura, the burden of vocals had fallen mostly on her. It had been fun, but she was more than ready to let the playlist on Libby's iPod take over. Ready to find Gabe and dance a little.

They finished and said their good-byes to the wedding guests, but when the crowd chanted and clapped for an encore, they played "Jingle Bell Rock," which they had practiced just in case. Then, with relief, they put their instruments aside and climbed off the stage as a Paul Simon number came floating through the speakers.

Gabe materialized at Sephy's side before she had time to look for him.

"Hey, that was just incredible," he said, reaching for her hand. "You are *so* talented."

"Thanks."

"Wanna dance?"

"I'd love something to drink first," she said.

"Great idea. Get you a beer?"

"Just water would be fine, thanks."

"Fine, I'll have the beer." He led her by the hand to the cash bar at the far end of the room, where he ordered a bottled water for her and a Coors for himself. He drank it as quickly as she drank her Poland Spring, took the empty bottle from her, set it on the bar with finality, and said, "*Now* we can dance."

He held her very close and danced slowly, although the song was a fast one. "You're beautiful," he whispered against her hair.

"Thank you. Gabe, do you realize we're supposed to be *fast* dancing?"

"That's for other people," he said, reaching under her hair to rub her neck.

The song ended, and without releasing her, he whispered, "Take a walk with me."

She was beginning to feel a little irritated. "Later, maybe. I haven't really had a chance to dance yet."

"You can *dance* later."

She spied David dancing with Amy. "I really should dance with my brother first. And my father." She extricated herself from his arms and hurried away. "Don't wait for me."

Their months of practice had paid off in spades. Bailey had come through for them like a star. But for Ivy, locking her violin in its case at the back of the stage, the day held a tinge of bitterness. Laura had called the night before to wish them all luck and congratulate David, but she should have been here. Still, thoughts like that didn't do anyone any good, she told herself, especially on a day like this one. Best to dwell on happier feelings.

She turned to search for Nick and found him standing on the other side of the room, talking with a man she didn't recognize. As though he felt her eyes on him, her husband looked up and saw her watching. He smiled, said a few words to his companion, and started toward her.

Ivy went to meet him. "Care to dance?" she said, holding out her hand to him.

Nick took it, his own hand warm and familiar. "I thought you'd never ask."

Sephy was dancing with her father and thinking what a restful man he was. She was tired and let down. Gabe had not turned out to be at all what she had hoped. Her best friend was married, and things would never be the same again. Now, even though they were practically sisters, there would always be someone else in Libby's life who came before Sephy. Maybe that was why she loved dancing with her father: he didn't change. She always knew where she stood with him; there was never any need to guess. Plus, he was an excellent dancer and had long ago taught all the girls to be good followers. Dancing with him made *her* feel like a great dancer, which she wasn't, really. They were doing a quick fox-trot, but it was soothing, all the same.

The song ended, and she reached up to plant a kiss on his familiar-smelling cheek. "Thanks, Dad."

A voice over her head said, "Excuse me, are you free for the next dance?"

It was Justice, and she remembered his request from earlier. "I am, as a matter of fact," she said. It was a slow number, and she had to reach way up to put her hands on his shoulders. She laughed. "You *are* taller than you used to be. I know, because I danced with you at prom and I didn't have to reach this far."

"You know," he said with mock seriousness, "you're the first person all day who's commented on my height."

She was instantly contrite. "Oh, Justice, I'm sorry. I know what a pain that can be."

"Really? You're not tall."

"People constantly mention how much weight I've lost. I hear it every day." Not for the first time, she considered the irony of this. "It's funny how some things are okay to say and others aren't. Like, for instance, no one would ever go up to a woman and say, 'You look like you've *gained* a lot of weight.' And you never hear people commenting to men about how short they are. Why is that?"

The light glinted off the lenses of his glasses, giving him a scholarly air. "Maybe it's because being tall and being slim are seen as desirable attributes; therefore it's acceptable to draw attention to them."

"While being short and being fat aren't," Sephy finished. "I know all about it. I've done my time in both of those categories."

"Do you mind if I ask how much weight you've lost?"

"I'll tell you if you'll tell me how tall you are."

"Six foot four."

"A hundred sixteen pounds." He was easy to laugh with.

"You really do look wonderful, you know. But more important . . ." He hesitated.

"What? Say it."

"More important, you were always one of the nicest people I ever knew. And I think you still are."

Tears rushed to her eyes, hot and surprising. She took her hand from his shoulder in order to swipe at them.

"Did I say the wrong thing?"

"No, of course not. Just . . . I think you're the first man who's ever thought to say that to me. It's a lovely thing to say. Thank you."

"It's a lovely truth," he said.

"Libby tells me you're headed to Africa."

"That's right. I'm going to vet goat herds in the Kalahari Desert for three months."

"Why are you doing that?"

"I make a trip like this every couple of years. I've had so many opportunities in my own life—this is a way of giving back, I suppose. Two years ago, it was donkeys in Peru."

"And before that?"

"A summer I would rather forget, spaying and neutering the stray dogs and cats of Mumbai."

She was impressed, and told him so. "When do you leave?"

"Ten days from now. I go back to Seattle on New Year's Day. I'll be there just long enough to pack a few bags before I fly out." He smiled down at her. "And what about you?"

"Still working at the hospital in Quahog."

"And do you like it?"

She considered this. "Yes and no. I like nursing, but I don't want to work in respiratory all my life."

"What do you want to do?"

"I'd like to try labor and delivery, but you have to have a year of general medical experience first."

"And your year is up . . . ?"

"In June. Then I can apply to L and D."

The song was coming to an end. "Well, I wish you the best of success, Sephy. In everything you do."

"And the same to you. I really, really hope you'll like Africa. What country will you be in, exactly?"

"Namibia. I've been there twice before."

The music faded, and she stepped away. "Will you be able to come to my parents' New Year's Eve party?"

"Are they still doing that?"

"For thirty-three years now," she said.

"I'll be there."

"Good." She smiled at him. "Then we don't have to say good-bye yet."

Amy had had enough of Mitch's nonsense. There he'd sat like a petrified log all night, while she and her sisters and Libby and Bailey had led practically the whole crowd in the Macarena and the Hustle and the Cupid Shuffle, and he had not once *attempted* to dance. Being shy was one thing, but he wasn't even trying to have fun. Well, if he went home at the end of the night without having once stepped foot on the dance floor, it wouldn't be her fault. So he couldn't actually go out with her for a year yet. Fine. She would approach him as a sister. Surely she had that right. She gathered her long green skirt about her and headed in his direction.

"Whoa," said Mitch, sitting to attention. "Here comes trouble."

"What's that?" Across the table, Kevin looked alarmed. He had been gloomily watching Bailey dance with Justice Hale.

"One of David's sisters," Mitch said. "I have a feeling I'm in for it."

"Why's that?"

"Because I usually am with this one."

Amy reached the table, looking like she meant business. Mitch tried to quash the thought that she was cute when she was angry.

"What'd I do?" he asked.

"It's what you *haven't* done. You haven't moved from that chair all night."

"Sure I did. I went to the bathroom."

She narrowed her eyes. "You haven't danced."

"Amy!" he protested. "I'm not a dancer."

She waved this away. "Everyone can dance, especially to the slow songs. All you have to do is shuffle your feet around and sway a little."

"I'd feel stupid," he muttered.

He saw her soften. "Dance with me, Mitch. Just one song, and I won't bother you again, I promise."

He looked at Kevin for support.

"Better do it, buddy," said Kevin, shaking his head. "She looks pretty determined."

Amy narrowed her eyes at him. "Aren't you Bailey's date?"

"Kevin O'Brien, friend and escort of Bailey Darling." He held out his hand across the table.

Amy shook it. "Are you her boyfriend?"

"Just a friend."

"Why aren't you dancing with her?"

Mitch winced. "Amy," he said, "leave the guy alone."

"Why? I'm sure it's not a secret."

"She's dancing with someone else." Kevin nodded toward where Bailey and Justice were doing a fast swing number. "Besides, I can't dance like that."

"But if the DJ plays another slow song, you could ask her, right? I mean, you should dance with your date."

"Amy."

She ignored him, and Mitch realized, not for the first time, that anyone might as well spit in the wind as try to stand in Amy Darling's way when she had a plan in her head.

At that moment, as if heaven itself were set against him, the fast song ended and a slow one began. "Go ahead," Amy prodded Kevin. "Ask her."

Kevin shot Mitch a look.

Mitch shrugged. "You heard the lady."

The other man stood up. "All right, all right, I'm going."

Amy turned to Mitch. "And you? Are you going to ask me, or do I have to ask you?"

"Either way, I'm not going to get out of this, am I?"

She made a face at him. "So charming."

He heaved an exaggerated sigh and stood up. Bowing low, he said, "Miss Amy Darling, would you do me the honor of having this dance with me? And I warn you ahead of time, I'm not very good."

"I would be delighted to dance with you, Mitch." She took his hand.

At the edge of the dance floor, he pulled her close and a pang of longing went through him. She smelled good. And she fit so well in his arms. She rested her head on his shoulder and he closed his eyes. "Amy," he said into her hair.

"What?"

"You are such a bully."

He felt her smile against his shoulder. "I'm no such thing."

"Yes, you are. Look at poor Kevin."

"Oh, 'poor Kevin,' nonsense. Look at him yourself. He's dancing with the woman he loves, and he's the happiest I've seen him all night."

Mitch understood how Kevin felt. "Well, your cousin doesn't love him back."

Amy raised her head and looked up at him. "Why not?"

"Says he's too short for her."

"That's the stupidest thing I've ever heard of."

"Me too, but that's what she told him."

"There will always be obstacles for people who look for them."

They swayed in silence for a minute. "You're doing just fine," she told him.

"Thanks."

"When do you go back to Florida?"

"Tomorrow."

"I wish you didn't have to go."

She didn't wish it half as much as he did, but Mitch said only, "My job is waiting for me."

Amy sighed. "I'll miss you."

"Me too," he said against her hair. A year, he thought, might as well be forever.

Leander held his wife close. Jane fit a bit more snugly into his arms than she had thirty-five years ago, but she still followed him in the same familiar, comfortable way. After a lifetime of dancing together, they knew the steps well.

"Janey."

She leaned back and smiled at him. "What?"

He loved the crow's-feet around her eyes, testimony to a lifetime of laughter. "You're beautiful," he told her.

She raised her eyebrows. "That's not what you were going to say."

Thirty-five years, he thought, *and there are no secrets left.* He told her what was on his mind. "I know we said we'd tell the kids after Christmas. But there's still the New Year's party. . . ."

She closed her eyes.

The hardest thing in the world, he realized, might not be facing death yourself. Far more difficult was to watch such lines of grief and loss become etched on the face of a person you loved.

"After the New Year, we'll tell them," she agreed.

He held her closer, and they waltzed on.

CHAPTER

23

THE DAYS FOLLOWING THE WEDDING left Sephy feeling flat and at odds with herself. Gabe had melted away, back to Virginia, the day after the wedding. Her father had driven him to the airport, and Sephy hadn't even said good-bye. Laura called to ask how the wedding had gone and to say that she was doing just fine. David and Libby, the lucky things, sent a postcard from Florida, telling her how much fun they were having in the sun on the apparently endless beaches. Meanwhile, a storm dropped thirteen inches of snow over the down east coast of Maine, most of which turned to slush in the rain that followed the next day. Since Sephy no longer lived in Copper Cove, she didn't see Justice, who was staying with his parents until the New Year. Her attempts at discreet inquiry of her mother and Amy netted her nothing. Apparently he hadn't so much as asked about her. The only thing to do was work, so she picked up a twelve-hour over-time shift and cleaned her apartment from carpets to closets, just to give herself something to do.

Amy gave her staff ten days off after Christmas and thought the days without work seemed endless. Crystal went home to visit her family. Paul flew out to Iowa, or Idaho—one of the *I* states, anyway—to visit a friend. Mitch went back to Florida the day after the wedding. Amy tried to be happy for him, to ignore the bitter sense that he had somehow betrayed her by leaving. In fact, the opposite was true. He had made it clear what his course was. For at least the next year, there was no future for them. She could not help it if the prospect of a year without him stretched before her as barren and endless as the Sahara.

As nothing had been decided yet about the spring musi-cal, there was nothing to plan. She compensated by giving the house a thorough cleaning. "For the New Year's Eve party," she reassured her mother when Jane tried to protest.

The day before the party, Amy hit the grocery stores at seven in the morning, as soon as they opened. She returned home to find that her mother was out. So, alone in the empty house, she began to tackle the list of food. She made puff pastry boats that her mother would fill later with slivers of rare roast beef and a horseradish cream sauce. Choux pastry bites for caviar and crème fraîche. Pumpernickel rounds to be spread with cream cheese and smoked salmon. Strawberries dipped in chocolate and set on the screened porch to chill. Ten dozen cookies. Crab dip to serve with crudités. Artichoke and spinach dip. White chicken chili to be served in little cups. Onion tartlets. Parmesan straws.

Her mother returned midmorning. "Amy!" Jane cried when she arrived home with her car trunk loaded with fruit and champagne. "What in the world are you doing?"

"Party food." Amy did not look up from the garlic she was mincing.

"But this is the kind of party where everybody brings something. And Sephy and Ivy are coming over tomorrow to cook all *day*."

"I know that."

"You didn't invite a hundred extra people and forget to tell me? Because if you did, we'll certainly have enough to feed them all."

"I just got in the mood to cook; that's all." Amy strove to keep her voice from sounding as brittle as she felt. She knew her mother was eyeing her with concern, but she ignored this and kept on mincing garlic.

"Do you think it'll be a good party?" Jane asked her husband. They were in the dining room, polishing and arranging trays of champagne flutes, which they would fill closer to midnight.

"Why wouldn't it be? It always has been before."

"I know. I was just thinking . . . the rehearsal dinner we had here on Christmas Eve was so wonderful. It'll be hard to beat."

"We don't have to beat it," Leander said. "This is a new day, new crowd."

"That's true." She held a flute up to the light and examined it for smudges, then put it down. "Leander, are the children going to be okay? When we tell them, I mean."

He put down his own polishing cloth. "They'll be all right. God will take care of them, as He's always taken care of all of us. For now, let's you and I concentrate on enjoying this party."

"It's just that . . . next year might be very different for all of us."

He pulled her into his arms then, smudging the glass she still held. She began to weep silently against his sweater. "I know," he said, patting her back. "I know."

When Ivy arrived at her mother's house on the morning of the party, she was astonished to see how much food Amy had already made. "Are we expecting the local frat house?" she asked, helping herself to a choux pastry.

"Those are for the party." Amy swatted at her hand. "And no. I got in the mood to do some cooking."

"These are good." Ivy took another pastry. "And don't worry that I'm going to eat everything. I could eat all day and not make a dent in this mountain." She squinted at her sister. "Are you okay, Amy? You look sort of . . . drawn."

Amy smiled at the adjective. "I feel drawn. My staff have the week off, and I'm going stir crazy."

"Hmmm. Is that all?"

"Of course it's all."

"I just thought it might have something to do with Mitch. Possibly. At the very outside."

Her silence was all the answer Ivy needed.

"Are you in love with him?"

Amy's eyes filled with tears. "We can't go out for at least a year."

"What do you mean?"

Amy told her.

"I never thought you would love an alcoholic."

Amy picked up a puff pastry and began to shred it onto the countertop. "It's not like I chose to."

"No." Ivy put her arms around her youngest sister. "No, you can't help who you fall in love with."

"Anyway, he's back in Florida. He might change his mind. I might never see him again."

"You'll see him. He won't be able to stay away."

Amy leaned against Ivy. "He might start drinking again."

Ivy had never been one to offer false hope. "It could happen," she said. "A lot of alcoholics never get sober." She kissed her sister's head. "If Mitch fights this demon for the rest of his life, then what?"

"I can't control what Mitch does. I'm getting to be an expert at letting go, you know."

"But you have such high ideals. If Mitch doesn't measure up, will you still be friends?"

Amy's smile was watery. "I can't imagine a world anymore where I'm not his friend."

The party had hardly begun when Jane pulled Ivy aside and whispered, "For heaven's sake, take some of this food home with you when you go! I don't know what Amy was thinking.

I've already put ten bags in the downstairs freezer with your name on them."

"What am I supposed to do with it all?"

Her mother eyed her shrewdly. "You have a teenage son, Ivy. You'll be through it in two days."

Sephy was at the door taking coats when the Hales arrived. "Hi," she said to Justice, feeling suddenly fourteen and fat again.

"Hi, Seph. Your family sure loves a good party."

"We always have. Are you all ready for Africa?"

She didn't know what she had been hoping for, but when he grinned and said, "Can't wait," her heart sank like a stone in her chest.

It was the roaring success that the Darlings' New Year's parties always were. There were at least seventy people there from the church, the school, the community arts center, the neighborhood. Jane and Leander had always been the kind of people who knew and loved everyone.

Ivy looked around the room with a surge of affection. She had so many memories among these people. There was Janet Little, her first Sunday school teacher, once tall and stern, now stooped over, with a sweet smile. David's old roommate, George the Frustrated Writer, was there. Bernard the postman, who had been delivering mail to 14 Ladyslipper Lane for the whole of Ivy's life, came to the party every year on the condition that he was invited as a friend (which he wasn't, strictly speaking) and not as a postal employee, which would have been against regulations. Ivy didn't even know his last name, yet he was, like so many there, a part of her life. She said hello to several of her old high school teachers, some retired, some still working at the same jobs, as her father was. Pastor Ken was there with his wife, Constance, and there were too many others from the church to count.

Ivy was exhausted. It had been a long week. A long month, really. By ten o'clock, Jada was drooping, her eyes nearly closed, against the corner of a couch. Nick had laid Hammer down on Amy's bed hours ago. Even DeShaun, who was hovering near the buffet, talking with Pastor Ken's son Wolfie, looked half-asleep. She saw Nick, talking to her father near the fruit display, and caught his eye. As if reading her thoughts, he nodded.

Knowing they understood each other perfectly, she went to find their coats and to collect her children, and her ten bags of food from the freezer.

Amy was refilling water pitchers at the kitchen sink when she heard her name.

She turned and nearly dropped her mother's white iron-stone ewer. *Mitch.* "I thought you were in Florida!"

"I was."

"Not anymore?"

In answer, he asked, "What are you doing?"

"Ah . . . mingling? That's what it's called when you walk around and talk to people at a party."

"I mean, are you busy? Can you get away?"

"Right now? Where?"

"Just get your coat and come with me. I want to show you something."

He drove to the outskirts of town, in the direction of Jefferson. "Where are we going?" Amy asked more than once, but he only shook his head and remained silent. It had snowed several inches that morning, and the world lay under a smooth, white blanket that muffled every sound. Overhead, a gibbous moon played hide-and-seek with the tattered clouds, first streaking the fields with silvery light, then abandoning them to blank, yawning darkness.

After twenty minutes, he turned left onto an unplowed road Amy had not even seen. "Hang on," he said, shifting the truck into four-wheel drive. She hung on. They fishtailed and spun their wheels, then inched along until the truck's wheels found some purchase and shot forward. She bounced off the seat and gave a little scream.

He laughed. "Almost there."

"I don't believe you!"

But all at once, they *were* there. He slowed to a stop and pointed the truck's high beams at a house that rose up out of the trees around it. It was big and bare and stark, with blank spaces where the windowpanes should have been and a sagging wraparound porch.

Amy shivered. "What is it?"

"It's my house. I just bought it."

"You paid money for this?"

"Wait 'til you see inside."

"Mitch—"

But he was out of the cab and around the front of the truck before she could think what she had been going to say. He opened her door.

"Come on." He looked like an eager boy.

"It looks scary."

"Nothing to be scared of. You're with me." He took her hand and more or less pulled her from the cab. But he didn't let go after that, and Amy thought that as long as he was holding her hand, she didn't mind braving a haunted house or two. They climbed the steps, brushing away the snow with their boots as they went. With his free hand, Mitch found the key on his ring and fitted it into the lock. The door creaked open, releasing a dry, musty smell. He pulled a flashlight from the pocket of his Carhartt coat and flipped it on.

It was dismal in every sense of the word. Great holes in some of the walls and floors. Nests that something had made in the corners. Freezing cold. But the rooms were large and high-ceilinged, and an enormous stone fireplace dominated one end of the ground floor. He pointed out to her that the original woodwork was intact around the doorframes and most of the windows. "I won't make you go down to the basement tonight," he said, though his tone indicated that he would gladly take her there if she were to insist. "But the foundation is sound. No moisture problems."

They had toured both stories and the attic and were standing again on the front porch while he locked the door when Amy asked, puzzled, "But why did you buy it? What are you going to do with it?"

"I'm going to renovate it," he said, as though it were the

most natural thing in the world. "And then I'm going to live in it."

"What about the job in Florida?"

He looked away, into the trees. "I thought I might, you know, stay around here awhile. Just try it."

She smiled in the darkness and followed him down the steps. He was not holding her hand anymore. "It's such a huge house. Why not something smaller? More manageable?"

Mitch turned to look up at the front of the house and smiled like a man besotted. "It has good bones," he said softly.

Amy knew what he meant.

It was eleven thirty, and Sephy had not spoken to Justice all night. A dozen times, she had tried to catch his eye as she was passing by, had started to approach him to talk, and every time he either had not seen her or had suddenly begun talking to someone else who would have been difficult to interrupt. She didn't want to think it was deliberate. She didn't understand it. She only knew she was exhausted and miserable and wanted nothing more than to go back to her apartment, crawl between the covers, and sleep.

She wandered into the kitchen, where the counter-tops were covered with leftover food, congealing on trays. Listlessly, she began to clean up. She put food in Ziploc bags and plastic containers and found room for them in the fridge. She consolidated the two-liter bottles of soda and tossed the empties into the recycling bin. She wiped the counters, loaded the dishwasher, and stacked the remaining dishes by the sink. The rest could wait for morning.

From the living room, she heard the piano strike the opening chords of "Auld Lang Syne." A new year. The cue for her to leave.

She went to the hall closet and found her coat. She had pulled it on and was extricating her long hair from the neck when she heard, "Sephy."

She froze, her heart leaping in her chest. She looked up. "Hi, Justice."

He was wearing a wool peacoat that didn't look nearly warm enough for January in Maine. His face was pained. "I wanted to say good-bye before I left."

She willed her heart not to break. "Good-bye. All the best to you in Africa."

"Well, the thing is . . ." He examined his hands. "I'm only going to be gone a few months. I thought maybe when I got back, I could give you a call."

They were singing now, in the other room. Welcoming in the New Year. She tried to keep herself from smiling like a lunatic.

"Happy New Year, Sephy."

He reached out and touched her face, and then he kissed her. A question at first, and then an answer. He pulled her close and slid a hand into her hair, and there was a stutter and then a stop in her chest that spiraled all the way into the depths of her stomach. He stepped away. And then he was gone. It happened as quickly as that. She might have thought she had imagined it, but for the sound of the door clicking shut behind him, the music dying away amid the cheers from the next room. The warmth of her neck where his hand had been.

Sephy touched her mouth with her fingertips and whispered his name, but she did not go after him. He would be back. They had all the time in the world.

DISCUSSION QUESTIONS

1. When Sephy and her honorary aunt Sharon follow the same unhealthy eating patterns, Sephy feels "the guilt of knowing they were like two drowning people clinging together, each too weak to let go and save herself, each trying to mitigate her own failure by pulling the other down with her." Have you ever found yourself in a similar relationship? How do the dynamics between Sephy and Sharon shift when Sephy decides to change her life? In her position, how would you have dealt with Sharon?

2. Laura goes to church looking for "a place where she belonged. A fundamental sense of roots. Maybe . . . okay, she would admit it: *family*. And with all its imperfections and potential for disappointment, church had always been a second family for her." What has your experience with church—and the people in it— been like? Did it surprise you that Laura would look for community in a church when she's not very interested in matters of faith?

3. In their first counseling session, Carl asks Sephy to envision who "the girl inside the fat suit" would be. Do you ever daydream about changing some part of yourself? If so, what would you change? What would your imagined self be able to do that you can't now?

4. When Amy brags to Mitch, "*Give yourself a break* is not part of my vocabulary," he responds, "You say it like it's something admirable, but it's not. You know what's admirable? Balance. *That's* what's not in your vocabulary." Do you think our culture puts too high a value on overwork or perfectionism? Do you, like Amy, struggle to reach your own high standard, or are you able to give yourself a break when needed?

5. Both Laura and Sephy feel at times that they need to stay away from their family. What are their reasons for doing so? Do you think they're justified in their feelings?

6. Laura observes, "Mom's highest aspiration for any of us is that we'll be nice and well-behaved and never make a scene," and Rob counters that his mother "always encouraged us to be ourselves no matter what." Which do you think is the better approach to parenting? Are there dangers in either strategy?

7. Moments of tension, like the clash over playing in the band for David's wedding, bring out the very different personalities of the Darling women. In your own family, what role do you play during a conflict? Are you a combatant, a peacemaker, a mediator, an avoider, or something else?

8. As she struggles to find her own voice, Sephy realizes that "she was always going to be a person who valued tact and kindness. But didn't she have a right, maybe even a responsibility, to say what she wanted to say? Surely both were possible." Do you struggle with either extreme—either speaking your mind too bluntly or keeping silent out of fear of what others will think? By the end of the story, has Sephy found the balance she's striving for?

9. When she realizes that Mitch has started drinking again, Amy wonders, "What did you say to one of the strongest people you knew when his strength was not enough to keep him from sliding into the pit again?" Is there anything helpful she could say to Mitch in this situation? How would you advise her?

10. Laura admits to Rob, "I know that if I were to have a relationship with God, I would have to let Him be in charge of my life. And right now, I'm not interested in that. I like things the way they are." Can you—or could you, at some point in the past—relate to her reluctance toward a relationship with God? What does Rob mean by his response: "If God wants your attention, He's going to get it, one way or another. I wouldn't want it to be harder for you than it has to be"?

11. As she looks back over her life, Sephy acknowledges that "maybe it was all grace. Because even the hardest things had shaped her for the good." What past pain or difficulty has shaped you in a positive way? Do you

agree with Sephy's conclusion that these things are "all grace," and that "grace—if you accepted it—was the only thing that could heal your soul"?

12. Jane and Leander decide to postpone telling their children about his illness, though Jane confesses to herself that she has mixed motives for waiting. Do you agree with their decision? If you were in the place of the Darling children, would you appreciate the delay or wish you'd been told sooner?

13. Jane comments that "next year might be very different for all of us." What do you think is ahead for Sephy and Justice? For Amy and Mitch? For Laura?

TURN THE PAGE FOR AN EXCERPT FROM

AVAILABLE IN BOOKSTORES AND ONLINE

CHAPTER

1

NICK WAS GOING TO HATE his birthday gift. Even as she taped down the ribbon and set the wrapped package on the kitchen table, Ivy Darling was already sure of this. It was a book of Mark Strand's poetry, and although she had gotten her husband a book of poetry every birthday for the six years they had been married, he had yet to open the front cover of one of them. That did not stop her from hoping, nor from appropriating the books for her own collection after a decent waiting period. Gifts, she thought, sometimes said more about the giver than the receiver. When you gave something you loved and thought beautiful, you were inviting another person into your world. You were saying, *Here is something that brings me joy. I want to share that joy with you.* She couldn't help it if her husband had never been all that much into joy sharing.

To be fair, it was also important to give something the

other person actually wanted. With this in mind, Ivy had bought Nick a year's membership to the Copper Cove Racquet and Fitness Club, which he would love, as well as a bathrobe, which he needed.

She would give him all three gifts when he got home from work, before they went to his parents' house for dinner. She did not want him to unwrap the things she had chosen in front of his mother, who would be hurt if her own gifts were upstaged. Nor did she want to give them in front of Nick's sisters, who would diminish them by being bored with everything.

She found the broom and swept up the scraps of wrapping paper, then emptied the dustpan into a plastic shopping bag and carried it to the back porch. The five o'clock sunlight flashed off the windows of the vacant house next door, making her squint. The place had been empty as long as she and Nick had lived here. It was a depressing sore on the pretty neighborhood: the house bleached and shabby in the summer sunshine; the grass growing high against the warped and splintered front steps, unstirred by human movement. A faded For Rent sign sagged in one window. She turned her back on it and went inside.

Ivy was sprinkling chopped nuts on top of the iced birthday cake when she heard Nick's car in the driveway. She met him at the door with the remains of the frosting and a kiss.

"What's this?" he said, frowning at the sticky bowl.

"It's your birthday icing. Did you have a good day?"

He stepped around her and set his briefcase under the hall table. "It was all right. What are you doing?"

"Making your cake. We're going to your parents' for dinner, remember?"

He ran a hand through his thick hair. "I forgot. I was hoping to go for a run. What time do we have to be there?"

"Six o'clock. I wanted you to open your presents here first."

He went through to the kitchen and began washing his hands, eyeing her over the top of his glasses. "You're not wearing that to my parents' house, are you?"

Ivy looked down at her T-shirt. It was yellow, with a picture of half a cup of coffee over the words *Half Full*. Below that, her faded cutoff shorts ended in ragged hems. "What's wrong with what I'm wearing?"

"You look like a slob."

She gave him a gritty smile. "You say the nicest things."

"I'm only saying it for your own sake. Don't you have anything with a little shape to it?"

"Yes, but it wouldn't be nearly as comfortable."

"Come on, Ivy."

"All *right*, I'll change before we go. But if we're going to be on time, you have to open your presents now."

He dried his hands and turned to survey the packages on the table. "What'd you get me?"

"A present you'll love, a present you need, and a present you'll learn to love."

"Hmmm . . . ," he said, pretending to think. "A Porsche, a Porsche, and a book of poetry."

"Close. Come on, you have to open them to find out."

She sat down across from him while he opened the packages. She had been right on all scores. He was indifferent to the poetry, satisfied with the bathrobe, and pleased with the gym membership.

"There's no excuse for me now," he said, pulling his wallet

from his back pocket and tucking the envelope into it. "I'll be in shape before you know it." Nick, who was already in great shape, was the only person Ivy knew who thrilled to the prospect of more self-discipline.

"You look great just the way you are," she said, standing and kissing him on the top of his head. "But if you want to half kill yourself in the gym five days a week, knock yourself out. We should probably leave in fifteen minutes, unless we want to give your mother an ulcer."

"Okay. Just . . . don't forget to change your clothes."

Her smile felt grittier this time but she did as he said, reminding herself that he was only trying to protect her from his mother, who had a finely tuned radar for her daughter-in-law's every shortcoming, fashion or otherwise.

Nick's parents lived across town, never a long drive even at the time of day considered rush hour in bigger cities. For three-quarters of the year, Copper Cove was small even by Maine standards so that now, in June, when the tourist season had filled the beach houses and hotels along the water, the town still did not feel crowded. Cars moved lazily along High Street, pulling in at Cumberland Farms for gas and at Blue Yew Pizza or Salt Flats Seafood for supper. Traffic, Ivy was sometimes surprised to realize, was just not something you ever thought about here.

At Nick's parents' house, his sister Tiffany met them at the door. "Oh, it's you."

"We thought we might show up," Ivy said. "You know, since it's Nick's birthday party and all."

"Happy birthday," Tiffany said grudgingly. "Everyone else is already here. The guys are watching the Red Sox game with Daddy." She aimed this bit of news at Nick. "And Mumma's in the kitchen," she added, a clear hint that Ivy should join her mother-in-law there and *not* join her sisters-in-law at whatever they were doing.

They followed Tiffany through to the kitchen, where Nick's mother, Ruby, was emptying fish market bags into the sink.

"Oh, wow, lobster," Ivy said. "Thanks for having a birthday, Nick."

"Nicholas!" cried his mother, turning from the sink and drying her hands on a towel. "Happy birthday, sweetheart. Thirty-two years old!" She tipped her cheek up for a kiss, smoothed down the sleeves of his shirt, and straightened his collar. Ivy had an image of a plump, pretty wasp buzzing around a pie at a picnic.

She set her cake carrier on the sideboard. "I brought the cake."

"Wonderful." Ruby brushed imaginary lint from Nick's shirtfront. "What kind is it?"

"Carrot cake with cream cheese frosting."

Ruby turned from Nick and eyed the cake as though Ivy had said it was made of sand and seaweed. "Oh . . . ," she faltered. "I *was* afraid one cake wouldn't be enough for all of us, so I *did* ask Jessica to make a cheesecake to go along with it." She smiled damply at her son. "You know how Nick loves cheesecake."

Ivy felt her nostrils flare. As a matter of fact, Nick did *not* love cheesecake. He preferred *carrot* cake. It had been one of life's long lessons, however, that objection was always futile with her mother-in-law. She felt her mouth twitch in a rictus grin. "Can I help with dinner?" she managed to choke out.

"You might set the table. We'll use the good china. The cloth is on the ironing board in the laundry room. You'll have to put the leaves in the table, but Nick can do that for you."

Nick trotted off to find the extra leaves and Ivy, having retrieved the tablecloth, began counting out forks and knives from the sideboard. The familiar task calmed her. "It's quiet around here," she observed as her mother-in-law added salt to two enormous canners full of hot water on the stove. "Where is everyone?"

"The men are watching television, and the girls are looking at Jessica's new scrapbook."

Nick had three sisters. His family, the Masons, and hers, the Darlings, had always belonged to the same church. In her growing-up years, none of Nick's sisters had seemed to object to Ivy as long as she had been just another girl in youth group. But from the moment Nick had brought her home as his girlfriend, Jessica, Angela, and Tiffany had circled like a pack of she-wolves guarding their kill. Together, they presented a solid, hostile wall designed to keep Ivy on the outside. They whispered with their heads together when she was in the house and stopped talking when she came into a room. They planned sisters' shopping trips in front of Ivy and did not invite her to come along. When Nick and Ivy were engaged and a family friend hinted that the groom's sisters might want to throw the bride a shower, they'd been offended and told Ivy so, with the greatest of umbrage.

Ivy liked people—all kinds of people—and in general,

people liked her back. She was unused to having her friendliness met with such stubborn, protracted rejection, and at
first she had been bewildered by Nick's sisters' antagonism.
"They hate me for no reason," she had once wailed to her
own twin sister, Laura. "I can't understand it. It's like being
in eighth grade all over again." By the time she and Nick had
been married a year, however, she was wiser. Nick's mother
doted on him, and this was at the root of her daughters' treat-
ment of Ivy. Nick's sisters were not horrible to her because of
anything she personally had done; they simply resented Nick
for being their mother's favorite and were punishing Ivy for
being his wife. It was a situation Ivy had gotten used to.

More or less.

When the lobsters were ready, Ruby sent her to call the
family to the table. She found Jessica, Angela, and Tiffany
upstairs, in Angela's old bedroom, looking at what appeared
to be paint chips from a hardware store. When they saw Ivy,
they stopped talking.

"Yes?" said Angela, who was Nick's middle sister, tucking
the paint chips under one leg.

"Your mother says come to the table." She would not give
them the satisfaction of being asked what they were doing.

"Thank you, Ivy. Tell Mother we'll be there in a moment."
Angela stared at her until she took the hint and went back
downstairs to the kitchen.

Nick's father, Harry, had muttered a long, rambling
grace and they were all cracking their lobster claws when
Angela rapped her fork against her water goblet. "Everybody!
Everybody," she called, half-rising from her chair. "Vincent
and I have an announcement to make."

"Angela, that goblet is *crystal*," her mother protested.

"Well, it's an *important* announcement, Mother."

Some blessed instinct of self-preservation warned Ivy of what Angela was about to say and gave her a heartbeat of time to compose herself for it.

"Vincent and I—" Angela looked around the table in delight—"are *pregnant*!"

It was evident that Jessica and Tiffany already knew, but that to the rest of them, it was a complete surprise.

"And here's the best part," Angela said, looking at Vincent and gripping his hand atop the tablecloth. "We're having the baby at *Christmas*! My due date is the twenty-fourth, but the doctor says if I haven't had it by then, he'll induce me so the baby can be born on Christmas Day. Won't that be so much *fun*?"

"Tell them how you planned it, Ange!" Tiffany said.

Angela looked around, ready to implode with pride. "Okay, ready for this? We knew we wanted to have the baby at Christmas, right? Because . . . *so* meaningful. Like Jesus. And obviously that meant we would need to get pregnant in March. But I didn't want to get really gross and fat while I was pregnant. So last January I went on this diet—"

"I remember," said Ruby, frowning. "I didn't approve. You're thin enough as it is."

"Right." Angela snorted. "I thought so too, because that's what everybody tells me? But then I thought, *Just wait until nine months from now.* So I went on this diet and got down to a size four, which was my goal, and *then* we got pregnant. Now it's just gotten warm enough to go to the beach, and . . . look!" She stood up and turned sideways, smoothing her

T-shirt down over her stomach, and Ivy saw what she had missed before. A small but very definite baby bump.

"So . . . showing, right? But still cute!" Angela beamed around at them.

Ivy stared back. She felt powerless over her own facial expression and could only hope she didn't actually look as though she wanted to vomit all over her lobster tail.

Angela was impervious to disapproval. She bubbled on. "You should see my maternity swimsuit. It's *so* cute! And by having the baby in December, I'll totally have time to get back in shape by next beach season!"

Her husband, Vincent, a caustic CPA who sipped black coffee as incessantly as most people breathe oxygen, said, "Tell them about the nursery." It turned out that the paint chips Angela and her sisters had been looking at were for the nursery, which would be done in a Beatrix Potter theme. . . .

It went on and on. The problem with Angela and Vincent reproducing, Ivy thought bitterly, was that they would create another person every bit as narrow and self-absorbed as themselves. Sometimes the world—or at least Nick's family—did not seem large enough to hold another person like that.

Nick had little to say on the drive home.

"The woman from Family Makers e-mailed me yesterday," Ivy said at last, breaking the silence. "She asked if we would consider foreign adoption." She looked at her hands but watched Nick from the corner of her eye.

He kept his own eyes on the road and did not answer her.

Which, she reflected, her heart lying in her chest as cold and heavy as one of Ruby's lobsters, was more or less an answer in itself.

ACKNOWLEDGMENTS

WRITING A BOOK IS, in many ways, a team project. I cast my grateful thanks at the feet of those who know more about any subject than I do and are willing to share their knowledge with me. To the builders in my family: my father, John Armstrong, and my brothers, Noble Armstrong and Jed Armstrong, thank you for helping me understand some of the problems Mitch encounters at the opera house. To Joyce Pelletier, licensed clinical professional counselor and national certified counselor, thank you for walking me through Sephy's first counseling session. Thank you also to my sister-in-law Laurie Hale, who helped me navigate the nomenclature of an airport. I continue to be all admiration for my editors at Tyndale for their commitment to excellence while still being fun, cool people. And as ever, love and thankfulness to my husband, Tim, and my kids, Sarah, Miles, and Mark. You deserve the best of soccer moms; instead, you have a harried woman who sits on the couch in yoga pants, pecking away at a computer, and forgets to sign up for your parent-teacher conferences. Yet somehow, you're still proud of me. I never cease to be amazed by this. I have the best family in the world.

About the Author

CARRE ARMSTRONG GARDNER was raised in the Adirondack Mountains of New York—the most beautiful of all possible settings—where she spent countless hours rambling through woods and beside streams, making up stories with herself as the heroine. It wasn't until well into adulthood that she realized not everyone in the world sat at traffic lights or passed the time in doctors' waiting rooms creating plots and characters in their heads. It was that realization that first gave her permission to think of herself as a writer.

Carre's favorite stories have always been those about the ordinary lives of ordinary people. She believes every life is a fascinating drama, every person is the hero of his or her own story, and Carre's desire is to tell those kinds of stories in a way that makes readers love her characters.

As a teenager, she was a pianist, and a teacher encouraged her to attend conservatory as a performance major. But in a fit of altruism she decided to become a nurse instead—a career that had the double benefit of assuring a paycheck while allowing her to pursue music and writing in her spare time.

From 2007 to 2010, Carre lived and worked in Russia with her husband and children. Now she lives in Portland, Maine, where she works as a nurse at a local hospital. She has three teenagers and two rescue dogs, which is far too many. (Dogs, not teenagers.)

RETURN TO MAINE'S ROCKY
SHORES FOR THE NEXT

Darling Family novel

IN BOOKSTORES
AND ONLINE

Fall 2015